PAYNE Avenue

PAYNE Avenue

M.T. BARTONE

MODERNPROSEPRESS

PAYNE **Avenue** Copyright © 2023 by **M.T. Bartone**

Published 2023 by **Modern Prose Press**
St. Paul, Minnesota

Cover Image Design and Illustration: Cherie Fox / cheriefox.com

First Edition 2023
Identifiers: / ISBN 979-8-9889830-1-9 (ebook) / ISBN 979-8-9889830-0-2 (paperback) / ISBN 979-8-9889830-2-6 (hard cover)
Subjects: BISAC: FICTION / Psychological Thriller / Crime Fiction / Domestic Thriller

Printed in the United States of America

Content Warning
This book contains mature content unsuitable for children and some adult readers, including: violence, strong language, animal death, sexual content, and grief.

Key words: psychological thriller, thriller, crime, crime thriller, crime fiction, domestic thriller, domestic psychological thriller, dark, dark fiction, murder, mystery, vengeance, revenge, love story, grief

DEDICATION

This book is dedicated to my husband, Geno Bartone, and his wonderful Italian family. After all, it is the Bartone family history that inspired this book. The "good old days" in St. Paul, Minnesota, specifically, on Payne Avenue, were unique, to say the least. Times were both magical and extremely difficult. Their strong Italian heritage and love of family have kept them together for generations, and have created memories and stories that are nothing short of legendary. I will forever be grateful to each of them for their unique role in bonding the Bartone family into the tightknit loving family it is today.

PAYNE Avenue

EDDIE

Spring

One

*E*ddie Bracchio rinsed the dried blood from his hands as he leaned in closer to the mirror. He flinched before gently patting the stinging gash on his forehead just below the hairline. He soaped it up and gingerly rinsed away the blood. A quick search of his bathroom drawers confirmed he had no bandages to stop the oozing. He'd have to improvise.

With his hands now blood-free, he could step out of his suit and into the shower. He frowned as he stripped. The evening hadn't gone as planned. He cursed himself as he thought about his near-miss with death.

Jay Morten, a tall and lanky drug-user with a sweaty pallor the shade of a gloomy rain cloud, had knocked on the door to the private club asking to see Eddie.

"Private club" was an inadequate description of the tiny, rundown room. Dark and dingy, its front door almost hidden, the club sat along the quieter end of a busy strip of stores and restaurants in Brooklyn's Dyker Heights neighborhood. Its sparse furnishings included a plain wooden bar against the far wall with three chairs pushed up to its front.

Behind the bar, stood long-standing bartender, Stooge. Other than a few old tables scattered about, there wasn't much to the place. Eddie and the rest of the boss's crew often spent their downtime there, discussing business and waiting for things to happen out on the street.

The door, always locked, was manned by Big Dog, the short, beefy and neck-less doorman of possible Mexican or Middle Eastern descent, Eddie wasn't sure which.

"Eddie," Big Dog called. "Somebody to see ya'."

Sitting at the bar, Eddie turned from his scotch and frowned. He stood and sauntered toward the door. "Jay—you piece-a shit. You got my money?"

Jay replied by pulling a knife and lunging at Eddie. Eddie jumped back, the knife narrowly missing his gut.

Big Dog pounced on Jay, sending him to the floor in a heap, the blade landing a few feet away.

"You miserable—," Eddie patted his pocket for his piece.

Big Dog kicked the knife and hurried to his knees to gain control of Jay, who kicked and slapped the bouncer in a frenzy. Flat on his back, Jay wriggled free and reached for a floor lamp standing near the front door. He whipped it back and forth, its small shade tipping and swinging. Big Dog tried unsuccessfully to grab the lamp as Eddie leaned in with his gun. As he waited for Big Dog to move out of the way, the pointed finial of the lamp smashed into Eddie's forehead, sending him stumbling back.

Stunned for a second, Eddie touched his forehead. Blood covered his hand and rage burned in his belly. He yanked the lamp from Jay and flipped the heavy metal base upward near his hands. He raised it high and smashed it down onto Jay's face. It connected with a squishy thud. Jay's body jerked before going limp. Eddie dropped the lamp and stumbled back.

Except for Stooge whispering "*shit*," and Eddie's heavy breathing, the room fell silent.

"Son-of-bitch," Eddie shouted, as he reached into his jacket pocket for his handkerchief. He pressed it on his forehead as he watched Big Dog check Jay for a pulse. He looked up at Eddie and shook his bald brown head.

"Dead."

"Shit."

Eddie paced the small room for a minute before pointing at Big Dog. "Make sure that door's locked. Nobody gets in. Nobody."

Big Dog moved to secure the lock. He double-checked the blinds and stood near the door.

Eddie pulled out his burner phone and dialed.

"Yeah. Gotta' little problem, here," he puffed. "At the club. Yeah. Need some clean-up." He paused. "Yeah. Now. Who? Some wacked out junkie. No one'll miss him. Yeah. Thanks. And ah', sorry 'bout this."

Eddie ended his call and went back to his drink.

"I'll have this cleaned up in a half-hour," he told Stooge and Big Dog. "Til' then, sit tight."

Stooge nodded and continued loading his fridge with beer cans, as Big Dog stood silently next to Jay's corpse, manning the front door.

Eddie returned to his drink at the bar and dabbed his bleeding forehead with his handkerchief.

"Jesus Christ. I'm gettin' too old for this shit."

Two

Eddie's early-morning call didn't surprise him. He knew there'd be questions about the events of the previous night. He dragged himself out of bed, his head-wound aching. He made sure to dress for the occasion and hurried so he wouldn't be late.

He strutted into the middle-class residential area, chuckling at the sounds of a fight coming from an apartment window above him. He then turned up the stairs to the home of his boss, Primo Simonelli.

Primo ran their criminal organization in the Brooklyn area. The territory was tightly managed and Eddie, one of Primo's long-time devoted lieutenants, had seen his responsibilities grow over the last couple of years. Narcotics and theft were his main priorities, but he also dabbled in extortion, loan-sharking and online gambling.

Inside the aged brick house, the pleasant smell of bacon lingered. Eddie entered the average-sized living room, making sure to wipe his feet before walking on the worn mahogany floor.

"Eddie, good morning. Come in," said Primo Simonelli.

"Yeah, morning, boss."

Eddie made himself comfortable in his usual upright chair, its lavender-flowered upholstery faded from years of harsh sunlight. He felt a slight breeze coming from the unlit stone fireplace decorated with Primo's family photos. Eddie crossed one ankle over his other knee, adjusted his gold pinky-ring, and looked across the room at Primo, who sat on the sofa across from him.

Primo's bodyguard, Vittorio, strolled past the kitchen door, taking a look at Eddie before disappearing.

A flip-phone rang from the coffee table in front of Primo and he leaned forward to grab it with his withered, veined hand.

"Micola. What's wrong, sweetheart?"

Eddie watched as Primo's expression turned to a frown, his gravelly voice strained. "Shooting? Who—who is shooting? In your front yard? What the hell? I told you long ago you should move from that neighborhood."

Primo stopped talking and listened, nodding and running his shaky hand across his bald head, combing back the few silver strands that sifted across the brown age spots. From his chair, Eddie heard a woman's frantic voice shouting through the phone.

Primo nodded. "God dammit, Micola. What's happened to St. Paul?"

On hearing the words, "St. Paul," Eddie straightened and leaned forward, a sense of dread washing over him. He watched Primo close his eyes and shake his head.

"I know, Micola. Yes. Forty years. Mm-hmm. Long time."

Primo widened his eyes. He looked at Eddie and jabbed his finger in Eddie's direction. Eddie whipped his head back-and-forth, reigniting its pounding pain as he mouthed the word "no." Primo again pointed at him.

Eddie stood and walked past Primo into the kitchen, eavesdropping for details of his new task in his hometown of St. Paul, Minnesota.

"I have someone who can help," Primo said. "Yes. He's good. Yes, Micola. I'll tell him you're family. Mm-hmm. Yes. I'll send him packing tomorrow—depending on the flights, of course."

With his hands on his hips, Eddie turned in circles as his gut tightened.

Shit.

"We take care of our own," Primo said. "You're welcome. And Micola, listen. Until we get this taken care of, be careful. I'll talk to you soon."

Eddie walked back into the living room as Primo finished his call. He stood in front of the old man, arms out to the side. "What? What happened?"

"The town's gone to shit, Eddie. I need you to go fix things."

"No disrespect, Primo, but what the fuck?"

"Listen to me, Eddie. Micola is my wife's sister, and she's got nobody else to turn to."

"I can't go to St. Paul, Primo. I got work to do. You know I can't take my eyes off-a those bums for one minute without somebody fuckin' somethin' up. I'm your best earner. I need-ta' stay here. Can't you send somebody else?"

"Eddie, St. Paul is your hometown. I need *you* to go. I'll get Freddy to handle things while you're gone."

"Freddy? Fuckin' Freddy's a dipshit and you know it, Primo. I worked a long time gettin' my crew the way I like it. That ain't easy these days, ya' know? Especially now that the whole world is watchin' every move we make. Cell phones and cameras everywhere. I can't afford to have Freddy fuck that all up after everything I-done to get things workin' smoothly."

Primo looked up at Eddie. "I'll handle Freddy."

"But ..."

"Eddie. You're goin' to St. Paul. And after that bullshit last night, you got no choice. We still need to talk about that. But for now, you're goin'. You grew up in St. Paul, and you know that town better than any-a the other guys."

"Don't remind me."

"Stop givin' me shit, Eddie. You know how that fuckin' aggravates me."

Eddie's broad shoulders fell as he looked at the floor, shaking his head. For a man of eighty-one, Primo still held tight reins on his business, and his loyal "muscle" always backed him up.

Eddie put his hands on his hips and looked up. "Alright. I'm goin' ta' St. Paul." He flipped his right shoulder. "Consider it done, Primo."

Primo smiled. "I won't forget this, Eddie."

"Good," Eddie said. He returned to his chair. "Now tell me what I gotta' do."

"Some punks are shootin' up my sister-in-law's neighborhood. Even shot at her house. I need you to go find out who they are and straighten-em out. Couple-a days, a week–tops."

A week!

Eddie took a deep breath and let it out quietly. "Okay, boss."

Primo leaned forward to pick up a nail file and started buffing his nails.

Eddie continued. "You know what I want, boss." He opened his palms and tilted his head.

Primo looked up at Eddie, still buffing.

"I've earned it."

Primo waved his hand and nodded. "We'll talk soon. Maybe when you get back, 'eh?"

Eddie waited for Primo to say more, but the room fell silent.

He tilted his head. "So? She's your sister-in-law, huh?"

Primo nodded. "My wife's sister. Micola Fortunato. She's seventy, seventy-two—somewhere around there. Came right off the boat from across the pond—Calabria—like my Marie. She's a widow—must be thirty years now. Been livin' in the same damn house for forty years. On Burr Street. A real shit neighborhood."

"Oh, yeah. I know Burr Street. Off-a Payne Avenue. Used to be a nice, quiet Italian neighborhood back when my folks first got married."

"Well, it ain't quiet no more. According to Micola, the Italians are long-gone. Now, you gotta' lotta' low-life whites, blacks, the ah'—Mexicans, and ah—'" he snapped his finger "—the what-da-ya-call-'em? Hmong."

"The-fuck's a Hmong?"

Primo shrugged his bony shoulders. "People. From Vietnam, I guess, or China. Who the fuck knows?"

Eddie looked at his shoes trying not to shake his head.

Fuck.

"She call the cops?"

"Yeah. She called 'em." Primo raised his fingers and made air quotes. "Said they're 'investigatin'. Anyhow, now they're shootin' up her fuckin' house and the whole goddamn neighborhood. She knows who's doin' it, too."

"That right?"

"Says one is a kid from across the street, and he's shootin at the kid next door, her side of the street. You believe that?"

"Fuckin' punks."

Primo nodded. "Sounds like some rival gang bullshit."

Eddie smiled. "Should be pretty easy, boss. Nothin' I like better than roughin' up some smartass punks who think they know everything. I'll handle it and be back in a day."

Primo raised his hand. "Hold on."

Eddie's shoulders fell. "What?"

Primo pushed the palm of his hand toward Eddie. "Don't rush it. I don't want any more calls from Micola about this. And I'm sure you won't want to go back again. So, clean up this mess, but good. *Capisci?*"

"What does that mean? You want me ta'—"

Primo shook his head. "Just scare the shit out of 'em."

Eddie nodded. "Easy."

Primo turned to gaze out the dining room window at some birds fluttering around an old birdbath. Eddie waited, saying nothing. When Primo turned back to him, he said, "Listen, Eddie. While you're there, check things out. See if there's any business opportunities. I'll give you some cash for your expenses."

"Yeah? How much?"

Primo shrugged. "Ten thousand."

Eddie frowned. "That won't last long."

Primo tucked in his chin. "Come on. It won't last long. What are you talkin' about, 'eh?"

Eddie sighed. "Fine. Ten-K. I'll work with that."

"Like I said, Eddie, take your time. This means a lot to my wife. And to me."

"Okay, boss," Eddie said. "I'll handle the punks and then check things out."

Primo nodded.

The room fell silent.

"You know anybody back in St. Paul who you can trust? Somebody to help you out while you're there?" Primo asked.

Eddie tilted his head, thinking. "Gotta' cousin. Sal. Haven't talked to him lately. Just got outta' the joint a while back. Stillwater Prison."

"What was he in for?"

"Attempted murder."

Primo nodded. "Where's he stayin'?"

"According to my source, he's staying with his mother."

"Who's your source?"

"My mother."

Primo let out a laugh. "Now that's a good source, am I right?" He laughed again, which caused him to choke and cough. Eddie watched as Primo's face transformed to a light plum.

"You alright?"

Primo waved his hand indicating he'd be fine.

"Jesus. I can't even laugh anymore. It's tough gettin' old."

Eddie nodded.

"Glad I got my Marie to take care-a me." Primo pointed at Eddie. "That's what you need. A nice younger woman who can take care-a you when you get old." He shrugged. "Who knows? Maybe you'll find a nice girl in St. Paul."

Eddie shook his head. "No way. I like things the way they are. I'm a free man. Don't wanna' be accountable to nobody."

"You'll wish you had somebody when you get old." He paused. "How old are you anyhow? Forty?"

Eddie wrinkled his nose. "Forty-three."

Primo's eyes widened. "That right? Holy shit."

Eddie didn't want to talk about his age. "So, your sister-in-law. She lives alone?"

Primo sat back and nodded. "She was married to Vince Fortunato. A long-time Payne Avenue Italian. Been dead for years, now.

"Was he connected?"

"Maybe. Micola's got money, I know that."

Eddie straightened. "Oh yeah? How much?"

Primo shrugged. "A few million—maybe more."

"That right?" Eddie rubbed his chin. This was getting interesting. "All that money and she stays in that shit neighborhood?"

Primo shrugged. "She won't leave. And be prepared. She speaks with a thick Italian accent. And I mean *thick*. Been here forty years, like I said, but ya' still can't understand her."

Eddie stood. "Let me get my travel plans figured out. I'll call ya' later—give you the details. You'll get the money for me? Cash? And her address?"

Primo nodded. "Gimme' a call when things are set."

Eddie turned to leave, but stopped. "About last night. We good?"

Primo flicked his hand. "This is important. Do this right, and I'll forget about it."

Eddie waved and shut the door behind him. That meeting didn't go at all as he'd expected.

Three

*K*ate De Luca felt a chill seep through the cracks in her old kitchen windows. She wrapped her oversized sweater across her body, though it didn't help. Minnesota's spring arrived with its typical sluggish, frigid entrance. After months of painful subzero temperatures, only a scattering of dirty snow piles remained. Yet, typical for March and April, more heavy, wet snow loomed in the short-term forecast.

As she flipped through the stack of bills on the kitchen counter—*pediatrician, surgeon, hospital*—Kate fought the familiar knot tightening in her stomach.

She didn't bother opening them. They were *"friendly reminder"* past due bills from her thirteen-year-old son's skateboarding accident. The amounts had been tallied a month ago, the final total now permanently seared in her memory:

Seven thousand, three hundred dollars.

Her thoughts were interrupted by her mother, Louise, walking in from the living room through the swinging kitchen door.

"Renzo and I had a nice chat. He said his ankle doesn't hurt nearly as much."

"Yes, Mom. I know." She tried to sound enthusiastic. "Good news, right?"

Louise kissed Kate's cheek. "Skateboarding is so dangerous, Kate. I mean, a broken ankle fixed with screws?" She shivered. "I can't even imagine."

"We've talked to Renzo about taking up a new sport," said Kate. "He's not very agreeable."

"I can't imagine he'd ever want to start it up again." Louise reached for her Burberry raincoat hanging over the chair. "He could use a haircut, by the way."

Kate held her breath for a second and let it out slowly. "Yes, Mom. I know."

"What's wrong? You look tired, dear."

Kate frowned, self-consciously pushing strands of loose dark curls behind her ears. "You always know how to make a girl feel pretty, Mom."

Louise laughed. "Kate. You're a beautiful girl. I don't need to tell you that all the time. But I do worry when I see you looking rundown. Get some rest."

"I will. I—"

"I'd better be going. Your father—"

The back door flew open and Kate's husband, Marco, rushed in.

"Kate—I got it! I got the—"

He stopped short, and Kate watched the joy fade from his big brown eyes, while maintaining some semblance of a phony smile.

"Oh. Louise, hi," he said.

"Hello, Marco." Louise tilted her head and smiled as her shoulder-length auburn hair bounced around her face. "I was just leaving. I take it from your grand entrance that you got the job." She smiled and folded her raincoat over her arm.

Marco gave Kate a quick glance. "Ah—yeah. I got the job." He stepped over to Kate, bending to give her a quick peck on her cheek.

She rubbed his arm as she looked up at him, smiling. "You got the mechanic's job?"

Marco nodded, giving her that smile she'd fallen in love with years ago. "Sure did."

Relief drifted through Kate's arms and legs, and she allowed herself to forget the doctor bills for the first time in a while.

"That's awesome!"

"Thanks," Marco said. He smiled uncertainly at Louise. "I—ah'—start on Monday. It's fairly close to us. Just off Payne and Maryland."

"That's wonderful news," Louise said. "Maybe now you can move out of this dreadful old house and this terrible neighborhood."

"Mom, stop—"

Louise shook her finger at them. "I'm not kidding. I heard on the news just this morning that there was another shooting the night before last." She pointed her finger toward the living room.

"Right over on Bedford Street."

Kate's jaw fell. "But—"

"That's right," said her mother. "Just a few blocks away from where we're standing. Gang related, they said." She put her hands on her hips, her green eyes looking sharply at them. "It's time, you two. You wouldn't want your only son—my only grandson—caught in the crossfire now, would you? This is serious."

"Mom. Please—"

"You could move out to Hudson, closer to your father and me."

"Mom. We're *not* moving to Wisconsin."

Renzo pushed through the kitchen door, and Louise moved to hold it as he struggled through on his crutches, his long brown curls falling across his face.

"We're moving?"

"No, honey. We're *not* moving," Kate said.

Louise grabbed her designer handbag from the kitchen table. "Suit yourselves."

She headed for the back door and turned. "At least *think* about it. This house is falling apart. A new house wouldn't be such a terrible thing, would it?"

Kate opened her mouth to speak, but she closed it after seeing Marco shoot her a look with a tiny shake of his head.

"Well, I'm off. Your father's probably pacing the floor wondering where his dinner is. Don't forget, darling. Lunch on Saturday. Just the two of us."

Louise then made the rare move of kissing Marco on his cheek, patting his arm as she pulled away.

"Congratulations on the new job."

She turned with a dramatic wave.

"Toodles!"

Four

*E*ddie Bracchio settled into his first-class seat and closed his eyes, letting the scotch and the purr from the plane's engine relax him. This was a nice change—this little bit of luxury. If anything good came from this trip, it was the chance to get away from Brooklyn on Primo's dime. He dozed as he thought about his new assignment.

The flight landed on time—7:00 p.m. Eddie looked around as he waited for a cab outside The Minneapolis-St. Paul International Airport. The city's crisp April air struck his face and cleared his mind.

As he settled into the back seat of an old cab, the familiarity of the drive tickled his memory. He closed his eyes and pictured his tiny, old gray house on the corner of Bedford and Beaumont Streets, just off the main drag—Payne Avenue.

He peered through the rain-coated window and tried to make out any familiar landmarks. Everything looked older, shittier than he'd remembered, with more traffic. It had been twenty-five years since he'd left. He was afraid of what other changes he'd encounter come sunrise.

The cab driver weaved through downtown St. Paul and pulled into a valet circle adjacent to a massive, creamy-stoned building. Its pillared front entrance emblazoned the hotel's name etched in Roman type:

THE ST. PAUL HOTEL.

A historic building, the hotel is a downtown landmark overlooking Rice Park, a popular hub for festivals, concerts and the *St. Paul Winter Carnival*. He was anxious to get checked into his room. He'd call Primo's sister-in-law first thing in the morning. He wanted to take care of the two punks as soon as possible; he was actually looking forward to it.

As he entered the hotel lobby, Eddie looked around and nodded to himself. Its lavish and extravagant décor suited him.

As a plus, it was only a few miles from Primo's sister-in-law's house. He didn't want to waste time traveling around in dirty cabs any more than necessary.

Eddie settled in and ordered room service. As he waited, he peeked out the window. The fractured moon shone brightly through the bare tree branches overlooking Rice Park. It felt strange to be back. He closed the blinds and contemplated his plans for the trip.

Five

Marco shut the door behind his mother-in-law.

"Dad! Grandma gave you a kiss!" Renzo said.

Marco smiled. "Yeah, she sure did."

"I *told* you she likes you," Renzo said, giggling.

Kate laughed at her son who was leaning on his crutches. He really did need a haircut. She pushed his curly brown hair away from his eyes.

Marco roughly rubbed Louise's kiss off his cheek. "Felt like a cold fish."

Kate shook her head at him while Renzo belted out his loudest musical laugh, one of Kate's favorite sounds.

"Alright. Go wash up. It's suppertime." She pointed at Renzo. "And don't argue. Wash 'em. And put on a warmer shirt. It's still freezing out."

"Fine."

Marco rolled his eyes at Kate as he held the door for Renzo to hobble through.

"I'll get him movin'. Be right down."

While she waited, Kate began plating their food. She looked up when she heard her son struggling back into the kitchen.

"All washed up," said Renzo. "And—a warm shirt."

She bit her lip as he banged his crutches into the cabinets and dragged his cast along her already heavily damaged wood floor.

"Come on, Renzo. Can you please try to be more careful?"

"Sorry, mom. Can't help it!"

She held her tongue and shook her head. The kid was oblivious, but what did she expect? She walked to the stove and lowered her head, breathing in the scents coming from the contents of the simmering pot she'd started earlier.

"Your gravy smells delicious, *Mother*."

"Okay. That's enough schmoozing. And it's *sauce*, not *gravy*."

"Grandma De Luca calls it *gravy*."

Kate frowned. "Don't start. Sit. Please."

Marco came into the kitchen and clapped his hands. "Let's eat!"

Kate delivered plates of spaghetti and Marco brought salad and buttered bread to the table. They held hands and said a quick prayer before passing the bread.

"So," Kate said, trying to sound casual, "what's the pay? Did they tell you?"

Marco frowned. "Yeah. Nineteen bucks an hour. Should be forty hours a week. I was hoping for more. I mean, I'm worth more."

Kate's heart sank, but she smiled and reached over to touch his arm. "You *are* worth more, but for now, we'll take it. You'll get more down the road. We have to be patient."

Marco sucked in a deep breath and smiled. "You're right. Thanks." He let out a chuckle. "Whoo! What a relief."

"And ... benefits?" She concentrated on twisting some pasta around her fork. "Did they say?"

He nodded. "Yeah. They're sending me some stuff on that. Don't get your hopes up, though. I don't think it'll be much."

Kate turned to her salad.

"Nice work, Dad," Renzo said, with a mouthful of spaghetti.

Marco smiled. "Thanks, dude. How's that ankle feelin' today?"

Renzo shrugged. "Pretty good."

"Good. Oh, I almost forgot," Marco said, wiping his mouth. He raised his brows and smiled at Kate. "My mom called."

Renzo giggled as Kate stopped chewing and frowned. "Uh-oh. I'm not sure I can handle both of our mothers on the same day. Was it the usual conversation?"

"Yep."

Marco raised his voice and started his perfect impersonation of his mother, Italian accent and all. He pinched his thumb and forefinger together and jerked them toward Kate. "*When-a you comin-a visit? I wanna' see my grandson.*"

Kate tilted her head. "Let me guess. She wants to see *me*, too. She misses me terribly."

Marco choked on his wine. "Yeah, right. It was more of the usual, '*I can't believe it's been two years since you-visit. I can't believe you-been away twelve years.*'"

Kate laughed and continued Marco's quoting of his mother, using the same hand-waving gestures. "*I can't believe you left New York for that girl.*"

Marco high-fived her, his eyes sparkling. "Very good impression."

She bowed her head. "Thank you. I'm here all week."

Renzo yanked off a bite of bread. "She likes you, Mama. She just doesn't like your *gravy*." Renzo's eyes sparkled as he giggled at his joke.

Kate put down her fork and leaned forward. "First of all, it's called sauce. Spaghetti *sauce. Not gravy.*"

Marco raised his eyebrows. "It's *gravy* at my ma's house."

"Well, here, in St. Paul, in our house, it's called *sauce*. And I make a fine spaghetti *sauce*."

"Alright Renzo. Let's leave Mom alone."

Marco turned to her, taking hold of her hand, which now held a forkful of wound-up spaghetti. He jerked her hand toward his. "I love your *sauce*."

She frowned. "Good. Now, can we just eat?"

"You alright?"

Kate paused before clanking her fork onto the plate. "I'm sorry, Marco, but nineteen bucks an hour? Seriously? How are we gonna' manage with that? Huh? Why did you take it without waiting for the other job? That could have been more money."

"Jesus. What's with you?" He threw down his napkin and pushed his chair back. "And while we're at it—what about *your* job? Huh? Zero commissions in—what? Three weeks? Maybe *you're* the one who should assess her job and income."

Renzo put his fork down and set his hands in his lap.

Kate's mouth fell open. "I…" Tears welled in her eyes.

Marco touched her arm. "Kate. I'm sorry."

She shook her head. "No. *I'm* sorry. I shouldn't have said that. I'm happy about your job. I am."

They finished their meal in silence, Renzo stealing looks at each of them as he spun his pasta around his fork.

Kate sat back and took a sip of wine. "Maybe we could take Renzo to see your mom after we get caught up on some bills. He should see her. We'd have to pay down one of the cards before we could even think about it. Plus the doctor bills … " She shook her head and kept eating.

Marco stared at her. "You've made your point, Kate. Money's tight, I know. It sucks. But, with this new job, things should loosen up—at least a little."

Kate shrugged. "I'm sure it will. Time will tell."

Marco stood and brought his plate to the sink.

"Okay," Renzo said, waving his fork with a meatball stuck to it. "Let's all try to get along. Money's not everything."

Marco turned to him from the sink, and Kate paused from taking another sip of wine. They both laughed as Marco tossed a dish towel at his head.

"Hey! My meatball!"

Kate rubbed Renzo's head and smiled. "It's movie night," she said. "Let's finish the dishes so we can relax."

Six

The following morning, Eddie opened the drapes to a view of the park. Rain continued to fall and the clouds cast a dark mood across the horizon. He fumbled in his pocket for Micola's number. The phone rang twice before he heard someone pick it up.

A cough and then the low, quiet voice of an older woman: "Hello?"

"Yeah. Is this Mrs. Fortunato?"

"Who is this?"

Whoa. Thick accent.

"This is Eddie Bracchio. Primo Simonelli told me to call you. I'm here—in St. Paul."

"Oh! *Sí*! *Grazie*! You-here to help me with those boys a-shootin' up my house?"

"Yeah. Ah, *sí, Signora*."

"*Bene*! *Grazie mille*!"

"Can I come by your house this morning? I need more information on these punks—I mean—boys."

"*Sí. Grazie.*"

"Um. And your address, *Signora*?"

"Oh! *Sí*! It's-a 1667 Burr Street. You need directions?"

"No, Ma'am. I'll find it. Eleven o'clock? Sound good?"

"Eleven o'clock. *Grazie, Signore*. You come. I make-a coffee, okay? I see you soon. Thank you for helping me, *Signore*."

"No problem. See you soon, alright?"

"*Sí, Signore. Arrivederci.*"

"Yeah. *Arrivederci* to you too, 'eh?"

Eddie hung up the phone and found himself smiling.

After a hot shower, he removed from his garment bag the one suit he'd brought with him. Suits displayed power and Eddie loved to dress the part. He adjusted his crisp white dress shirt and gray silk tie before donning the finely tailored black Italian jacket and matching slacks. He stepped back to admire the final look. This would certainly give him the attention he wanted. Nothing too over-the-top. These people were simple, laid-back. He didn't want to stick out too much.

Subtle power. He looked perfect.

The ride to Bedford Street was a quick ten-minutes. As the young Somali cab driver weaved through downtown and crossed over to Seventh Street, Eddie looked out at the rainy city. It was older, drab; more rundown than he'd remembered. As they passed an old, tan brick building on the corner, Eddie sat up.

"The Gopher Bar? That dive still open?" he asked the driver.

"I guess so," said the kid. "Never been there."

"They got the *best* Coney Islands in town. Not as good as the ones in Coney Island, but really good. Boy does that take me back. Been there *forever*."

"I don't know what that is," said the kid. "Coney Island?"

"You don't know what a—? Oh my God. You kiddin' me?" He looked across the front seat at the driver's face in the rearview mirror. "It's a hotdog with chili, cheese and onions. You should really try one. They're fuckin' delicious."

The kid laughed. "Hotdogs? No. I don't eat those."

"Too bad. Ya-missin' out."

Eddie felt a twinge of nostalgia as they moved along. Turning left onto Payne Avenue, Eddie noticed the Minnesota Music Café on his left, a small music venue known for attracting big acts, like Minnesota's own superstars: Prince and Bob Dylan. The slight gray building wore a sign painted directly onto the brick in red and white:

"Where the Food's Great & the Music's Cookin'!"

As they continued their way down Payne, Eddie saw only nondescript single-story buildings with worn and faded paint, obviously untouched for decades. Across on the right, however, Eddie noticed what looked to be a new townhome development. Its clean, updated look and landscaping gave the area a fresh feel. Past the development was a row of trees that lined the east side of the street. Eddie knew Swede Hollow Park was just beyond those trees.

Despite the new development, little had changed. The Asians he saw walking down the street, and in cars driving alongside the cab, were new to the ethnic mix. If there were any remaining Italians, they were hiding on this bleak day.

The cab approached Tedesco Street and stopped for a red light. Morelli's, a small Italian Market and Liquor Store, stood across the street on the corner to their left.

Eddie sat up. "Jesus. Morelli's? That place is still open?"

"Yes sir. Still open."

He looked out at the old building. The Italian flag was prominently displayed above the door of the once-white brick exterior, now faded and chipped. Hand-painted green vines crawled upward as though reaching for its last bit of heritage. He sat back in his seat.

"I used to shop there with my grandmother."

The light changed to green and the driver turned left. Eddie kept his eye on Morelli's, now on his right. A beautiful woman in a fitted navy dress and tan high heels walked out of the market struggling with two bags of groceries.

"Hey," Eddie said to the driver. "Slow down here."

The cab slowed as Eddie rolled down his window. The woman's long brown hair flowed behind her as she caught sight of the slowing cab.

Eddie called out to her. "Hey gorgeous! Ya' need any help with them bags?"

She gave him a hesitant smile as she looked around and behind her. When she realized he was speaking to her, she shook her head.

"No thanks. I'm good. My car's right here." She crooked her head toward a white sedan.

Eddie waved. "Alright. Keep doin' what ya' doin. Ya' lookin' real good!"

He watched the woman laugh as she called back to him.

"Thanks!"

The cab picked up speed and Eddie turned to watch her until she was out of sight.

He sat back. "You should never pass on a chance to talk to a beautiful woman. Know what I mean?"

The driver chuckled.

Eddie continued to look around as the cab slowly traveled up Tedesco Street. He recognized the rundown apartment complex to his left; the petite old clapboard houses on his right looked exactly as he'd remembered, each the same as the next.

As the driver turned right onto Burr, Eddie closed his eyes and pictured his old house on Desoto, a few blocks away. He was anxious to see the old place and made a note to drive by before flying back home.

He looked side-to-side through the rainy windows of the cab, noting the strange, nostalgic emotions stirring in his gut. He never would have guessed the old neighborhood would have affected him this way.

He looked up at the passing branches of mature maple trees draping overhead. They formed an arch—almost like a roof— across the deserted road. Cars parked on both sides left barely enough room for the cab to pass.

He couldn't help feeling disappointed, though. The old neighborhood looked like shit—rundown houses, yards littered with old toys, trash cans and crappy lawns. It destroyed his fond memories.

A faint thump of rap music muffled by the cab's closed windows jarred Eddie from his thoughts. The cab passed a group of five young Black men in baggy jeans and sweatshirts standing near a parked car. Oblivious to the rain, but not the approaching cab, they stopped their business and turned to stare at Eddie, snarls on their faces as the cab passed.

No one else was out on this cool, rainy morning. This encounter further disillusioned Eddie. No more old Italian ladies laughing as they walked along the sidewalk. No old Italian guys sitting on their porches playing pinochle. The neighborhood of his childhood was definitely gone.

The cab continued along, crossing Minnehaha Avenue and slowing to a stop three houses down on Burr Street. To Eddie's left, loomed a dark brick house sitting high on a hill. Extravagant and grand, it dwarfed its neighboring homes with its two stories and roofed front porch. The grandiose mansion appeared to be in pristine condition. Eddie guessed it was built in the twenties. The lush, emerald grass appeared freshly mowed, in stark contrast to the dumpy yards on either side.

He paid the driver, tipping generously.

"Thank you," said the kid.

"Yeah. See ya' 'round."

Eddie pulled down his black fedora as he exited the cab, rain pelting its fine fabric. The cool, damp air moistened his lungs as he hurried across the street and onto the cracked sidewalk. He looked up at the house for a second before jogging up six cement stairs and then started on the next four leading to the heavy wooden front door, its roof protecting him from further drenching.

A slight motion from the curtain to his left caught his attention as he pressed the yellowed doorbell and waited. He heard the click and release of the deadbolt as the hinges of the heavy mahogany door creaked open, revealing a short, heavy-set woman of about seventy. She smiled.

"Buongiorno."

Seven

*E*ddie tipped his hat. "Mrs. Fortunato?"

"*Sí.*"

The plump, stocky woman wore her wiry gray hair pinned back, loose and messy. She smiled, her wrinkled, sagging cheeks turning pink with warmth as she waved him in.

"Come in. Out of the rain."

Eddie wiped his feet on the mat at the foot of the door as he removed his hat and leather jacket.

"I'm Eddie Bracchio." He palmed his hair with his free hand. "Primo Simonelli sent me."

The subtle scent of garlic and sauce tickled his nose.

"*Sí! Grazie, Signore* Bracchio." She waved her veined hand, ushering him in. "Please, *entra*, come in," she said, in a thick Italian accent. Her cheery smile warmed her brown eyes, twinkling behind drooping lids.

Eddie smiled as he bowed slightly. "Thank you—*grazie.*" His Italian was rusty, but he enjoyed its musical lift. It reminded him of his family.

Her strong grip surprised him as she pulled on his arm drawing him to her for a quick kiss on his cheek. He caught a hint of soap that disappeared as he pulled away.

"Well," he said, "I wasn't expectin' such a nice greeting."

Micola clapped her hands and brushed them down a white marinara-stained apron. "Look at you. So handsome, *Signore* Bracchio." She rubbed her chin. "I like this—how you say—?"

Eddie stroked his salt-and-pepper goatee. "This? My goatee?"

"*Sí.* Goatee." She laughed. "I'm so happy you-here, *Signore* Bracchio."

"Please. Call me Eddie."

"Okay, Eddie. And you—call me Micola, okay?" She smiled as she put his jacket and hat into a closet near the door.

"Okay, sure. 'Micola' is it?"

"Mee-koe-la. Sí?"

"Sí," Eddie said, smiling. Her charm was irresistible.

Micola guided Eddie across the tiny threshold of black-and-white-checked linoleum and led him down a short, dark hall, the old mahogany wood floor creaking under their weight. Photographs of smiling people lined the walls.

They turned left to the entrance of a decent-sized living room decorated with outdated furniture in a beige and rose floral print, worn and faded from years of sun and use.

Straight ahead was a massive picture-window overlooking Burr Street and the front yard and steps Eddie had just climbed. Facing him beneath the window, was an extended sofa. Across it, were two chairs and a mahogany coffee table. Under it all, was an oversized rug covering the worn wooden floor.

Micola's house was brighter and cheerier than it had appeared from the outside, and it reminded Eddie of his grandmother's house not too much further down the road.

Micola turned and asked him to sit. Eddie hesitated. Each seating option was covered in fitted, clear plastic. He chose the sofa, cringing at the sound of the stiff plastic under his weight.

Micola smiled. "You-like some coffee?"

Eddie nodded. "Sure. Thanks."

"Okay. I'll be back." She turned with a quiet giggle and bustled out of the room.

While he waited, Eddie looked around the old-fashioned living room. To his right, sat a built-in mahogany cabinet pushed tightly against the wall. Above it hung a large mirror framed in shiny gilded metal.

Eddie stood and walked to it, frowning as it captured the honesty of his reflection. He straightened his posture and leaned in, fingering his hair where the hat had misplaced some of the strands, before standing back to assess his appearance. The sound of the old lady shuffling down the hall sent him back to his seat on the sofa.

Micola approached the living room with a silver tray holding a set of dainty China. Eddie stood to help her.

"Please," he said. "Sit. Let me pour."

"Grazie, Signore," she said, taking her seat in the chair across from him.

Eddie held his gaze with a smile as he poured two cups of steaming coffee. Micola smiled nervously until Eddie handed her a cup and returned to his place on the sofa. He took a sip before beginning their conversation.

"Now, Micola." Eddie smiled, pointing at her. "I notice you gotta' *bit* of an accent."

She nodded before he continued. "How long you been in the states?"

As Micola spoke, Eddie did his best to listen intently, grasping what he could from her thick accent. She told him about meeting her husband in Calabria, Italy, moving to St. Paul, and raising her family there for many years. She was sweet and jolly, and he instantly liked her.

At a pause in their conversation, Micola excused herself to the kitchen. She returned with two small plates holding generous pieces of lemon cake with a light lemon glaze.

"*Mangia'*," she said. "I make-a this cake for you today, Eddie." She returned to her seat, crossing her arms.

"You did? Well ain't that sweet-a you'se? Thanks."

She watched with a smile as Eddie took his first bite.

He raised his brows. "Mmm, that's good."

"You like?"

"Like? You kiddin' me? I *love*."

Eddie took another bite and wiped his mouth with the elegant cloth napkin. He flipped his fork up-and-down as he spoke. "One thing about me," he said. "I never lie about food—especially homemade sh—" he caught himself—"cookin'."

Micola beamed. "You come tonight, Eddie. I make you something. What-you like?"

Eddie took a gulp of coffee and said, "Well, my favorite is eggplant parmigiana. You know how to make that?"

Micola nodded, a proud look on her face. She waved her hand. "*Sì*. You come tonight. I make-a you eggplant parmigiana. You come?"

"Yeah, sure. I got no plans. Six o'clock?"

"*Sì*. Six o'clock. *Bene*."

Eddie set his coffee cup and plate onto the table and sat back, crossing one leg over the other. "Now, tell me about these punks shootin' up the fuckin' neighborhood."

Micola's eyes widened as she put her hand to her mouth.

Eddie wiped his mouth and leaned forward. "Oh my God. 'Scuse my language, Mrs. Fortunato. I gotta' work on that, ya' know?"

She chuckled as she pointed her finger. "*Nessun problema*. It's okay, Eddie."

Eddie stroked his goatee. "Thank you." He started again. "So, do you know who they are? These guys?"

Micola frowned. "There is a Black kid, Dario. He—" she frowned and looked toward the ceiling—"maybe twenty years old." She pointed toward her left in the direction of the stairs and front door. "He lives over there. In the house next door."

She then pointed toward the front window at Eddie's back. "And the other kid, Tau. Same age—twenty, I think. Hmong. He live across the street."

She stood and walked toward the picture window, pointing furiously, getting angry.

"There."

"Oh yeah," Eddie said. "'Hmong.' Primo mentioned that. I ain't never heard-a that before." Eddie stood to look out the front window and across the quiet street.

"That house, right there?"

She nodded. "*Sì*. That is Tau's house."

"So, what happened the other night?" Eddie asked.

"Okay, Eddie." Micola pointed to the sofa. "Sit. I-tell you."

Eddie eased back onto the plastic, hoping, but failing, to keep the noise at bay. He leaned forward, elbows on his knees. "Let's hear it."

Micola moved to the other side of the coffee table, but remained standing. She began throwing her arms around as she told her story.

"It was the other night—like I tell Primo. But—," she shook her finger, "—this-no-is the first time, Eddie." She shook her head.

Eddie frowned. "No?"

She raised her fingers. "Two other times this happened."

"I go upstairs in my bed, sound asleep. I think it was—maybe two-three o'clock in the morning. I hear noises—on the side of my house by my bedroom window. The side by Dario's house." She raised her hands toward the sky. "*Molto forte!*"

"Loud?"

"*Sì.*"

"The bullets—they hit my house." She clapped her hands. "Bam, bam, bam! I sit up fast. The house was cold, Eddie. I keep the heat down real low at night. Too much money."

Eddie smiled as he recalled Primo saying she had millions. He nodded. "Yeah, I hear ya'. Go on. Then what?"

Micola continued. "I hear many shots and I think to myself, why-they hit my house? These boys, they need shooting lessons, no? I don't think they know how to do it."

Eddie chuckled and Micola stopped talking. "Why-you laugh, Eddie?"

He raised his hand. "Sorry. Go on."

She nodded. "Then, it's quiet. I wait. Then—" she clapped her hands again as her usually low voice went into a high shrill— "they shoot my house some more. Almost break my windows. Oh, Eddie, I was so afraid!"

Eddie leaned forward. "No cops? Nothin'?"

She shook her head. "I get outta' my bed—my feet-so cold on that floor. I get to the phone on the nightstand. I call *la polizia*."

"And how'd you know it was *those* two boys?"

"Because, I look out the window. I gotta' big light on the side of the house. It shined down—right on Dario! I see him! And he—he look-up at me and he do this to me." Micola gestured the finger to Eddie who shook his head.

"Micola. You should *never* go to the window when you hear gunshots. *Never*." He shook his head. "Very dangerous. You coulda' been shot, ya' understand me?"

Micola pursed her lips. "*Sì*, Eddie. I know this. But Dario—he *never* do that to me. His mother. She's a nice lady."

Eddie shook his head. "I don't give a sh—" He paused. "S'cuse me. I mean, I don't *care* about his ma'." He waved his hand for her to continue. "Go ahead. What happened next? Did you see that other kid? What's his name, Tar?"

Micola smiled. "No. Tau. Like 'cow' but with 't.'"

"Tau. Got it. You see him? This Tau-guy?"

She shook her head. "No. I can't see his house from uppa-my bedroom window. But Dario—he shouted his name when he shoot his gun over to Tau's house. Those two boys—they no-like each other." She folded her arms and shook her head. "Never did. Maybe is-because Dario is black and Tau is Hmong?" She shook her head. "I don't know too much about this, but I think this is how it is in this neighborhood. There are gangs now, Eddie." She jammed her finger toward the floor. "Right here in this neighborhood."

Eddie shook his head. "What-a shame. I used to live here—long time ago."

"Oh, Eddie, really? Here?"

"Yeah. Do you know the Sabatinos?"

She put her hand to her chin, thinking. "Sabatinos? I think so, *sì*."

"Yeah. That's my family. My grandparents—my ma's parents." He waved his arm across the room. "We all lived here. Right down on Desoto."

Micola's eyes widened as she smiled. "You-kiddin' me, Eddie. That's so nice. You remember the neighborhood?"

Eddie nodded. "Sure I remember. Great old Italian neighborhood." He frowned. "Gone now though, am I right? Swede Hollow? The Italians? We used to have a lotta' fun. Nobody shot nobody. Everybody got along—well, mostly. Too bad it's all changed."

Micola sat back in her chair and shook her head. "It's bad, Eddie. But I no-move." She jabbed her finger into the arm of the chair. "I'm here in this house forty years. I die here."

Eddie chuckled. "Understood. Now, Let's get back to these kids. So you *did* call the cops?"

"*Sì*. The policeman—he come to my house. He go outside with a flashlight. He say, 'yes, there are bullet holes.' He say 'yes, he-talk to those boys.'"

Eddie stood to leave. "Well, I'm gonna' talk to 'em, too. Time fa-me to take care-a business. That's why Primo sent me. I'll go straighten-em out right now."

"Eddie, please don't hurt them. They-boys—causing a little trouble."

He put his hand on her shoulder. "Don't you worry 'bout nothin'. I'm gonna take care-a this problem. And those two boys? They won't bother you no more. *Capisci?*"

"Okay, Eddie. *Grazie.*" She walked him to the front door, retrieving his leather jacket and hat from the closet.

Turning toward the front door, he said, "Do you know if these guys are home right now?" He looked at his watch. Eleven-thirty a.m.

"Dario—he's home. He leaves at night. Tau, I think he works. I see him go in the morning."

Eddie tipped his head toward Dario's house next door. "I'll start with this punk and take it from there. Be back soon, 'eh?"

"Okay, Eddie. *Grazie.* Be careful."

He laughed. "You ain't gotta' worry 'bout me."

Micola gave him a nervous giggle. "Okay."

He waved his hand. "Alright. See you'se later."

As Micola shut the door behind him, Eddie walked down the steps to the sidewalk, plotting his moves with the two idiots who liked shootin' up the old lady's house—and the neighborhood. Afterward, he'd call Primo with an update.

Eight

Kate came into the kitchen with her bag from Morelli's Market and placed it on the counter before taking off her jacket.

Marco walked in and opened the fridge. "Hey babe. What'd-ya get at Morelli's?"

Kate dug into the bag. "Ground beef and pork chops for later this week. Bought you some beer and a bottle of wine for me. I stopped in after my showing this morning to save us a trip later."

Marco kept his head in the fridge. "Nice."

"You gonna' keep your head in there much longer?" she asked.

He stood with an apple in his hand and saw her holding the packages of meat.

"Oh, sorry." He set the apple down. "Give me those."

Kate pulled the rest of the stuff from the bag. "Oh!" she said. "Guess what happened to me on my way out?"

"Out of Morelli's?"

"Yeah. Guess."

Marco shrugged. "No idea." He took a bite of his apple.

Kate smiled and did a twirl.

"What? What's with the dance?" he said, grinning.

Kate flipped her shoulder and flashed him a beautiful smile. "I got hit on."

Marco leaned against the counter. "Oh yeah?" He nodded as his eyes swept across her. "Well, you *do* look amazing. I've always liked that dress."

She wiggled her eyebrows. "Apparently this guy liked my dress, too." She laughed at herself as Marco rolled his eyes. "Anyway, as I walked out of the store, I saw this cab slow down."

Marco swallowed a bite of apple. "A cab?"

"Yep," Kate said. "The passenger in the back seat rolled down the window to ask if I needed help with my bags. When I said 'no thanks,' he said 'keep doin' what you're doin' cuz you're lookin' good.' Or somethin' like that. Isn't that hilarious?"

"Wow," Marco said. "That's different."

"I know, right? From a cab?"

Marco smiled. "You've still got it baby. I'm the luckiest guy on earth." He kissed her cheek. "As soon as this rain stops, we'll go to your mom's and then to the park."

Kate nodded. "Okay. It's supposed to stop by noon." She kicked off her pumps and put away the liquor.

Marco called out to her as he left the kitchen. "And when we get back, we can have some of that wine you bought."

"That's *my* wine!"

Nine

Whistling his favorite Sinatra tune, Eddie strolled the short distance to the house next door. The air felt damp and cool on his face, but he barely noticed. He was too focused on the little puddles dotting the cracked, weed-infested sidewalk. With genuine concern for his new Italian leather shoes, he cursed the spatters of mud touching their tips.

He turned to face the small and shabby, two-story house. The shadow of Micola's house loomed over it like a giant guarding its tiny prisoner. He familiarized himself with any potential obstacles before his inevitable confrontation.

He pushed open the broken gate of the rusty chain-link fence and walked the short sidewalk to the house. A screen door—minus the screen—hung and wobbled from its upper hinge. Eddie moved it out of his way and pounded on the dirty wooden front door. Muffled swearing and banging came from inside.

The sound of pounding footsteps grew as the door swung open, revealing a tall and reedy light-skinned Black teenager with a medium-length Afro and angry brown eyes. Eddie guessed him to be nineteen, maybe twenty. His shirtless torso revealed slight muscles on bony arms, tight, narrow abs and a hairless chest.

In a surprisingly high voice, the kid shouted at Eddie. "The-fuck *you* want?"

Eddie stared at him for a few seconds, setting the tone. "You Dario?" His voice quiet, calm.

"Yeah," said the kid, giving Eddie the cocky tough-guy once-over. "Who the-fuck are you?"

Eddie's swift two-handed shove to the chest stunned the young man who found himself tripping backward into the house. Stumbling and cursing, Dario landed hard-assed in his own dimly lit living room. He paused for a second to look up at Eddie, who stood over him, daring him with his angry eyes to get back up. The kid surprised Eddie by doing just that.

Dario scrambled to his feet, but he was no match for Eddie's speed or strength. In one swift move, Eddie had Dario's arm twisted around to his back, using his other hand to shove Dario's face against the living room wall. The force of the blow sent a cheaply framed drawing crashing to the floor.

At the same time, the sound of a woman yelling came from the back of the house. Dario's cocky attitude had quieted, replaced with a steady grunt and cry as he tried to adjust himself to lessen the pain. For good measure, Eddie put an upward and twisting pressure on Dario's wrist, ready to break the hand, if necessary.

The screaming woman ran into the room, and Eddie freed his other hand to prepare for what might come next. Dario was fully under his control, so he relaxed and stood ready for her. The smell of stale smoke and fried food suddenly burned his nose.

The woman was followed by a black and golden German Shepherd prancing behind her, the click of its toenails loud on the grimy linoleum. Behind the big dog, came a young boy who appeared to be about six years old.

The tall Black woman stopped short, hands on her hips, as she stared at the scene before her. "What the hell is goin' on here? Who are *you*?"

Standing firm, she glared at Eddie with cold, brown eyes as wild as her short, wiry hair. Eddie smiled calmly at her, almost casually, the twisting of Dario's hand a seemingly effortless task. Still firmly pressed to the wall, Dario moaned quietly, his eyes pleading to the woman.

Eddie assessed her for any potential danger, noting that her black sweatpants and oversized gray t-shirt might be hiding her size and strength. She turned her gaze to Dario.

"What is goin' on, Dario? Who is this guy?"

Dario coughed, his head still pressed against the wall. "Mama, help me. I don't know who he is."

She lurched toward Eddie, but he was too quick. He grabbed her throat, stopping her short. His grip was firm but not lethal. The woman's hands instinctively grabbed onto Eddie's fingers, while at the same time, she pulled herself back and away from him.

The dog began to bark and snarl, so Eddie loosened his hold on her. He noticed a faded bruise under her right eye as he released his hand and shoved her away. The dog stopped barking but stayed close to her heels. At the same time, he put more pressure on Dario's wrist causing him to squeal.

The woman moved toward her cellphone sitting on the coffee table next to an old worn-out sofa. "Get offa' my son! Get the hell outta' my house before I call the cops!"

"I wouldn't do that, lady," Eddie said, shaking his head and pressing a little harder. Dario whimpered.

Eddie pointed at the woman with his free hand. "Now, who the fuck are *you?*"

"I'm his mom," she said, her hands trembling. "Marian Tucker." Eddie stayed calm while the dog's barking increased as it circled Eddie's feet.

"Shut up, Barkley. Sit," she said. The dog immediately stopped barking and sat next to her.

"And the kid?"

"My son, Cody. Dario's brother."

"Alright," Eddie said, nodding. "I want everybody to do what I say and no one gets hurt. Not today at least." Eddie pointed at the little boy. "Send Cody upstairs. Now."

Eddie watched the woman's shoulders sink and her confidence wane, fear visible on her tired face. She bent down and spoke quietly to the crying boy. "Cody, go on upstairs, baby. Everything's fine."

The boy hesitated, squeezing her thigh. Her voice grew firmer. "Now." Cody let go of his mom and ran upstairs. "And don't you dare come down 'til I tell ya', you hear?"

"Yes ma'am," the boy cried.

"Very good, Ms. Tucker," Eddie said, looking around the room. "Now, is there a *Mr.* Tucker around here today?"

She shook her head. "No. He took off four years ago."

"I see." Eddie smoothed his goatee with his free hand, his other hand still gripping Dario's twisted wrist, his face still planted against the wall. "Well, Ms. Tucker, as you can see, we have a *pretty* big problem with your son."

"Come on man," Dario choked. "Let me go. *Please!*"

Barkley's quiet rumble grew angrier.

"Shut that dog up."

Ms. Tucker ignored Eddie and folded her arms in defiance. "Let go-a my boy first. *Then,* I'll shut the dog up. Who are you, anyways? What do you want with Dario?"

"All due respect, Ms. Tucker, I'll do the fuckin' talkin'. Now sit right there on that sofa and shut the fuck up. And get this damn dog away from me."

She lowered her arms and did what she was told. She grabbed Barkley by the collar and sat on the sofa, pulling him next to her feet.

Eddie continued. "Your son is in a *lotta'* trouble."

"What are you talkin' about?" She asked. "What kind-a trouble? You a cop? You don't seem like no cop."

Eddie shifted his feet. "Did you know that Dario's gotta' gun? And likes shootin' up the neighborhood with it?"

Eddie gave the kid's wrist a hard turn. Dario cried out. "Come on, man! Let me go, please. My hand's 'bout-ta break."

Eddie ignored his pleas. "I'm here-ta put a stop-ta all this trouble he's causin'."

Ms. Tucker stood and looked at her son, his face still pressed into the wall. "Dario? You gotta' gun?"

Dario squirmed and moaned but didn't answer his mom. With the increased volume and tension in the room, Barkley started barking again.

"No disrespect, Ms. Tucker," Eddie said, "but ah'—if you had better control over your son, we wouldn't be in this predicament right now, am I right?"

She shook her head, her hands balled into fists, head thrust forward. "Well, what am I supposed to do? Huh?" She pointed at Dario. "He hits me all the time." She pointed to her eye. "See this?"

Eddie scowled at Dario and released his grip enough to allow Dario's head to come up from the wall. Eddie then dug his free hand into Dario's cheeks, and twisted his face and head to the left, while still twisting the right wrist. "Are *you* the one who gave her that bruise? *You* hit your mother? Huh, tough guy? That-what you do?" Dario moaned and a tear rolled down his cheek.

"Please," he whispered. "Please stop, man."

Eddie released Dario's face with a firm shove but kept pressure on his wrist. "You piece-a shit." He backhanded Dario's cheek and Dario screamed.

"That shit stops right fuckin' now," Eddie said. "You hear me?"

Eddie felt his blood boil. This kid was too much. "You hit your mother again and she'll come to me, you understand?"

Dario sobbed, but nodded. "Okay. I got it. Please, man. Let me go."

Eddie gave him one last press before tossing him loose. Dario stumbled away and brought his right arm in front of him as he bent forward, gasping. He fell to his knees, rubbing his wrist and wiping his tears.

Eddie stood over him, scowling. "Stand up you piece-a shit."

Dario jerked back and struggled to his feet until he was straight, his head held high. Face-to-face, Dario had two inches on Eddie, but height couldn't help him now. He gripped his damaged wrist and gave Eddie his best tough-guy stare-down despite the leftover tear stains streaking his cheeks.

Eddie leaned in close, inches from Dario's face, his hand out. "Gimme' the gun."

Dario looked at the ground as he shook his head. "Can't do it man. I need that piece for protection."

Barkley closed in on Eddie's ankles, snarling and exposing his sharp teeth, a low, angry rumble growing in his throat.

"Get this fuckin' dog away from me." Eddie attempted to kick the animal away. "I mean it!"

Dario's mom pulled on Barkley's collar, struggling to keep him in check.

"Let's go, Dario," Eddie said. "I won't ask again. Gimme' your fuckin' gun."

Dario stood motionless, so Eddie bent down and frisked him, starting with the pockets of his sweatpants. The dog continued to pull away from Ms. Tucker as he growled at Eddie, his fangs exposed.

Dario wiggled and frowned. "Come on, man. Get outta' my pants."

Eddie reached further down Dario's leg until he felt something. He yanked out a silver twenty-two from its ankle holster.

Holding the revolver barrel-up, Eddie palmed it, examining it. "Where'd you get this?"

Ms. Tucker's hand went to her mouth, her eyes wide. "Dario! Where'd you get that gun?"

Dario adjusted his sweatpants with his one good hand before slouching forward, struggling for oxygen.

"Got that from my friend, Sage."

Eddie pushed his jacket aside and slid the gun into his belt. He gave Dario an angry grin. "Well, it's mine, now."

"Come on, man. Gimme' back my piece. You can't keep that. It's mine."

Eddie shrugged. "Call the fuckin' cops."

Dario pursed his lips and kicked some invisible rocks. "Come on man. I need that piece."

Eddie ticked his head up. "Tell Sage to get you a new gun. This one's mine."

"But—"

Eddie smacked him across his head. "Don't argue with me you little shit."

Dario grabbed his head and ducked away from Eddie. "Okay, man. Come on. Please, stop."

Ms. Tucker rushed in to protect her son, but Eddie gave her a light shove and she stumbled backward. Barkley leapt onto Eddie's leg, growling and snapping at his hand, nipping it twice and causing him to bleed.

"Jesus Christ," Eddie yelled. He jumped back and pulled out the gun he'd just put into his belt. Without hesitation, he pointed it at the dog and pulled the trigger.

The blast exploded through the room rattling everyone into stillness. Barkley let out a quick yelp before falling limp to the floor. Crimson spattering crossed their bodies as a pool of dark liquid swirled under the dog's short fur.

Ten

The ringing in Eddie's ears made him pause. Killing the dog had not been in his plan.

Dario's eyes popped. "Barkley! No!"

Ms. Tucker raised her hands to her head as tears filled her eyes. After a second of disbelief, she and Dario fell to the floor next to their now-dead dog, while Eddie shook his bitten hand and checked his pants and shoes for any residual mess.

From the floor next to Barkley, Ms. Tucker looked up at Eddie, her face twisted with anguish. "What are you doin'?" she squealed. "Why'd you do that?" She turned back to the dog. "Barkley!"

The sound of Cody running came from upstairs. He cried out for his mom.

"Don't you come down here, Cody!" she sobbed. "Everything's okay, baby. Stay up there. Turn around and go back. Now!"

Cody obeyed his mother and his footsteps faded back up the stairs.

Eddie watched, unmoved, as Dario knelt next to his mother and the two of them cried over the lifeless body of their beloved pet. Eddie felt bad about the dog, but the damn thing had attacked him. He was comfortable with his decision.

Eddie stepped away from the bloody heap and returned the gun to its new home—tucked inside his belt. He walked to the front door and peeked out. He checked left, then right, for any neighbors who may be running out to check on the gunshot. Nothing. He waited another minute before he closed the door and locked it.

He returned to the bloody scene. "Alright," he said. "Everybody calm down."

Ms. Tucker, still on her knees with blood soaking into her sweatpants, held her dog as she sobbed. Eddie bent forward and gave Ms. Tucker a stern look. "You can blame your son for this."

Ms. Tucker looked up at him.

Eddie continued. "Your neighbors came to me cuz' Dario's been shootin' bullets into their houses and breakin' their windows. He could-a' killed somebody. Did you know about any-a this?"

Ms. Tucker's pained expression turned to shock. She shook her head, wiping the endless tears with the bottom of her gray t-shirt, now darkened with Barkley's blood.

"No. I *never* know what he's doin'," she cried. She scrambled to her feet and Eddie took her arm to help her.

"He's gone all hours of the night." Her cracking voice grew louder, angrier through her tears. "He don't respect me. He don't listen to me." She pointed at her eye. "And this is how he treats me. What am I supposed to do?"

Eddie scowled at Dario. "You don't gotta' worry about that no more, Ms. Tucker." He walked over to Dario and slapped him across his face. Dario cried out as he bent forward, bringing up his arms, bracing for more.

Ms. Tucker came between them. "Stop it—please! Stop hurting him!"

Eddie dropped his hand and stared at her. "The-fuck's the matter with you, lady?"

She wrung her hands. "What?"

He pointed at Dario. "Why are you protectin' him when you just told me he don't respect you? Or listen to you? And … hits you?"

Ms. Tucker looked at Dario. "He's my son," she whimpered. "I love him."

Eddie shook his head and threw up his hands. He leaned in to her. "Un-fuckin-believable." He turned to Dario and jammed his finger at him. "This shit stops right now."

"What? What shit?"

"What are you? Some kinda' fuckin' idiot? Everything you're doin'—and *not* doin'. It all stops. Right now. *Capisci*? From this moment on, you're mine. You will *listen* to your mother. You will *respect* your mother, and you will stop the bullshit in this neighborhood. No more shootin', no more nothin'. You answer to me and you'll do whatever the fuck I tell you. You got that?"

Dario looked at his feet but nodded.

"Now. Are there any other *weapons* in this *fu-cking* house?"
Eddie moved back in on Dario and jabbed a finger at him.
"Don't fuckin' lie to me, kid."

"Got one in my dresser."

Ms. Tucker threw up her hands. "Dario!"

"Get it."

Dario walked toward a short hallway.

Eddie followed close behind, careful to step around the pool of dark blood now doubled in size around the lifeless animal.

They crossed through a small but tidy kitchen and turned left into a room off the back door. Dario flipped on the light and kicked away a pile of clothes and shoes strewn across the floor as he made his way to an old, beat-up dresser. He yanked open the third drawer, tossed around some underwear and t-shirts, and reached in for the piece.

"Uh—nope. Don't touch it," said Eddie. He wrapped his fingers around the first gun still tucked inside his jacket and pushed Dario aside. A black .38 snub nose with a brown wooden handle sat near the back of the drawer along with a box of shells. Eddie bent down and grabbed them both. He examined the piece quickly and stuffed it into one of his jacket pockets and put the box into the other.

Dario shook his head and threw up his hands. "Come on, man. You can't leave me with nothin'."

Eddie snarled. "Move. Back into the living room."

They returned to the living room. Ms. Tucker quickly stood up from the sofa when she heard them reenter.

Eddie spoke to the two of them. "Ms. Tucker, like I told ya'—" Eddie tipped his head at Dario—"Dario's been shootin' at some kid across the street and bullets have been flying into my friend, Mrs. Fortunato's, house. In case you don't know, she's your next-door-neighbor."

Ms. Tucker nodded. "Yes, we know Mrs. Fortunato."

Eddie nodded. "Oh, so you *do* know her." He gestured for them both to sit.

He paced in front of them a few feet in either direction. "Well, what you might *not* know, is that Mrs. Fortunato has lived in this neighborhood—"Eddie pointed at the wall in the direction of Micola's house—"that house—for over *forty* years."

He turned to face the two of them. "*Forty* years. Think about that. She's been here longer than *anybody* in this neighborhood. And you know what? She's a nice lady and she don't deserve nothin' but your respect." He looked at Dario. "You understand me?"

Dario nodded. "Yeah."

"I'm not gonna' let you or that kid across the street, whatever the fuck his name is, or anybody else, upset her by shootin' up her house or whatever else you punks like to do."

Eddie put his hands on his hips. "Now, does that other guy live right across from you?"

Dario stared at him.

Eddie leaned forward. "Don't play dumb with me. The Asian kid." He snapped his fingers. "What the fuck's his name? Chow?"

Dario straightened and nodded. "It's Tau. He lives right across the street from the old lady."

Eddie lightly smacked Dario across his head.

Dario bent sideways. "Owe, man! Come on! What's wrong with you?"

"The-fuck did I just tell you about respect?"

"Sorry! I meant, Mrs. *Fortunato*."

"That's better. You're finally gettin' the picture. You start respectin' your mother, Mrs. Fortunato, *and* this entire fuckin' neighborhood, or you'll be answerin' to me the hard way, you understand?"

Dario said nothing. Eddie smacked him in the head again and leaned in. He spoke slowly, quietly. "Do–you–understand me?"

"Yeah! Yes! I understand. Please stop hittin' me."

"Okay." Eddie stepped back and nodded. He folded his arms, admiring his progress.

He turned to Ms. Tucker. "I'll be leavin' now."

She let out a breath and nodded, wiping her cheeks.

"And your son? He's comin' with me."

Dario and his mother jumped to their feet. "What?" she yelled. "No! You can't *do* that. Please, mister. Don't take my son. I'm beggin' you."

"Yeah, come on man," Dario said. "What do you need with me anyways? I promise I'll stay outta' your business."

"Actually," Eddie said, "you're now *in* my business."

Ms. Tucker straightened and opened her mouth to speak, but Dario beat her to it.

"Say what now?"

"As of this very fuckin' minute, you work for me."

Dario started pacing in a circle in front of Eddie. "Oh, hell no. I ain't workin' for you, man. You'll kill me. I know it."

"Damn right I'll fuckin' kill ya'."

Eddie looked at Ms. Tucker and gave her a quick smile and a wink. He continued. "I'll kill you right fuckin' now if you don't get your shit and come with me. And I *might* kill you later if you fuck up. So shut up and get your shit."

"What am I supposed to do with Barkley?" asked Ms. Tucker. "I don't want Cody seeing him like this."

Eddie looked down at the poor dead dog. "You know what? You're right, Ms. Tucker. You got a shovel 'round here?"

"Out back, in the garage."

Eddie patted Dario on the back. "Take care-a the dog. Bury it in the backyard. I'll be back in an hour to pick you up."

Dario put his good hand to his head. "What? Man, why do I got to clean this shit up? You killed him."

Eddie's hand was quickly around Dario's throat, giving it a gentle but firm squeeze. Dario blinked and choked.

"Just do it, Dario," cried Ms. Tucker. "Stop agitatin' the man. *Please*."

Dario's eyes bulged as he tried to peel away from Eddie's strong grip. "Okay," he said, gagging. "I'll do it."

Eddie released his fingers. "Like I said, I'll be back in an hour. Make sure this floor's cleaned up, too."

Dario flipped up his one good hand, flinching. "Man, I'm gonna need more'n an hour." He raised his hand as a reminder. "Look at my hand. It's practically broken."

Eddie grabbed Dario's wrist and looked at it closely, twisting it. Dario flinched but kept quiet. "Broken? This ain't broken." Eddie abruptly released it and walked to the front door. He turned back and looked at the two of them.

He pointed at Dario. "Two hours."

Eddie turned to Dario's mother. "Now, Ms. Tucker. You will *not* call the police. Do you understand? If you do, Dario's blood will be on your hands. Got it?"

Ms. Tucker nodded. "Yes. Please don't hurt my boy."

"If he behaves, he'll be fine."

Turning to Dario, Eddie said, "Bury the dog out back and keep your mouth shut. Both-a-ya's. Understand?"

Dario and his mom nodded silently.

Eddie turned and opened the door. With his back to them, he said, "See you in two, Dario."

He closed the door and walked out, a humid breeze straining his meticulously styled mane. He immediately heard shouting coming from inside the house which made him smile. That over-confident smartass kid now belonged to him. That was pretty easy. He chuckled as he headed back to Micola's house.

As he strutted along, he patted the guns and smiled. Now, he needed a car.

Eleven

Micola opened the door, her eyes searching Eddie's. "Eddie. Everything okay?" She waved her hand. "Come in."

Eddie smiled. "Yeah. Everything went great."

Micola stepped aside and waved her hand toward the kitchen. "Come, Eddie. Tell me what happened with those boys. I have meatballs."

Eddie threw out his hands. "That sounds fantastic!"

He followed her down the hall past the staircase into the kitchen. The scent of the marinara sauce he'd whiffed earlier was even more potent. He inhaled deeply.

They entered an average sized kitchen with a petite, round table surrounded by four dark wooden chairs. On the table, sat a bowl with two huge meatballs covered in a thick red sauce. Next to the bowl was a plate holding three pieces of Italian bread and a bowl of salad greens and vegetables tossed in a creamy dressing.

Eddie stopped and smiled as he looked at Micola, his arms open. "All this fa' me?"

She smiled and bobbed her head. "Si, Eddie. *Siediti, per favore.* Sit."

He laughed. "Micola, you're gonna' make me fat." He was about to take his seat when he paused. "Join me, 'eh?"

She shook her head. "No. I already-eat."

He gestured to one of the chairs. "Well, at least sit with me so we can talk."

"Okay, Eddie. You want wine?"

He looked at his watch and chuckled. "Ah, very temptin'. But, no thanks. Still got work to do, ya' know?"

Micola took a seat and leaned on her elbows, hands under her chin, as she waited for him to take a bite.

Eddie sliced the soft meatball and moaned as the first bite of the hot, flavorful sauce and perfectly seasoned mixture settled onto his taste buds.

He closed his eyes for a second before wiping his mouth with the cloth napkin. "Micola, this is delicious."

Micola smiled. "You like?"

"Like? I love!"

He dug into the salad and Micola patiently waited for him to settle into his meal before asking him how his morning went.

Eddie gave her most of the details from the events at Dario's house, leaving out the part about Barkley. She seemed pleased but slightly concerned about how rough Eddie had been with Dario. Eddie assured her there'd be no further problems from him.

He pointed his fork at her while chewing. "Still gotta' go to this Chow's house across the street."

"Thank you for talking to the boys, Eddie. I feel better already."

"Forget it. It's my pleasure." He clinked the empty wine glass with his forefinger. "Know what? Maybe I will have a small glass-a that vino."

"Sí!" Micola stood and grabbed a bottle of Merlot from the counter, already opened and breathing.

They sat in the kitchen and talked about the two boys, but mostly, Eddie talked about Micola's food. She offered him more of the lemon cake but he put up his hand.

"Are you kiddin' me? Thanks, but I got no more room."

He slapped his thighs as he stood. "I gotta' call a cab, get back to the hotel and sleep off this meal and the wine. After that, it's back to work. I'll pick up Dario and then go to the other kid's house."

They walked to the living room and Eddie pulled out his phone, but Micola shook her head.

"No, Eddie. No cab. No hotel." She pointed up the stairs. "I got so many bedrooms. You stay here. I feed you, I wash-a-you clothes."

Eddie opened his mouth to protest, but she continued. "And I gotta' nice car for you. No cab. Come." She headed back toward the kitchen.

Eddie protested. "Micola. No, really. I don't wanna' take your car."

She ignored him and marched to the back door and out to the walkway that led to a detached, double-car garage made of the same dark brick as her house.

She reached into her floral apron pocket and pulled out a set of keys. She unlocked the side door and stepped inside. Eddie followed her. She flipped on a light switch, and there, in front of them in the clean but musty smelling garage sat a car covered by a dusty white tarp. Eddie moved to the car and pulled back the tarp. Underneath sat a black Honda Accord. It was an older model, but appeared to be in excellent condition.

"Whoa," he said. "Will ya' look at that? What's the year on this? 2008? '09?"

"2008. Eddie, you take this car. Use it while you are here in St. Paul. I-no use it."

"Really? You don't need it?"

She shook her head.

"Why don't you use it?"

"I-no drive. My friend—she drive. She pick me up and we go shopping. She take me to my appointments and to the casino. That's all I need."

She pulled a key fob from her pocket. "Here. You take."

Eddie smiled. "Alright. This is great. Beautiful car. Thank you. I'll take good care of it."

"I know you will."

Micola hit a button and the garage door creaked open. He planted a kiss on her cheek.

"Thanks for this."

Before getting into the car, he paused. "I think I'll take you up on that offer, too. I'll run to the hotel and pack up. Be back later."

He watched her eyes light up as she clasped her hands. "That-make me so happy, Eddie."

He guessed he was Micola's first real visitor in a while. He thought about that and smiled as he climbed into the car and backed down the driveway.

Low, gray clouds had reappeared and raindrops pelted the car as he exited. He stopped to admire the lush green lawn and massive old mansion towering before him. Dollar signs danced in his head and rustled up feelings of optimism he'd never felt before.

Despite killing a dog this morning, Eddie realized he'd enjoyed himself. Something about their fear really got his juices flowing. He'd enjoyed the confrontation and was looking forward to his next one with the Asian kid.

He made the short trip to the hotel and had the valet hold the car nearby while he raced up to his room to pack. He checked out of the hotel and was back in the car in thirty minutes. He thought about the money—Primo's money—he'd be saving by moving into Micola's house. It was money he could now use for other things. The drive back was quick. He pulled the car up Micola's driveway and rolled his suitcase to the front door.

Micola greeted him. "Come in, Eddie. I'm so happy to have you stay with me."

"Yeah, this is great. Thanks again."

"This way," she said, as she turned to climb the steep staircase.

Eddie followed her up, each step lined in thin, burgundy carpet—its rich wood peeking out on either side. The stairs creaked under their weight, and Micola was slow in her ascent, which gave Eddie a chance to survey the family portraits adorning the wall to his right.

They followed the burnished wood banister up and around a corner to their left leading to a substantial landing. Another left turn and up four more stairs took them to the top.

He looked around the spacious area surrounded by four doors. "This is nice up here, Micola. How many rooms you got?"

"Three bedrooms, two bathrooms."

He followed her to the small bathroom. She flipped on the light. "You use this. I have one in my room." Eddie peeked in. The dated tiled bathroom had a tub and shower covered by a simple white curtain. The vanity had minimal counter space but would suit Eddie's needs.

Micola flipped off the light and returned to the hall. She directed him to one of three other doors and flipped on the light. "This okay for you, Eddie?"

Eddie smiled. "Yeah, very nice."

The spacious bedroom had a queen-sized bed to the left of the door flanked by a mahogany nightstand and bronzed lamp on either side. The spread was an old-fashioned white quilt with embroidered flowers at the foot. A mound of pillows lay under the spread and two navy throw pillows decorated the center.

A bulky old trunk sat at the foot of the bed and Eddie set his suitcase on it. Directly across from the bed to the right, was a single door that Eddie assumed was the closet. Next to the closet, sat an antique dresser with four drawers and a mirror directly above it. One small window, its white shade pulled, was adjacent to the head of the bed and adorned with a simple, white lace valance draped over the top.

"This'll do just fine, Micola. Thanks again fa' lettin' me crash here."

"You-welcome, Eddie. I'm happy to have you stay with me."

"Let me get unpacked. After that, I gotta' go across the street and have a little talk with the other kid."

"Okay, Eddie."

After Micola left and Eddie had unpacked, he checked himself in the mirror, headed downstairs and out the front door. The rain had let up which was good for the hair. He palmed it as he turned down the sidewalk toward Dario's house.

He should-a buried the dog by now.

Twelve

*E*ddie rammed his fist on the Tuckers' front door and waited. In seconds, it was opened by Ms. Tucker, who stepped aside and let him in. Dario, sitting on the sofa, stood and passed his mom. He stopped in front of Eddie.

Eddie nodded at Ms. Tucker and looked around, his arms outstretched. "Look at this fuckin' floor, 'eh? Sparklin' clean." He backhanded Dario's chest. "Nice work, kid."

Dario scowled and rubbed the spot where Eddie had slapped him.

Eddie lowered his chin as he smirked at Dario. "Nice to see you so quiet, Dario. It suits you." He laughed and hooked his arm around Dario's neck. He pulled his head down to meet Eddie's eyes. "You're pretty tall, kid."

He let him go and Dario adjusted his t-shirt and palmed his short Afro.

"One more thing before we go," Eddie said.

Dario flinched as Eddie continued. "There's somethin' you'se two need-ta remember." He jammed his finger in Dario's direction. "I don't give a fuck about you, your mother here, or your little brother. None-a ya's."

Ms. Tucker gasped and placed her shaking hand over her lips.

Eddie continued. "So you," —he poked his finger into Dario's chest—"better shape the fuck up. We can play this two ways. Either you're with me or you're against me. And trust me," —Eddie waved his finger—"you don't wanna' be against me. Understand? *Capisci*? You'll all regret it. Do what I say, and we'll get along. If not, we got a serious fuckin' problem."

He looked at Dario's mom. "Ms. Tucker. Besides all-a that, I want you-ta come see me if Dario gives you even the tiniest fuckin' problem. I'll handle him. I don't have an office yet, but I will. Dario will tell you where-ta find me. You come see me anytime you need help—understand? For anything."

Ms. Tucker twisted her lip but nodded. "Okay."

Eddie noticed her hesitation. "I mean it. Come see me."

She gave him a forced smile.

Eddie took Dario's arm and shoved him as they headed out the door.

The sun had dipped below the ceiling of trees on Burr Street and the cool breeze invigorated Eddie as he walked around to the driver's side of Micola's black Honda. He looked at Dario from across the roof.

"Get in."

They sat in silence for a while—Eddie in the driver's seat, Dario in the passenger seat.

After a few minutes, Dario spoke. "Man, where we goin'? You takin' me somewhere to kill me?"

Eddie looked at him and laughed. "Not yet, kid. I'm givin' you a chance. I told-ya: you work-fa me now. Don't worry. I won't kill ya'—'less you deserve it."

Eddie chuckled and gave Dario's shoulder a shove. "It's easy. Just do as I say. Be loyal to me and you'll live." Eddie laughed. "Calm down. Shit. You might even make some money."

Dario brought his fist to his mouth to hide a slight smile. He raised his brows. "For real?"

Eddie nodded. "For real." He jabbed his finger in Dario's direction. "Fuck me over, though—go to the cops—or whatever and your momma's dead. Your little brother—what's his name?"

"Cody."

Eddie casually twirled his gold pinky-ring with his thumb. "Cody's dead too."

"Man, you can't do that. He's just a kid."

Eddie's eyes darkened as he looked at Dario. "I can and I will. Make it easy on everyone, Dario. Do as I say and your family will be fine. Fuck me over and you'll all be as dead as your damned dog. What was the dog's name again?"

"Barkley."

Eddie shrugged. "Seemed like a nice dog, Barkley. Too bad. Keep him in mind when, or *if*, you ever consider fuckin' me over, you hear?"

Dario nodded, his head hung low. "I hear ya' man. I won't fuck you over. I promise."

Eddie slapped him on the side of his head. "Good!"

Dario brought his arm up and rubbed his head. "Man, please stop hittin' me. That shit hurts."

Eddie shook his head. "Jesus, you really gotta' toughen up, Dario."

Dario gave Eddie a side-glance. "Where we goin', man? Why are we in this car?"

Eddie continued. "Your first assignment, whether you like it or not, is to bring me to Chow."

Cheering up a bit, Dario nodded and said, "I can do that. You gonna' pay me? What I gotta' do?"

"No, I'm not payin' you for that."

"How come?"

Eddie shook his head. "Jesus. You don't get it, do ya'?"

Dario gave him a blank stare.

"You and Chow—you'se two gotta 'pologize to Mrs. F."

"What? Come on, man. Why you—"

Eddie put his hand up and pointed. "That's his house there, ain't it? Across from Mrs. F.'s house?"

Dario nodded. From the car's window they looked over at the big, dirty-white two-story house.

"Yep."

Eddie nodded. "Okay. You go in first. I'll come in after."

"Man, why'd we even get in this car? How 'bout I wait right here while you go in and bust up their house like you did mine? Huh?"

"Too many fuckin' questions, Dario," Eddie said. "Too many."

"Ok. One question, then—"

"Because I want Chow—"

"Man, his name is *Tau*. Tau Vang."

"Whatever. I want this Tau to see *you* as you are right now. Scared shitless." Eddie laughed. "It'll help him realize his predicament. Know what I mean? Let's go." He opened the driver's side door and got out.

Dario got out from his side of the car and followed him across the street. "What predicament is that?" he asked.

Eddie stopped and stared at him. "Same predicament as you. The *predicament* that *he's* comin' to work for me, too."

Dario stopped. "What?" He shook his head. "No way, man. Uh-uh. I ain't workin' with that piece-a shit. No fuckin' way."

Eddie shoved Dario's shoulder. "Keep movin'."

They stepped onto the boulevard and, before Dario got a chance to say another word, Eddie pushed his face up against the rough bark of a tree.

Eddie's voice turned cold as he whispered in Dario's ear. "Listen, you motherfucker. You gotta' short memory, don't you? You *will* do whatever I tell you to do, and you will keep that big fuckin' mouth-a yours shut, you hear me?"

Eddie pressed and twisted Dario's face around in the bark. Dario moaned. "Alright, alright. I hear you man. Stop! Please!"

Eddie abruptly released Dario, who tripped backward. Dario frowned at Eddie but kept his mouth shut.

They walked the short distance to Tau's house in silence. Eddie stopped and pointed. "This it?"

"Yep."

Eddie looked around. "Big house. Bigger than yours."

Dario shrugged.

It was similar in size to Micola's, but instead of a brick exterior, it had dirty cream-colored siding with green painted shutters and door, now faded from the sun and neglect.

"Move," Eddie said.

They climbed five wide wooden steps up to an enormous front porch. Several pairs of shoes of varying styles and sizes were scattered around either side of the front door.

"Jesus," said Eddie. "What's with all the shoes?"

"Hmongs," said Dario. "Big families—tons-a kids."

Eddie rang the doorbell and stepped to the side with his back against the wall, out of sight of the door, pointing to Dario.

Dario looked over at him, arms outstretched. "What?"

Eddie pointed to the door and put his fingers to his lips.

A stampede of footsteps and giggles interrupted his response as the door slowly opened. Four little black-haired children, two boys and two girls, looked up at Dario.

Dario glanced at Eddie and then bent down to speak. "Is Tau here?"

One of them turned and shouted "Momma!" The others continued to stare.

A short Asian woman approached from down a hall toward the front door. Her black hair was pulled back and she wore a flower-printed apron over a dress, both of which were too big for her tiny frame. In a high, squeaky voice, she spoke in broken English. "I help you?"

"Yeah," Dario said. "I'm lookin' for Tau."

"Tau not here."

"Okay. I'll come back later," said Dario. She started to close the door.

Smoothly and quickly, Eddie appeared in the doorway. He grabbed Dario by the elbow and shoved his way past the four children and into the dark front hallway.

"We'll wait," Eddie said. "You Tau's mother?" The woman's head came only to his chest. He continued down the hall.

"Hey, wait a minute," shouted the woman, looking first at Eddie, then Dario. "Who-you-think-you-are coming in my house? I call police!"

"Tell her Dario," Eddie said, looking down at the woman. "Tell her she don't wanna' do that."

Dario put his hands together like he was praying and bowed down to her. "Believe me when I say to you, ma'am, you do *not* wanna' call the police."

She pointed at Dario. "You that boy always fighting with Tau. You get him in trouble?" She looked up at Eddie, jerking her thumb in his direction. "Who is this guy?"

Eddie pushed back one side of his jacket to expose the handle of the pistol in his belt. He let his stare and the gun speak for themselves. Her shoulders sank.

"Call him," Eddie said. "Tell him to get here. Now."

Tau's mother continued down the hall and turned the corner. Eddie and Dario followed her into a surprisingly spacious living room, though sparsely furnished. A strong odor of pork and ginger burned Eddie's nostrils but not in an unpleasant way. Toys were strewn everywhere. A bird cage near the picture window held a tiny yellow parakeet screeching his annoyance at the disturbance of his afternoon nap.

The children gathered behind the woman, hanging onto her stained apron. She shooed them away in a language Eddie had never heard before and picked up an out-of-date cordless phone.

She dialed with trembling fingers and then spoke to someone on the other end of the line in the same unfamiliar language.

"No!" She yelled. "You get here now!" She listened for a second and then hung up the phone. Visibly shaken, Tau's mother informed her unwanted guests that Tau would be home at four o'clock.

Eddie looked at his watch.

"We'll wait."

Thirteen

*E*ddie made his way to an old and worn, gray velveteen sofa covered with toys. He cleared them with one sweep and sat down. Dario sat at the other end, away from Eddie. He tried to play it cool, but his knee began to bounce as he started gnawing on his thumbnail.

The woman poked her finger and yelled at Eddie.

Eddie shook his head at Dario who shrugged his shoulders. "Don't look at me, man. I don't know what she's sayin'."

Eddie ignored her and examined his manicure, but she continued to shout at him. He reached into his leather jacket and pulled out the .38 he'd taken from Dario and rested it on his thigh.

On seeing the weapon, she stopped short.

Eddie smiled. "That's more like it."

He fingered the gun and turned to Dario who was rocking front-to-back. Eddie shot him a side-glance and leaned over. "Look, kid," he whispered, "I know you don't like being in your enemy's house, but stop that shit. You're embarrassin' yourself."

Dario stopped rocking and straightened up.

Tau's mother moved to a chair across from them, arms folded, occasionally yelling over their heads toward the kitchen behind them. Eddie had no idea what she was saying, which put him on edge. He shrugged at Dario.

"Hmong," Dario whispered.

"Huh?"

"Hmong. It's a *language*, man. That's what she's speakin'."

"You understand her?"

"I told you. I don't understand that shit."

"Then how come you know so much about it?"

"Man, you're makin' it too obvious you ain't from around here," Dario said. "'Hmong.' They're people? From Vietnam?" He pronounced 'Nam' like 'ma'am.' "Or China?" He shrugged. "I don't know. Not really sure where they're from. But man, they're all over this town."

Eddie shrugged. "Never heard of 'em 'til I got here."

After waiting ten minutes, Eddie heard a door open from behind them. He and Dario turned to look back toward the kitchen. Two male voices could be heard yelling. The woman sitting in the chair stood and raced toward the kitchen. She joined in the yelling. The screaming voices mellowed to a whisper and then stopped.

Eddie sat back and smiled at Dario.

"Tau's mom is pissed," he whispered and laughed.

He sat back, waiting, listening. He wasn't sure what they were talking about, but he didn't care. Tau was in deep shit with his mother for having "company" come barging in.

A smooth, low voice came from Eddie's right. "Can I help you?"

Eddie turned to see a tall, good-looking and thin Asian kid of about twenty looking down at Eddie's gun. His black hair was cropped short on the sides, but full on top, swooping stylishly back. He wore a Lakers jersey, jeans—about two sizes too big, clean white sneakers, and a long, gold chain around his neck.

The petite woman hovered behind him. She was now accompanied by a short, round Asian man of about fifty, who was pointing and yelling at Tau, and then at Eddie, in the now-familiar—yet still foreign, Hmong language.

Eddie ignored the outburst and remained seated. He turned toward the front window as he addressed Tau. "English," he said. "Good."

He waved his hand toward the chair the woman had been sitting in. "Have a seat."

The kid sat down.

"You Tau?" Eddie asked.

Glaring at Dario before answering, he said. "Yeah."

Dario smiled. "Sup, Tau? Gotta' little company today, huh?"

"Shut up," Eddie hissed.

Tau jerked his head in Dario's direction. "What's this piece-a-shit doin' in my house?"

Eddie sat forward as his dark eyes narrowed. "Shut the fuck up, Tau."

Tau sat back in the chair and casually picked at his fingernails. Chuckling, he said, "Man, who the fuck are you?"

Eddie turned to Dario. "Tell him."

"Man," Dario said, "don't even try. Mother-fucker killed my dog today. Better do what he says, man."

Tau stared Eddie down for a second before Eddie picked up the revolver and waved it in Tau's direction. "You the one shootin' up Mrs. Fortunato's house?"

Tau's face twisted. "Who?"

Eddie stood, quickly grabbed the shoulder of Tau's mother, and pointed the gun at her head. She let out a slight yelp as Tau made a move toward them, but Eddie shook his head, the click of the cocking gun louder than expected.

"Don't even fuckin' try."

Except for the distant sounds of children and a cartoon playing on a television, the room was silent.

After a few seconds, Eddie spoke. "You see what I mean, Dario?"

He pressed the gun against Tau's mother's temple, forcing her head to lean to the right. She moaned quietly. The older man put his hands to his mouth to muffle his cries.

"You fuckin' punks. You got no respect. Mrs. Fortunato is your *neighbor*."

Tau gave Eddie a blank stare.

"Across the street?"

His eyes flashed his understanding.

"Oh, so *now* you know who I'm talkin' about?"

Tau kept his cocky composure. "Yeah. So?" He spread his arms wide, his head tilted to one side. "Big deal. I shot at the old lady's house." He shrugged. "And you killed a dog." He looked over at Dario and smirked. "So?"

Eddie took one quick stride and clocked Tau in the forehead with the butt of the gun. Loud but brief screams erupted from Tau's mother and the man.

Tau tipped sideways and fell to his knees with his hands out in front of him. Blood poured down the side of his face as he let out two stifled groans. His mother cried and moved toward her son.

Eddie put out his hand and yelled to her. "Nope. Stay back." He dropped to one knee, wrapped his arm around Tau's throat and squeezed.

Dario let out a chuckle, but quickly put his fist over his mouth to stifle his amusement. He stayed back, entertained, as Tau unsuccessfully scratched and pulled at Eddie's muscular forearm. His eyes bulged as his throat let out strange gagging sounds.

Eddie looked down at him, his face calm, except for pursed lips. He loosened his grip as Tau stared up at him.

"I'm here to teach you two little pricks some respect," Eddie said. He released Tau from his grip and returned to his feet. Tau remained on his hands and knees as he gasped for air, a pool of blood forming on the worn carpet. Eddie looked down at him for a flash before stepping on Tau's fingers with his dress shoes.

"Respect for your neighbors, your family, and your fuckin' neighborhood," he said, twisting his toes as he pressed.

He turned to Tau's mother. "Get him a bandage. He's comin' with me."

Tau's voice screeched up in pitch as he attempted to rise from the floor. "What? No way, man. I'm not goin' anywhere with you."

Blood covered one side of his face and had dripped onto his jersey. He put his hand to his wound and looked at the bloody result.

Eddie returned to one knee and pressed Tau's wounded head into the floor. He sensed Tau's fear, and smiled as he released him. Eddie stood back up, and Tau pushed himself up to his knees, panting, moaning. Tau stared at the floor, watching streams of his blood flow onto the carpet beneath him.

He scowled and tried again. "I'm *not* goin' with you. No way."

Eddie again moved fast, raising the gun high over Tau's head.

Tau covered his head with his arms as he let out a quiet whimper. "Okay. Please. Stop!"

Eddie lowered the gun just as Tau's mother came in with a towel and bandage. She helped her son back into the chair, whispering angrily to him in Hmong. Eddie waited for her to clean him up. When that was finished, he looked at Tau and stuck out his hand.

"Gimme your piece."

Tau glanced at his mom. "I don't have a piece."

"Bullshit. You-been shootin' up the neighborhood haven't ya'? Gimme your goddamn piece."

Tau shook his head. "Not mine. That's my father's gun. I don't have it. He does."

Eddie shook his head in disgust. "Let's go."

Tau stood, gently touching the bandage now covering his forehead just under the hairline. Eddie grabbed his arm. With a tight grip, he jerked Tau toward the front door. Dario followed, chuckling quietly.

Eddie turned back to speak with Tau's parents, first shooting a nasty look at Dario. The Hmong couple stood in the center of the living room clinging to each other. Tau's mother covered her mouth with her hands as she cried.

Eddie turned to Tau. "Tell 'em this—what I'm about to say."

Tau paused for a second, looking at his mom.

Eddie jerked Tau's arm. "Tell 'em."

"Okay!" Tau whispered, flinching.

Eddie spoke slowly. "Don't worry."

Tau translated.

"Your son is coming to work for me. If he behaves, he'll be fine."

Tau shot Eddie an uneasy glance but again told them what he'd said.

"And if you know what's good for you *and* your son, you will *not* call the police."

Tau relayed that message.

"But also, if you'se two need anything, you let me know." Tau paused, a confused look on his face.

"Go on. Tell 'em that," Eddie said, giving him another jerk.

Tau translated Eddie's last sentence. Eddie watched as their expressions eased. He nodded. They returned his nod. Eddie then moved to leave. He jerked the gun in the direction of the front door.

"Move."

Tau gave his parents one last look before walking out the front door with Eddie and Dario.

Fourteen

*E*ddie was the last to walk down Tau's front steps. The temperature had dropped with the setting sun. Dario and Tau turned and waited for him. As he approached, Eddie gestured toward Micola's brick house across the street.

"Awe, man!" Dario said. "Where we goin now?"

Eddie ignored him as he crossed the weeded boulevard and stepped onto the street. He didn't turn back, but heard their rumblings and footsteps behind him. When he reached the bottom of the stairs in front of Micola's house, he stopped and turned to them.

Dario, holding his injured hand, and Tau, gingerly touching his bandaged forehead, paused at the boulevard.

"You'se two punks are goin up there to apologize to Mrs. Fortunato for shootin' up her house. *Capisci*?"

"Man, do we have to?" Dario asked.

Eddie scowled, before climbing both flights of stairs leading to the front door. He rang the doorbell as they trudged up behind him.

The door opened. On seeing Eddie, Micola smiled and moved to let him in, but she frowned as she peered over his shoulder to see the two tall figures behind him.

"Eddie. Why you bring these boys?" Her voice elevated. "They shoot up my house!"

"Mrs. F., I know. But like I promised, I got it under control. They're here to apologize. They won't be shootin' up your house or the neighborhood no more."

She narrowed her eyes. "Okay, but I-no want them in my house. They say it there, on the steps." She crossed her arms and frowned.

Eddie looked up at the sky and sighed. "Alright. I thought we could sit down and talk, but fine. We can do it here."

He stepped aside. "Have at it, boys." He whispered in Dario's ear loud enough for Tau to hear. "Make it good."

Dario and Tau stepped forward and Micola stepped back.

Dario spoke first. "Um. Mrs. Fortunato? Yeah. I just wanted to say that, um. I'm very sorry for shootin' up your house and all. It was a dangerous and stupid thing for me to do. It won't happen again. So, ah'. Yeah. Sorry."

He stepped aside and looked to Eddie for approval. Eddie nodded as Tau stepped forward.

"Mrs. Fortunato," he said, "I would also like to apologize for my behavior. I promise it won't happen again. We understand we were wrong and I'm sorry." He turned to Eddie, who smiled, almost as if he were proud.

"Very good, boys. Nice work. What-d-ya' think Mrs. F.? That-make ya' happy?"

She nodded. "*Sí*, Eddie. *Very* happy. I won't be so scared when I go to bed now. *Grazie*."

"Ya'-welcome. Now we gotta' go."

"I see you tonight, Eddie?"

He nodded and waved. "Yeah. See ya' soon."

Dario and Tau followed him down the steps as Micola closed the door.

"Now, that wasn't so bad, am I right?" Eddie laughed.

Dario nodded. "I gotta' admit. Not bad at all. Seems like she don't like us, though."

Eddie smacked the side of his head. "Would *you* like somebody who shot up *your* house? Come on, don't be stupid."

Dario rubbed his head as they walked toward his house.

Eddie stopped in front of Dario's yard. "Alright. Good start. Go home. Do somethin' good for your families."

"Are we done with you now, Eddie?" Tau asked.

Eddie folded his arms as he chuckled. "Ah', no." He raised his finger. "No you are *not* done with me. In fact, we're just gettin' started." He laughed at their disappointed expressions. "You'se two start thinkin' about ways I—" he put out his hand in a slicing motion—"we—I meant 'we'—can make some fast money 'round here. Okay?" He smacked Tau's shoulder. "Take care-a that head-a yours, huh Tau? Dario? Take care-a that hand-a yours. And I-ah', I'll see you'se two soon. I'll be in touch."

Eddie turned and headed back toward Micola's house. After a few steps, he spun back and called out to them. "Oh! One more thing. Get me three burner phones. One for each of us. Drop one off later tonight and give me your numbers. Then I'll call you'se."

Dario called out. "Man—those cost money!"

Eddie reached for his wallet. "Come here!"

Dario ran to get the cash. Tau followed.

"Guess I'm doin' it," Dario said, snatching the money.

"Don't complain," Eddie said. "I want change, too. Tomorrow, we work. Get some good rest. You meet me right here at the car. Both-a-ya's. Ten sharp."

Dario's voice rose in pitch. "In the morning?"

"Yes, in the goddamn morning. And don't make me wait. Always remember, I know where you boys live. I know your mommies, your daddies, your baby brothers and sisters, and your doggie—well—not Dario's doggie, cuz he's dead." He threw his head back and laughed.

Dario frowned. "Man, that ain't funny."

"Just keep quiet and do as I say and you'll be fine."

Eddie turned back toward Micola's house.

"Sure, Eddie. See you at ten," Tau called out.

"Don't make me wait, ya' hear?"

Eddie checked his watch as Tau crossed the street and up the stairs to his house, and Dario walked down the street toward his front walk.

He couldn't hold back a chuckle as he headed toward Micola's house. Big, badass kids shittin' their pants. He laughed to himself as he climbed the stairs.

Not bad for his first day in town. Quite productive, in fact.

Fifteen

*E*ddie climbed the stairs and gave his new living quarters the onceover, stopping at the window to get his bearings. He pulled on the navy blue shade and peered out, getting a good look at the dark street below. A light drizzle patted at the windowpane, the last of the evening sun hidden behind thick, gray clouds. The upper level of the house was high off the street, dwarfing the other homes around it. He could see Dario's house next door to his left and Tau's house across the street.

He returned to his suitcase sitting on the old trunk at the foot of the bed and began unpacking his things. He frowned at his limited wardrobe, and made a note to spend some time getting fitted for new suits and other items.

After a quick shower, he dressed for dinner. He checked himself in the mirror, smoothing and patting his hair and adjusting the tuck of his shirt, before turning out to the hallway. The digital clock on the bedside table said six-ten.

He was late.

The sweet aroma of red sauce and garlic pleasantly tickled his nose as he descended the squeaky old staircase. He peeked into the kitchen to let Micola know he'd arrived. She shooed him to the living room where he took his place on the sofa, frowning at the now familiar crackling of plastic under his weight.

As he studied the room, he eyed the built-in cabinet under the mirror. A bar. He hadn't noticed it earlier. He walked to it and looked through the glass doors at its contents. Several bottles of wine lay tucked inside on a built-in rack. He opened the door and reached in, randomly pulling out a bottle of Merlot. On the other side, wine glasses hung upside down on a track. He opened that door and slid out two glasses and set them up on the bar's countertop. He opened the bottle, but didn't pour.

The sounds of lumbering down the hall made him look up. Micola greeted him with a light clap of her hands and a smile that made Eddie's day.

"Eddie," she said. "Did you rest?"

Eddie moved in for a quick hug. She leaned in, giving him a strong bear-hug, much stronger than anticipated.

"No. Took a shower. Unpacked my sh—stuff. Didn't wanna' be late, but I am anyways. Sorry 'bout that."

She batted a hand at him, smiling. "I'm so happy you-here with me, Eddie."

"Yeah, me too."

Her eyes flickered. "Oh, I have something for you." She left the room and returned with a plastic bag. "From Dario."

Eddie peeked inside. "My new phone. That was quick. Good."

He pulled out a note and saw his new number and both Dario and Tau's numbers written on it.

"Thanks. Remind me to give you the number." He waved his arm toward the bar.

"You ready for a little vino?"

"*Sì.*"

Eddie poured the wine and handed her a glass.

"A toast," she said, clinking her glass to his. "Eddie. I'm so happy you-here. And *grazie* for talkin' to those boys."

Eddie took a sip. "My pleasure. And thank *you* for lettin' me crash here."

"I love the company, Eddie. I'm always alone. So, this is nice. Someone to talk to, no?"

He nodded. "Very nice."

Eddie strolled around the living room admiring her artwork and antique furniture. He came to an old stand-alone mahogany stereo console, a speaker covering its front. He smoothed his hand over the top and lifted the lid.

"You gotta' lotta' nice records in here," he said, flipping through a neat stack of vinyl albums.

"Sinatra, Martin, Louis Prima." He stopped and looked closer at one of the albums. "What's this? *Vikki Carr?*"

She walked over to him and smiled. "*Sì.*"

"Oh my God. This takes me back." He pulled it from the stack and flipped it to read the songs. "*It Must Be Him?* My ma' used-ta' *love* this song. I ain't heard this in years. Mind if I play it?"

She raised her brows and smiled brightly. "I-like to hear it, *sì.*"

Eddie removed the pristine vinyl album from its sleeve and placed it gently onto the turntable. The sound of the needle crackled through the speaker until the sweet sound of Vikki Carr's voice filled the room. He raised the volume.

They stood near the stereo holding their glasses of wine, listening. Micola's eyes lit up and she began tipping her head side-to-side. He took a quick sip of wine before swaying with her.

After a moment, he reached out his free hand to her. "Shall we?" He set his glass on the nearby coffee table without waiting for her reply.

Micola put her hand to her mouth and giggled. "Oh, Eddie."

He took her glass and placed it next to his. He then reached out, putting one hand around her waist and his other hand in hers. She laughed as they danced a few steps before he gave her a slow, gentle twirl. When the song ended, he gave Micola a final spin that left her breathless.

"How'd-ya like that, 'eh?"

Eddie laughed as he helped her back to the sofa. He lowered the volume and returned to sit in the chair across from her.

They sat in the cozy-lit living room chatting about music from the old days. Eddie listened attentively, trying to understand her broken English, as Micola reminisced about her earlier years with her husband. Her brown eyes sparkled with animated joy and her voice was light with laughter as she told Eddie story after story.

After an hour, Micola's eyes popped. "Oh! Eddie. We eat, no?"

She rose quickly, brushing away his offer of assistance. He followed her into the kitchen and took his spot at the table, while she busied herself at the stove.

"You hungry Eddie?"

He grinned. "Am I hungry? Does a cat have an ass?"

Micola frowned, hands on her hips. "I-no-like that, Eddie."

Eddie laughed. "'Scuse my language. Gotta' work on that, ya' know?"

She gave him a fake frown and shook her finger. "*Sí*."

As the food arrived, Eddie noticed a low growl in his belly. The bubbling eggplant parmigiana was still piping hot despite the delay in serving it. With it, Micola served a cold, crisp Caesar salad with homemade buttery garlic croutons, and pizza fritta (deep-fried bread dough). The strong aroma of garlic and Italian seasonings made Eddie's mouth water as the mixture of flavors, subtle and savory, took him back to his early days in St. Paul. The sauce was a release of flavor on his palate that he hadn't experienced in years.

Micola beamed as Eddie continuously praised her cooking. "I gotta tell ya', Mrs. F.," he pointed his fork at his plate. "That right there—that's gotta' be some-a the best food I ever ate. I'm not kiddin' ya'."

"Thank you, Eddie. I'm glad you-like."

After their meal, Micola stood and took Eddie's plate. He stood, too. "Here. Let me help you clean up."

She shook her finger. "No, Eddie. I—"

"I insist."

Micola smiled. "Okay."

The music floated into the kitchen and they laughed and sang as they cleaned. They then returned to the living room for dessert—two more slices of Micola's lemon cake.

Eddie shoved in a mouthful and waved his fork at her from across the coffee table.

"How come you never opened a restaurant? A fancy one, ya' know? I don't see no fancy Italian food around this neighborhood. That's a tragedy, am I right?"

"No, Eddie. We have Yarusso's. On Payne Avenue."

Eddie's eyes popped. "Yarusso's? That-still around? God bless-em. Been there a long time." He shrugged. "But, that's pretty casual, right?"

"Maybe that's enough," she said. "This neighborhood is no good for high class *ristorantes*."

"Micola. Let me tell you, *everybody* loves Italian food. Everybody."

Micola giggled. "*Si*. Everybody."

"And people come from far away for *good* food, am I right?"

She nodded.

They finished their cake and sat quietly listening and nodding their heads to Frank Sinatra's *My Way*. A comfortable mood had spread across the room. When the song ended, the room fell silent. Micola leaned across the coffee table toward Eddie.

"Eddie?"

"Yeah?"

She paused, biting her lip.

He shrugged. "What?"

"You help me with my *ristorante*?"

Eddie's head jerked back. "What-? Me? No." He tilted his head. "Help you? What'd-ya' mean?"

"*Sì*, Eddie. You help me find a place? Help me get started? I always ..." she opened her arms wide ... "*always* want to open my own *ristorante*."

Her excitement caused her to start speaking rapidly and her accent became muddied.

Eddie raised his hands. "Whoa. Slow down, Mrs.-F. I can't understand ya'."

"Oh, Eddie. You make-a me laugh."

Eddie chuckled. "That's good, but slow down, alright?"

"*Sì*. Okay. I tell you Eddie, I *always* want to open a *ristorante*." She frowned and shook her head. "But nobody—they don't help me, Eddie. I no-can-do it by myself. I need help. My daughter— she say, 'no, Ma.' You-too old.'" Micola slapped her hand on her thigh, her eyes bright despite the wine. "I'm *no*-too old, Eddie. I make-a the good food, no?"

"No doubt," Eddie said. "You'd make a fortune sellin' what you-got goin' on in that kitchen-a yours."

"*Sì*. I make-a lotsa' money." She giggled. "Eddie, I know we just meet, but no one help-me. You help me, Eddie?"

Her pleading eyes and look of hope weakened him. He sat back on the sofa, wondering how he'd get out of this without makin' her cry.

He shook his head. "Micola, listen ... I can't—I gotta' get back, ya' know—to Brooklyn? I got work I gotta' do there. Your brother-in-law, Primo, he needs me back there. You understand, right?"

Micola's enthusiastic expression fell. She nodded. "*Sì*. I understand. Is-okay." She batted her hand at him. "Bad idea." She stood, collected the dessert plates and headed back to the kitchen.

Eddie pressed his temples. He felt bad for disappointing her, but setting up a restaurant? That was a helluva lotta' work. Primo would *never* let him stay longer than a week or two without some lucrative business opportunities. He was workin' on that, but he'd only been there a day. He sat back and listened to Micola run the water. He knew she was taking longer than necessary. Stalling.

He stood and walked back into the kitchen. Micola looked up as he entered, her hands busy drying glasses and other dishes.

"Look, Micola," he said. "Let me talk to Primo about this, huh? Maybe I could at least stick around long enough to help you find a nice spot, and maybe hire somebody to get you up and runnin'. I could probably help with that, alright? Sound okay?"

Her eyes brightened. "Oh, *sí*, Eddie. Thank you."

Eddie smiled down at her. "Yeah. Sure thing."

This *was* a bad idea, but Eddie kept his thoughts to himself. Hopefully, Primo would talk her out of this pipedream.

She pulled his head down to her and kissed both sides of his face.

"*Grazie!*"

"Now, don't get too excited. Let's see what Primo says first, right?"

She nodded. "Okay, Eddie. Tell Primo, I have lotsa' money. I pay you."

Eddie raised his brows. *Hmm. Pay me?*

He tried to play it cool. "I'll talk to him in the morning, okay?"

Micola nodded furiously, smiling and rubbing his arm. "*Sí.* Thank you, Eddie. *Grazie!*"

"Alright. Yeah."

Eddie leaned way back, hands on his hips and yawned. The long day had suddenly hit him.

"So, that meal, the wine? *So* good, Micola. I mean it. But ..." he slapped his belly. "I'm beat. Been a long day." He pointed toward the stairs. "Mind if I head up?"

She flapped her hand. "You go."

"Alright. We'll talk in the mornin'. And listen—thanks again. I had a good time."

She put her hands together. "Me too, Eddie. You don't know. It's-a long time since I smile, listen to good music and have company." She touched his arm. "Thank *you.*"

He kissed her cheek. "See you'se tomorrow, 'eh? Ga-night."

"*Buon anotte*, Eddie."

He waved and headed upstairs.

Before climbing into bed, Eddie called Dario from the burner. He'd changed his mind about the time. Ten was too early.

"Yeah. You and Tau meet me outside Mrs. F's house at Eleven." He paused, rubbing his hand across his face and eyes. "Yes, *in the morning*. Eleven o'clock *in the morning*."

He ended the call. "Dipshit."

The queen-sized bed felt a little soft under his hands. He stripped down to his t-shirt and underwear and climbed in. He stared up at the ceiling, thinking about his unexpectedly pleasant evening. He had to admit, he'd enjoyed dancin' with the old broad and listenin' to her collection of nostalgic records.

He turned off the light and thought about his happier days as a child, reminiscing until he finally drifted off.

Sixteen

*K*ate and Marco sat on the sofa, their feet up on the coffee table, while Renzo limped with his crutches over to the "good" chair—the brown leather recliner. Settling in, he propped up his feet and threw his arms above his head.

Kate turned to Marco, remote in hand. "Sweetie, can you turn off the music? I want to start the movie."

As Marco walked toward the speaker, the *Tango* song came on from their favorites list. Kate jumped up.

"Ooh! Turn it up!"

Marco frowned but did as she asked. When he returned, she grabbed his hand, pulling him toward her.

Marco moaned. "Come on, Kate. Not now."

Renzo rolled his eyes. "Why do you guys always have to dance when you hear this song?"

As Marco swirled her around in front of the coffee table, Kate looked over her shoulder at Renzo. "Because—it reminds us of when we first started dating."

Renzo slapped his forehead. "Geez. I thought that *other* song was your song. The one where it spells out the word 'love.' You said *that* was your song."

Kate laughed.

"Oh, yeah. That's our song, too. But this one—*this* was our song from the very beginning, back when I could have been a star." She whispered the last word—*star*.

Renzo frowned. "Huh?"

Marco nodded. "Yep. Your mom wanted to be a professional dancer. Like a ballerina."

"No way."

"Way," Kate said, smiling. Marco moved as she'd taught him, holding her close. "I auditioned for *Juilliard*, a very prestigious school for the arts."

The violins grew louder as Marco straightened his arm and pushed Kate away, before pulling her arm back to him, twirling her. She chuckled as he bent her backward, her long, chestnut hair falling toward the floor. From her upside-down position, she saw her son smiling. Marco pulled her back up, and she listened to Renzo's laughter as he watched his parents move gracefully across the living room floor.

As they continued their moves, dodging the coffee table and TV stand, Renzo said, "What happened?"

Marco and Kate continued swaying around the room as Kate responded. "I didn't make it. *Worst* day of my life."

Marco twirled her again. "Well, until that night—when she met me."

Kate nodded and smiled. "True."

"Where'd you guys meet? In a bar?" Renzo laughed at his joke.

Kate and Marco stopped dancing. "How'd you know that?" Marco asked.

Renzo's jaw fell and he covered his eyes. Dragging his hands down his face, he said, "You guys actually met in a *bar*? That's *so* embarrassing."

Kate put her hands on her hips. "What's so embarrassing about meeting in a bar? Lots of people meet in bars."

Marco put his arms around her and looked over at Renzo. "Yeah. It doesn't matter where you meet. Just that you actually meet."

Renzo raised his brow. "If you say so. I still think it's embarrassing."

The song ended and Marco and Kate flopped back onto the sofa.

Kate pouted. "*Not* embarrassing."

Marco started the movie but paused it as the microwave beeped.

"Popcorn!"

He returned with a bowl of popcorn for Kate and him, and another bowl for Renzo who dove in, shoving a fistful into his mouth, residuals falling around his lap.

"Okay," Marco said. "Let's get this movie started."

Kate watched Renzo's face turn pensive as he turned to his parents and said, "Ah'—wait. Since we're talking about"—he made air-quotes with his fingers—"love and stuff ..."

Kate tilted her head. "Yes?"

Renzo pushed out his hand. "Don't freak out or anything. It's not a big deal, but there's this girl at school, and I—" he paused, his face unsure. "I kinda' like her."

Kate smiled and stood up. "That's so great!"

His prepubescent voice cracked and squeaked. "Mom! Stop. It's not a big deal."

Kate's shoulders sank as she slid back down. "Well, who is this girl? Have you talked to her? Does she like you?"

Renzo rolled his eyes. "Mom. Please."

"Are you guys gonna' go *steady*?"

"Seriously Mom? Nobody says that anymore."

Marco chuckled. "Yeah, 'seriously Mom?'"

Kate ran her fingers through her snarled hair, messed from her recent dancing. "Sorry. I'm just curious, that's all."

"I'll let you know if anything happens. For now, I like her and I think she likes me. Her name is Stella, and she's in my class. That's *all* I'm telling you."

Kate nodded. "Okay."

They settled in and Marco started the movie. After it finished, Kate turned to Renzo. "Bedtime, dude."

Renzo pushed himself out of the recliner and whined about going to bed so early.

"This is bullshit," he said.

"Renzo!" Kate shouted.

Renzo twisted his mouth. "Sorry. I didn't mean it. I'm going."

"Better watch that mouth-a yours, Renz," Marco said.

"I said I was sorry, geez. It's *not* a big deal."

Marco shook his head and followed Renzo upstairs.

Kate listened to the yelling, which had become more frequent of late. The argument was quick. Marco's message was usually solid, and so far, Renzo hadn't fired back.

Marco returned downstairs to help Kate clean up.

"It's fine," he said. "Don't overreact."

Kate nodded.

They deposited the wine glasses and popcorn bowls on the countertop and straightened things up. Marco turned to Kate and kissed her forehead.

"I'm sorry we met in a bar."

She set her head onto his shoulder. "Best day of my life."

He leaned down and kissed her. Pulling away, he said, "Hmm. Maybe we should get to bed, too."

She smiled. "Maybe we should."

They walked upstairs and Kate sat on the edge of the bed for a minute before reaching over to turn off the bedside lamp. She snuggled in next to Marco. The darkness of the room mellowed with the moonlight through the slates of the blinds above their heads.

"He's still awake," she said. "I can see the light from his phone at the bottom of his door."

"He sure loves his phone. Hope he's not lookin' at boobs again."

Kate moaned and reached over to smack him. "Stop!"

"Or," Marco said laughing, "maybe he's texting his new *girlfriend.*"

"God."

She hooked his arm in hers and leaned over to give him a gentle peck on the lips.

He adjusted her under the crook of his shoulder.

"Love you."

"Love you, too."

They held each other in the dark for several minutes before Kate turned on her side to face Marco, his profile lit by the moon, eyes closed.

"I keep thinking about what my mom said. Do you think we should move?"

Marco jerked a little and sniffed loudly, pulling his head back to look at her. "What? No," he said. "I just got my job. We can't move. Renzo's got his friends, his school. His *girlfriend.*"

Kate shook her head. "I hate to admit it, but she's right. This neighborhood is getting more dangerous. It's not like it used to be."

Marco opened his mouth to object but she continued. "And if he gets hurt or starts getting into trouble ..." She shook her head at the thought. "Then having friends or school won't matter."

"I think you're getting ahead of yourself, Kate." He sat up on his elbow and turned to her. "Usually, things are fine around here. The neighbors are great; we come and go as we please; no problems."

"I know. All of that's true, but ..."

Marco patted her arm. "*But*—let's keep the thought of moving on the back burner. Can I at least start my new job?"

She pushed him away. "Fine."

Marco rolled over as Kate turned onto her back. She stared at the dark ceiling for another hour before finally falling asleep.

Seventeen

*E*ddie awakened to the rich aroma of freshly brewed coffee ambling in through the cracks of his closed bedroom door. He rose and sat on the edge of the bed, shaking the cobwebs from a restful night's sleep.

A tinkering sound lured him to the window. He pulled up the shade and moaned. Tiny snowflakes popped like little seeds off the window and onto the street below. He shook his head, grateful for his leather jacket and fedora.

After a nice shave and shower, he dressed in the same black dress slacks from yesterday, but grabbed a warm black sweater from his nearly empty dresser drawer. Once satisfied with his appearance, he sat on the bed and made a call to Primo using the landline phone sitting on the bedside table.

"Yeah. It's me."

"How's my sister-in-law?" Primo asked.

"Good. Made some nice progress yesterday."

"You find those bastards who shot up her house?"

"Yeah. Straightened their punk-asses out. Even got them to apologize."

Primo chuckled. "Yeah?"

"Yeah. Pretty funny. They're scared shitless. They'll do whatever I want. Gonna' get them workin' on some leads, like you asked. Could be some promisin' stuff here."

"That right?"

"Yeah. I'd like to stay another week or so, feel things out. See what I can get my fingers into that'll benefit the business."

"Good, Eddie."

"But Primo, one thing I need to mention."

"What's that?"

"Your sister-in-law wants to open an Italian restaurant here in the neighborhood."

"Jesus Christ. She on that again?"

"Yeah. She wants me to find her a place. And then she wants help findin' somebody to help her get it opened. I told her I had to get back to Brooklyn, but ah', she wanted me to ask you if I could stay and help her with that."

"What a waste-a fuckin' money, 'eh?"

"I mean, I agree with ya' Primo. But maybe I could look around for a place. When I can't find one nearby, I tell her that. Then it's done. Off the table, right?"

"Excellent point. You'll *never* find a spot in that neighborhood. I assume she insists it be near her house?"

"Yeah. She made a point-a that."

Primo grumbled. "That's what I figured. The woman don't wanna' leave that place. Keep an eye on her. Don't let her waste her money, ya' hear?"

"Sure thing, boss. I'll go through the motions. Look for some spots. We'll see what happens after that. Sound good?"

"Keep me posted."

The phone went dead. Primo's usual manner of saying goodbye.

Eddie hustled down the squeaky steps, his nose drawn to the coffee. He heard the rustle of paper to his right and walked down the hall to the kitchen. Micola sat at the table sipping a cup of coffee, the St. Paul paper in front of her.

She looked up at him with a grin. "*Buongiorno*, Eddie. How was you-rest?"

"*Buongiorno*. Slept great. Thanks again. It's a lot better than that stuffy hotel, ya' know?"

"*Sì. Bene.*" She smiled as she pushed herself up from the table. "Coffee?"

"Yeah, thanks." He took his now-familiar seat at the table. "So, I talked to Primo this morning."

She turned, her hand at her chest. "Primo? He say-you help me with my *ristorante*, Eddie?"

"Yeah. He said I could help."

Micola looked up to the ceiling and shook her hands at the heavens.

"But, Mrs. F., do you got any idea how much this is gonna' cost you? Cuz lemme' tell you, it ain't gonna' be cheap."

"*Sí*, Eddie. My husband—Vincenzo—he leave me a lotta' money. This house? Is-all paid. I spend my money on nothing. It sits in the bank. When I die, it goes to my daughter. What good is that to me, 'eh? *Niente*. Nothing."

"Okay. I just wanna' be sure you know what you're gettin' into. I mean, your food is amazin' and I think you could make a lotta' money. But up-front?" He twisted his mouth into a frown as he shook his head. "Very expensive, know-what-I-mean?"

She flapped her hand at him. "I don't care about money, Eddie."

Her words made Eddie's heart soar.

"No? What then?"

"I always wanna' do this, but Vincenzo—he say no. He say, his wife stay home where she belong. Then, when he die, I think—now, I do it. But my daughter? She say 'Ma,' you-too old.' So?" She threw up her hands. "I forget it. I-no wanna' fight with my daughter. So, I do nothing. Get lonely. That's all I do."

Eddie gave her a sad smile.

"But you, Eddie. You come-a my house. I like you." She pointed toward the living room. "I like the music you put on. You dance with me and make me laugh. I-no laugh in a long time, Eddie. And you like my food! It makes me feel so good, you know? And my little *ristorante*? It make-me so excited. Is-my dream, Eddie. My dream! So I say 'pssh' to the money."

Eddie sipped his coffee as Micola continued.

"Eddie. I pay you, okay?"

Eddie nearly choked.

There she goes again. I pay you ...

Easy money. Plus, he was already gettin' paid from Primo to help her. If Micola wanted to throw him some cash, too, who was he to say no?

"That sounds real good, Mrs. F. I'll try ta' find you a nice place. We'll make sure it's just what you want. Somethin' small, where you could cook and serve those delicious meals-a yours and share it with others—for a price, a-course." He laughed. "Am I right?"

Micola grabbed a tissue from her apron pocket and dabbed her eyes.

"Eddie, thank you for helping me. I am so excited!"

She walked over and put her hand to his cheek.

He looked up at her from his seat, took her hand, kissed it, and winked at her. He leaned back in his chair and smiled.

"Let's do this, 'eh?"

"*Sí*. Let's do this, Eddie."

He slapped the table. "Okay, then. I'll make some calls to realtors and you call your banker, or whoever, to figure out how much you wanna' spend."

Eddie felt an exhilarated rush. He sipped the last of his coffee. "Now, I got some business-ta take care of today, but I'll try-ta make some calls—see what's out there for locations. We can talk about it some more after that—start makin' plans, okay?"

He checked his watch. "Gotta' go."

He stood and headed down the hall. Micola followed, pulling his jacket from the closet. She handed him his hat and walked him to the door.

He smiled and grabbed her cheeks. "Excitin', huh?"

She giggled. "*Sí*, Eddie. *Sono molto emozionata.*"

He kissed both of her cheeks. "Good. I'll call ya' later."

"Okay. *Ciao*."

"*Ciao*."

Eighteen

The freezing pellets had transformed into sloppy flakes. Eddie frowned at the wet mess as he headed down the steps of Micola's house.

The air felt cold, but not bitterly so—a typical spring morning in Minnesota. Both the grass and Micola's car were covered in a light coating of slush. He cursed himself for forgetting to park the car in the garage. He carefully placed his fedora onto his head and tiptoed along, mindful of his shoes.

His mood lightened when he saw Dario and Tau walking toward the car.

Right on time.

He chuckled and gave himself an imaginary pat on the back.

Dario, wearing oversized blue jeans, a black leather basketball bomber and white sneakers, paced the sodden sidewalk. White flakes settled on his short, black Afro, then quickly vanished from the heat of his head.

Tau, donned in a heavy gray and white sweatshirt, the hood over his head, attempted a laidback appearance by leaning against Micola's car.

Neither could fool Eddie. They were uncertain of their fates, and he wanted to keep it that way. He slid his Ray Bans up to the bridge of his nose as he clicked open the car doors.

"Get in."

At the sound of his voice they scurried. Dario quickly moved to the front passenger seat. Tau frowned, but quietly piled into the back, scooting into the middle so as not to miss anything.

Eddie's mood was upbeat, but he concealed it. He needed them on edge. He wanted his unhinged wrath always at the forefront of their minds. He took off down the quiet street.

"Where we goin'?" Dario asked.

Eddie noticed he seemed fidgety. "Takin' you boys to breakfast. Magnolias. Wanna' talk about the neighborhood and what kinda' businesses are makin' money on the streets."

Dario smiled. "Alright. I'm starvin'."

After the short ride down Payne Avenue, Eddie turned left onto Magnolia Avenue and parked on the street. Magnolias Restaurant, a classic American diner, is best known for its home cooking. Its bright green awning is the only spot of color near the drab, worn-down intersection.

The bell jingled above the door as they entered. Eddie slid into a green vinyl booth away from the door and window, his back to the kitchen. He never sat with his back to the windows or entrance. Dario crawled in on the other side. Tau moved to sit next to Eddie, who shook his head and flicked his fingers in the direction of Dario, across the table.

"Over there."

Tau glared at Dario and then at Eddie, who frowned. "Sit down, Tau." Eddie shook his head. "You'se two better learn-ta get along before I kill the both-a-ya's." He picked up his menu. "Christ almighty."

Tau said, "Yo, man. Move over."

Eddie's eyes lit up as he put up a hand. "What the hell, Tau? I know you speak English, but why does it sound so stiff?"

Dario laughed and nodded. "Right? Sounds like Mary Poppins or somethin'."

Tau did not reply as he slid into the booth. He set his hands in his lap and frowned.

Dario leaned in near Tau's face, smiling. "Yo, Tau. You need more attitude, man." He patted his stomach. "Like this." Dario tipped his head back and forth, his grin exposing straight, white teeth. In a high-pitched voice he said, "'Yo, man.'" He smiled at Tau's shrinking posture. "Like that."

Tau shook his head but made the attempt. "Yo, man."

Dario turned his head sideways for a second and frowned. "Man, you need a lotta' work on your street-hood. But don't give up. You'll get it." He picked up the menu and started scanning it.

"I can't help the way I talk," Tau said. "My family speaks Hmong. I learned English from the kids in the neighborhood and school. I keep trying, but then I go home and it's all messed up."

Eddie rubbed his temples. "Yeah, yeah. Enough of this shit. Back to business. Let's order."

After their food arrived, it was time for the meeting. Eddie took a bite of his pancakes and spoke with his mouthful.

"Now, since it looks like I might be in town for a while—"

Dario stopped chewing and gave Tau a side-glance. "Wait. What's that now?"

Eddie nodded. "Yeah. Mrs. Fortunato wants to open an Italian restaurant. I'm gonna' help her find a place."

"Thought you was leavin' right away."

"No, Dario. Sorry to disappoint. I'll be watchin' you'se two for a while."

Dario sucked in a deep breath. "Okay. That's cool."

Eddie chuckled and continued. "While I'm here, let's figure out where we can make some cash. He swallowed and licked his fingers as he spoke. "What-d-ya got? What do you'se two do fa' money?"

"Mostly sell weed," Dario said. "A little meth sometimes. Sometimes I ah', try to sell some ah'," he looked around and whispered, "ya-know stolen shit."

Eddie hooked his lip. "You steal it yourself?"

"Naw, my boy Nick—he does some shopliftin', burglary and shit. Pretty good at it, too. Gives me a piece-a the action if I can move it."

Eddie turned to Tau. "And you?"

"Same. Mostly hot property. Weed. Meth. The usual."

Eddie raised his brows and waved his fork at them. "Alright. And where do you'se get the product? The drugs, I mean?"

Dario and Tau exchanged a quick glance, enough to heighten Eddie's radar. He frowned.

"What?"

Dario shrugged, rubbed his chin and leaned in. "There's a guy." He waved his fork in the air. "And he's got a couple-a guys. We deal with them. They get us the stuff, we sell it and we get some-a that cheddar."

He shrugged nervously before looking at Tau again.

Eddie put down his fork and sat back. "What the fuck are you'se two lookin' at each other for? What?"

Dario elbowed Tau.

Tau leaned in. "Mr. Bracchio there is a system here."

"Yeah? So? I know about systems. What's yours? Who's the guy?"

"First off—" Tau looked around the restaurant and whispered, "—it's part of the cartel."

"Whoa, whoa, whoa."

Eddie pressed his back into the vinyl cushion of the booth as he lowered his voice. He stuck out his chin, tilting it to make sure he was hearing right.

"You talkin' 'bout the *Mexican* Cartel?"

"Yeah," Dario whispered. "That's where *all* the shit comes from. But we don't deal with them. We just get it from the guy who gets it from the guys. Those *guys*—they get it from the cartel. We don't even deal with that shit."

"How much-you think the guys'-*guy* makes dealin' with you'se two losers?"

"He's gotta' lot of us runnin' around for him, Mr. Bracchio," Tau said. "I have no idea, but I'm gonna' guess he's making bank."

Eddie smiled. "I like the sound-a that."

Dario shook his head. "You like the sound-a that? That ain't your business, man. You can't just go in and take it."

"Well, *you* can't go take it. But *I* could. *I* could take it."

"How?" Tau asked.

"Yeah. How?" Dario repeated.

Eddie scratched his cheek. "I'm gonna' need more information before I can answer that."

Dario shook his head. "Don't like the sound-a this, Mr. B."

Eddie ignored him. "What's this guy's name—the one you deal with here in the neighborhood?"

Dario looked over at Tau. They stayed silent as they looked back at Eddie.

Eddie flicked his fingers toward himself. "Just gimme' the name."

Dario looked behind him before turning to whisper the name.

"Guy's name is O."

"O?"

"Yeah. O. Like L-M-N-O." He waved out his hands. "O."

"Oh," said Eddie.

Dario laughed and smacked his hand on the table. "That's what everybody says."

Eddie smiled at Tau, tipping his head in Dario's direction. "Well at least he knows his fuckin' ABC's, am I right Tau?"

Tau smiled and nodded. "That is special."

Eddie spit out a loud laugh. "I like you, Tau." He knocked his knuckles on the table. "Yeah. I like you."

Dario flapped his hand at them and looked in the direction of the wall. "Man, forget you two."

Dario continued. "Anyway, like I was sayin'. We stay far, far away from those cartel dudes, man. They'll string you up, gut you and hang you from a bridge. They mean serious business, for real."

Eddie laughed and snapped the edges of his jacket. "Where do ya' think they got all-a them bright ideas, 'eh?"

The two boys looked at him, straight-faced. Dario shrugged his shoulders.

Eddie frowned. "Seriously? You'se two gotta' lot-ta learn, you know that?"

Dario laughed, his high voice carrying across the restaurant.

"Oh! Okay." He covered his mouth and sank into the booth. "I get it. Yeah. You're talkin' 'bout the mafia, right?"

Eddie looked around the restaurant. "Keep it down. Don't call attention to yourself, ya' fuckin' idiot." Eddie shook his head. "This is gonna' be harder than I thought. You'se two don't know nothin'."

Dario leaned in and whispered across the table. "Hold up. Eddie—I mean—Mr. Bracchio—Mr. B. Are you in the mafia?"

Eddie knocked his knuckle on his own temple. "You must be slow learners." He looked around the restaurant and leaned in, whispering. "I'm the one—" he pointed at his own chest—"who's gonna' shoot you down like dogs, so don't disrespect me, and don't ask me stupid fuckin' questions."

Eddie let that simmer for a beat. The three of them sat quietly eating their meals. He knew the silence wouldn't last.

Dario swallowed a mouthful of scrambled eggs. "But you're a gangster though, right?"

Eddie stopped chewing and frowned. "Gangster? No." He returned to his breakfast. He took in a slow breath as he wiped his mouth. "I'm a businessman."

Dario laughed. "You killed my dog. Normal businessmen don't do shit like that, man. That's somethin' gangbangers 'round the neighborhood would do."

Eddie sat back. "Let me tell you somethin' kid. Even if I *was a* gangster—which I'm not—and even if I *was* in the mafia—which is none of your fuckin' business—"

Dario turned to Tau and laughed. "That means he *is* in the mafia—I knew it!"

Eddie gave Dario a death-stare. "You finished interruptin' me you piece-a shit?"

"Whoa, whoa. Eddie—Mr. B—what's with all the hostility?" While Dario laughed and looked over at Tau, Eddie's fingers curled into a fist.

This fuckin' kid.

He reached across the table causing dishes to tumble, some to the floor. A few gasps were heard from nearby customers. Before Dario could blink, Eddie's hand gripped his throat. Dario reached up and clawed at Eddie's hand, but Eddie leaned in and pulled Dario toward him, his stomach now lying across his sticky pancakes. Eddie wanted to snap his neck right there, but instead, he tightened his grip just enough to make the kid's eyes bulge a bit. Then, just as quickly, he let go. Dario's head snapped back as he gasped for air.

"You ever fuckin' interrupt me and disrespect me like that again, you're dead. You hear me?"

Dario fell back against the booth, syrup and butter staining the t-shirt under his jacket. Tau leaned away from Dario, as Eddie popped his arms to adjust his jacket.

Dario choked and coughed. His eyes watered as he held his throat with both hands.

"S-sorry, Eddie. Sorry."

Eddie frowned. "You alright?"

Dario nodded, still coughing.

"Okay, then. As I was sayin'. There's one big difference between the mafia and your fuckin' gangbangers, right?"

The boys listened intently, Dario still rubbing his neck.

"First off, gangbangers—what do they do, 'eh? They sit around all day in their mother's fuckin' basement, plottin' who to screw over or who to take out." He put his hand to his chest. "The mafia builds businesses. Right? A lotta' times, legitimate businesses. They're organized. They make money. They have a team—they call-em soldiers—all workin' together." He waved his finger. "A lotta' of 'em are loved by their community. They *help* their community." He shrugged. "Gangs? What? They're scumbags. They don't work. All they do is fuckin' screw each other over. Kill each other. Retribution. All day long." He shook his head. "*Not* the same thing. That's the difference between Mafioso and gangs."

The boys kept quiet, fascinated with Eddie's poise and confidence. His fearlessness.

He leaned across the table and whispered to the two young men, feeding on their energy. "This is gonna take you'se two some time, but you—you're gonna' learn to show power and confidence. And not just on your face, ya' know? In your body language. Your walk, your voice. How you dress. It's about respect. Fear." He shook his head. "But that don't come overnight."

Dario shrugged. "Confidence I got. But it don't always work, man."

Eddie nodded. "You're right. Not at first and not all the time. Take it from me. One time … I got cocky with this guy—big guy, too. He fucked me up real bad. Kicked my ass and then he shot me. Believe that?"

Eddie shook his head, as he laughed at the memory. He slid to the edge of the booth and stood up to face Dario and Tau, who were still seated on their side of the booth.

Eddie pulled up his pant leg. "See that there?"

He showed them a rope-like scar running down his leg.

Dario couldn't contain himself. "Whoa, man!"

Nearby customers stopped talking and looked over at the commotion.

Eddie chuckled at his response. "Yeah. Hurt like a bitch." He smiled at the customers and waved. "Sorry for the disturbance. We're leavin'. Enjoy your breakfast."

He reached for the check. "Let's go."

Tau and Dario scrambled to finish their last few bites before they made their hasty exit to the car.

Outside, Eddie inhaled the cool spring air. Brooklyn's air never seemed to be as fresh as this. It cleared his head and brightened his mood. Cars whizzed past them as they walked down Minnehaha toward Micola's car.

"Good talk. We're done for a while."

He returned to Micola's house and parked on the street. As Dario and Tau headed in the directions of their homes, Eddie shouted out to them. "You see me callin', you answer."

They waved back at Eddie as he climbed the stairs. Breakfast had reaped a nugget of information.

O.

He paused near the steps of Micola's house to consider a trip to the Mall of America for new suits and other personal necessities. He changed his mind and continued up the stairs. First—a nap. He'd need a little more energy for that shit.

Nineteen

Steam from the shower filled the small bathroom. Marco threw back the shower curtain just as Kate flipped her thick, brown hair upside down, scissors in hand.

"What the hell are you doing?" he asked, reaching for his towel.

She looked up at him sideways, her hair falling around her face. "Cutting my hair—just a trim." She grinned at him. "Don't worry."

Patting himself dry, he said, "Shouldn't ya' have someone do that for ya'?"

She brushed the ends together into a bunch and started snipping. "Too expensive." She continued cutting inch-long chunks of hair and let them fall into the sink.

"Do you have any idea how much it costs for me to get a haircut these days?"

"No. And I don't wanna' know."

She straightened up and let her hair fall wildly around her face.

"*Very* expensive."

"I hate this," Marco said. He wrapped his towel around his waist and moved next to her in front of the mirror, combing his damp black curls.

"What?"

"All this scrimpin' to get by."

She continued clipping her ends. "Me, too."

Marco drew up his sweatpants. "I just wish I was makin' more money, ya' know? Maybe I could find somethin' else, too. Part-time to supplement my job at the shop. If I could do that, we'd be fine."

"That'd be nice, but I think we'll be okay."

Marco pulled her close. "Look at you."

She smiled. "What?"

"You know what." He pushed his face into her neck and inhaled. "After all these years, you still get me goin'."

She watched his eyes wander and leaned in.

"Mom!"

"Oh, God."

Kate ran out of the bathroom to yell downstairs.

"Coming sweetie! Do you have your backpack?"

"Yes! Come on. We're gonna be late!"

"Your homework assignment?"

"YE-us! Come on!"

She returned to the bathroom. "Do you hear how low his voice is getting?"

Marco frowned. "Yeah. But he's closing in on fourteen. Nothin' we can do about it."

"I'm not ready."

She ran to the bedroom closet to look for her shoes while she buttoned her blouse. "Gotta' go!"

She felt a smack on her ass. She turned and smiled.

Marco smiled back. "Have a great day today, baby. Sell some stuff."

"And you have a great first day. See you tonight. We'll grill some burgers. Sound good?"

"Sounds awesome. Hopefully, this snow stops later on. It's supposed to."

She blew him a kiss as she grabbed her briefcase and yelled to Renzo as she hurried down the stairs.

Renzo sat impatiently in the front passenger seat of Kate's beat-up Ford. He shook his head at his mother as she climbed in, tossing her briefcase in back.

"Sorry," she said, ignoring his crabby preteen attitude as he sat quietly stewing.

She backed down the long driveway, realizing her son was right. They were late. She tried not to rush through traffic as they headed for Cleveland Junior High.

After driving a few blocks, Renzo turned to Kate. "Can I go to the movies with Michael and his parents tonight?"

"It's a school night. No."

"No, it's not. It's Friday."

"Oh! It is." She shook her head. "I need to get my head in the game. I guess it's okay."

"Can I sleep over, too?"

"Sure, I suppose that's ok."

She pulled her car behind a row of others lined up for drop-off in front of the old brick school building. The usual kids mulled around the front sidewalk and trampled lawn. Renzo pulled himself out of the car and turned to say goodbye.

Kate smiled at her son, longing for the days of a quick kiss and hug before he left her. "I'll have to check with Michael's parents about tonight," she said.

"Okay," Renzo said.

"Bye, sweetie! Have a great day!"

He gave her a backhanded wave as he ran to meet up with Sean and some other boys. Kate stared after him, frowning.

When did he get so tall?

She shook her head and pulled back onto Lawson Street and headed toward her office.

She spent her day looking at properties with prospective buyers, replying to e-mails and returning calls. After lunch, she remembered to call Michael's parents to confirm that the movie and sleepover were okay with them, and made arrangements to drop him off after work.

Her desk phone rang just as she was packing up to leave for the day. She was tempted to let it go to voicemail, but instead, picked it up after three rings.

"Kate De Luca. How may I help you?"

"Yeah, Ms. De Luca. How you doin'? My name is Eddie Bracchio."

Kate was so thrown by the New York accent she almost chuckled.

The caller continued. "I was told by Jim Schmeising from your office that you were the agent in charge-a stuff in the Payne Avenue area."

"That's right. I am. Are you looking for residential or commercial property?"

"Commercial. I'm ah' … wonderin' if you got any places for a little Italian restaurant in that area—Payne Avenue somewhere's."

"Sure. Um ..." She flipped her hair behind her ear and sat back in her chair, thankful she hadn't yet logged off her computer. She pulled up her available properties near that area and scrolled through.

"It looks like I have a few places on the northern end of Payne and one at the far south of it, close to Seventh Street, although I'm not sure whether that one is suitable for a restaurant. It's a former office building. It's been vacant for quite some time. I—"

"Those sound great. We can save that last one for the end. How about tomorrow morning? I know it's Saturday. Would that work anyway? Say ten o'clock?"

"Sure. Saturday is no problem. She gave him the address to the first place. I'll meet you there and show you around and we'll take it from there."

"Sounds real good. Appreciate that. See ya' tomorrow then, Ms. De Luca."

"Kate. Call me Kate."

"Alright, Kate. And you call me Eddie."

"I will. See you tomorrow, Eddie. Thanks for calling."

"Ya' welcome." Eddie hung up.

Kate looked at the phone and let out a chuckle.

"Okay. That was different."

She logged off her computer, grabbed her purse and briefcase and left for home, excited to tell Marco about her new prospective client.

Twenty

Kate had just finished emptying the dishwasher when she heard the back door to the kitchen open. Marco walked in and she greeted him with outstretched arms.

"Hi baby. How was your first day?"

Marco smiled back as he wrapped his arms around her waist and pushed her hair behind her ear. "Pretty good." He kissed her forehead. "Let me take a quick shower and I'll tell you all about it. How was your day?"

Kate smiled. "Pretty good. Got a new client today."

"That's great," Marco said. "Can't wait to hear all about it." He walked to the door to the living room. "Renzo upstairs?"

"Nope."

Marco stopped. "Where is he?"

She lowered her eyes and wiggled her eyebrows. "Sleeping over at Michael's."

Marco gave her a dirty grin and pretended to stumble back. "No way."

She nodded. "Yep. We're *all* alone. For the *whole* night."

He did a fist-pump. "Yes!"

Kate laughed. "So, no burgers tonight. I made chicken. Go clean up."

She squeezed her breasts together with her arms and gave him a sultry look as she shimmied her shoulders.

"Hurry back," she said, in her sexiest whisper. "Sorry. Lame."

"Not lame to me!" Marco chuckled as he hurried out of the kitchen.

Kate was tasting gravy at the stove when Marco came into the kitchen. He hugged her from behind, brushing his whiskers against her neck. She turned and they embraced. He lowered his head and gave her a warm kiss.

"Hmm. Nice," Kate said, as Marco slowly dragged his hands down her arms.

"That smells delicious," he said. He turned to the wine rack on the counter. "Care for a glass?"

"Dumb question, sir."

He poured two glasses of chardonnay and turned on some quiet bluesy music. As Kate plated the food, Marco set the table and dimmed the overhead light. They talked quietly about Marco's first day on the job and Renzo's sleepover.

After cleaning up, they moved to the living room. Marco set the music and lighting, leaving on the hall light near the front door. He then lit the candle sitting on their beat-up coffee table. They propped up their feet and snuggled next to each other as they sipped their wine.

After a couple of glasses, Kate felt a flush of heat rise up her face and a tingle of warmth in her belly. She placed her hand inside his thigh and turned up to him, kissing his soft lips, tasting the wine on his tongue as his hand gently caressed her breasts over her shirt. Their passionate breath intensified and Marco moaned softly, pulling away to look at her.

"Should we go upstairs?"

She smiled and nodded. "Definitely."

Marco blew out the candle and grabbed their wine glasses while Kate turned off the lights. He struggled to hold the glasses upright as they giggled, groped and kissed their way up the stairs and into the hallway. At the bedroom entrance, Kate flipped on the hall light and pulled away from Marco, their fingers the last to release before she turned to climb onto their king-size bed.

She kept the bedside lamps off, leaving the dark room lit only by the sliver of illumination from the hall. She sat on the bed's edge, facing Marco, and pulled her t-shirt up over her head, tossing it to the floor as he approached her.

Kate felt his heat and quickly pushed off her sweatpants while backing herself further onto the bed. Marco's gaze intensified as he drew near.

He stripped down and joined her. Kate caressed his smooth skin as he straddled her, lowering his mouth to her breasts. She arched her back, letting him linger before pushing him away, moving back toward the pillows. He watched her, his gaze hungry as he crawled toward her. She reached out her hand and he gently took it as he moved on top of her. He lowered his head to her chest and they held each other tightly, kissing and caressing as they rolled side-to-side, front-to-back. Their passionate breathing grew. Kate again pulled away, pushing Marco aside as she flipped herself around and straddled him. She lowered her head and watched him through her long, wild hair.

She smiled and slowly slid back, crouching between his knees. Through tousled hair, she watched him watching her. It wasn't long before he tipped his head back and closed his eyes.

She retreated and climbed on top of him and they moved in unison, continuing until Kate could take no more. She let out a suppressed cry and grabbed Marco's shoulders, pulling his body to her. They slowed their pace and Kate looked down at him as he held her hips.

Marco gently pushed Kate's mass of hair from her face, and she rolled next to him. He sucked in a breath and popped it back out.

"Whoo! Goddamn, girl! That was fuckin' amazing." He turned on his side and propped himself up on his elbow, looking down at her. "Why don't we do that more often?"

"Good question."

He brushed a strand of hair from her forehead. "I mean, are we losing our touch? Are we getting boring in our old age?"

She rolled onto her side. "Obviously, we're not losing our touch. It's just—we never get this kind of alone-time."

"Well, that's bullshit. Let's try harder."

Kate giggled and yawned. "Okay. It's a deal." She ran to turn off the hall light and climbed back into bed. "Gotta' get up early tomorrow. Nine o'clock. Have to meet my new client at ten."

In the silhouetted light from the window, she saw Marco's head lift and turn toward her.

"Tomorrow's Saturday. It's my *only* Saturday off for a while. Starting next week, I'm on two Saturdays a month."

"You know I have to work on Saturdays sometimes."

He flopped his head back on the pillow. "Shit. For how long?"

She patted his chest. "Just a couple hours. I'll be home a little after noon. Now go to sleep. I'm exhausted."

He lifted his head and turned to kiss her quickly on the lips.

"Night. Love you."

"Love you."

Twenty-one

Kate had already showered when Marco entered the bathroom and kissed her neck.

"Morning," he said, his voice gravelly.

"Morning, sleepy-head."

He stood at the toilet while she worked on her hair at the bathroom mirror, makeup, hairspray and brushes strewn across the tiny sink.

"So, who's the new client?" Marco asked.

"Someone interested in that crappy old building down on Payne and Petit."

"You're kiddin'."

With her curling iron locked up near her head, Kate smiled.

"Nope."

"God. You've had that place for a long time and no nibbles."

"Don't remind me. He called just as I was packing up yesterday. He's looking for a place to open a little Italian restaurant. I told him I wasn't sure this place was a good fit, but he was very specific about the location. There are only a couple of places that might work in that area."

Marco laughed. "Jesus. You get all kinds, don't cha'? Do you think this guy's serious?"

Kate shrugged. "Who knows? It'll probably be a waste of time."

She turned to the mirror and ran her fingers through her long curls finishing her look. "Interesting-sounding guy, though. Thick Brooklyn accent. Like yours."

She gave him an exaggerated bopping of her head as she produced her best Brooklyn accent, her finger and thumb pinched together as she waved it at Marco.

"He said, 'Yeah. How you'se doin' ta-day? You got any buildins' I coo-look at?"

She shrugged her shoulders and wiped her nose with her thumb.

Marco laughed. "Hey, that's a good impression!"

She grabbed her crotch. "Hey. What-aya' gonna' do? 'Eh?"

He shook his head. "Jesus. Will ya' stop?"

She laughed and sighed, returning to her reflection in the mirror.

"I love my job."

With a quick motion, he moved her hair from her face. "Be positive. I know it's a sore subject, but we could use a break. I mean—*you* could use a break. You've made half of what you made last year."

She pushed him away. "Yeah, so you've reminded me."

"Come on, babe. I'm sorry. I'm just sayin'—maybe this is it. The break we've been waitin' for. I mean, with my new job, and, ya' know, maybe this turns out for you, who knows? Maybe we'll be in Fat-City."

She gave him a flat smile. "I hope you're right."

"What time's the meeting?"

"I told you. Ten." She leaned out of the bathroom door to check the clock on the nightstand.

"Right. I forgot. The wine, ya' know?"

"Yeah, I know. Me too."

She pressed her navy skirt and white blouse into place and walked back into the bedroom.

Marco flopped onto the bed, his arms folded under his head, watching Kate run around the room searching for her shoes and digging through her bag.

She walked to the edge of the bed, the sheets and blankets in a tousled mess from their lovemaking the night before.

"I'm off," she said, bending to kiss him.

He pulled her down on top of him and she screamed and laughed. He muffled her with a passionate kiss, lingering for a couple of seconds. Kate melted into him, but he teasingly yanked her away.

"Have a great day. Sell lots-a stuff."

She gave him a fake frown. "Now I have to fix my lipstick."

She returned to the bathroom to adjust her hair and lipstick and walked back into the bedroom, grabbing her bag and jacket.

As she hurried down the stairs, Marco called out to her.

"Bye gorgeous. See you in a couple hours."

Kate hurried out the back door to her car, the chilly wind penetrating her unbuttoned, cream-colored raincoat. She scowled at the looming gray clouds.

Who says April in Minnesota is nice? It's never nice.

She backed down the driveway and headed for the first rental location on Payne Avenue.

Twenty-two

Kate pulled up behind a black sedan parked outside the old brick building near Payne and York. A silhouette of a man sat behind the wheel.

She grabbed her bag and stepped out of the car. A cold wind swirled around her legs, cutting through her coat. The steely sky held the impending rain in its grip, ready to let loose at any moment. Kate cursed herself for forgetting her umbrella — especially this time of year.

As she shut her car door, a blustery gust took up her hair — high over her head — swirling it in place for a second, before letting it flop down in a heap around her shoulders. She let out a quiet shriek, stopping short to pat it back into place with her free hand. She heard a car door shut and looked up to see a stocky, muscular man heading her way. Unfortunately, she couldn't take back this embarrassing first impression.

The man appeared to be in his early forties. His salt-and-pepper hair was swooped back and held in place by a thick gel. His entire ensemble was black. Black shirt, unbuttoned at the top, expensive looking black leather jacket, black dress pants and black shoes, buffed to a shine. The only hint of color Kate noticed, was a gold chain hanging around his neck, a gold cross dangling in the middle.

As he approached her with an outstretched hand and a smile, Kate noted his broad shoulders and deep-set brown eyes. His olive complexion was mostly hidden beneath a neatly groomed salt-and-pepper goatee, which gave him a bit of a menacing appearance. She thought him ruggedly attractive — in a gangster sort of way.

She'd given up on her hair, and reached out her hand as he approached.

"Mr. Bracchio?"

"Yeah, that's me," he said, giving her hand a rough shake. A few cars whizzed past, making it difficult to hear.

Kate paused for a second, remembering the man from the cab who had called out to her. She thought this might be that guy. She kept that memory to herself though, as she noted his impeccably manicured hands.

Money.

"It's very nice to meet you," she said, returning his handshake with her own strong one.

"Yeah. Nice ta-meet you'se too." He gave her a creepy up-and-down look and said, "When you said your last name was De Luca, I thought you was Italian." He scratched his chin, still ogling. "But you don't look Italian. Irish. Am I right?"

Kate smiled politely and nodded. "This way." She pointed to the door of the first location.

"I'm impressed. I am Irish. What gave it away?"

Eddie leaned back and threw out his arms. "You kiddin' me? Those baby-blues? That beautiful pale skin? An easy guess. Know what I mean?"

She smiled, but didn't reply.

"So," he said, "I take it you married an Italian then?"

"I did. I mean—I'm married, yes. His name is Marco." She paused. "He's from Brooklyn. Like you."

Eddie smiled and jerked his head up a smidge. "How-you know I'm from Brooklyn?"

She smiled. "Please. That accent?" She flapped her hand at him. "Fu-ghet-abowd-it."

Eddie threw back his head and laughed. "That's pretty good, you know that?"

She laughed, too. "Really? You think?" She let out a big sigh. "Oops, sorry. Unprofessional."

"Nah'," Eddie said. "I love it."

"What-you say your husband's name was? If he's from the neighborhood, maybe I know him."

"Marco De Luca."

Eddie looked up toward the gray sky for a second. "Marco De Luca. De Luca. Hmm." He shook his head. "Nope. Never heard-a him."

He turned to look at the old dark brick building in front of them.

"So this is it, 'eh? You weren't kiddin'. Don't look like much."

Three stores lined the front. To the left was an old liquor store long since shuttered. To the far right, was a narrow and battered wooden door, scarred by scratches and gouges, its stain faded to a dull gray. This entrance had no front window, only a worn-out sign on the door that read:

Accountants. No Appointment needed.

Kate frowned. She hadn't recalled the building being this dilapidated. They moved to the middle door and she cupped her hands around her eyes and peeked through the grimy plate-glass window. It was bigger than she'd remembered. Empty, except for an abandoned stool sitting nearly dead-center.

She pulled away from the window and looked at Eddie with a frowning smile.

"What?" He asked. "No good?"

With hands on his hips, he leaned back to scan the entire front of the building, and then turned in a circle to check out the area. The streets and sidewalks were deserted, but it was still early on a Saturday morning.

Kate scanned the building one more time and turned back to Eddie, her brows raised as she crinkled her nose.

"Thoughts?"

Eddie shook his head. "I don't like it. This center unit. It feels, I don't know—"

"Claustrophobic?" Kate asked.

"Yeah. Claustrophobic." He turned to her. "What else ya' got?"

"You don't want to go in?"

Eddie frowned. "Nah'. Seen enough."

"Okay. Let's see." She flipped the pages of her notepad, the cold wind biting her face. "I have a few more places up and down Payne." She headed to her car. "Why don't you ride with me? It'll be easier. I'll bring you back to your car once we've finished."

Eddie nodded and got into the passenger side of her car. They looked at three more places that morning, traveling up and back down Payne Avenue. One place was too close to Yarusso's Italian Restaurant, and the other two didn't give Eddie the vibe he was looking for.

"I can tell from your reactions that nothing is clicking with you so far," Kate said, as they walked out of the last place. She padlocked the door, and they turned toward her car.

"Not yet," said Eddie. "But I know these things take time. You got any more places we could look at?"

Kate shook her head as they climbed into her car. "Unfortunately, none for today, but ..."

Eddie gave her a side-glance. "What?"

Kate let out a sigh. "I do have one more place." She frowned as she clicked her pen on the notepad, thinking.

"What? Somethin' wrong with it?"

"Well, as I mentioned over the phone, this place is just—it's not set up for a restaurant. It's an old warehouse down closer to Seventh Street near the *Minnesota Music Café*. There would have to be major—and I'm talking *major*—renovations to convert it into a restaurant."

Eddie nodded. "Yeah, I don't know about that. Sounds like a lotta' money."

They fell silent on the ride back to his car, but as she pulled up behind it, Eddie rubbed his chin. "I don't know. I guess I could look at it. My client—I'm not sure she'd wanna' put that much money into it, know what I mean? But the location would be perfect. Near Seventh. Right outta' downtown."

Kate nodded. "I guess it couldn't hurt to take a look. I can set something up for Monday. In the meantime, I'll try to find more prospects. I'm afraid we might have to move beyond this area, though."

Eddie shook his head. "Nope. Gotta' have it 'round here. That's for sure. She wants it near her house. She's older, ya' know? She don't wanna' spend a lotta' time driving back and forth."

He opened the passenger door.

Kate nodded. "I understand." She reached over and they shook hands. "I'll call you later today with the time for early next week." She felt him linger his grip on her hand, but she let it slide.

"Alright then," Eddie said. "I'll wait for your call, Kate. Good ta' meet ya'."

She smiled and nodded. "Good to meet you, too. I'll be in touch."

As Kate drove away, she noticed Eddie in her rearview mirror standing next to his car, watching her.

Twenty-three

*E*ddie pulled into the driveway of Micola's house and came in through the back door. He called out to her from the kitchen.

"I'm here, Eddie."

He walked down the hall to the living room where Micola sat, hands on her knees, looking anxious.

"How did it go, Eddie? You find my *ristorante*?"

He shook his head and moved to sit in the chair across from her.

"Not yet. They weren't right. Dumps, really."

She nodded, her expression flat. "Oh. I see. Dumps. But ... you look for more? You keep checking, *sì*?"

He smiled. "Yeah. The realtor's gotta' place. She's gonna' call me with a time to go look at it next week. It's more money than we talked about, though."

She flapped her hand at him. "Eddie, I got money. You no worry about money, okay?"

His chest fluttered with excitement. "You sure?"

"*Sì*, Eddie." She pulled herself up from the sofa. "Now, I make you breakfast."

Eddie chuckled as she passed him. "I ain't gonna' turn that down."

Micola placed a hot cup of coffee next to Eddie before sitting next to him at the kitchen table. With his mouth full, he nodded his thanks to her. She leaned on her elbows and smiled as she watched him eat her homemade spinach and mozzarella omelet with toast and jelly. A simple meal, rich and creamy, with a hint of garlic, yet, unique—unlike any other egg dish Eddie had tasted.

After taking his last bite, Eddie wiped his mouth and sat back, his hands resting on the table.

"Let me tell you, Mrs. F.," he pointed at his empty plate, "you got somethin' real special here. Too good to be true, know what I'm sayin'?" He gave her a quick chuckle of disbelief as he shook his head. "I'm not kiddin' ya'. Every dish has been fantastic. Your restaurant? It's gonna be great."

Micola smiled. "Thank you, Eddie. You-like-a dream to me. You come here. You give my life a spark. I am nervous about the *ristorante*. But excited, too."

"That's good."

Eddie went up to his room for a quick nap. His burner phone rang and he was happy to see it was from that beautiful realtor.

"Kate. What'd ya' find out?"

"Hi Eddie. We can look at it tomorrow morning. I know it's a Sunday, but–are you available around eight-thirty?"

"Too early, Kate. How about ten?" He listened to her chuckle and imagined her beautiful smile.

"Well, I'd have to confirm that. Tell you what. If you don't hear back from me, you can assume ten o'clock works, okay?" She gave him the address.

"Yeah. That's great. Thanks, Kate. I'll see ya' tomorrow unless I hear back."

"Sounds good, Eddie. See you then."

Twenty-four

*E*ddie closed the door to his bedroom and called Primo.

"Yeah. It's me."

"Yeah."

"Been over to your sister-in-law's house a few times," Eddie said, "and, you're not gonna' believe it but, she had me move in." He paused for Primo's reaction. After a breath of silence, he added. "Saves money anyways."

"Good," Primo said. "My wife will like that you're there."

Eddie was pleased he'd given him no pushback.

Primo let out a gurgling cough and then said, "You talk more about the restaurant?"

"Talk about the restaurant? Are you kiddin' me?" Eddie put his hand on his forehead. "Primo, that's *all* she wants ta' talk about. I don't think she's gonna' let me stop lookin'. I told her there was nothin' but garbage for locations, but she insists I keep tryin'."

"She's a stubborn old broad, that's for sure."

"I'm beginnin' to see that. Her food is unbelievable, though. It could be a great place."

"Yeah, no doubt she's got a nice product."

"Christ, she's already got me talkin' about menus and what type-a place she wants. You know, a deli, a bakery, or a full-out dining room?"

"What she say?"

"Full dining."

"Figures. Jesus. At her age. The whole thing is fuckin' stupid."

"She's no spring chicken, that's for sure. Seems up to it, though. Tough. I told her I'd try to find a place close to her house. Gotta' real estate agent workin' on it now."

"Jesus. Do your search and forget about this bullshit restaurant. I need you back here. I can't have Freddy handlin' your business for too much longer. You were right. He's a mess."

"Hey, no disrespect, Primo, but I told you he was a no-good prick." Eddie stood and started to pace the room. "And, I mean— I hate to remind you—but you was the one that made me come to this piece-a-shit town. Now, I gotta' at least *try* to help Micola find a place. I can't leave yet. It was my big mouth that started all-a this shit." He paused. For a moment, there was silence on Primo's end, too.

"Shit," Primo said. "What a mess, 'eh? Now, my wife's all excited about this stupid restaurant, too."

"I'm sorry, boss. I know this is puttin' you in a tough spot. And if I'd-a known what I was startin'? I'd-a kept quiet. Believe me. But I didn't. Now, Micola's *really* excited about it. I'd hate to break her heart, know what I mean?"

"Hmm."

Eddie continued. "And helpin' her find a place is gonna' take time."

"How much time?"

"I don't know. Three weeks?" Eddie braced himself for Primo's wrath.

"Three weeks? Shit, Eddie."

"I know. I'm sorry, Primo. But she's your sister-in-law. And, your wife? She's gonna' want me to help her, am I right?"

"Don't try to play me, Eddie. Who do you think you're talkin' to, 'eh?"

"Come on, Primo. You know what I mean. I'm not tryin' nothin'."

Silence lingered over the line before Primo spoke. "Alright. You gotta' finish this."

Eddie smiled and nodded to himself, surprised he was so happy to be staying. "Okay then. I'll keep you posted."

"You do that, Eddie. I mean it."

"I will, Primo. You got my word."

"Alright. You-got enough money ta' last for a while?"

"Yeah. I'll let you know if things get tight."

"Good. Did Micola offer to pay you?"

"Naw. Not yet, anyway," Eddie lied.

"I'll talk to Micola about payin' you."

"No," Eddie said. "I'll talk to her. She'll pay. I'll let ya' know when I'm runnin' low."

"Alright. Make this quick, Eddie."

"Right, boss. I'll be in touch."

Eddie looked at his phone as the line went dead. Good. Now, he had a little breathin' room to get things goin' with the restaurant and work on some extracurricular activities with those punks.

He headed back downstairs and peeked around the corner into the living room.

Micola turned off the vacuum. "Where you go, Eddie?"

He waved his hands down the sides of his body. "Gotta' get some new clothes. Looks like I'm stayin' awhile." He took his jacket from the back of the chair. "I'll be back in a few hours. Not sure how long things'll take at this Mall of America. Gotta' *find* the place first, know what I mean?"

Micola nodded. "See you, Eddie."

He waved to her and shut the back door behind him.

Twenty-five

*E*ddie slammed the snooze button on the screaming alarm clock and squinted to check the time. Eight-forty-five. He rolled onto his back and grunted. It was an early wake-up call for any day, let alone a Sunday morning. He dragged himself out of bed and peeked out the window. The weather showed promise. The clouds had broken up and the sun was shining.

He showered quickly and donned one of his new ensembles from the many he'd purchased the day before during his shopping spree at the Mall of America. He'd blown a ton of cash on the clothes, but impeccable style builds reputation, and reputation was what he was after.

He didn't want to waste a suit on this morning's simple warehouse viewing, but he did want to impress the beautiful realtor.

Kate.

He paused to relive that first moment yesterday. Her hair had swirled over her head. He'd never seen anything like it. So spontaneous. Like it was meant for him to see. She'd swept him up right then.

He flipped through his new selections, now hung neatly in the closet, and chose some designer jeans and a cherry and white paisley dress shirt. He put on his usual chain, ring and bracelet, and this time, he added a splash of new cologne. Couldn't hurt.

He arrived at the warehouse a few minutes early. As he sat in his car waiting for Kate, he checked out the surrounding area. The place was directly on Payne Avenue, just as Micola had hoped. The rest of the area was pretty rundown. Old brick buildings lined both sides of Payne, and Swede Hollow Park was behind him.

The stand-alone building before him had a rust-colored brick exterior, stood two stories tall, with a flat roof. The old but solid structure appeared to be in good condition, although the tan painted windowsills were chipped and faded.

Kate pulled in behind him, and he again watched her from his rearview mirror. He admired her beauty as she stepped out of her car. As it did yesterday, a brief gust encircled her walnut-colored hair and flew it wildly about her face, not quite like the vision of yesterday, but he couldn't believe it had happened again. He watched her quickly brush it down and push it behind her. She bent back into her car and Eddie smiled as her high-heeled foot lifted.

Goddamn.

He could look at her all day long. Unfortunately, the moment was brief. Kate had stepped back out of her car, briefcase in hand. She closed the door and gave him a smile and a quick wave as she walked toward him, her cream-colored raincoat blowing behind her. He opened his car door and tried not to scan her body. He did admire her legs under the black, pencil-thin skirt. Her blazer hid the prize package up top.

She called out to him. "Good morning."

"Mornin', Kate."

She shook his hand as they turned to face the front of the building. Eddie felt a twitch of pleasure at her touch.

She opened her arms to the building.

"Well? This is it. Let's check it out. And just to warn you, I have not seen this one yet."

As they approached, Eddie peered through one of the glass windows, noting the beat-up cement floor. Kate unlocked the lockbox and opened the front door. She waved her hand. "After you, Mr. Bracchio."

Eddie leaned back and put out his hand to stop her. "Please. Call me 'Eddie,' remember?"

"Right. 'Eddie' it is."

Eddie bowed and waved his hand across his waist. "After you."

Except for the light from the front windows, the main room was shrouded in darkness. Kate moved along the nearest wall to her right, searching for a light switch. When she found one, she flipped it up and fluorescent bulbs popped to life overhead.

"Okay!" she said. "Let's explore!"

As they moved to the center of the front area, Kate put her hand to her nose. "It seems this place hasn't held fresh air in a while."

Eddie nodded. "Yeah. It sure don't smell like a restaurant, know what I mean?" He laughed and Kate smiled at him as they continued the tour.

Those blue eyes. Like crystals.

He tried not to stare.

They toured the empty, hollowed interior, their shoes clicking on the cold, cement floor. There was something Eddie liked about the place. Though the framework was unfinished and the plumbing exposed, he loved the high ceiling and the spaciousness of the front room. And after talking money with Micola, it seemed the price was right, too.

As they returned to the front of the building near the corner door, Eddie swung his hands open wide. "Now this place, I like."

Kate nodded. "I know what you mean. I'm pleasantly surprised. There's something about it, right? It has character. Potential."

"It does. I'd like to show my client. Can we come back this afternoon?"

She looked at her watch. "I have a couple of personal matters in the next couple of hours. How about three-thirty? Will that work?"

She turned to exit the building and Eddie followed.

"Sure," he said. "We can do that. My client lives a few blocks away. I think she's gonna' like it."

"Well," Kate said, "now that I have the keys, I can bring you in anytime you'd like."

Eddie loved the sound of her voice.

"That's great," he said.

She locked the door and they walked to their cars.

He turned to her. "Three-thirty then?"

Kate nodded and smiled as she reached out her hand. "See you then, Eddie."

He took her hand and shook it gently. "Lookin' forward to it, Kate. And thanks for your help."

"You're welcome."

He watched as she walked to her car and drove off.

No matter what happens, meetin' her was worth it.

He drove back to the house, excited to tell Micola about her new *ristorante*. He walked in through the front entrance and called out to her.

"In the kitchen, Eddie."

Eddie walked down the hallway to the kitchen. Micola stood at the stove, stirring something creamy that smelled of garlic and onion.

He peeked over her shoulder. "Smells delicious. More sauce?"

"*Sì.*"

She set down the spoon and turned to see him smiling. She clapped her hands. "You find my *ristorante*, Eddie?"

He took her by her elbow and led her to the table. "I think so, Mrs. F. Wait ta' ya' see it. I think this might be the place."

She put her hands to her mouth.

"You okay, Mrs. F.?"

She nodded. He could see a smile form across her cheeks as her eyes began to glisten.

"I don't know what to do—I'm so excited—my heart—" She patted her chest with one hand. "I thought it stopped." She giggled and Eddie laughed.

"Alright. Calm down. Take a breath, 'eh?"

"I can't wait to see it. When? When can we go?" She moved to stand. "I'm ready. Anytime."

"We go at three-thirty this afternoon. We'll leave a few minutes before that. The place is *that* close."

"Today? That's wonderful, Eddie. Tell me—what is this place? Beautiful, no?"

He shook his head. "No."

She gave him a sharp look. "No?"

He smiled. "Not yet." He pinched his thumb and forefinger together, shaking them in front of her face. "But it's got *potential*. *Capisci*? So I need you to be prepared. It's gonna need a *lotta'* work, okay?"

"Okay."

"Now, go finish your sauce. I got calls to make and a few errands to run. I'll meet you back here at three-twenty."

They rose from the table and Micola embraced him.

"Okay, Eddie. See you soon."

Twenty-six

*E*ddie pulled up Micola's driveway at exactly three-twenty to find her waiting on the front porch. She wore a bright green spring coat, buttoned up tight, with her hands clasping a white handbag. Eddie put the car in park, and ran up to help her down the stairs.

He grinned. "Look at you." He reached out his hand. "You look more than ready."

"I am ready Eddie." She giggled. "Oh, that rhymes."

Eddie joined her with a laugh at her little joke.

He stuck out his elbow. "Let's go check out your new place."

Micola hooked her arm through his. "You really think this is the one?"

"I do."

He helped her into the passenger's seat and chuckled to himself. This whole setup just might work.

They drove down to Payne Avenue and turned right. After driving several blocks, Eddie slowed the car and parked in front of the old building on their right. Kate's car was parked up ahead.

Micola's shoulders slumped as she frowned, her wiry salt-and-pepper eyebrows nearly touching as she turned to Eddie.

"This place?"

Micola stared at the old brick building and looked back at Eddie.

"Hey. What's with the face?"

She opened her mouth to speak, but Eddie stopped her with his best charming grin. He patted her hand.

"I know. I told ya', dint-I? It don't look all that great right now. But you gotta' trust me. This is the place. It's got a-lotta' potential, *capisci*?"

"Okay. But right now?" She shook her head. "I no-like."

"Come on, lemme' show you."

Eddie got out and jogged around to help her from the car. He gently placed his arm around her waist, as they walked toward the front door.

He leaned in near her ear. "Believe me. With my ideas? And your food? This place'll be a gold mine."

"I hope so."

"You'll see. Trust me."

"Okay, Eddie. I trust you."

Eddie raised his hand to knock just as Kate opened the door.

"Hello," she said, smiling. "Come on in." She held the door and stepped aside.

Eddie ignored the smell of the damp, musty air but watched as Micola wrinkled her nose. She raised her hand to block it.

"Oh, Eddie. What is that smell?"

"I know. But hear me out, okay?"

Micola frowned as she lowered her hand.

"Kate, I'd like you to meet Mrs. Micola Fortunato. You can call her Micola."

Kate reached out her hand. "It's a pleasure to meet you, Mrs. Fortunato. Micola." She waved her arm across the room. "Please. Take your time."

Eddie wrapped his arm around Micola's shoulder and began to work his magic. "Now, close your eyes, Mrs. F."

"No. I-no wanna' close my eyes. I wanna' leave this place. It stinks."

Eddie turned and smiled into her brown eyes. "Come on."

"Fine. I-close my eyes."

He walked behind her and leaned his face close to her right cheek as he guided her across the room. He winked at Kate, who was watching with amusement.

Even though Micola couldn't see what he was doing, he reached out his arm and slowly spread his hand across the room.

"Imagine, Micola. Freshly painted walls, in maybe some-a-that fancy mud stuff they use to troll across the walls—maybe a caramel color or a warm cream—or maybe both."

With her eyes still closed, the old woman nodded. "I like that. *Sí.*"

Eddie continued whispering as they walked slowly across the room, painting the imaginary picture.

"We buff up the floors to a shine in a color you like, lights comin' down outta' the ceiling on those long wires, and maybe a big chandelier dead-center."

"Hmm-hmm," Micola murmured.

"Beautiful tables with white linen tablecloths and flower centerpieces, the place filled with all kinds-a people laughin', and drinkin', and eatin' your food. Beautiful Italian music comin' outta' the speakers." He turned her toward the door. "And maybe a little bell that jingles when people come in."

Micola giggled and clapped her hands. "Oh! Yes, a bell. I love that."

She opened her eyes and turned to him. "Or maybe no bell because it will be too much ringing from all of the people coming in, yes?" She bent forward and laughed at her joke.

Eddie laughed, too. "Good point. All that jinglin' could get annoying."

He watched as she examined every corner of the spacious unfinished area. She came to a space with broken bricks exposing a set of black PVC pipes and frowned.

Eddie came to her side. "Don't worry about stuff like that, alright? All that stuff'll get fixed."

He turned to face her, his right hand on his stomach, his left hand stretched out, fingers snapping, head bobbing as he sang out the words to *Oh Marie*. He took her hand and twirled her under his arm, as she giggled.

He caught a glimpse of Kate standing off to the side near the back, watching and smiling.

Eddie continued his singing as he took Micola's hand and did the same little dance they'd done in her living room. He stopped after a few seconds and continued his pitch.

"And that food-a yours? I can smell it and taste it already."

Micola's face broke into a great smile as she opened her arms for a hug.

He had her. He *knew* he did.

"Okay. If you think this is the place, then I-do it. It's-no-what I think I like, but I trust you, Eddie."

"You okay with the price?"

She flapped her hand. "*Sí!*"

And in that instant, with those few words from Micola, Eddie knew he had the investment capital he'd need to start his very own organization—without Primo breathin' down his neck. It looked like they both had their dreams comin' true. Dollar signs floated in his head.

He took her hand and kissed it as he looked her in the eye.

"You won't regret it, Mrs. F. It's gonna' be great."

He turned to Kate. "Kate. Good news. We'll take it."

He watched Kate's smile bring a sparkle to her blue eyes.

"That's wonderful! I'll get the paperwork started right away. We can talk about the details tomorrow."

Eddie gave Kate a slight bow. "Thank you."

He held the door for his two new favorite women, one young and beautiful, the other old and rich. He soaked in the crisp spring air, not even slightly bothered by the gentle drizzle falling on his hair.

"You have my number, Kate. We hope to hear from ya' real soon, alright?"

Kate reached out her hand. Eddie took it, feeling her soft warmth.

"Thank you," she said. "I'll give you a call as soon as I can."

She turned to Micola. "Mrs. Fortunato, it was a pleasure meeting you. Congratulations. I'm so happy you like the place and I can't wait to come here for dinner."

She waved to them as she headed toward her car.

Eddie put his arm around Micola's shoulder. "Let's go home and talk business."

"Okay, Eddie. I better get out my checkbook." Micola laughed again at her own joke.

Eddie joined her, pleased that she'd said it first.

Twenty-seven

*A*s Eddie opened the glass door to Magnolias, the bell chimed above his head. He frowned as the entire room of patrons glanced over at him. He made a mental note to tell Micola the bell was a no-go.

He did a quick scan of the restaurant, the aroma of freshly brewed coffee, eggs and syrup kindling his appetite. He spotted Kate sitting at a booth near the back, sipping coffee and flipping through some papers. She looked up and gave him a smile and a wave. Eddie waved back and crossed the maroon carpet through the narrow rows of tables and booths lined up along the front window.

"Mornin', Kate," he said, sliding into the seat across from her.

"Good morning," she replied.

They placed their order and began looking over the documents for the restaurant. He took every opportunity to casually look into Kate's blue eyes. When a silky brown curl fell in front of her face, he resisted the urge to reach over and gently move it away. He pinched the top of his hand to stay focused. Her voice was so soothing, calm and quiet, with a hint of sweetness that drove him wild. He could listen to her all day.

When their business had finished, they rose from the table. Most of the patrons had left and the restaurant was quiet. Eddie paid the bill, took the papers from Kate and opened the door for her. They walked together to her car and shook hands. He lifted her hand to his lips and gave it a quick peck.

"Thank you, Kate. You've been a big help with all-a this." He flapped the paperwork. "Mrs. Fortunato is gonna' be real happy."

He thought he saw a glow rise in her cheeks as she chuckled.

"You're very welcome," she said. "I'm happy to help."

He smiled and nodded. "Alright then. I'll be in touch."

"Have a wonderful day, Eddie."

Kate waved and got into her car.

Eddie smiled and nodded as he strutted across the street to Micola's car, satisfied with his productive morning with the beautiful Kate.

Twenty-eight

*B*ack at the house, Eddie and Micola sat in the dining room at a long mahogany table and spread out the paperwork. Micola cut two slices of pumpkin cake and poured two cups of coffee, while Eddie worked on their ideas and plans. As she set his cake and coffee in front of him, Micola looked down at Eddie who was furiously taking notes.

"Eddie."

He stopped writing and looked up at her, shrugging his shoulders.

"Do you need me to write a check yet?"

He gave her his softest effort at a smile. He'd love to get a check from her, but what he really wanted to know was how much money she actually had. Still, he couldn't ask. It was too soon. That question had haunted his dreams the past few nights. What had Primo said? A few million? Maybe more?

"You okay, Eddie?"

Micola held her cup to her lips, staring down at him, a worried look crossing her face.

He let the vision of hundred-dollar bills slip away.

"Yeah. I'm fine." He tapped his temple with his pen. "My mind is goin' crazy up here, know-what-I-mean?" He chuckled as she let out a breathy laugh. "But 'ah, yeah. I am gonna' need a check pretty soon."

"Okay, Eddie. You let me know. I got money."

He heard a bit of a melody in her statement and he looked up to see her smiling.

"*Lots*-a money."

He smiled at her, but held his tongue. He didn't want to appear greedy. He'd find out soon enough how much she had.

"That right?"

She clasped her hands like she was praying and nodded. "Mm-hmm. Lots."

His heart flip-flopped. "Okay," he said, keeping his cool. "That's good. Cuz we're gonna' need *lots*-a money. I hope you're ready to spend it."

"*Sí*, Eddie. I'm ready."

"Good. Now, let's get-ta work."

Over the next three hours, the two of them sketched and planned the layout for her new restaurant. As the afternoon turned to evening, Micola prepared plates of pasta and salad.

She peppered Eddie with questions. She wanted his opinions and sometimes challenged his ideas. Eddie had expected this. She knew what she wanted, and he loved her enthusiasm. The whole concept was exciting, but in different ways for each of them.

As Eddie finished up the last of his notes, he glanced over at Micola.

"Tired?"

She nodded. "*Sí*, Eddie. My head—it's exploding."

He put down his pen, stretching as he let out a loud groan. "Yeah. It's a lotta' work."

He stood and leaned over to kiss Micola's head. "Got some other work to do, some calls to make. We'll talk some more tomorrow. You should get some rest."

"Okay, Eddie."

She looked up at him from her chair, took his hand and kissed it. "Thank you. Your help is—" Her voice cracked and her eyes moistened. "It's—"

"I know. Ya' welcome. Gonna' be fun, 'eh?"

He turned and walked out of the dining room.

"*Buona notte.*"

"*Buona notte*, Eddie."

Twenty-nine

*K*ate strolled confidently into Magnolias, leaving Eddie momentarily concerned with the skip in his chest.

She wore a fitted black and gray striped dress, just covering her knees, a thin, black belt cinched tight around her waist, and her perfect breasts were featured discreetly at the neckline. Her long and slender bare legs guided the eye downward to her stylish slate-gray heels. Her shiny dark hair fell in waves around her pure, pale features and flowed backward as she effortlessly crossed the room.

Eddie soaked in the vision. She'd looked pretty yesterday, but today? Stunning. In a sea of ordinary broads, she was fuckin' exquisite. He'd been with plenty-a beautiful women over the years, but this one? He'd never seen anyone who came close. She had a certain brightness in her personality and an intelligence unlike any woman he'd ever encountered. The best part was, she seemed unaware of her beauty. She was sincere. Kind.

As Kate approached the table, that same clear sparkle in her eyes seemed to light up the room. Eddie tried not to gawk, struggling to keep his gaze casual.

He rose, adjusted his tie and waited to greet her.

She stood taller in the heels which forced Eddie to look up toward her eyes. He didn't like that but ignored his discomfort. He reached for her hand, kissing it gently. Kate lowered her head and brushed a strand of hair from her face. He watched her blush, which stirred something in him.

"Good morning, Eddie."

"Mornin', Kate."

He pulled out her chair before returning to his seat across from her.

Kate rustled through her briefcase, taking a moment to gaze around the diner. "You sure like this place. I haven't been here this much in years. I must say the food is very good."

She pulled out an envelope. "I have the papers I mentioned. I marked the places where I'll need Mrs. Fortunato's signatures."

She handed the package to Eddie.

"Yeah, sure. I'll get those signed fa' you."

She smiled. "Would you like me to go through them one more time?"

He shook his head. "Naw. I'll call you if I got any questions. I'm sure they're good."

Kate nodded and motioned to leave. "Great," she said. "Give me a call. I'll stop by to pick them up."

"Sure. Hey. You wanna' join me a for a cuppa' coffee?"

"Ah," Kate looked at her watch. "I'd better be going. I have a few more stops to make before heading back to the office."

She and Eddie rose from the table.

"Thanks again, Kate. For everything."

"It was my pleasure, Eddie."

"Maybe we could have dinner sometime. I'd like to thank you for all your hard work."

Kate shook her head and opened her mouth to respond.

Eddie raised his finger. "Ya' married. I know. What's his name again?" Eddie snapped his fingers, thinking.

"Marco."

"That's right. From Brooklyn. Like me."

Kate nodded. "That's right."

"What's he do again?"

"He's a mechanic."

"Alright, okay. Great profession."

An uncomfortable silence grew.

"No, but anyways" Eddie continued, "I thought, ya' know, you could bring your husband. Marco." He shrugged. "We could talk business. I mean, ah', I like cars, right? What'da-ya' say Kate?"

Kate opened her mouth again to respond, but he interrupted her.

"Saturday night? St. Paul Grill?"

"I should really check with Marco—I should ... check ..."

Eddie pushed in his chin. "Listen. I'll be there Saturday night at seven. You don't come? I order. No big deal, *capisci*?"

"Sure. Sounds great." She put her hair behind her ear as she reached out to shake his hand.

Eddie took her hand and kissed it, looking into her beautiful blue eyes and inhaling her scent. "Alright then, Kate. Thank you. And, ah' ... so, maybe we see you'se Saturday night, 'eh?"

"I'll try—*we'll* try to be there. Seven o'clock."

"I hope so."

She turned and headed for the door, but looked back. "See you soon." She smiled and waved.

Eddie smiled and pointed at her. "See ya' soon, Kate."

He stood to the side of the window, watching, as she walked to her car.

Thirty

*E*ddie crossed the carpeted lobby of the St. Paul Hotel, its luxurious settees mostly empty of patrons. Rounding the corner, he headed for the entrance to the hotel's trendy St. Paul Grill nestled in the far corner of the historic building. Hypnotic aromas of seafood, garlic and char sparked his appetite, as did the attractive tall blonde waiting with a smile at the hostess stand. His feet echoed as he crossed the pale wood floor of the restaurant's foyer.

"Good evening, sir."

Eddie raised his voice to be heard over the restaurant chatter and clatter. "Good evening. Bracchio, party of three. I'm a little early."

The hostess checked her computer screen before taking three menus. "Right this way, Mr. Bracchio."

Eddie followed her, enjoying the view of her curvy young figure as they passed the long, mahogany bar and rows of dining tables. She took him to a recessed area of the restaurant, near a set of enormous windows. A dimming view of Rice Park was on display across the street, the sunlight fading quickly in the west.

Eddie took a seat at the square table for four, its wood buffed to a gleaming shine, place-settings elegantly arranged. He folded his hands as he waited for the server.

A tall, thin young woman, in a long, white apron approached and began filling water glasses.

"Good evening, sir. May I bring you a cocktail while you wait for the rest of your party?"

He looked past her for any sign of Kate. "Ah', no. Thanks. I think I'll go to the bar and grab one. Wanna' watch for my guests."

"Very good, sir. I'll check back later."

"Yeah, thanks."

Eddie rose from the table and walked across the dining room toward the bar. He stood at the end nearest the foyer, so he could watch for Kate.

Pushing the stool aside, he ordered a Johnnie Walker Black on the rocks and sipped it as he waited. Oblivious to the crowded and noisy room, his thoughts fixated on Kate. He took a quick look in the mirrored wall behind the bartender, lowering his head to see his reflection between the rows of liquor bottles. The lighting was dim, but he didn't see any obvious hairs out of place.

A sudden crowd of excited voices jarred Eddie from his thoughts. He turned to see a group of young women at the hostess stand talking and laughing. Still no sign of Kate. Maybe she wasn't coming.

He was about to return to his drink when he saw her. She'd entered the lobby with a tall, extremely handsome, dark-haired man whose thick waves of black hair stung Eddie's ego.

The husband.

Kate looked elegant in yet another classy dress, this one a black and white floral, flowing just above the knees. Her husband wore a pale pink dress shirt and black slacks.

Standing just inside the door, they stayed clear of the group of women, waiting patiently to be greeted by the hostess. Eddie watched as her husband leaned down to listen to Kate who had said something and then smiled, touching his arm.

Eddie took a moment to admire her. Oblivious to his gaze, Kate bent slightly to adjust the strap on one of her high-heeled black sandals. Eddie's breath caught in his throat as he watched her shiny chestnut hair fall, briefly hiding the side of her face. His gaze fixed on her hand as it slid down her long, slender leg to her shoe. As she came back up, her hair fell around her face, but she quickly flipped it behind her. Eddie couldn't get enough of that hair.

She leaned in and whispered again to her husband. Eddie imagined himself in that man's place. The couple pulled away from each other and smiled as she began to look around. He watched her walk toward the hostess podium. She carried her tall physique with smooth grace, her subtle curves swaying with each step.

When the hostess started guiding them through the restaurant, he grabbed his drink and hurried back to the table near the windows. He took his seat, and pretended to study the contents of the menu.

"Hello, Eddie."

He looked up and feigned surprise as he rose to greet them.

"Oh, hey. How you'se doin'?"

"We're doing great, how are you?" Kate asked.

"I'm doin' great, too. Glad you could make it."

Kate turned to her husband. "Eddie, I'd like you to meet my husband, Marco. Marco, this is Eddie, the client I told you about."

Marco smiled and leaned in to shake Eddie's hand. "Nice to meet you, Eddie. Thanks for the dinner invitation."

Eddie leaned back, his hand on his chest. "My pleasure. It's the least I could do after all-a Kate's hard work." He waved his hand over the table. "Please. Sit." He turned to the hostess. "Can you send our waitress over for some drinks?"

"Certainly, Mr. Bracchio." The young blonde smiled and left. Eddie returned to his seat at the table.

Kate, sitting across from him and next to Marco, leaned in. "'Mr. Bracchio?' Aren't you new to town? How does she know your name already?"

Eddie smiled. "What can I say, Kate?"

The waitress arrived and they ordered drinks. "Ladies first," Eddie said, his hand out toward Kate.

"I'll have a glass of your house chardonnay."

"Manhattan for me," Marco said.

Eddie wiggled his near-empty glass. "Johnnie Walker Black. Rocks."

After the drinks arrived and the order was taken, Eddie sat back, relaxed and ready to talk. "So, Marco. I hear you're from Brooklyn, like me. A mechanic?"

Marco nodded. "That's right." He raised his glass to Eddie. "Cheers to Brooklyn."

Eddie smiled. "Cheers to Brooklyn."

Marco continued. "I've always loved cars. Love workin' on 'em. Love drivin' 'em."

"Marco's an experienced race car driver," Kate added proudly.

"That right?"

Marco nodded. "Did some drag racing in local circuits. East coast. Nothin' major. That was years ago. Back in my early twenties. I do love it though."

Eddie leaned forward, taking a sip of his scotch. "If you're interested in some extra work, I-gotta' drivin' job you might like."

Marco nodded before taking a sip of his drink. "I *am* interested," he said. "I have a full-time job at a station down Payne Avenue a few miles, but I—" he looked at Kate "—I'd be interested in drivin', too. Some side work would be nice if you've got it."

Eddie nodded. "We could all use a little extra cash, am I right? So, like I told your beautiful wife, I'm gonna' be in and out–what with gettin' this restaurant up and runnin' and other business I gotta' take care of, so yeah, I could use a driver. A good one."

"He is a good one," Kate said, smiling.

Eddie nodded at Marco but kept a discreet eye on Kate. He was enjoying the closeup view. Her beauty was enhanced by the glow of the candlelit ambiance, but it was her smile that truly captivated him.

Eddie finished his scotch and waved the waitress over for another. He smacked his hand on the table. "I trust your wife. So, you can have the job if you want it. I'll pay you six hundred a week if you drive me around in the eve'nins. Say, eight-thirty, nine, to whatever time I need you. Most nights, I like to get to bed by one or two. Gettin' older, ya' know?"

Kate and Marco chuckled at Eddie's joke.

"Thank you, Eddie," Marco said. "I appreciate your trust in my wife. I hope you'll soon see you can trust me, too."

Eddie raised his glass, and Kate and Marco joined him.

"*Salute e cent'anni.*"

"*Cent'anni,*" they replied.

After their food arrived, Kate and Marco proudly talked to Eddie about their son, Lorenzo.

The mood was jovial. Everyone was feeling the drinks and raving about the food when Kate turned to Eddie. "What about your family? Are you married? Your mom and dad?"

Eddie shook his head and frowned. "I was married. She died though. Don't wanna' talk about that." He put his head down and picked at his food.

"Oh, I'm so sorry. I didn't mean to—"

Eddie smiled and shrugged, barely pausing. "My father was a piece-a-shit. 'Scuse my language." He waved his finger at her. "For sure don't wanna' talk about him."

Kate nodded. "Sorry, again. Your mom? Are you close with her?"

He smiled and nodded. "My ma'? Yeah. We still talk." He let out a chuckle. "She's a real good cook. Lives in Brooklyn. She raised me and my brother all by herself after my ol' man was ah' ... killed." He raised his brows. "There I go talkin' about him again."

Kate gave Eddie a sensitive smile. "Any kids?"

He waved his fork at them. "No kids. For the best." He ignored the awkward silence as he continued to eat.

They made small-talk about the restaurant and the food, which led them to talking about the neighborhood and again about Renzo.

Eddie put down his fork and wiped his mouth with the cloth napkin. "Sounds like you'se two gotta' nice kid. And you—" he pointed to Marco. "You sound like a good father."

Marco smiled. "I appreciate that, Mr. Bracchio. I try."

Eddie put up his hand. "Please. Marco, like I told your wife. Call me 'Eddie.' We're friends here, am I right? No need for formalities, 'eh?"

Marco smiled. "Okay, 'Eddie.'"

"But," Eddie pointed his forkful of food at him, "when you're workin' fa-me, try-ta be professional in front-a people and *then*," he smiled, "I want you-ta call me 'Mr. Bracchio,' *capisci*?"

Marco smiled. "*Capisci.*"

"You understand. It's about respect." Eddie chewed and talked at the same time, occasionally waving his fork, pointing it at them. "And if you don't got respect, you got nothin', am I right?"

"You are," Marco said.

This guy, Marco, Eddie thought. One handsome son-of-a-bitch. It pissed him off. Respectable, too. And being married to this beautiful woman? Goddamn irritating.

"So," Eddie said, with a mouthful of linguine, how'd you'se two meet, if you don't mind my askin'?"

Kate looked at Marco, smiled, and turned back to Eddie.

"I was in college at NYU, and had gone to this very crowded bar with my roommate, Nora. I had battled my way to the restroom and when I came back, I ran smack into this guy."

She nudged Marco with her elbow. Eddie watched as they looked at each other.

"That's it?" Eddie asked. "A bar? The way you'se two look at each other, I'd-a thought maybe it'd be more romantic than that, know what I mean?"

He laughed loudly at his own joke, and Marco and Kate laughed with him.

Marco took a sip of his Manhattan and said, "Our son, Renzo, would agree with you, Eddie. And you're right. So *cliché*, meeting in a bar and all. But, seriously. Look at her. I couldn't help but fall for her."

Eddie smiled and nodded as he buttered a piece of bread. "Obviously." He pointed the knife at Kate. "Go on. What happened next?"

Kate finished a bite of halibut, wiped her mouth and said, "I felt the same way. He was *so* handsome. He had on this old black leather jacket. And his hair. I mean, look at it," Kate said, laughing.

Eddie looked at Marco and shrugged and nodded as he chewed.

Kate turned to Eddie. "Anyway, he had this tough-guy persona. Played it cool for quite a while. He was everything my mother didn't want for me in a man."

Kate chuckled at the thought of disappointing her mother.

"That right? She want you to marry a churchgoer? A lawyer or a doctor, am I right?"

"Exactly. And maybe that's why I pursued the relationship even though, at times, I thought maybe he was too much for me. The crowd he hung around with, some of the things he used to do—"

"Like what?" Eddie pointed his fork at Marco. "Kind-a stuff you do back then?"

Marco took a deep breath and flipped out his hands. "Ya' know. Nothin' too crazy. A little collections, a few scores. Small-time stuff like that."

Eddie smiled. "That right?" He nodded as he cut his food. "Okay, alright."

Marco continued. "And, ya' know, for a while, I thought, maybe Kate was right. We'd had some problems. She didn't like my line-a work. We fought about that—like a *lot*."

Eddie looked at Marco and then at Kate. "So? You'se two break up, or what?"

Eddie watched her look over at Marco as if to ask whether she should tell the story. Marco shrugged.

"What?"

Kate turned to Eddie, pausing. "I can't believe I'm telling this story to someone I've only just met." She let out a nervous chuckle.

Eddie noticed she was feeling the wine and he enjoyed seeing her so relaxed.

Eddie tipped his head. "So? We're all friends now. Go ahead. Tell me."

Kate moved her plate to the side and folded her hands, resting them on the table. "I got pregnant and he couldn't deal with that. So I left." She raised her brow as she gave Marco a side-glance. "Came back here—to St. Paul. Back home. Had the baby and didn't hear from him for a while."

Eddie sat back before slapping his hands on the table. "Whoa! Marco! That's heavy shit."

"Very heavy," Kate said, again looking over at Marco who lowered his gaze.

Eddie tried listening to her story, but his peripheral vision caught Marco's hand reaching over to Kate's, his fingers weaving through hers as they held hands. For some reason, this tiny gesture stirred something inside Eddie. He wasn't sure what it was. Jealousy, maybe? Loneliness? Whatever he was feeling, Kate and Marco's intimacy changed his mood, though he tried not to show it.

He sat back in his chair. "Well, at least you'se two figured things out. You seem like a pretty happy couple, am I right?"

Kate turned to Marco and nudged his shoulder. "We are."

Marco raised his glass. "Here-here."

They clinked their glasses and took a sip.

"You're a lucky man, Marco. I'm not sure I've ever met a more beautiful woman than Kate, here." He reached across the table, took her hand and leaned in, kissing it gently before releasing it.

Kate gave him an awkward grin.

Marco turned to Eddie with a smile. "If I didn't know better, Mr. Bracchio, I'd think you were makin' a pass at my wife." He laughed at his own joke.

"No, I wouldn't disrespect you'se like that," Eddie said.

Marco smiled at his wife and moved to stand.

"Excuse me. Restroom."

Eddie stood until Marco left.

"I like him, Kate. Seems like a good guy."

Kate leaned on her elbows and nodded. "He is. Thanks for offering him the driving job. He's gonna love it."

"My pleasure. I hadn't thought about it until you brought up what a good driver he was. Plus, I never thought I'd be hangin' around this long. Now? Looks like I'll be here for a while."

"The restaurant will keep you *very* busy."

"Yeah, it will. I gotta' say, I'm lookin' forward to it."

The waitress stopped by. "Dessert? Coffee?"

"Yeah, sure. Kate? Dessert?"

"Nothing for me, thanks." She looked at her watch. "We should really get going. I don't like leaving Renzo home alone for too long. He might get himself into trouble."

Eddie laughed. "Kids can't help themselves, am I right?"

Kate laughed, too. "So true."

She looked up at Marco as he returned to the table.

"Ready to go honey?"

Marco nodded. "Yeah, okay."

Kate and Eddie both stood.

"You'se two go ahead," Eddie said. "I gotta' take care-a the tab here."

"Oh, right. I'm so sorry. Can we—"

"Kate. Please. Don't insult me, now. I invited you'se two. I got this. You go on. Get home to Renzo." He turned and shook Marco's hand. "Marco, a pleasure-ta meet ya'. You call me. Kate's got my number."

"I will," Marco said. "Thanks again."

He turned to Kate as she reached out her hand. He took it and again kissed it gently. "Always a pleasure, Kate. Don't be a stranger, now, ya' hear?"

"Thank you, Eddie, for dinner. It was wonderful."

Marco nodded. "It really was. Thanks again, Eddie."

Eddie watched as they left the table and rounded the corner until they disappeared. He returned to his seat and called out to his waitress.

"'Scuse me? Ma'am? Another one please?"

Thirty-one

Marco turned onto Seventh Street and headed toward Payne Avenue.

"Wow. That Eddie—he's some character, right?"

"He sure is."

They were quiet for a while and then Kate said, "He seems so tough, ya' know? Doesn't he? So unafraid. And his dad? I wonder what that was all about."

She reached over and took his hand. "I'm glad our son has a happy family life."

He gently squeezed her hand. "Me too. Obviously, Eddie turned out alright. He can handle himself. He's tough as shit. Hell, he's probably killed some people."

Kate whipped her head to look at him. "He has *not* killed anybody. Why would you even say that?"

"Kate. Come on. It's *so* obvious."

"What? What's obvious?"

"The guy's a mobster. Don't you see that?"

She let out a short laugh. "No. No, he's not." She paused before turning to stare at Marco through the darkness, the lights from the streets moving across his face. He turned to her and shrugged before bringing his eyes back to the road.

Kate sat back, silent, as they headed down Payne Avenue.

As Marco rounded a corner, she said, "Do you really think he's in the mafia? I mean *really*? I know it's his persona. It's how he wants us to *perceive* him."

Marco shook his head, his eyes still on the road ahead. "Do me a favor, Kate. Don't be naïve, alright? This guy could be dangerous."

"Oh, God. Too dangerous for you to work for? I mean I don't want you—"

Marco raised a hand. "Kate. I said '*could be*' dangerous. I'm only warnin' you. Besides, I can handle myself. I've been around wise-guys like him my whole life. I'll be fine drivin' him around and stayin' outta' his business. And you need to be street-smart, okay? I want you to know what you're dealin' with. Eddie's a smooth-talker. Charming. Just don't be fooled, alright?"

She nodded. "Okay. You're right."

She said nothing more the rest of the ride home. The road to their house seemed darker than usual. Shadows from the trees danced on either side of the car, as though trying to reveal some ominous secret.

Summer

Thirty-two

June in Minnesota brought some of the finest weather of the year. Bright, cloudless blue skies, a soft, gentle breeze, and temperatures lingering near the ideal eighty degrees. The warm weather had lifted Eddie's mood, and after weeks of heavy, sometimes problematic and very expensive renovations, Fortunato's Italian Restaurant was nearing completion.

Weekly calls to Primo appeased him enough to allow Eddie to remain in St. Paul. The construction proved to be a continuing pain-in-the-ass, but Eddie's side-business with the boys was gaining steam. This pleased him. He'd noticed real promise and, more importantly, a surge in income from the streets. He'd kept Primo *partially* in the loop on this aspect, and even had sent cash to pacify him.

Dario and Tau had been the real surprise. They'd quickly stepped into their management roles over the past few months, though it was difficult to ignore Dario's obnoxious confidence. Tau had been especially impressive, gaining new customers and bringing in profits. Eddie was impressed by how quickly word spread on the street that they now were the ones to seek out for product, loans, and betting.

Weekly meetings to split cash and discuss strategy had worked well, but Eddie decided the boys needed a little oversight—oversight he'd soon have no time for. They both were producing cash. Cash that grew exponentially each week, and he didn't want that getting lost as he tended to the restaurant's opening. In other words, he didn't want to get ripped off. He had someone in mind to oversee the street business: his cousin, Sal. He made a mental note to check in with him soon.

As for the restaurant, the once hollowed and musty warehouse had been transformed into an old-world setting of authentic, rustic beauty. Creamy plastered walls were graced with rustic Italian art pieces. Sconce lighting and petite crystal chandeliers hung from the ceiling and set the perfect mood. The once drab and dirty cement floors now glistened in chocolate and cream swirls dotted with specks of gold. Massive rugs rested on the floor throughout the dining room and bar. The unsightly metal beams had been artistically painted to look like walls of old bricks, and then wrapped from ceiling to floor in tiny, twinkling amber lights and buttery tulle. Similar twinkling lights hung near the ceiling and flowed down the plate-glass window, wrapped around in more sheer cream tulle on either side, all of it loosely pulled back to create a sophisticated and inviting mood. An antique floor-to-ceiling mirror with an etched heavy mahogany frame gave dimension and magnitude to the room, while hiding the broken brick and pipes that had been one of Micola's biggest concerns.

Eddie continued his stroll through the dining room, inspecting the details. The mahogany bar with its cream and gold swirled marble top, set up against the back wall, was polished and ready for product. He checked himself in the full wall of mirrors behind it, as he pushed in the leather stools and straightened wine glasses.

He continued his wonder at the alien sensation of glee he'd felt since arriving in St. Paul those many weeks ago. Now, with the restaurant nearing completion and the grand opening just weeks away, he was especially ecstatic.

As Eddie looked out the restaurant's newly arched front windows onto dreary old Payne Avenue, he said a silent prayer that Mrs. F.'s food would bring the customers and the money. He wanted it for himself, but he was surprised by how much he wanted it for her, as well.

He checked his watch and headed to the end of the dining room, turning down a short hallway which led to three stairs. At the bottom of those stairs stood an old wooden door, its forest green paint faded and chipped. He shook his head and whispered to himself as he unlocked it.

"Gotta' get this door painted. It's embarrassin'."

Eddie flipped on the overhead office light and headed to the old beat-up wooden desk that would be his workplace for the next few months. At the center of the desk, papers had already begun to pile up. Bills, mostly.

The lighting was dim, and more than a hint of mildew irritated his nose. He sat in the cheap, squeaky office chair and jotted "paint," "air freshener," and "chair" on his notepad. He generally liked the office. Nice and private. He removed his .38 from the back of his belt buckle and began sorting through the paperwork and paying bills.

Eddie then made his way back upstairs. Micola's angry bellowing grew louder as he approached. He pushed through the doors and walked into the kitchen. Micola was pointing her finger and scolding the new staff about dinner salads. He walked over and put his arm around her as he pulled her from the group.

"Mrs. F? Can I see you for a minute?"

"But Eddie I—"

"Leave'em alone. They got this. Come on. We need to finish this menu. We're almost done."

He took her hand and they walked out to the dining room to one of the round tables near the front window. As they scrutinized the menu and pricing, a team of electricians testing the sound system put on the song, *Come Fly With Me*, by Frank Sinatra, blasting it through the speakers. Micola and Eddie looked around and laughed.

"Oh! This is happening, Eddie. My dream!"

He touched her hand. "It is. I'm so happy for you, my dear." He put out his hand. "May I have this dance?"

Micola giggled. "*Sí, Signoree.*"

He helped her up and wrapped an arm around her waist and took her hand. They sashayed along the sleek floor as Eddie quietly sang to her. When the song ended, he gave her a twirl and an ever-so-slight dip. After pulling her up, he bowed.

Micola could barely hold her laughter. "*Grazie, grazie.*"

Eddie smiled and guided her back to the table.

"My pleasure, Mrs. F. Now, back to work."

Thirty-three

*F*ortunato's Italian Restaurant opened for business four months after Micola signed on the dotted line. A crimson awning fluttered atop the front window in the hot August breeze, "*Fortunato's*" emblazoned across it in grand, gold cursive.

Eddie dressed for the occasion, wearing his best black Armani suit. Micola wore her new plum dress and matching low-heeled pumps, purchases Eddie insisted on for their opening day.

The two of them strolled nervously through the dining room, as the staff bustled about making last-minute finishing touches. The heavy wooden tables were dressed in crisp cotton. Chairs were pushed in, fresh floral centerpieces adjusted, and candles lit. The kitchen and waitstaff were ready, and two bartenders stood stoic behind the marble-topped bar.

After setting the music and lighting, Eddie and Micola could do no more. Together, they watched as Regina, the manager Eddie had hired, expertly handled everything. Patrons began to trickle in, greeted by the intoxicating aromas of garlic, sauces, seafood and smoky char.

For the first week or two, business was slow, which was expected. This didn't bother Micola. She couldn't contain her excitement. Her dream had finally become a reality. She mainly stayed in the kitchen, ensuring her recipes were followed to the letter.

It wasn't long before word spread and business began to pick up. The true jumpstart, however, came after a review in the *St. Paul Pioneer Press*. The glowing comments from the city's top food critic was the turning point to the restaurant's success. Patrons began to fill the place.

Eddie felt like a celebrity, as some customers pushed through the crowded dining room to introduce themselves. He relished the attention and did his best to remember their names and faces, as he showered customers with attention and charm.

With Regina at the helm, the restaurant had begun to run well. The time had come for Eddie to turn his attention to Dario and Tau. Their work on the street was where the real money would be made. Their crews had grown, moving stolen goods and expanding the sports-betting and loan-sharking businesses–all easy money-makers. The drug sales weren't meeting Eddie's satisfaction, but he was intent on fixing that.

It pleased him that Dario and Tau were trying to get along. Eddie was getting a good read on their personalities and also sensed their growing loyalty toward him.

They checked in often with small, discreet bags of cash in hand. Their regularly scheduled meetings were held downstairs in Eddie's office where the earnings were immediately split. Eddie kept seventy percent. It was risky to give them such big cuts, but Eddie wanted their trust and knew if he didn't, they'd skim at least that much anyway.

As the weeks passed, the cash grew, as did Eddie's street employees. Dario and Tau's hustle for new business was slowly multiplying.

Thirty-four

On a steamy Sunday morning, Dario approached Micola's front door and rang the doorbell. Eddie opened it and walked away, leaving Dario at the entrance.

Dario followed him into the living room. "You wanted to see me, Eddie?"

Eddie sat on the sofa and waved him in. Dario sat in the chair across from him.

"I met your uncle, or whoever he is, last night. Terrence? He came into the restaurant with his family."

Dario smiled. "Oh yeah. I told him to come by, check out the restaurant. I told you I'd send the customers, Mr. B."

Eddie smiled. "Yeah, ya' did." He plucked Terrence's hundred dollar bills from his shirt pocket and flipped them in the air. "He gave me this. Said he owed it to ya'. He said you fronted him some cash for the game."

Dario reached across the coffee table, smiling, but Eddie shook his head and shoved the cash back into his pocket.

"Come on, man. Gimme' my money. That's mine. Terrence owed me."

"Your first mistake," Eddie said, "was lettin' anybody 'owe' you. You always get *all* the money up front. Uncle or no uncle."

Dario's shoulders sank. "But—"

"Shut-up. Your second mistake was bringin' your street business into my fuckin' restaurant. That guy took me by surprise. I ought-a' slap you across your fuckin' head right now for that stupid shit. If you-was around last night, I would've."

Dario giggled nervously. "Ey-man. Sorry. I got busy last night and ran outta' time. But, like I said, I told my uncle to come into the restaurant, didn't I? Told-him he couldn't deal with me unless he ate at your restaurant. You-know. Give you some-a-that business you're always pressurin' me about."

Eddie shrugged. "Don't have people comin' into the restaurant tryna' to do street business, you got that? It can't happen."

"I got it, man. It won't happen again. Now, can I get my two hundred?"

"No fuckin' way. Deal with it."

Dario frowned as he looked at the floor and shook his head.

"Now," Eddie said, "about these customers you're bringin' in, you did good on that. I see you're workin' on that part."

Dario whipped his hand across his body. "Man, I know a *lot*-a people. A *lot*."

"Alright. Keep-em comin'. And as far as the street work goes, you keep that comin' and I'll keep splittin' any profit with you'se two seventy-thirty."

Dario's eyes bugged out, his arms spread outward. Eddie laughed because he knew Dario's high-pitched voice was about to reach an even higher level. He was right.

"Seventy-thirty? Still? Man, you're killin' me—and Tau. You said you was gonna' change it to sixty-forty. I'm doin' all the grunt-work. You *gotta* do better-n that." He made a *psst* sound and flapped his hand at Eddie, whispering, "seventy-thirty."

Eddie's eyes narrowed and his lip snarled, as he jabbed his finger in Dario's direction.

"Don't you disrespect me, Dario. That attitude-a yours is why you ain't movin' up. It'll be sixty-forty soon. But, you gotta' short fuckin' memory. I'm the one coverin' the up-front on all-a this shit." He paused and then pointed at Dario. "Do *you* want to cover it?"

Dario opened his mouth to argue, but Eddie put up his hand.

"You also seem to forget that you ain't got shit without me."

He watched as Dario's fight drained from his face.

Eddie continued. "Now, if things start comin' around, we'll talk. We could start the sixty-forty. And *maybe* we'll do fifty-fifty. *Later*. For now, stop your fuckin' whinin' and get-back-ta work."

Dario stood to leave. "Okay. Don't worry, man. You can trust me."

Eddie gave Dario an angry laugh. "I *barely* trust you, Dario. This is no fuckin' joke."

Dario frowned as he waited to be excused.

Eddie flipped his hand. "Get the fuck outta' here."

Dario paused, but Eddie had nothing more to say, so he left.

When the front door closed behind Dario, Eddie picked up his burner phone and dialed.

"Primo. Eddie. You get my FedEx yet?"

Primo let out a mucus-filled cough into the mouthpiece. Eddie frowned, as he pulled the phone away from his ear.

"Got it. Nice work."

"Told you, 'eh? Things've been good."

"I see that. You stay out there a while longer. Let's see how things go."

"Yeah. Okay," Eddie said. "I guess I don't mind. I'd hate to leave Micola until I found a decent replacement. Those books are a lotta' work."

"Yeah." Primo let out another hacking cough.

"What about you, Primo? How's business? You keepin' an eye on Freddy? Who's handling my books?"

"I'm handlin' your books. Things are slow. You're better off where you're at."

"Slow, 'eh?"

"Yeah. Slow. Did I fuckin' stutter?"

"Alright then, Primo. I'll be in touch."

Primo hung up.

"Slow, my ass," Eddie said to himself. No doubt Primo was screwin' him. But that was fine, cuz' Eddie was screwin' Primo, too. If Primo had half an idea of the amount of cash that was comin' in, he'd have Eddie's head.

Fuck Primo.

Eddie smiled and went upstairs to finish dressing for the day.

Autumn

Thirty-five

*F*all was officially underway and the cool temperatures suited Eddie just fine. He sat at the bar watching the Vikings game as he went through the day's receipts. The dinner crowd had been good, but the place had emptied out except for a few tables in the dining room.

A short, busty blonde woman in her mid-forties walked up and pulled herself onto a stool two seats from him. She ordered a vodka tonic and turned to Eddie just as he looked her way. His eyes immediately fell to her breasts overflowing from her low-cut black dress. She appeared somewhat attractive, but the bar's dim lighting often played tricks. He returned to his work.

"You're workin' hard," she said. Her deep voice suggested a tough life of drinking and smoking.

Eddie looked up to see the broad was talking to him.

"Ah, yeah," he said. "Gotta' lot-ta do tonight."

"Mmm," she said, sipping loudly. "This your place?"

Eddie put down his pen and turned to her. Never disrespect a customer.

"Yeah. It's mine. First time here?"

"It is."

She twisted her chest in his direction, her glass in hand, as she drew a long sip from her straw.

Eddie's eyes once again drifted to her exposed breasts. She smiled up at him. Her dull ash-blond hair appeared dry and brittle, and her solid size was heftier than he usually liked. But those jugs—they were enormous and jiggled as she breathed, talked and laughed, almost as though they were speaking to him.

"It's nice," she said. "I haven't eaten here yet, but I like the ambiance."

"Thanks."

"Maybe I'll order somethin'. Can I eat here? At the bar?"

Eddie smiled and nodded. "Sure. Eat wherever ya' want."

The bartender handed her a menu and she looked it over as she sipped her cocktail.

"Try the Ravioli Alla Calabrese," Eddie said. "It's like a cheese ravioli, only better." He kissed the tips of his fingers. "Fantastic."

She shut her menu. "Okay, I'll try it."

The bartender took her order, and then brought Eddie his usual Johnnie Walker Black on the rocks.

The woman talked to Eddie occasionally as she ate her ravioli. After she'd had three more vodka tonics and Eddie had had one more than his usual three scotches, the conversation blossomed. Eddie moved to sit next to her. She seemed to enjoy his wandering gaze.

"What's your name?" she asked.

"Eddie. Yours?"

"Shari," she said, slithering a bite of ravioli, sauce spilling around her mouth.

Eddie flinched at the sight, but with each drink, her obvious flaws became blurred. Her breasts became his focal point. It'd been quite some time since he'd been with a woman, and he was enjoying the warm feelings of arousal.

They talked and laughed until it was time to close up. The waitstaff had been gone for a couple of hours when the bartender said goodnight. Eddie walked Shari to the front of the restaurant.

"Wait here," he said. "Gotta' lock up."

Feeling optimistic he might get lucky, Eddie pranced through the restaurant doing a less-than diligent shutdown.

"Okay," he said. "All set."

He held the door for her and then turned to lock up. Payne Avenue was deserted and the crisp, cool air sobered him a bit.

Shari bent over to adjust her skirt, giving Eddie a brilliant view of her chest. When she came back up, she pushed a strand of her dull hair behind her ear and giggled.

"So," she said. "Ya' wanna' maybe come to my place? It's just down the block here." She pointed up the side street from the front door. "We can walk. Maybe have a nightcap?"

Eddie's heart skipped. He *was* gonna' get lucky.

"Yeah, sure. I'd like that."

She leaned in and kissed him, the taste of cigarettes and alcohol confirming his earlier assumption.

"Come on, Eddie," she said, taking his hand.

She guided him up the darkened sidewalk, the streetlights dimly lighting the way. They traveled a block and a half, arriving in front of an old brick three-story apartment building. The hallway smelled of stale food and old carpet, but Shari's unit was clean and neatly decorated.

Eddie got what he'd come for. At his insistence, Shari turned off the bedroom lights, swallowing the room into darkness, and making it easier for him to imagine Kate's beautiful face looking up at him. He imagined her long chestnut hair sprawled across the pillow below him, as she whispered softly.

Eddie rolled roughly off Shari, her face thankfully invisible in the lightless bedroom. She panted and rolled onto her side to face him, setting her hand on his hairy chest, as he lay next to her fighting for breath. He patted her arm with a false sense of thoughtfulness.

After waiting a reasonable amount of time, he sat up.

"Gotta' go."

"What? No! Eddie—why? Why can't ya' stay?"

He swung his feet over the edge of the bed. "Gotta' work in the morning. I told ya'. Don't bust my balls."

She slapped the mattress. "Fine. Go."

Eddie pulled up his pants and slipped into his shoes, as he buttoned his dress shirt. He headed to the bedroom door and Shari called out to him.

"Wanna' do it again sometime?"

He turned down the hall without responding.

"Fuck you, Eddie!"

"Jesus Christ," he whispered, before grabbing his jacket and slamming the door behind him.

It never fails. One way or another, there's always a price for a piece-a ass.

Thirty-six

Eddie sat in his office, adjusting the numbers from the previous night's receipts. He removed most of the cash, but left some to avoid suspicion. He placed the cash into his pocket and made the new, adjusted notations in the accounting log. No computers for him. Too much accountability. The cash in his pocket would later be transferred to a safe he'd hidden under a loose floorboard in the closet floor of his bedroom at Micola's house. The total was growing nicely.

As he cooked the books, he took calls from Tau and Dario, who were handling some hot prospects. He then went upstairs to meet with a couple of restaurant purveyors.

Next, he met with Regina to discuss staffing and scheduling issues, and then—there was Micola. He loved her, but still, she talked his ear off about stupid shit like, waitresses puttin' too many sprinkles of *parmaseana* on the risotto. He could barely stand it on a normal day, let alone with the hangover he was nurturing from his fling with Shari the night before.

He'd finally escaped to his office for some peace and quiet and a quick nap after the lunch rush. It wasn't more than fifteen minutes when he'd heard a light tap on the door. He flipped his feet off the desk and sat forward.

"Yeah," he called.

The door opened. "Hi-ya' Eddie. Ya' busy?"

Shari. Shit.

He frowned as he picked up his pen. "Yeah, I'm busy. What-d-ya' want?"

Shari opened the door wider and walked in, wearing an uncertain smile. Eddie's eyes immediately fell to her exposed cleavage, as she walked toward him. She adjusted her tight floral dress and clicked her fingertips on the desk.

"I-ah'. I didn't like the way we left things last night, so I came to apologize. Hope we can get back on track, ya' know? Try things again?"

"Listen, yeah," Eddie waved his hands over the desk. "I gotta' lotta' work-ta do, so I ain't really got time for this. But, yeah. It's fine. Forget it."

He went back to his books hoping she'd leave, but she made her way around his desk and bent forward, her chest near his face as he turned.

"You *sure* you're busy?" she giggled.

Eddie smiled and dropped his pen. "I suppose I gotta' few minutes."

He grabbed her by her waist, and pulled her onto his lap. She wrapped her arms around his neck and kissed him passionately. He started to moan but checked himself and kept it quiet. He thought about pulling away to lock the door, but things got hot pretty quickly, and that idea faded fast.

A quiet tap on the door startled them. The door opened abruptly and Kate leaned in.

"Hi Eddie. I'm—Oh! I'm so sorry. I—"

She attempted to retreat out to the hallway but instead backed into the doorframe.

Eddie shoved Shari off his lap and hurried to stand. He had to grab her arm before she fell on her ass.

"Jesus, Eddie," Shari snapped. She collected herself and adjusted her dress.

"No, Kate," Eddie said, as he tucked in his shirt and straightened his tie. "It's fine. Come in. Please."

Eddie grabbed Shari's shoulder and pushed her toward the door.

Kate raised her hand. "I didn't mean to—"

Eddie shook his head. "No-no. Shari was just leavin'—weren't ya' sweetheart?" He nudged her toward the door. "I'll see ya' tomorrow."

Shari let out a whine and stomped her foot.

"Come on, Eddie. Can't ya' come over ta-night?"

Eddie pinched the bridge of his nose and shook his head.

"No. Tomorrow. Now, come on. I gotta' get-ta work."

He gave her a gentle shove.

Shari jerked her arm from him.

"Just forget it, Eddie. Don't bother."

She gave Kate the once-over, before storming past her and out of the office.

Kate gave Eddie an awkward smile as they listened to Shari's swearing. Her high heels pounded heavily down the tiny hallway, the sound fading as she climbed the stairs.

Eddie smiled, flipping his hand. "Sorry about that, Kate. This is embarrassin'."

Kate chuckled as she shook her head. "I think you're in *trou*-ble," she sang.

Eddie laughed and set his hands on his hips. "Yeah. I think I am." He paused and turned toward the desk.

"Please," he said. "Where are my manners?"

He pulled out one of the chairs in front of his desk for Kate. He pressed his hair down at the sides, as he returned to his seat at the desk.

"Eddie, I'm so sorry to interrupt. You didn't have to send her off. I was just looking for Marco."

Eddie shook his head and frowned.

"It's no problem. I was already tryna' get ridda' her. You helped me out, really."

Kate laughed. "Okay. Well, anyway ..."

"You're lookin' lovely today, Kate. Did you ah' ... do somethin' new with your hair?"

She pushed a strand behind her ear. "I—ah'. No. It ... maybe it's ... it just works out different sometimes ...."

Eddie nodded, but said nothing as he tried not to stare.

"So," Kate said, "the restaurant seems to be doing well, right?"

Eddie perked up. "Yeah. Doin' great." He put his hand out toward her. "Couldn't have done it with you, right?"

She laughed. "Well, I'm glad we were able to find this location. It really worked out perfectly." They talked briefly about the bustling lunch crowd and the restaurant's business. Once the small-talk was over, the room grew silent.

"And Marco seems to be enjoying driving you around town."

"Marco's great," Eddie said. "Great guy. Great driver, right?"

She nodded. "He is. I'm glad that's working out—for both of you."

Eddie nodded. "Yeah. Me too."

Kate stood. "Well, I'd better get going."

Eddie stood too, and walked around the desk.

"Marco?" Kate asked. "Is he around? I need to talk to him about Renzo's soccer schedule."

"Yeah. Sorry. He's out back. I think he's workin' on the car."

"Okay," she said. "Thanks. I'll see ya' later. And again, I'm so sorry for interrupting."

Eddie shook his head and his finger at the same time. "No, Kate. I'm the one who's apologizin' here. Take care, now. Good to see ya'."

"Good to see you too, Eddie."

She nodded and left the office.

Eddie shut the door behind her, and walked in a circle mouthing the word 'fuck' over and over. After thirty seconds of that, he stormed out of the office, down the hall, up the stairs and around the corner, through the dining room and into the kitchen. He passed a couple of cooks, and then the dishwasher, to get to the backdoor. He stopped to listen and then cracked it open.

He couldn't hear what Kate and Marco were saying, but he had a good view of them. They talked quietly for a moment, then, smiling, Kate leaned in. Eddie watched them as they kissed each other slowly, neither touching the other so as not to get grease on Kate, but it was passionate.

Eddie shut the door and stormed back to his office. He slammed the door and circled the small room before returning to his desk. He sat there for several minutes thinking about Kate and that kiss she gave to Marco.

Thankfully, the phone rang and he was forced to shake the image from his mind and get back to work.

Thirty-seven

A light tap interrupted Eddie's thoughts. He frowned. "Yeah."

Marco peered around the door.

"You wanted to see me, Eddie?"

Eddie waved Marco in. "Sit down."

Marco sat in one of the chairs in front of Eddie's desk, folded his hands across his waist, and waited for Eddie to finish what he was working on.

When he was finished, Eddie looked up.

"We gotta' talk, Marco."

Marco flipped his hands open and shut. "Okay."

"I need you around here," Eddie said, leaning back. "Can't wait for you while you're at your other job."

Marco frowned as he glanced sideways at Eddie. "I don't know, Eddie. I need that money."

"How much?"

"What?"

"How much you makin'—at that garage?"

Marco shrugged and twisted his mouth. "It's embarrassin', but I make about thirty-eight K."

Eddie leaned his elbows on the desk. "That's it?"

Marco nodded.

Eddie scratched his head, thinking. "I'll pay you double what you're making, plus bonuses. Cash."

Marco's eyes popped. He leaned forward as a grin crossed his face. "What? Are you kiddin' me?"

Eddie shook his head. "I don't kid about money. I'm serious." He threw the pen on his desk. "This is bullshit. I need you when I need you. I can't wait around for my rides."

Marco looked up at the ceiling for a second. "Wow. I don't know what to say."

"Say 'yes.'"

"Kate—"

"Kate's gonna' love this. It's good fuckin' money. I pay on time and in cash. Go tell her. I'll let you lovebirds talk it over. Let me know what she says tomorrow. We can start this thing fulltime as soon as you ditch the other job."

Marco stood and reached over the desk to shake Eddie's hand. "Thanks. This is great, really. I'll talk to Kate and let you know tomorrow, alright?"

"You do that. And tell Kate I said hello, will ya'?"

Marco nodded and turned to leave.

"Saw her earlier today. Kate. She was lookin'-fa' you."

Marco turned back to Eddie. "Oh, right, yeah. She had some stuff to talk to me about."

"Renzo. Soccer stuff."

Marco nodded again, shifting his feet.

"How long they play that here—Soccer? I mean, winter's comin'."

"They'll finish up soon," Marco said. "Sometime in October, I think. Playoffs and stuff."

Eddie smiled.

Marco reached out his hand. "Hey, maybe you could come to one of his games. He's really good."

"Yeah?"

"Yeah."

"I'd like that," Eddie said. "Gives me a chance to get to know him, right?"

"Right. I'll let you know when the next game is."

"Good."

"Thanks again, Eddie."

"Ya' welcome. It'll be good."

"Oh, and hey," Marco added. "Kate mentioned having you over for dinner sometime."

"That'd be great," Eddie said. "Let me know when and I'll be there."

"Yeah, I will."

Marco left and Eddie again spent more time thinking about Kate. Kate and her nice little family.

Thirty-eight

Rush hour traffic on I-94 near downtown St. Paul was always gridlocked. Marco inched his black 1986 Mustang, buffed to a sparkling shine, around the winding and twisting lanes known as Spaghetti Junction, but any attempt to get past the sea of cars was futile. Eddie leaned back in the passenger seat, happy to let Marco maneuver through the mess.

"Fuckin' traffic. Jesus Christ," Eddie said.

Marco shrugged and kept his eyes on the road. "Rush hour. What'd'ya gonna' do?"

Eddie smacked Marco's arm.

"Will ya' look over there? Ain't that the guy who stiffed Dario for that meth from a couple-a weeks ago?"

"Where?"

With the Mustang paused in traffic, Eddie could have been pointing to any of the cars ahead of them, each trapped at a standstill in the four lanes.

"Up there," said Eddie. "One lane over, two cars up. That white piece-a shit Camaro. See it? I'd know that rusty-ass car anywhere."

"Oh, yeah. That's him," Marco nodded. "What's his name again, Snap? Sap?"

"It's Snack," Eddie said.

Before Marco could say another word, Eddie was out of the car.

Marco poked his head out of the driver's side window and shouted. "Eddie! What the fuck?"

As Eddie walked around the front of Marco's car, he adjusted his Ray Bans and flicked his hand, before walking in and around the mass of cars as they inched around the curve at a snail's pace. Eddie ignored the honking horns, and continued until he reached the white Camaro. He gave the trunk of the car a solid pound with his fist before walking to the passenger side door and climbing in.

Snack, a middle-aged white man who dressed like a young hip-hop star, whipped his head as his bulging eyes locked on Eddie.

"The hell?" Snack looked side-to-side and back at Eddie. "Where'd you come from?"

"Nice to see ya', Snack. You got my two grand?"

"Holy hell, Eddie! How'd you get here—in the middle of the freeway?"

"Don't worry about that. Gimme' your wallet."

Snack's shoulders sank as he leaned into the steering wheel.

"Come on, Eddie. I don't have your money."

Eddie raised his fist and smashed it into Snack's cheek, his head jerking from the blow. "I'm not fuckin' playin'."

Snack put his hand to his face as he leaned away from Eddie.

"I mean, I don't have it *now*. Here. In the car. I was totally gonna' come by the restaurant and drop it off."

Eddie grabbed Snack's hand from the steering wheel and bent his fingers backward. Snack moaned and fought, without success, to yank away his hand.

"I should fuck you up right here, you little piece-a shit," Eddie said. "You're lucky, though. Too many witnesses. Come by tomorrow. Parking lot across the street. Five o'clock. Got it?"

"Got it. I'll be there."

Eddie poked his finger in Snack's cheek. "You better be there. Cuz' if I have-ta come lookin'-fa you, you'll be a *snack* for my fuckin' dog, you got that? Huh? Snack? And don't come in-ta my restaurant. I'll have somebody waitin'."

Eddie shook his head. "Ya' know, Snack, that idiot Dario never learns. I told him no more frontin' people. So *you*? You learn now, or you'll learn later. Money up front from now on. Got it?"

Snack bobbed his head up and down. "Yeah, Eddie. Up front. Okay."

Eddie wanted to pop him in his jaw again, but instead, he left the car without saying another word, leaving the passenger door wide open. He heard it slam behind him as he walked back through the traffic. He ignored the honking and shouts, and the uptick in traffic speed, as he continued to saunter around the cars as though strolling in the park.

Once back in the car, Marco started yelling. "Jesus Christ Eddie. What the fuck was that?"

Eddie adjusted his shirt sleeves. "Just conductin' a little business." He looked over at Marco and grinned. "Nothin' to worry about."

Marco shook his head as he got the car moving again. "Okay."

Eddie patted Marco on the back as the car started crawling through the traffic.

"Let's get back-ta the restaurant. Can you pick me up around eight tonight? Gotta' make a few stops. Collect on a few more notes."

Marco kept his eyes on the road. "Sure, Eddie. No problem."

"This is workin' out nice, ya' know? You drivin' me around so I can make these stops quicker?"

"Happy to help," Marco said. "It's been … interesting."

Eddie chuckled as he reached into his jacket pocket and handed a wad of cash to Marco.

"Sorry about the late-night shift. Hopefully, this'll make up for it."

Marco took the cash without looking at it, and leaned sideways to stuff it into his jeans pocket. He glanced over at Eddie with a smile. "Thanks."

"Oh, and that piece-a-shit Snack is comin' by the restaurant around five tomorrow to give me my two grand. Can you handle that? Meet him in the parkin' lot across the street? I don't want these losers comin' in my restaurant."

"Sure, I'll handle it."

At the restaurant, Eddie got out of the Mustang.

"Tonight, then. Eight o'clock?"

Marco nodded. "Pick you up right here."

Eddie shut the car door and walked into the restaurant as Marco pulled away, headed for home.

Thirty-nine

*K*ate kicked off her shoes just as Marco came in through the back kitchen door.

"Oh hi, babe," she said. "I just got home, too."

Marco leaned in to kiss her cheek. "How was your day?"

"Pretty good," she said. "I got a few nibbles on that place over on Maryland. I'm gonna' run upstairs and change into my sweats. I'll be down in a minute to start dinner."

She leaned her head out the door to the living room. "Renzo! You home? Come down here and set the table!"

She pulled back into the kitchen for a second. "How about you? How was your day?"

Marco went to the fridge and stuck his head in to snoop around. She folded her arms, waiting. He lifted his head and smiled at her.

"Oh, pretty good. Ya' know. The usual. Stopped in the middle of Spaghetti Junction while Eddie walked through freeway traffic to slap a guy around. Nothin' too exciting."

Kate frowned as she walked over to him.

"What? Are you serious?"

He nodded. "I'm serious." He flicked his hand. "Go on upstairs and change. We'll talk later. I don't want Renzo hearing this shit."

"Are you okay? Were you scared?"

Marco chuckled and folded his arms.

"Scared? No. You seem to forget, Kate, I did stuff like this *all* the time back home. I just—I never thought I'd get back into it again, ya' know?"

Kate opened her mouth to speak, but Renzo came barreling down the stairs and into the kitchen.

"Mom! Can't you hear me? Why do I have to come down? I'm in the middle of a game!"

Kate raised her brows at him, arms folded.

"Well, geez, Renzo. I haven't seen you move that fast in a while," she said. "I see your ankle is feeling better since you got your cast off."

"What's wrong?" Renzo asked. "You guys look so serious."

Kate put on a fake smile. "Nothing. We're fine. I'm going upstairs to change. I'll be down in a bit. Get the table set. Marco, are you coming up? To change, I mean?"

"Ah', no. I can't."

Kate stopped and turned to him. "What? How come?"

"Gotta' go back out after dinner. Eddie needs me to take care of a few things."

"You've *got* to be kidding me. You worked all day."

Marco shrugged. "What can I say? My role is expanding. Now, I gotta' help with the neighborhood watch and handle some collections."

"Neighborhood watch? What the hell is that?" Kate asked.

"It's no big deal, Kate. We just keep an eye on a few businesses, make sure they're secure. I'll be gone no more than an hour and a half. Go on upstairs and change. I'll get the chicken ready for the oven."

Kate frowned and shook her head. "Fine. But I'm not happy about this."

She turned to address Renzo's look of concern.

"Everything's fine, honey. I'm just a little mad that dad has to work tonight. But he's right. He'll be back before we know it." She headed for the living room. "I'll be right down."

She gave Marco a quick look and left the kitchen.

As they finished dinner, Marco wiped his mouth and pushed back his chair.

"Okay. Gotta' go."

He stood and kissed Kate on the head and fist-bumped Renzo.

"Later, dude."

"Later, Dad."

Marco grabbed his keys. "Sorry I can't help with the dishes, Kate. Renzo, help your mother, okay?"

"Okay."

Marco gave Kate an air-kiss before closing the door behind him.

***

Later that evening, Kate sat in bed reading as she waited for Marco. Renzo was asleep in his room. She heard the car pull into the driveway and looked at the clock.

Eleven-thirty.

She closed the book and waited for him to come upstairs. After some rustling noises from down in the kitchen, she heard his footsteps as he climbed the stairs.

He walked into the room, unbuckling his belt. "Hi."

"Hi," she said. "That was a long hour-and-a-half. Everything go okay?"

He sighed. "Yeah. Fine. Just had to run Eddie around to a couple-a places. That's all. Waited in the car the whole time. Pretty boring stuff. A nice change."

She patted the mattress.

"Come and tell me what happened today. I thought this was supposed to be a simple driving job."

He sat next to her as he untied his shoes.

"It is, technically. Most of the time, I just tote the old lady around to the stores, and back-and-forth from her house. Same thing for Eddie, usually.

But today, I drove Eddie around town on a bunch of errands. The next thing I knew, I was watching him rough up a guy who owes him money. You should have seen him, Kate. Walking right down the middle of Spaghetti Junction. I couldn't believe it. People honkin' at him, screamin'." Marco rubbed his hands through his flopped, tired hair. "Fuckin' unbelievable."

Kate frowned as she folded her arms across her stomach. "Are you sure you're okay with all of this, babe?"

He reached over and patted her leg. "I'll be fine. It's just—I don't know. This isn't at all what I'd expected."

He stood and walked toward the closet, stopped and patted the sides of his jeans.

"Oh, I almost forgot."

"What?"

He turned to face her. A bright and unexpected smile crossed his face. He reached into his pocket and pulled out a wad of bills. He shook it at her, as he walked back to the edge of the bed.

"Got a bonus today." A strand of curled black hair flipped down into his eyes. "Can't believe I forgot to tell ya' about this earlier. I put it in my pocket and got worried about your reaction to me going back out tonight. Must have slipped my mind."

Kate opened her mouth and reached for Marco's hand. "*More* cash? How much?" She couldn't help but giggle.

He yanked his hand away. "Wait a minute."

Kate got onto her knees and watched, as he started counting the bills, laying them out on the bed.

"One, two, three, four, five, six, seven ..." He continued counting until he slapped down the last bill.

"Two thousand?"

Kate put her hands over her mouth to hide her smile.

Marco put his finger to his lips as he looked out into the hallway. "Shh!" He smiled and nodded, whispering, "Can you believe it?" He pointed at the money. "I'm not even sure if this is for a week? A month? No idea. But Eddie didn't even bat an eye when he handed it to me."

Kate put her hand on top of her head, her eyes wild. "Oh my God, Marco."

"I know, right?" He shook his head. "Eddie's amazing. He's already got his hands in a ton-a shit and it's pickin' up fast."

Kate's smile fell. "What kind-a shit?"

He put his hand out to stop her.

"Kate. Don't ask. It's best you don't know. I'll try to stay out of it as much as I can. He seems to be okay with that. It's almost like he doesn't want me knowin' too much of his business."

She frowned. "I'm guessing it's all illegal."

Marco shrugged. "Well, no. Not the restaurant part. At least I don't think so." He flipped his shoulder. "Yeah, probably the restaurant, too. But what we don't know, won't hurt us. So, don't worry. I'll know when to get out."

"Yeah, but will you be *able* to get out?"

"I'm no idiot, Kate. I know how this shit works. It'll be fine. Eddie would never hurt me. It's weird, but I think it's because he likes *you*."

She frowned. "Well, I don't know about that."

He rolled his eyes. "Don't be naïve, Kate. I watch him watch you. He's got the hots for you."

She wrinkled her nose and leaned back. "Eew. Don't say that!"

He shook his head and shrugged. "Just sayin'."

Kate looked at him and then at the cash on their bed.

Marco scooped it all up and shoved it into the nightstand drawer.

"But seriously, Kate. For now? This is amazing, right?"

He laughed and Kate joined him.

"If this is the kind-a money I'll be makin', I can handle the hours and the weird stuff I'll have to do. It'll all be worth it. We'll be in fat-city in no time."

She sat back on the edge of the bed next to him, clapping her hands quickly and quietly.

"I can't believe it. Wow!" She reached for the cash in the drawer. "Can I have some for—"

He pulled her hand away.

"Uh-uh. Hang on. I need some of this for my image. I can't walk around without cash. It'd be embarrassin' if Eddie asked for some, and I had to tell him I gave it all to my wife to pay for milk and doctor bills."

"Fine." Kate took one of the bills out of the drawer. "For milk and bread and stuff. The doctor bills can wait."

She leaned in and kissed him and he kissed her back.

"Mmm."

He stood and closed the bedroom door, before stripping down to his underwear and climbing into bed with her. She pushed him onto his back and straddled him, her hair falling around her face.

"This is for my hard worker."

Forty

Marco stopped the car in front of Magnolias and Eddie got out.

"See ya' in an hour or so, 'eh?"

"You got it, Eddie."

Despite the approach of October, the humid air clung to every part of Eddie as he hurried into the restaurant. The air conditioning felt weak but cooler than outside.

"Charles, how you doin ta-day?" Eddie said to the muscular Black teen standing at the podium. He patted him on the back.

Charles laughed, shaking Eddie's hand. "Hey, Mr. Bracchio. I'm doin' good. How you doin'?"

"Good. Sure is a hot one out there, 'eh?"

Eddie rounded the corner and headed toward the booth where Dario and Tau were seated.

"Oh hey—Mr. Bracchio," Charles called out.

Eddie turned back, "Yeah?"

"Thanks for helpin' out my dad the other day. We all appreciate it."

Eddie smiled and pointed at him.

"My pleasure. See you'se at the restaurant sometime. Bring 'em all in."

"You got it, Mr. Bracchio."

Eddie continued to the table. He tipped his head at Dario to move to the other side of the table next to Tau. He obliged without argument.

Dario pointed in the direction of Charles. "What's Charles talkin' 'bout?"

"Nothin'. His dad needed help with some problems he was havin' at his shop. I helped him out. No big deal."

Dario opened his mouth for a follow-up question, but Eddie shot him a look, so he snapped it shut.

After their sandwiches and salads arrived, they settled in to eat and discuss their miscellaneous business matters.

Eddie dug around in his salad before taking a bite.

"Alright. Next? What-d-ya-got?"

"Yo, man. Tau's got some news. It's big. Really big. He—"

Eddie raised his hand. Their table went silent for a moment.

"Tau? What-d-ya-got?"

Dario sat back in the booth and rocked his head as he chewed his thumbnail.

Tau, always with perfect posture, leaned in, speaking in his usual calm voice with proper English.

"I have a friend. He drives a truck for a big distributor."

Eddie shrugged. "So?" He stuck a toothpick in his mouth and waited.

Dario leaned forward and opened his mouth to speak, but Eddie raised his hand again. "Uh-uh. No, Dario." He turned back to Tau. "Go on."

Tau gave Dario a side-glance before continuing.

"So, my friend—his name is Lang—he told me he delivers lots of different stuff, including cigarettes. I talked to him, and he would be interested in lifting some product for a price. Fifty percent of the take."

Eddie sat back against the booth. "Tell Lang we'd give him thirty percent. Otherwise, it ain't worth our time."

Tau stared at Eddie.

Eddie raised his brows. "What?"

"Lang said fifty percent or forget it."

Eddie smiled and shrugged, pausing for effect.

"Listen, Tau. You got a few things-ta learn about business, but I like your creativity. Now, you go back to Lang and tell him thirty percent, or he can go fuck himself. Got it?"

Tau looked over at Dario who held his fist to his mouth to hide his chuckle.

"Okay. I'll tell him."

"Good. And now that things are pickin' up and you're both makin' new contacts and doin' good work, I wanna' talk about the problem you mentioned before. You said word on the street is that some folks ain't too happy with me steppin' in."

Tau and Dario nodded, but said nothing.

"Who?" Eddie asked.

"O," Tau answered.

Eddie nodded and continued. "So, this O." He snapped his fingers. "Last name?"

"Jackson," Dario said.

"Alright," Eddie said. "*That* guy, I'm interested in. He's the one in charge-a the drugs in this neighborhood, right? Just *this* neighborhood?"

The boys nodded.

"But Eddie, why? Why-you interested?" Dario asked. He shot a quick glance at Tau, who's eyes betrayed his concern.

"Because," Eddie said, "O, I can take. We just need his supplies. Then, we—I mean *I*—take his place. Get what I'm sayin'? Just take over the piece—for just this neighborhood."

The boys shook their heads.

"No," Dario said. "I *don't* get it. That sounds like a *bad* idea. They don't trust me, they don't trust Tau, and they don't trust *you*. They don't even *know* you. Know what I'm sayin'? It's all about the trust."

"I know all about trust, Dario, okay? Listen, I take over for O, and before they even find out about it, we got the business runnin' like a top. Hell, they won't even know I'm involved. It'd be all the same people, except for O. And I wanna' do it quick. Before they even know what happened."

Dario let out a slow breath as he shook his head.

"Listen," Eddie continued, "this is business. And I know what I'm doin'. So, O's distributor-guy—it'd be nice to have a name, by the way."

Eddie saw Dario's eyes pop.

Eddie paused. "What?"

"Well, ah'," Dario lowered his head as he looked around the restaurant. "Let me tell you—" he put up his hand "—this is what I know." He flicked his thumb across his nose and looked around again before continuing. "One time, this dude came up to us over in Swede Hollow. Big Mexican dude, right? Came up to us waving a forty-five around our faces—"

Eddie cut him off. "Yeah, yeah. Get to the fuckin' point. This is O's distributor? He brings O the drugs?"

Dario nodded. "Yup."

"He gotta' name?"

Tau and Dario exchanged a look before Dario finally mustered up some courage.

"Magic Man," he said. "Dude's the leader of F.A.M."

Eddie shook his head and frowned. "Nice fuckin' name. What the hell is F.A.M.?"

Dario leaned in and whispered, "That's a Mexican gang. Their colors are green, white and red. Name stands for *'Forever After Money.'*"

Eddie smiled and tipped his toothpick toward the boys. "Okay. Alright. Now we're gettin' somewhere's. You got the local cartel contact—this ah' Magic Man character; then, you got O Jackson—the guy in charge-a this neighborhood. That it? I need to be sure that's it."

"That's it," Dario said.

Eddie continued. "So, O's just the middle man? Magic Man's flunky, right? The guy who distributes and takes in the cash and drugs for the neighborhood?" He jammed his finger into the tabletop. "Just for this neighborhood?"

Dario didn't hesitate. "Yep. That's right. O Jackson, Jr."

Eddie wiped his mouth with his napkin and pushed his empty salad plate to the side.

"So, Magic Man, he don't care who sells his shit, right? He cares about the *money.*" Eddie swished his thumb and middle finger together. "Sure, he'll be suspicious at first, when O don't show up, but we'll step into O's shoes before he even gets a chance to question it. We keep O's crew, everyone and everything—it all stays the same." Eddie smiled. "For all he knows, O's outta' town. And for all O's boys know, O's outta' town. And they can tell Magic Man that."

He paused for affect. "You see what I'm sayin'? We start handlin' the sales, give the guy his money, and we keep the cut that normally goes to O."

Dario rubbed his face before burying it in his arms on the table.

"No, man. You can't do that. What do you think O's gonna' do about this? Huh? You're gonna get us all killed. You're makin' this sound too easy. It don't work like that."

Eddie frowned at Dario and ignored his pleas. "Don't you worry about O. I'll handle him." He paused to let that sink in. "So, where do we find him?"

Dario looked up at the ceiling appearing to say a silent prayer, before he leaned in. He spoke quietly. "So, O's ol' man, O, Sr.? His garage is over on Desoto and East Beaumont," Dario said. "There's a back alley. They come and go through the back entrance most of the time, especially at night. No cameras in the back. Only in the front of the garage. The main entrance."

Tau nodded. "During the day, that's when the regular customers come in. O and his crew—they hang out back. The owner—O, Sr.—he lets them hang there—I think cuz' he's scared to say no."

Eddie sat back and smiled. "I like the sound-a this." He knocked his knuckles on the table. "Dario, I need you to take me to see O."

Dario let out a sputter. "Wha-? Come on, man. Why me?"

Eddie shrugged. "Okay, you *and* Tau. Both-a you'se."

Dario and Tau snuck a glance at each other, as Eddie leaned in and whispered to them.

"Listen, if we pull this off, it'll be the start of somethin' *real* big for us. I can feel it. And remember, you'se two'll get a generous piece-a the action. But—" he pointed his finger at both of them— "you fuck me and I'll know. As soon as I know I can trust you, your piece-a the action will grow. Got it? I need your loyalty. You gotta' prove it to me. After that?" He leaned back. "Sky's the limit, my friends."

Dario nodded furiously. "Okay, Eddie. Cool, cool. We'd never fuck you over, man. Come on, now. We know who's boss. Who's got the brains."

Tau nodded and smiled. "You can trust us, Eddie. I'll make sure of that."

Eddie pointed at Tau. "You? I believe." He pointed at Dario. "You? You gotta' lotta' work to do to prove your loyalty."

Dario let out a breath and closed his eyes for a second.

"Fine. I'll prove my loyalty. Let's go. I'll show you the garage where O hangs out right now."

Eddie shook his head. "Tonight. Show me tonight."

Dario's jaw fell open as he exchanged a glance with Tau.

"Tonight?" He shook his head. "Come on, man I—," Dario shut his mouth for a second before starting up again. "Look, man. I can't tonight. I got this thing ..."

Eddie's eyes narrowed as he pressed his finger on the table. "Tonight."

"Okay man," Dario said, laughing nervously. "Sure. I can cancel my plans. It's cool."

Eddie continued. "We'll start small. With O."

"Small? O?" Dario said. "He ain't small." He raised his hand high above the table. "Big dude."

Eddie shrugged. "That right? Well, that's important information, I guess. Now, here's what I want the two-a you'se to do. I want you to go over to this garage and give this O mother-fucker a message from me. You tell him—"

Dario's voice whispered in a higher-than-usual range. "Are you crazy man? That guy'll shoot us down like dogs if we go anywhere near his territory. He don't like me man, I'm serious." Dario rocked forward and backward as he rubbed his thighs under the table.

Eddie frowned at Dario. "Jesus, Dario. Man the fuck up."

Dario stopped his fidgeting and sat up tall, as Eddie turned to Tau.

"What's O's story, anyway?" Eddie asked. "What's he into?"

Tau leaned forward. "Mostly meth. Weed."

Eddie nodded. "They makin' money with this shit?"

"Yeah, they're makin' bank," Dario said. "O may be workin' outta' that shitty car repair shop, but he's livin over on one-a them lakes over in Minneapolis. Gotta' real nice house, too. That's what I heard, anyway. I ain't never been invited over for a cup-a tea, know what I'm sayin'?"

He smiled and fist-bumped Tau before he remembered they were sworn enemies. His smile fell.

Eddie eyes narrowed as he shook his head. "You'se two better start gettin' along. You're business partners now. You got that? You work fa-me now, and this feudin' shit's gonna' get in the way-a all of us makin' money. So figure it out."

"Yeah," Dario said, "but we might be dead before we make a dime."

Eddie slapped the table and smiled. "Come on, Dario. Don't be such a chicken-shit. Listen, you stick with me—do as I say—and not only will you live, you'll prosper."

Dario and Tau gave him blank stares.

He pinched his thumb to his forefinger. "It means you'll make money. You'll be successful without havin' to shoot people—well, not very often anyway. Trust me. You'll be fine."

Tau spoke up. "Mr. Bracchio. You say we'll be fine because we're with you now."

"That's right."

"Well, how is O Jackson going to know that? He'll shoot us on sight."

Eddie looked at the table, thinking. "Yeah, yeah, you're right, Tau."

Tau smiled and folded his arms. He shot a cocky look at Dario who flapped his hand at him.

"When is O usually at the garage?" Eddie asked.

"Most nights, I guess," Dario said. "Probably after eleven."

"Okay. Here's what you're gonna do. You'se two are gonna' go down there tonight. Walk into that garage—"

"Say what now?" Dario brought his hands to his head. "Oh my God."

"Jesus, Dario. Man-the-fuck-up. Christ-almighty."

Dario lowered his hands and held his tongue. Tau remained quiet. Calm.

"Don't worry about it," Eddie whispered. "You'll be fine. I guarantee it. You'se two make the introductions, and then," he slapped his chest, "I come in. Come on. It'll be fun."

Dario's eyes bulged. "Fun? That ain't fun, man."

Eddie turned to Tau. "Tau. You in?"

Tau nodded. "Yes, Eddie. I'm in. I like this idea, actually. I had a run-in with O a while back. I don't like him."

Eddie stood, ready to leave the restaurant. "Good. It's set." He pointed at Dario. "Do *not* disappoint me."

"You can trust us," Tau said. "We'll be there."

Eddie nodded. "Alright then. Good."

After paying the bill, he moved toward the door putting one arm around each of their shoulders.

"Cheer up. You guys are gonna' make me proud."

Marco stood outside his car waiting for Eddie.

"My ride. Gotta' go." He turned to the boys. "Okay. I'll see you'se two outside the house. Tonight. Eleven o'clock."

"Okay, Eddie," Tau said.

He felt the eyes of the boys on his back, as he climbed into the passenger seat of Marco's shiny black Mustang. He gave them a dismissive wave as the car pulled away.

He was looking forward to the evening. It had been too long since he'd had any fun.

Forty-one

*A*fter his lunch with the boys, Eddie made a stop that was long overdue. The sweltering afternoon and cloudless blue sky left the sun burning his head and shoulders. He hated to sweat, but was losing that battle as he pulled open the heavy wooden door. The day's light streamed into its dark entryway as he stepped in, letting the door slam behind him.

Aptly named *The Corner Bar*, the place had seen better days. The smell of stale beer and old popcorn drifted up Eddie's nostrils, as he lingered near the entrance waiting for his eyes to adjust to the gloom.

After a moment, he looked around the outdated tavern. To his left stood a long wooden bar, its shine long-gone, the polished beauty scuffed away, one sliding bottle of beer at a time. Along the bar sat three lone patrons, each hanging their head as though waiting for hope to jump out of their drinks. To his right, several beat-up tables and a wall lined with booths, sat empty.

Eddie's cousin, Salvatore Gagliardi, sat in the furthest seat of the bar near an unmarked door, a red and purple neon sign in the shape of an arrow pointing at it from above. Restrooms, Eddie presumed. Mirroring the mood of his bar mates, Sal's head hung low, his mouth close to the tip of his bottle of beer. The bartender and the other two patrons turned as Eddie entered, but not Sal. Eddie walked to him and gave him a heavy slap on the back.

"Sal! How's it goin'?"

Sal raised his elbow as he turned to see who'd just assaulted him. On seeing Eddie, Sal's eyes lit up. He lowered his battle-ready arm and smiled.

"Eddie! What the fuck?"

He stood and gave Eddie an enthusiastic embrace. Eddie patted Sal's huge back, still as muscular as always, and pushed him away, holding him at arm's length.

"Lemme' look at-cha', cuz."

Sal's salt-and-pepper hair, usually swooped back in a high wave, was flat and overgrown, looking more *salt* than pepper. His oversized mustache was, as usual, over-dyed a harsh black, but his beaked nose covered half of it.

Eddie quickly let go of him and spread out his arms. "Huh? Surprised?"

"Surprised? I can't believe it!"

Eddie laughed. "Your ma' told me you'd be here. She was her usual bowl of sunshine when she heard it was me on the phone."

Sal let out a sharp, short laugh. "Yeah, I'll bet she was."

He gestured toward the stool next to him. "Sit down. Lemme' get-cha' a beer."

Eddie straddled the stained and worn bar stool, its peeling red pleather poking out in the shape of a star. Sal waved his hand at the hunched-over bartender who appeared to be at least seventy-five.

"Yo Frank, can we get a couple-a beers over here?"

"Sure thing," said the old man.

Eddie looked up and down the bar. "This place sure has gone to shit since the last time I was here."

"The whole neighborhood's gone to shit," Sal said. "Payne Avenue all the way up past Minnehaha." He shook his head. "It's all changed."

Frank delivered their beers and grabbed Sal's empty bottle.

Eddie looked at the bottles and pointed. "What's this?"

Sal took his bottle. "What?"

"Where's the fuckin' glass? I ain't drinkin' outta' some filthy beer bottle."

Sal looked around. "Come on, Eddie."

"Hey—ah', bartender! Frank!" Eddie shouted.

Frank looked over at him.

"Can we get a couple-a glasses here? We ain't animals."

Frank rolled his eyes. "Pardon me." He returned with two room-temperature mugs. "Shall I pour for you fine gentlemen?" he asked.

Sal waved him away, obviously embarrassed.

"Jesus, Sal," Eddie said. "We gotta' get you outta' this dump."

He poured his beer and took a sip, frowning at the taste, before leaning in to Sal with a smile as he smacked his arm.

"Hey. 'Member when we was kids? We'd go door-to-door exchangin' food?"

Sal looked straight ahead at the rows of bottles behind Frank as though seeing those days long since passed. He nodded.

"Yeah. I'd bring bread, 'member? Your ma' would give me meatballs. Mrs. Tarluzzo—she'd give me lettuce."

Eddie looked straight ahead, too. "By the time we were back home, we had a full dinner."

Sal looked at Eddie. "And when we got older, we'd go bowling at the Arlington Bowling Alley with our parents. And to the ice cream shop to look at the pretty girls sittin' at the counter."

Eddie laughed. "Now, those were good times, am I right?"

"Yep," Sal said, quietly. "Good times." He sipped his beer. "Then you had to move to Brooklyn, and I was stuck here—*all* by my-lonesome. Watchin' the Italians move out and the riff-raff move in."

The two men sat in silence.

Eddie took a swig of beer. "So, how long you been out?"

"'Bout six months now."

"What they get ya' for again?"

"Assault with a deadly weapon. Wacked a guy over the head with a baseball bat."

"That's right. I remember my ma' tellin' me about that."

"He owed me money." Sal shook his head. "Prick almost died. Shit."

Eddie lifted his beer and air-toasted Sal.

"Got what he deserved. Man's gotta' pay his debts, know what I'm sayin'?"

Sal nodded. The two men stayed silent for a moment, and then Sal turned to Eddie and said, "What-cha doin' back in town anyways?"

Eddie smiled and flipped his head side-to-side. "Oh, you know. Business. Got a few irons in the fire, as they say."

Sal nodded. "That right? Good fa' you."

Eddie turned back to Sal. "So, yeah. I gotta' restaurant now, too. Down Payne a bit from here. I'm helpin' this old lady run it."

Sal smiled. "Oh yeah? What kinda' restaurant?"

"Italian. It's called *Fortunato's*." He smiled. "Surprised, right?"

Sal chuckled. "Yeah, actually. I am surprised. That don't sound like somethin' you'd get into. How come you doin' it back here and not in Brooklyn? I thought that was home fa' you now."

Eddie tilted his head. "Well, yeah. Brooklyn's home. But I got called back here to help my boss take care-a some bullshit and help this old lady. Turns out she's alright, ya' know? Sweet old lady. Hundred-percent *eye-talian*. Can barely understand her."

Sal nodded, listening and drinking. But mostly drinking.

"Think I heard-a that place. Fancy shit."

"Fancy is right. And her risotto?" Eddie kissed his two fingers. "Top class. You ain't even gonna' believe it, Sal. I'm tellin' ya'."

Eddie sensed he was losing Sal's attention.

"So ah', yeah, anyways. That's why I'm here. I been lookin'-fa' you."

Sal turned to him and touched his chest. "Lookin'-fa' me?"

"Yeah. Yeah!"

"Fa' what?"

"I wanna hire ya'. Ya' know, run some operations I'm startin', right?" He looked around as he lowered his voice and leaned in closer to Sal. "Stuff in addition to the restaurant."

Eddie saw a flicker in Sal's eyes and watched him straighten his spine. Sal lowered his head to get his ear closer to Eddie's mouth. "You got work fa' me, cuz?"

Eddie's voice went a few breaths higher despite his smiling whisper. "Yeah. I got work." He straightened and grinned as he took a swig of his already-warm beer.

Sal's head bobbed, his eyes hopeful. "I mean ... seriously, Eddie. I ain't had a job in a while now. My ma's been houndin' my ass. Wants to kick me out. I could really use the work—get a place-a my own, ya' know?"

"I knew you'd be interested," Eddie said. "I mean—I hadn't heard you was outta' work or nothin'. I just always remembered you liked your money and your nice things. And from the looks-a ya', you could use that right now."

Sal frowned and looked down at his stomach, pulling on the old black and red flannel shirt he was wearing, tattered at the edges, tight around his belly.

"Man, you got that right. What kind-a work you talkin' about?" He shook his head. "I mean, I don't know what I'd do, ya' know? I don't got no connections like I used to. When I got outta' the joint everything was different."

He splayed his fingers as if to say "*poof.*"

"Don't you worry about that. I got some punks workin' fa' me. Neighborhood kids. They got connections. They'll do the dirty work. But I need *you* to oversee what *they're* doing. *Capicsi?* You'll be their manager. You just make sure the money they're bringin' in comes to me. *All* of it. I'll pay them their cut and give you fifteen percent of my cut. How's that sound?"

Sal smiled and moaned. "Mmm. Manager, huh? I like the sound-a that." After a minute though, he shook his head. "I don't know, Eddie. I'm still on paper. Sounds too risky."

Eddie leaned in. "Come on, man. What'd'ya got to lose? You ain't doin' shit. You got no money." Eddie straightened his spine. "And believe me …" he pinched his thumb and forefinger together and waved them near Sal's face "… there's *lots* to be made. Come on. What'd'ya' say, 'eh? I need your help. You're the only guy I can trust. I need somebody to watch these punks. Make sure they ain't robbin' me blind."

Sal sighed heavily and nodded as he turned to Eddie.

"Yeah, okay. What the fuck? You talked me into it. Anything's better than sittin' around like this all fuckin' day, every day."

Eddie laughed loudly. "That's the spirit, cuz!"

He took out a pen and used a bar napkin to write down the address of the restaurant. He slid it over to Sal.

"You come see me at this address tomorrow around four o'clock. We'll talk some more."

Sal took the napkin and put it in his flannel shirt pocket. "Got it."

"Don't say nothin'. Not to your ma', not to nobody."

Sal frowned. "I got it, I got it. I won't say nothin', alright?"

Eddie finished his beer and stood to leave. He reached into his wallet and threw a twenty on the bar.

"Don't be late."

"I'll be there."

"Oh, and tell Aunt Rita I said hello," Eddie said, as he turned to leave.

Sal took his last swig from the bottle. "You know she hates you," he laughed. "Says you're the one who got me into all-a this trouble."

Eddie grabbed his chest in mocked surprise. "What? Me? Naw."

Sal chuckled.

"Well," said Eddie. "I guess I'm gonna' have to change her thinkin'."

He reached into his pocket and again pulled out his wallet. He rifled through the wad of bills he'd taken from the restaurant's register, pulled out a couple hundred dollars, and tossed it onto the bar in front of Sal.

"Here."

Sal raised his brows. "What's this for?"

"Go buy some clothes. You look like a bum. If you work fa' me, you dress the part. And buy your ma' some flowers. Tell her they're from me. There's many ways to make people happy. You just gotta' know how-ta do it."

"It's not easy with her."

"Do me a favor. Try being nice-ta her. Then, when we meet tomorrow afternoon, you let me know how she reacts, alright?"

Sal frowned and shook his head. "Yeah. Alright Eddie. I'll give it a try. It'd be nice, actually, to get her back to the way she used-ta be."

"I'll see you'se later."

"Thanks, Eddie," Sal said. He gave him a short wave.

Eddie pulled open the heavy old door, the sun spilling inside. He turned and pointed at Sal with a grand smile. "Ya' welcome."

He walked out onto the street and strutted toward Marco's Mustang, a slight grin crossing his lips.

The boys ain't gonna' like Sal.

Forty-two

Dario and Tau paced in the darkness as they quietly waited on the sidewalk in front of Micola's house. It was eleven o'clock sharp, as Eddie backed down the driveway. The three of them spent the short ride in silence, Tau up front with Eddie, Dario in back.

Eddie pulled up to the curb on Desoto Street and shut off the headlights. The surrounding neighborhood homes were quiet, everyone settled in for the night. The back of *Jackson's Garage* stood in the shadows two blocks ahead. Tiny homes surrounded it, and an apartment complex stood just beyond.

From the backseat, Dario pushed his arm through to the front of the car near Eddie's head, his finger pointing.

"That's it up there," he whispered. "See that light?"

Eddie saw the light above the door facing a small parking lot that appeared to accommodate only four cars. The lot was empty.

Eddie turned back to Dario. "So what do you know about this O? What's his weakness? He got family or somethin'?"

Dario nodded. "Gotta' little girl. I think she's three, four years old, maybe. Like I said, they live on one-a them fancy lakes in Minneapolis. But I think he stays 'round here a lot. Don't know where, though."

"Alright," Eddie said. "Let's go."

The three men exited the car and made the short walk down the old sidewalk toward the garage. An aging billboard stood on the rooftop facing the front of the building, its message unseen from their vantage point.

"Yo. Eddie, man. You lookin' fly tonight," Dario said, as they walked. "That suit is nice!"

Eddie smiled as he flipped his suit jacket open and closed and then secured the middle button. "You'se two could learn a few things about dressin' up for meetin's."

As they approached the old, cement-block building, Eddie heard the deep bass of a rap song vibrating against the rusted metal door just ahead. They crossed the dilapidated parking lot, Dario and Tau walking behind Eddie. He pounded the door with the side of his fist.

A voice from behind the door yelled over the music. "Who is it?"

Eddie heard Dario whisper to Tau. "Man, we gonna' die tonight."

Eddie turned and gestured with his hand as if to air-slice their throats. "Shut-up," he mouthed. He hid his smile as he pushed Dario to the door.

"Yo man. It's Dario. Dario Tucker? I gotta' message for O."

They heard some clicking and watched the doorknob turn. Light spilled through a slight crack as the door opened, showing a sliver of someone's face peering out at them.

The music drowned out the deep, angry voice. "What kind-a fuckin' message? From who?"

Dario replied. "Some new dude in town. He's got a message for O. Wants me to give it to him."

The unknown person on the other side of the door said, "Oh this-gonna' be rich."

His voice faded as he slammed the door shut. Eddie and the boys looked at each other and then back at the door. They could hear the voice yelling and laughing from inside.

"Hey O! You gonna' love this shit, man!"

The doorman returned. Again, only a slit of the door opened as the music wailed loudly in the background.

"O don't wanna' see nobody right now, Dario. Get the fuck outta' here."

Before he could shut the door, Eddie slid in his foot and wedged it next to the doorframe, his fingers wrapped around the door's edge as he pushed it open using the side of his body and shoulder.

"Whoa, whoa, hold-up GQ," said the tall, heavy Black man, now illuminated by hanging lightbulbs scattered overhead.

Eddie and the boys stood near the man in an open and spacious, but filthy auto repair garage, the fumes of gasoline and rubber filling Eddie's nostrils. Racks of equipment, tools and supplies were packed onto shelves and in crates all around the floor, though no vehicles were inside for repair.

Eddie gestured with his hand, low and behind his back, for Dario and Tau to stand behind him. They quickly obeyed.

Addressing the doorman—who had stepped back from Eddie's unexpected intrusion at the door—Eddie calmly looked up at him and said, "You tell that prick O—" his head tipped side-to-side as he spoke—"or whatever the fuck his name is, that he's got a fuckin' visitor, and it's goddamn disrespectful not to accept that visitor."

He stared up at the man, whose eyes bulged in surprise by the balls of the stocky Italian man in front of him.

Eddie's argument on etiquette always worked. Criminals often thought of themselves as businessmen, though most times, in Eddie's experience, calling them businessmen was a stretch. The doorman glared at Eddie for a second, giving him his requisite stare-down. Then, he shrugged and said, "Hold on."

The hefty man turned and sauntered across the grease-stained cement floor toward a closed door in the far-right corner of the garage. He opened it, closing it behind him. Eddie watched until he disappeared, noting his loose clothing: a Timberwolves jersey, old and worn; jeans, sagging at the back of his ass, the handle of a piece showing at the waist.

The rap continued to blare into Eddie's ears. He looked around in hopes of finding the source of the noise so he could shoot it dead.

"Jesus, I hate this rap shit," he said to Dario and Tau. Neither responded to his comment. Instead, Tau shuffled his feet and Dario continued to look over each shoulder, turning in circles now and again.

Eddie chuckled. "You'se two look like you're about to shit your pants." He smiled and stood between them, putting his arms around their shoulders. "Relax," he said. They each gave him a weak smile. The little weasels were his punks and he loved it.

After a minute, the door re-opened and the doorman gestured at Eddie to head toward him. Eddie strutted in his direction. Dario and Tau followed.

At the door's entrance, the man placed his hands on the chests of the two boys. "These two shitheads stay right here."

He turned to Eddie and tipped his head. "You can go back." He looked past Eddie and shouted, "Frisk this guy, Dax." Eddie turned to see another Black man walk out of a second door he hadn't noticed.

The second guy, Dax, also black, also substantial in size, sauntered confidently toward Eddie, cold-staring him down as he approached. Unlike the first guy, though, who was overweight and slow, Dax was in excellent shape. Muscles bulged through his skintight black t-shirt. In Eddie's estimation, he was at least six-three, two-hundred-eighty pounds. He couldn't spot a piece on this guy, but he definitely had one. No doubt about it. Probably strapped around his ankle.

Dax stopped in front of Eddie and shouted directly into his face. "Turn that shit down!" His breath puffed across Eddie's face, a hint of onion offending the nostrils. Eddie closed his eyes for a second at the offensiveness of the gesture but said nothing. The volume of the music dropped.

"Thanks," Eddie said. "Thought I'd bleed from the ears from that shit, ya' know?"

He laughed at his comment, but Dax did not.

Eddie looked up at him and smiled, as he spread his legs and raised his hands. He knew the drill.

"This ain't my first frisk," he said to Dax.

It most certainly was not his first frisk. Dax gave Eddie the familiar once-over before patting him down, inside and outside of his ISAIA navy-and-white-checked suit jacket. He stopped at Eddie's waistband and pulled out Dario's .38. Eddie never would have shown up without it. A show of strength and appearance was half the battle.

The man looked at Eddie and took the piece, before finishing the frisk down the sides of Eddie's dress pants, and up the middle of his legs. Eddie's eyes followed the man as he frisked him.

When he finished, Eddie said, "I'll be wantin' that back." Dax tipped his head upward as if to say, "we'll see about that," before opening a dirty, wooden door with a hole near the bottom. He nodded and stepped aside for Eddie to enter.

Eddie walked in.

Dax paused at the door. "You want me to stay boss?"

The man looked at Eddie. "For this old man?" He chuckled. "Naw."

Dax left, shutting the door behind him.

Forty-three

*E*ddie found himself standing in a tight, windowless room, with barely enough space to hold the cheap wooden desk and two mismatched office chairs that stood haphazardly before him. He assumed the tiny room was the meager headquarters of the garage owner's business.

Behind the junky desk covered with greased-stained customer invoices, sat yet another Black man. This guy was better looking and not quite the size of the other two. Strong, but not overly muscular. Thinner, too. His head was shaved bald and buffed to a shine.

Several bricks wrapped in silver electrical tape sat in neat piles on the far end of the desk, along with a black .45. A larger load of the bricks lay on the floor next to the desk. Meth, Eddie assumed.

Based on the man's youth and attire—a loose white muscle shirt—as well as tattoos covering his light-skinned muscular arms, it seemed unlikely this guy was the owner of the establishment, Mr. O Jackson, Sr. No, sitting before Eddie was *the* O Jackson, Jr.

The bald man, who appeared to be in his mid-twenties, busied himself with some sort of handheld video game. He gave Eddie a bored glance before returning to it. His cockiness indicated to Eddie a confidence borne from a tough life. He'd likely be more difficult to take down than his appearance indicated.

"You O Jackson?" Eddie asked. "Jr.?"

The man lifted his gaze to assess Eddie, seemingly for the first time. His voice was quiet, nonchalant.

"The-fuck are you?"

Without an offer, Eddie took the seat closest to the door and threw his right knee across the left one. He leaned back and folded his arms.

"Name's Eddie Bracchio. Thought I'd be polite." He shrugged one shoulder. "Introduce myself."

O had no reply and continued with his game. Eddie sat in the chair in front of the desk and began to study O's tattoos. "Interesting tattoo. The-fuck is it? A buncha' broads having an orgy or somethin'?"

O's chest and shoulders shook a little before a grin crossed his face, revealing a gleaming set of white teeth, except for one gold one at the top right.

"Somethin' like that."

Eddie's brows raised as he smiled. "That's different. Ain't never seen nothin' like that before."

O placed the game in a bag on the floor behind him and then rested his forearms on the desk. He leaned forward and stared at Eddie with a dead-eyed expression.

"How can I help you, Mister—what'd you say your name was?"

Eddie put his leg down and leaned in, too.

"Bracchio. Eddie Bracchio. Call me Eddie." He smiled and put up his hands. "No formalities, please."

O leaned back, his hands still resting on the desk. "Listen, man. Honestly, I don't give a fuck who you are. Either state your business or get the fuck outta' my office."

Eddie smiled. "Alright." He nodded three times. "O." His smile quickly turned to a frown. "A man who means business. I respect that. I'll get to it, then. The reason for my visit today, is to tell you—" Eddie's voice hardened as he pointed at O— "that *I'll* be takin' over these operations." Eddie waved his hand in the direction of the bricks. "Your services are no longer required."

O's eyes narrowed for a second and then he chuckled. "That right?"

Eddie nodded. "That *is* right."

He sat back, looked at his gold pinky-ring, buffed it with a quick breath, and then folded his arms to wait for the news to sink in.

For the first time, O took a good look at Eddie. He raised his right brow and scrunched his face almost into a smile as he snarled.

"Fuck you talkin' 'bout?"

Eddie stayed firm, un-wavering, as he watched O's confidence begin to fade. O stood and slammed his hands on the desk, causing it to wobble loudly under its aging legs. Eddie never flinched and remained seated.

O leaned across the desk toward Eddie and did a rapid shake of his head, his finger raised and waving.

"Naw, naw man. I don't know who the fuck you think you are, but that shit ain't happenin', and you can go fuck yourself if you think you're takin' over my shit."

A slight smile formed across Eddie's lips. He was enjoying this new sense of concern in O's tone. This crack in his confidence. Eddie adjusted himself in his seat and crossed his arms, waiting for more from O.

O tipped his head forward as he laughed, his cold eyes fixed on Eddie.

"I'll hand it to ya' though, man. You got some balls walkin' in here like you did." He laughed again, his hands on his stomach, the desk between the two men. "Yep, some kinda' mother-fuckin' balls." He paused, still smiling. "What are you, Italian or somethin'?" O grabbed his crotch. "*Cajones*? Is that what you call 'em?"

He shook his head and waved his hand to the side. "Man, fuck you. Get the fuck outta' here 'for I pop your silly ass."

O sat back down and turned to reach for his game as though bored with Eddie.

Eddie used that opportunity—O's lack of focus—to slip his right fingers into the left sleeve of his jacket at his wrist and pull out a petite, solid steel screwdriver about the length of his hand. Held securely and discreetly in a tiny elastic loop just inches from the edge of the shirt cuff, it was a tool of his trade, and always missed in body searches.

Just as O's eyes returned to face Eddie, Eddie jumped from his seat causing it to tip and crash back. He leaned in across the desk toward O and, with his left hand, grabbed O's right hand and slammed it onto the desk. At the same time, he raised his right arm high over his head. O had only a second to look up at the small screwdriver, as he fought to wriggle his hand from Eddie's powerful grip.

"Wait!" O shouted.

He fought with Eddie's grip, while trying to stand, but Eddie was faster, stronger. Eddie held O's right hand with a power O could not overcome, and jammed the screwdriver down into his hand, crushing bones as it penetrated, before lodging firmly in the wooden desk underneath it. O's hand was now pierced into the desk, a bonus Eddie had not planned on.

O's eyes bulged as he screamed out a sound resembling that of a dying animal. Eddie heard voices and commotion outside the door, but his hand held the screwdriver firmly in place. O tried to fight him off with his other hand, but the agony made this effort futile. Eddie wiggled the screwdriver a bit, further slowing O down.

Eddie then grabbed the .45 from the pile of meth and pointed it at O.

"Sit down," Eddie said. "And shut the fuck up."

O's face contorted in anguish, as he slowly sat down behind the desk. He was now firmly under Eddie's control.

Both Eddie and O turned to the closed door, as they heard footsteps and yelling from outside. Eddie maintained his grip on the gun in his right hand and O's speared hand in his left. He wiggled the screwdriver just slightly between O's bones, causing him to groan in agony. He could now see that the tiny point of entry between O's forefinger and third finger had punctured a vein. Blood spilled over onto the table and onto the bricks of meth, which had jostled a bit in the struggle.

The office door was yanked open. Dax stood just outside of it, his gun pointed at Eddie. Eddie sensed the guy looked nervous, unsure of the scene before him.

With the gun aimed in Eddie's direction, Dax yelled, "The fuck you doin'?"

"Shoot this motherfucker!" O cried, pushing the desk toward Eddie with his waist. It barely moved, though. Eddie's hold of the desk with his thighs was stronger, and O's pain and blood loss were weakening him.

"I wouldn't do that," Eddie said to Dax. "I'm a good aim. You shoot me, I could shoot O first, then you, before I go down." He laughed at the guy with the gun. "What're ya' gonna' do, 'eh? It's a big chance you'd be takin', am I right?"

Dax held his gun at Eddie, but Eddie never flinched as he stared down its barrel. He continued holding the screwdriver, and gun at O, as O squirmed. Dax looked away from Eddie and back at O.

Eddie held on as he grinned at O. "Tell him to back off, O. I've got eyes on your nice house. The one on the lake? Your little girl?"

O stopped squirming and stared at Eddie. "No!"

Eddie raised his brows as he whispered, "Yeah."

He gave the screwdriver another tug sending a shriek from O's lungs.

"Tell him to back off," Eddie said. "Now. Or I give the orders at your house."

O moaned, his face contorted in pain. "Stay back, man! Stay back!" He shook his head. "Maddie!"

Dax continued to point the gun at Eddie, unsure of what to do.

"Back away, man," O said, grunting through the pain.

Eddie and O hadn't moved, their faces nearly touching. Sweat dripped down the sides of O's forehead. Eddie's firm grip remained on the screwdriver's handle, with O's left hand still pinned to the table and bleeding. Eddie's other hand held the .45 near O's face.

Dax lowered his weapon. "Okay, man. It's cool, it's cool. I'm movin' back, okay?"

Eddie hissed at Dax. "Get the fuck out and shut the door."

Dax lowered his weapon, backed out, then reached to shut the door. Eddie waited. Once the door was closed, he turned back to O, his hand still tightly holding the screwdriver.

"Keep that screamin' down, O. You don't want your boys out there thinkin' you're some sort of pussy now, do ya'?"

O's face remained twisted in pain, but he went silent.

"Okay then. I'll repeat myself, which I don't like doin'," Eddie said. He wiggled the screwdriver another fraction. "*Do* we have an understandin'?"

O squeezed his eyes shut and nodded. "Please man. Please stop. Please get that thing outta' my hand."

O begged Eddie with his eyes for relief, but Eddie just smiled at him, unflinching, as he held his grip.

After a moment, Eddie's smile faded. He leaned into O's face, and with cold eyes, he spoke quietly through gritted teeth. "Now you listen to me you *mother-fucker*. Like I was sayin': you, and your stupid-ass friends out there, got a *new* boss."

Eddie jiggled the screwdriver around O's bones. O squirmed, bouncing his legs uselessly. Except for a brief moan though, he stayed quiet.

"That's me," Eddie whispered. "You answer to *me* now. You got that? Huh? If you don't, there's a lot more where this came from," he said. "But if you *do* get it," Eddie pulled back a bit and smiled. "We'll make some money together. Yeah?"

Eddie laughed as he tightened his grip on O's wrist before quickly yanking out the little screwdriver. O screamed as he pulled his mangled hand away from Eddie. He held it gingerly in his other hand, close to his chest.

Eddie reached across the table, pulled on O's white muscle shirt, and wiped the bloody screwdriver clean.

He paused, smiled, and then whispered through his teeth.

"You piece-a shit."

Eddie moved back, his legs brushing the tipped chair as he took a handkerchief from his inside pocket and wiped the blood and skin off his hands. He threw the bloodied cloth onto the table in front of O and stepped to the door, whipping it open.

Dax was there, pointing the gun at Eddie, but Eddie was pointing O's .45 at Dax.

Eddie spoke calmly. "You gotta' fuckin' problem, asshole?"

Dax lowered his gun. "Man, fuck you."

Eddie stared at Dax, challenging him until he blinked. Eddie continued to point the gun at him as he put out his other hand.

"My piece?"

Dax frowned as he retrieved Dario's .38 from his sweatpants pocket and handed it to Eddie. Eddie slipped it into his jacket pocket and smiled.

He then moved past Dax and lowered O's gun, adjusting his suit jacket as he walked toward the front of the garage, not once, losing his stride or swagger.

Upon seeing a third door, he stopped and turned back to Dax.

"What's behind that door?"

"None-a' your fuckin' business."

"Alright." Eddie smiled. "For now."

He walked up to Dario and Tau, who stood near the exit trying to look calm, but Dario was fidgeting. Tau kept tight eye contact with Eddie.

Eddie gestured with his arm for the boys to leave first.

"Let's go."

Before leaving, Eddie turned back to face the men one last time.

"Until we meet again," Eddie called to them.

"Fuck you," Dax shouted.

Forty-four

Outside the rundown service station, the boys scrambled across the dark parking lot and headed for the sidewalk.

"Slow down," Eddie whispered. "Stay cool."

They turned and looked back at him, as he exited the door. Dario had regained his strut, and Tau jogged behind him until they were on the sidewalk. Once they were a block away from the shop, Dario started in, walking backwards to face Eddie, as they moved toward the car.

"Man, what happened in there? Was that O screaming? What'd you do to him?"

Eddie put out his hand as he looked around at the dark houses on either side of the street. "Keep it down. People are tryna' sleep 'round here."

He understood their racing adrenaline, he was feeling it too. He grinned as they walked briskly ahead of him.

"Come on, Mr. B.," Dario said. "Tell us what happened in there. What was all the screamin' and yellin' goin' on in that back room?"

"Yeah, what happened?" asked Tau.

Eddie smiled as he pulled out the tiny screwdriver from his pocket and showed it to the boys.

"Jammed O's fuckin' hand with this."

Dario covered his mouth and laughed.

"Oh shit! No way, man!"

Eddie lowered his chin and smiled, nodding.

Tau said nothing, a touch of surprised fear glowing in his eyes.

Eddie continued, "I just let him know — all-a them know — that I'm their new boss." He laughed, mostly to himself. "I think they get the picture."

"Wait," Dario said. "You just *told* them? 'I'm your boss?' That's it? No proof? No names? No fuckin' backup?"

Eddie pushed his lips into a smiling frown. "Yeah."

"Goddamn!" Dario whisper-shouted.

Tau turned back to look at Eddie as they walked. "I thought they frisked you."

Eddie explained how he keeps the screwdriver in his sleeve and showed them the elastic loop that holds it securely in place, and how easily and discretely it can be removed.

"Man, I never woulda' thought a tiny thing like that would do any good," Dario said.

"Yeah, but you wouldn't believe how many times I've used this little screwdriver. I've had it for years. It always comes in handy. Every time—and I mean *every* time—I raise my hands and spread my legs, and say to them, 'this ain't my first frisk,' they miss it. Every fuckin' time." Eddie laughed at his brilliance.

"Aren't you scared he's gonna' come after you? Kill you?" asked Dario. "Or call the cops?"

"Oh, he will *not* call the cops. He doesn't want that kind of attention. But yeah, he's comin' after me, that's for sure. I'll be waitin'. In fact, I'd be surprised if he *didn't* come. Am I scared? Hell no."

As Eddie and the boys opened the car doors, Eddie said, "Don't you boys worry. I got it all taken care of."

He didn't really have it taken care of—yet. He'd need a little help for that.

They got in and Eddie drove off, his brain whirling. Taking on O like that was a gamechanger. Other people's fear had always been Eddie's key to success. Tonight was just the beginning.

Eddie made the quick drive back to Micola's. As the boys headed to their houses, he called out to them.

"Hey!"

They turned to look at him.

"Check in with me tomorrow afternoon."

"Sure thing, Mr. B.," Dario said.

Tau waved.

Eddie listened as they continued their whispered conversation about the evening's events. He smiled and headed up the stairs to Micola's house.

Forty-five

The following afternoon, Eddie heard a light rap on his office door.

"Yeah," he shouted.

The door opened and Tau and Dario walked in.

"Take a seat."

The boys sat in chairs in front of Eddie's desk. Dario began talking about the cash he'd made the previous week when the sound of approaching footsteps and muffled voices interrupted him. Eddie stood, as the boys turned toward the door just as a light knock was heard.

"Come on in," Eddie shouted.

Two large men walked into the tiny office, now crowded with five people.

"Sal! Marco!" Eddie called out.

With arms outstretched, Eddie walked around his desk to greet them.

"Welcome to my new place-a business, Sal."

Sal smiled and reached out his hand to Eddie. His dark sunglasses and mustache, along with his stocky, muscular build, gave him an intimidating appearance.

"Eddie. How you'se doin'?"

Eddie took his hand and patted it. He gave Sal's new attire a nod of satisfaction. The black dress slacks and light blue cotton dress-shirt were major improvements.

Marco shook Eddie's hand.

"Marco, yeah. How you'se doin?"

"I'm good, Eddie. Thanks."

Eddie clapped his hands. "Alright. First order-a business—introductions."

Tau stood, but Dario didn't, so Eddie leaned over and smacked the back of his head. "Don't be disrespectful. Stand up."

"Owe, man!" Dario rubbed his head. "Sorry, Mr. B."

He stood and tried to look serious. Professional. He put his hands behind his back as he waited for Eddie to continue.

"Dario, Tau, this here's my cousin, Salvatore Gagliardi. But you can call him Sal."

Dario reached out his hand to Sal just as Eddie said, "He's gonna' be your boss on the street."

Dario jerked his hand back. "Wait—say what now?"

Eddie hooked his brow. "You gotta' problem with that, Dario?"

"Well, um. I just thought, you know, Mr. B., I thought I was in charge."

Eddie couldn't contain his laughter. He shook his head. "What the fuck, Dario?"

"No." Dario let out a nervous laugh. "That ain't what I meant, Mr. B. I ah'—what I meant was—ya' know. *You're* the boss. We come to you, but um ..." He wiped his nose, stalling. "I thought I, ya' know, I could run my own shit on the street."

Eddie squeezed his eyes and pinched the bridge of his nose for a second, shaking his head. When he opened them, he stared at Dario before waving his arms around the room.

"*I* am the boss, Dario, of all this shit. But Sal here—he's *your boss*—out on the street. You go to him with questions, and keep him posted on your comins'-and-goins' and shit, and give him the cash, *capisci*? You run your business, but you *answer* to Sal. You *pay* Sal."

Dario looked at Tau and frowned. "Yeah, I *capisci*."

Sal chuckled as he took off his sunglasses. He flipped his thumb in Dario's direction.

"What's with this guy, Eddie? Why you got a fuckin' punk like this workin' fa' you, 'eh?"

Eddie watched Dario jerk as if to make a move on Sal, but he knew Dario didn't have the balls. Sal didn't flinch. Eddie's cousin was a couple inches shorter and much beefier than the tall, lanky Dario, and Eddie loved how uncomfortable he'd already made Dario feel. Sal still held power in his appearance and presence. He was just what Eddie needed.

"Alright," Eddie said, laughing. "Everybody's gotta' learn to get along here. This is business, right? Now Sal," he flicked his thumb in Dario's direction, "Dario here—he knows the neighborhood like you *used*-ta' know the neighborhood. Things have changed, as you already know. We need Dario to flush out the business, right?"

Sal nodded.

Eddie continued. "And by *'business'* I mean, both the restaurant business *and* the street business, got it?"

"And Tau—he's gonna' be good. He has a whole 'nuther connection with the Asians—what are they called again, Tau?"

"Hmong, Eddie," Tau answered quietly, standing tall.

"Right. 'Hmong'." To the group, he said, "Did you'se know 'Hmong' starts with the letter '*h*'?" He laughed, shaking his head. "Don't make no sense-ta' me, know what I'm sayin'?"

The others joined him in a quick laugh, except Tau, who smiled faintly.

Eddie then turned to Marco who stood next to Sal. "And Marco, here—you boys already know him—he's my driver."

Eddie pointed at his chest as he looked at Dario. "*My* driver. You hear me? Do not expect him to drive any-a you'se around."

The other three nodded.

"He's got other stuff to do that are none-a your business. But remember," Eddie pointed at Dario and Tau, "he's always watching, too. So do your jobs and you'll have no problems with me."

Dario opened his mouth to speak, but quickly closed it.

Eddie walked around to his seat at the desk. "Alright, gentlemen. We'll need a couple more chairs. Let's get down-ta' business."

Marco left the office and returned with two folding chairs. The group of men huddled around Eddie's desk, as he leaned back in his chair, listening—loving the concept of running the show.

"Hit me," he said. "What'd-ya-got?"

The five men spent an hour discussing everything from sports betting, loan-sharking, cigarettes and liquor, product heists, to drugs.

Finally, Eddie leaned back and smiled.

"I like it. This is good. I think we got plenty-ta' work with here. Now, go on. Get out there and start drummin' up business."

The four of them stood.

"Dario," Eddie said, "run across the street to the parking lot and get Snack's two grand. He'd better fuckin' be there. Let me know if he ain't. And remember, I don't want any-a you'se comin' 'round here too much unless it's an emergency."

The rest of them nodded and turned to leave.

"Sal. Marco. Stay for a minute."

After Tau and Dario left, Eddie asked Sal and Marco what they thought of Dario and Tau.

Sal shook his head. "The Asian kid's gonna' be good. I'm worried about Dario. He's gotta' big fuckin' mouth."

Eddie looked over at Marco, who nodded. "I agree, Eddie," Marco said. "He's a loose cannon. But the guy's got ideas. And, I hate to admit it, but he's got the most connections outta' all of us."

"Shit. I know." Eddie shook his head. "I gotta' keep him. I actually *need* him. Don't tell *him* that, right? Keep a close eye on him. He's nervous now. Keep him that way. We don't want him gettin' any cockier than he already is."

"Okay, Eddie," Sal said. "Consider it done."

Marco nodded. "Yeah, I'll keep watch, too."

"Alright then," Eddie said, rising from his chair. "Gotta' get back upstairs for the dinner crowd. Marco, pick me up tonight?"

"Sure, Eddie. I'll be here."

"Good."

Sal and Marco left Eddie to prepare for the evening rush.

Forty-six

Eddie set the alarm and flipped off the lights to the restaurant before stepping out onto the dark street. The temperature had plummeted. It finally felt like October. Eddie turned as he heard Marco pull up. The streets were empty and quiet. He checked his watch as he walked to the car, squeezing his tired and burning eyes.

Eddie opened the passenger door of Marco's car and climbed in. "Jesus," he said, throwing his jacket in the back. "I'm ready for bed."

"What's this?" Marco asked, pointing at a car driving slowly toward them from the opposite direction.

"Shit. I don't like the looks-a that," Eddie said.

As the car approached, a burst of gunshots exploded from the driver's-side back window.

"Shit! Get down!" Marco shouted, grabbing Eddie's arm.

Marco and Eddie lowered their heads as the car sped past.

"They hit the restaurant! Go after those mother-fuckers!" Eddie shouted.

Without hesitation, Marco spun the car around, tires screeching, until the Mustang was traveling north on Payne. He picked up speed, whipping in and out of the occasional car, as he closed in fast on the dark blue Ford. The sedan whipped around until it was heading south on Payne. Marco screeched the car's brakes and whipped the wheel until they too were back heading south. He hit the gas and followed the car past Fortunato's, and then turned right on Seventh toward downtown St. Paul.

"Those mother-fuckers were aiming for us!" Marco yelled, as he maneuvered around a pick-up truck.

"They will die!" Eddie yelled. He pointed ahead, his other hand clinging to the dash. "Stay with 'em."

Marco chased the car past the Highway 52/Lafayette Bridge as they headed toward downtown. The car braked before turning right at the Gopher Bar.

"You gonna make that turn?" Eddie yelled, bracing himself.

Marco ignored Eddie and spun the car to the right. He pressed the gas as they entered Wacouta Street, and revved up his speed as the car in front of them crashed into a parked truck.

"Holy shit!" Marco yelled.

He slammed on the breaks, skidding and screeching the car to an abrupt stop at an angle just behind the smashed car. Eddie jumped out and ran toward it. A woman opened her front door, looked at the scene outside of her house and ducked back in, slamming the door behind her.

"Stay cool, Eddie," Marco yelled.

Eddie appeared calm as he stormed the vehicle. The driver's head lay on the steering wheel. No movement. The head of the passenger sitting directly behind the driver rested on the backdoor window. No movement.

Eddie drew the .45 he'd lifted from O Jackson and yanked open the back door. The man stirred and shook his groggy head, his eyes unfocused. Eddie noted the gun on the floor, as he pulled the arm of the passenger—the shooter—who screamed, "Don't shoot, man. Don't shoot!"

Eddie threw the young white man onto the street and called out to Marco. "Come and get his piece!"

Marco ran to the back of the car, leaned in and took the gun. He then brushed past Eddie to open the driver's door. He held the gun at the unconscious driver, breathing heavily, his legs spread.

Eddie leaned over the shooter who appeared to be in his early twenties. He was now on his knees in the street, his hands in the air. Eddie pressed O's gun into his temple.

"Don't do it, Eddie," Marco shouted.

Eddie lowered the gun and instead, hit him over the head with the butt several times. The guy fell to the ground, his arms covering his head, as he pleaded with Eddie to stop. Eddie continued to pound him to unconsciousness and gave him two more hits after that.

When Eddie straightened up, he saw Marco shaking his head.

"Okay man. He's down."

Marco continued to hold the pistol on the driver who had begun to stir. Eddie moved up to the driver. He nodded at Marco to back away. Marco lowered the gun as he stepped back, but remained ready.

A dark-skinned teenager raised a heavy hand. He looked at Eddie as blood poured from his forehead.

"Please man. Don't kill me. Please. I'll tell you anything you want to know. Please."

"What's your name?" Eddie shouted.

"Mike. Mike Parker."

"Well, *Mike*, you sure got a lot of fuckin' balls comin'-ta' my place-a business and shootin' it up. Were you tryin' to shoot me? Or what?"

"I don't know, man."

Eddie sideswiped the butt of his gun across Mike's chin.

Marco moved in. "Come on, Eddie."

Eddie gave Marco a cold look, so he stepped back.

Blood from Mike's new wound began to trickle from a deep gash on the side of his face.

"Please stop," he whispered.

"What's your address, Mike Parker?"

"My address? What do you need that for?"

"Are you *that* fuckin' stupid? You're gonna' ask *me* questions? Give me your fuckin' address before you end up like your friend down there."

Mike Parker gave his address on Chesapeake Street.

Eddie turned to Marco. "You got that?" Marco wrote it down in a notepad he kept in his shirt pocket. "Got it."

"And, what's this half-dead fucker's name and address?" Eddie flipped his head in the direction of the shooter, who lay motionless at Eddie's feet.

Mike looked over at his friend and let out a quiet moan. "That's Stevie. Stevie Mason. He lives by me. I don't know the number, but it's like, three or four houses down. Same side of the street as my house."

"Okay, *Mike* Parker. Now, tell me why you and your piece-a-shit friend here had the stupid idea of shootin' up my business. Was I the target?"

Mike's eyes welled, his arms still up. "Yeah."

"Well your friend, Stevie here, sure fucked that up. Who ordered the hit?"

"This guy—his name is O."

"That right?"

"Yes, sir. O's probably gonna' kill me now for tellin' you his name."

"He pay you to do this?"

"Yes, sir. He paid us a grand each."

"Did you get paid up front?"

"Yeah—yes, sir. Half up front."

"Give it to me."

Mike's head seemed to clear. "What?"

"You heard me. Give me the fuckin' thousand bucks."

Mike leaned to the side, moaning. He fished five hundreds from his wallet and handed them to Eddie.

"Now get Stevie's money," Eddie said.

Mike dragged himself out of the car and walked tentatively toward Stevie, who, to Eddie, looked dead. Eddie watched as Mike pushed Stevie onto his side. Stevie moaned, opened his eyes for a second and then closed them.

Eddie nodded to himself. *Good. Not dead.*

Mike reached into Stevie's back pocket and dug out his wallet. He flipped it open and took out five crumpled hundreds and tossed the wallet to the ground near Stevie. He stood and handed Eddie the cash. Eddie snapped it from him as Mike stepped back.

Eddie moved in, leaning close. He flapped the hundreds in Mike's face.

"I'll be usin' this to fix the front window on my restaurant. You're lucky nobody was in there. And Stevie's damn lucky he's a shitty shot." He shook his finger at Mike. "Next time you see this mother-fuckin' O piece-a shit, you tell him that his plan didn't work. You can also tell him that you, and that fuckin' half-dead Stevie over there, work for *me* now. You got that?"

Mike's mouth opened and then shut. "I can't tell him that, man. He'll kill me."

Eddie laughed. "You're right, little Mike. He *will* kill you."

He and Marco headed back to the car just as Eddie heard sirens.

Mike yelled out to Eddie. "What am I supposed to do?"

Eddie turned and walked back to him.

"Quit your fuckin whinin', Mike. Get Stevie in the car and get outta' here. Now. Then, you and Stevie come-ta my restaurant tomorrow afternoon, ready to work. I want to know all the deals you got goin' and be ready to hit the streets."

Mike's voice lowered. "What about O?"

"Don't worry about it. O won't touch you."

Mike nodded, even though Eddie could see in the kid's eyes he didn't believe it.

Eddie jabbed his finger into Mike's chest. "You'se *better* be there tomorrow."

Marco yelled out to him. "We gotta' move, Eddie!"

Eddie grabbed Mike's cheeks with his fingers and thumb and squeezed them. Mike closed his eyes as he raised his chin.

"You know where it is, right? The place you just shot up?"

His eyes still closed, Mike nodded.

Eddie let go of his face and headed to Marco's Mustang.

"Five o'clock tomorrow afternoon." He pointed at Mike. "And if I don't see you both there, remember, I know where you live. And you and your mama don't want me comin' 'round to your house, now do you?"

Mike shook his head. "No, sir. I'll be there. *We'll* be there."

"Don't come in-ta my restaurant." He pointed past Mike. "The parkin' lot. Somebody'll come-ta you. Wait in your car." Eddie waved the .45 in Stevie's direction. "Now, get him in the car and get outta' here before the cops come."

Marco was already in the Mustang when Eddie got in. They drove off, leaving Mike to tend to Stevie.

In the car, Eddie turned to Marco. "You're some fuckin' driver, you know that? Nice work."

"Thanks," Marco said.

"Now, let's go see what kinda' damage those two pieces-a shit did to my restaurant."

When they arrived, Eddie was relieved to see it was just the window to the front door and not the large plate glass window. Still, it was the whole door.

Marco helped Eddie clean up the glass, tossing bigger pieces and sweeping the rest. They found a cardboard box, cut it up, and covered the door using masking tape—the only thing Eddie could find.

The two of them sat at one of the dining tables. Eddie let out a deep breath. "Jesus," he said. "What a fuckin' mess."

Marco nodded, as Eddie poured two snifters of brandy.

"Seriously though. That was some fine drivin' you just did, Marco."

They clinked their glasses and Marco smiled. "Thanks. Gotta' admit, the drivin' part was pretty fun."

They spent the next half-hour reliving the early morning's events. When the room went silent, Eddie pinched his nose and squeezed his eyes.

"I think I'll sleep here in this chair until morning. I can't leave the restaurant like this."

Marco nodded. "I can stay too, if you want."

Eddie waved a hand at him. "Na'. You go home-ta your family. I got this."

"You sure?"

"I'm sure. I'll get somebody over here first thing to get the glass fixed. Go home."

Marco stood to leave. "Alright. I'll check in with you in the morning when I drop Micola off. See if there's any runnin' around you need me to do."

Eddie raised his now empty glass. "Appreciate that."

Marco paused. "Say, Eddie. About tonight."

"Yeah?"

"I'm not sure I'm up for all-a this—"

Eddie waved him off. "I know. Sorry about that. Things got outta' hand. I gotta' little too rough with those punks."

He stood and reached into his pants pocket and pulled out a wad of cash.

"Here."

Marco waved him off. "No. Eddie. I'm not asking for—"

Eddie frowned. "I know. But take it. That was a lot tonight. I wanna' make it up-ta ya'."

Marco took the cash, as Eddie looked at his watch.

"Jesus. Kate must be wonderin' where you're at. Go home."

"Yeah, okay. Thanks. I'll see ya' in a few hours."

Eddie smiled as he took his seat again. "You drop Micola off and that's it. Take the rest-a the day off, ya' hear? I'll have Dario bring us home."

Marco nodded. "Sounds good. Thanks, Eddie."

Marco left and Eddie locked the broken door behind him, which made no sense, but he did it anyway. He returned to his chair and watched the morning light filter in through the front window.

He thought about O Jackson, as he put the .45 in his lap and closed his eyes.

It was time to take care of him.

Forty-seven

Kate heard the car pull into the driveway and looked at the clock. Marco shuffled into the bedroom a few minutes later.

"It's morning. Time for me to get up. What the hell, Marco?"

"Sorry, babe. I know. Things got crazy last night after I picked up Eddie."

"It was supposed to be a quick pick-up, and you'd be back before I knew it, remember?"

He nodded as he stripped, threw on some sweats and climbed in next to her.

The early morning sun slipped through the blinds like stripes running down his tired face. He closed his eyes, as Kate lifted her elbow. She looked down at him.

"You okay?"

He nodded and touched her bare arm.

"What was so crazy? What happened?"

Marco turned onto his side and looked into Kate's blue eyes.

"Don't freak out, okay?"

Her eyes widened and she sat up quickly.

"Okay, now I *am* freaking out."

"Let me tell you what happened, but just know that everything is fine. Everyone is fine. Okay?"

She frowned. "Okay. What happened?"

Marco told her the whole story about the drive-by shooting, his participation in a car chase and hostage situation, and holding a gun at one of the perpetrators.

"Oh my God, Marco. What the absolute hell?"

He sat up, too, smearing his hand down his face.

"I know, I know. It's fucked up. This isn't what I wanted. I was worried the whole time. Worried about the cops arresting me. Worried about you. Renzo. I kept thinking, this is not how we wanted to live." He shook his head. "And Eddie? I mean, you should've seen him, Kate. His rage was somethin' I haven't seen in a long time, or … maybe ever."

"This is bad, Marco. You have to stop working for him."

"I tried to tell him that that shit was more than I signed up for, Kate."

"What did he say?"

Marco frowned and crawled out of bed. He grabbed his jeans from the chair and dug into the back pocket. He threw the wad of cash onto the bed next to Kate.

"He apologized and gave me this." He pointed at the money. "Said it won't happen again. He wouldn't even listen to me."

Kate picked up the bills and counted them.

When she finished, they both looked at each other, bug-eyed.

"Three thousand?" Kate whispered.

"Jesus," Marco said.

"Where is he getting all of this money, Marco? Do you know?"

He started to pace. "Well, I know the restaurant's doing pretty good."

"Oh, come on, Marco. Don't patronize me. This is drug money, isn't it? Drug money—sitting right here—on our bed!"

He nodded. "Yeah. I'm pretty sure it is. He's got that, and a bunch of other stuff with the two kids, and now this Sal guy—his cousin—he's in the picture, too. They've really moved fast on infiltrating the neighborhood."

"I'm getting scared, Marco. Between this cash and what happened tonight, it's what we've been afraid of, isn't it?"

He nodded. "It is."

They stared at the cash.

"I think it's time I get out, Kate."

She nodded. "I think so, too."

"But I'm worried that I know too much."

Kate sucked in a breath. "God."

Marco sat next to her. "Let's just think about this—about how to handle it, okay?"

She nodded. "You're right. We have to do this right. We need a plan."

Forty-eight

Eddie stayed at the restaurant into the next morning waiting for the window repairman. He wanted no evidence of the incident when Micola arrived around eleven. He swept up the rest of the broken glass and sent the repairman on his way fifteen minutes before she arrived.

Unfortunately, the jig was up when a cop arrived asking about the shooting. Micola came running when she saw the tall, Black officer at the front door talking to Eddie.

"Can I help you officer?" Eddie asked.

"Morning, sir. We received a report of a shooting in the area early this morning, followed by a lot of screeching tires." He turned in the direction of the newly repaired window on the door. "Just saw the window repairman leave. Thought I'd check that out."

Micola bustled toward Eddie and the cop. "What is this, Eddie?" she asked nervously.

Eddie shook his head at her before addressing the cop.

"Officer," he said. "I don't know nothin' about no shootin', but I came in this morning to find my front window shattered to pieces."

"Were you planning to file a police report, sir?"

"Ah', no. I wasn't plannin' on filin' nothin'." Eddie smiled at him. "Look, officer. To be honest with ya', I don't wanna' know what happened to that window, right? I don't need bad press about the restaurant. We're just gettin' started here. Business is good. Pickin' up. People find out somebody shot up the place—we're done. Understand what I'm sayin'?"

The cop nodded. "Sir, I understand, but we can't let random drive-by shootings go unreported, if that's what this is."

"But we don't know, do we?" He turned in a half-circle. "Look. No bullets or nothin'."

The cop smiled and looked at Micola for a second. "Have you checked your security footage?"

"Well, ah', no. But I will."

He started walking toward the door and the cop followed.

"Thank you for stoppin' by officer. I appreciate your concern. And hey, I'll be sure and check that footage and get back to you. You gotta' card or somethin'?"

The cop nodded as he reached for his wallet and pulled out his business card. "Call me any time and leave a message. I'll get back to you as soon as I can."

Eddie shook his hand. "Thank you. You stay safe out there, ya' hear?"

"Thank you. Have a nice day."

"Yeah, thanks. You too."

When the officer left, Micola started spewing out broken English and Italian. It took Eddie several minutes to convince her there was nothing to be concerned about. He told her it was probably some kids vandalizing. He reminded her it was to be expected in that neighborhood, and she finally agreed. He took her back to the kitchen and suggested she forget all about it.

Once Micola was back to work, Eddie went to the office to make some calls and then handled the lunch rush. When he returned to the office, he picked up the burner and dialed Tau. A meeting was set for four o'clock that afternoon. Dario was to come, too.

The boys arrived promptly. The three of them discussed various matters for a half-hour. They were standing to leave when Eddie stopped them.

"Oh, I almost forgot. One more thing." Eddie raised his hand and pointed. "Dario, there should be two kids across the street in the parkin' lot waitin' for you. That'd be Stevie and Mikey. I told them five o'clock. You'll know 'em by the fuckin' bruises all over their faces."

Dario frowned. "What do they want?"

"They work for me now, so you're in charge-a them. You wanted to be boss? You can boss the two-a them around. Have 'em start doin' some-a this shit we've been talkin' about."

A huge grin spread across Dario's face. "Boss, huh?" He nodded and started pacing the room. His pitch rising. "I'm the boss-a them?"

Eddie grinned. "Yeah."

Dario clapped, as he bent forward and laughed.

"Hot-damn! I'm the boss." He gave the stink-eye to Tau. "That's right, Tau. You the boss-a somebody? No. You ain't."

"Alright, alright. Don't get cocky, Dario. It's just a matter-a time, and Tau will have some flunkies he's in charge of, too."

"What should I do with these fools?" Dario asked, laughing.

Eddie leaned forward and pointed his pen at Dario. "First, I want them to take care-a whoever is messin' with your mom's beauty salon. She came in the other day. Told me somebody's been vandalizin' it. They keep comin' back and breakin' windows and shit. Get them workin' on that. Figure out who's doin' it and get them to stop."

Dario's eyes bugged out, as he put his hand on his chest. "Wait. What? *My* mom? Vandalized? What cha' talkin' 'bout Eddie?"

"You're a shitty son, do you know that? You don't know nothin' about this?" He shook his head in disgust. "She asked me for help, so it makes sense that *you* should be the one handlin' it. She's *your* mom." He flicked his hand to dismiss them. "Make sure this gets taken care of. Tonight."

Dario frowned and shook his head, as he and Tau turned to leave. From the hallway, they heard Eddie shouting after them.

"I don't want *none-a* these punks in my restaurant. You hear?"

Dario peered back into the office. "Got it. I'll handle this, Eddie."

"Good. Now, shut the door!"

Forty-nine

Eddie stayed in his car after dropping off Micola, telling her he had to make a couple of stops. The street outside her house was quiet and dark. He pulled the burner out of his pocket and dialed Primo.

The old man was slow to answer. "Yeah?"

"Yeah," Eddie said.

"How's it goin' out there?"

"Good. I could use some help, though."

"With what?"

"A little clean-up. Not a big deal. You got anybody close by?"

There was a pause before Primo spoke. "Gotta' couple guys in Milwaukee. Could be there in what? Six hours?"

Eddie frowned. It'd be daylight by then. "How about tomorrow night? Eleven or eleven thirty? Tell 'em to meet me near the river, just outside-a downtown St. Paul. Give-em this number. I'll tell 'em where I'll be."

"Done."

Eddie heard the phone click. He looked at his watch. Just after eleven. He dialed again.

"Yeah?"

"Sal. I need a favor."

"Sure, Eddie. Now?"

"Yeah. Now. Meet me at Desoto and Beaumont. Stay a couple-a blocks north of Beaumont. You gotta' piece?"

"No. But I could get one. Might need a little time. Couple hours, maybe."

"Okay. Need-a silencer, too."

Eddie hung up and waited in the car for ten minutes before heading back to O's garage. A little surveillance never hurt.

He pulled into a spot along the curb near where he'd parked during his first visit with O. The neighborhood was quiet and he chose a spot away from the illuminating street lights.

He kept an eye on the back parking lot of the garage. All seemed quiet, so Eddie rolled down the window and shut off the engine. The cool air slapped him awake and generated the energy he'd need for the task at hand. He'd feel better once this was handled.

A little over an hour later, headlights shone in his rearview mirror just as the phone rang.

"Yeah. I'm here. Where-you at?"

Eddie flicked his lights on and off one time.

"Gotcha'," Sal said.

Eddie watched the car behind him slip into a spot along the curb, five cars back.

"What now?" Sal asked.

"We wait. I'm watching that parking lot. Lookin' for a tall, bald guy. He'll come outta' the door under the light."

"Is he in there?"

"Not sure. This could be a while."

"Ten-four."

Sal hung up. The occupied cars sat in darkness for the next two hours. Finally, the back door to the garage opened.

Eddie dialed Sal.

"We got action."

"I see it. That him?"

"No."

Eddie watched as the heavy-set guy from before, waved to someone inside the garage, and strolled down the street to an awaiting car. The car stayed parked for five minutes before driving away.

Eddie and Sal's wait continued.

Fifteen minutes later, two more men left the garage. This time, O was one of them. Eddie saw his hand had been wrapped with a bandage. He dialed Sal again.

"That the bald guy?" Sal asked.

"That's him," Eddie said. "With the bandaged hand."

"What's the plan?"

"I'd like to take him there. No cameras."

"What about the other guy?"

"Naw. We're leaving him alone. For now."

"How do you know they won't leave together?"

"I *don't* know."

Eddie hung up. He watched as the two talked excitedly about something. Then the second guy, Dax, walked around to the driver's side of a car and O came to the passenger side and got in.

"Shit."

He dialed Sal.

"What-d-ya wanna' do boss?"

"Follow 'em," Eddie said.

"Ten-four."

They hung up and, one at a time, pulled out, staying well behind the dark car as it traveled through the sleeping neighborhood. It turned right onto Payne, and Eddie and Sal followed. They passed Fortunato's before turning left onto Seventh, and then a quick right onto Mounds Park Boulevard, which led them to the I-94 ramp going westbound.

Eddie smacked the steering wheel. "Dammit."

They followed the car, each of them mixing in with the sparse early-morning traffic, as they traveled along the freeway toward Minneapolis. Eddie cursed himself for letting O get this far. It should have been taken care of right outside the garage.

The car took the Snelling Avenue exit and turned right.

Hmm. Not Minneapolis. Staying in St. Paul.

The car passed University Avenue and turned right onto Charles Avenue. Sal turned first, then Eddie. Eddie continued past them, as the car pulled over to the curb a few houses down from the corner. He watched Sal's car in his rearview mirror take a right on Albert.

"Shit. Where's he goin'?" Eddie pulled over and dialed Sal.

"I got him," Sal said. "They're parked on Charles. I'm turnin' around."

"Meet me there."

Eddie saw Sal again appear in his review mirror. He had rounded the block and pulled up on the right, several cars back, headlights off. Eddie turned and headed around the block.

Sal pulled his car over to the curb. Tail lights from the sedan glowed red several houses up the street. Eddie had pulled in a few cars behind Sal's, just as O exited the passenger's side of the car. He leaned back in to talk to the driver. Eddie inched down his window hoping to hear what they were saying.

He watched as Sal silently slipped out of his car. He was still quick for his age. He dodged low around parked cars and then hid behind a tree near O and the car. Eddie quietly exited his vehicle and ran to Sal's. He got in, ready to move. Sal waited, motionless behind the tree, shrouded in darkness, as he took aim with his gun.

The car took off, and Eddie watched as O turned. He headed toward a set of stairs leading to an old brick apartment building, muffled rap music thumping loudly from inside. The front entrance was dimly lit with one aging bulb.

Eddie put Sal's car into drive and pulled out slowly. He moved closer to Sal's position, lingering along the line of cars parked on either side of the narrow residential street.

Tension burned in his neck, as he watched Sal pull something from his back pocket and run like a quiet cat behind O, who turned at the sound of Sal's footsteps. Sal dropped the gun to the ground and quickly pulled his hands from behind and over the head of O. He yanked the item around O's thick neck, as he slammed him to the ground.

"Shit!"

Eddie quickly put Sal's car into park in the middle of the street, engine still running, as he ran to assist with whatever the fuck Sal was doing.

The item Sal had pulled from his pocket was a plastic bag, and he now held it tightly over O's head. Eddie leaned in to help hold down O as Sal squeezed the bag tight around O's neck.

"We gotta move!" Eddie whispered, pushing O's fighting arms to the ground.

O moaned and gurgled loudly, as he kicked and punched for air, sometimes making contact with Sal's face, but Sal never flinched. O's heavy and panicked air-sucking caused the bag to pull deep into the crevices of his face, displaying his horrified and twisted expression. He flailed and snorted and desperately tried to scream, as he ferociously fought to break loose.

Eddie moved fast, grabbing Sal's gun from the ground and smashing it onto O's skull. His body fell still. Eddie and Sal then worked furiously, as they dragged the heavy, dead weight across the grassless boulevard and into the street. They struggled to heave him up and into the trunk of Sal's car, but finally succeeded.

Sal lowered the trunk until it was nearly closed and then took the gun from Eddie. Peering through the slight opening of the trunk, he popped two bullets into O's temple, the silencer doing its job with quick, thumping bursts. Sal slammed the trunk shut and looked up at Eddie, smiling at him in the darkness.

"That plastic bag worked good," Sal said, breathlessly. He wiped his hands on his jeans. "Better than blood spillin' all over the sidewalk." He pointed at the trunk. "Gotta tarp in there. Glad you knew to move my car and not yours."

Eddie ran his hand through his hair, as he smiled at Sal. He patted him on the back. "Nice work, Sal. Good thinkin'. For an old man, you're still pretty fast, you know that?" He pinched Sal's cheeks.

Sal chuckled. "Yeah. How 'bout that?"

"Gotta' crew comin' in tomorrow night," Eddie said. "I'll have 'em call you. Leave the car in your garage 'til then."

Sal nodded. "Alright. I'll take care-a everything. Go home."

"Let's get outta' here. I'll talk to you'se tomorrow."

"Yeah. Tomorrow."

Sal drove off with O's dead body in the trunk. Eddie took a quick scan of the neighborhood before getting into Micola's car. He drove back to her house, and slipped quietly up to his room.

The clean-up crew would arrive tomorrow night and that would be the end of O Jackson.

Fifty

Several days after Primo's crew met up with Sal to clean up the O Jackson mess, Eddie joined Dario and Tau at the back table of Fortunato's. His mood had lightened considerably once that had been taken care of. He felt relaxed. Normally, he'd conduct this business down in the office, but he hadn't eaten and ordered the special—grilled halibut with an asiago cream sauce.

The lunch crowd had dissipated, leaving only the lingering scent of garlic and fish. It was just the three of them in the restaurant. One bartender manned the whole place while Micola busied herself with Eddie's lunch order before preparing for the dinner rush. Eddie could hear her humming in the kitchen.

He sat down and slapped his hands on the table. "Okay. Wha-d-ya got for me? What's this big news you're talkin' about?"

Tau looked at Dario, who was leaning in, looking excited. "Alright, man," Dario said, "I found out from my boy, B.B. Stylz, that—"

Eddie raised a hand and tilted his head to the side. "B.B. who?"

"Stylz. B.B. Stylz."

"That's the guy's name?"

"Yeah. Why? What's wrong with that?"

He flicked his hand at Dario. "Nothin. Go on."

Dario smiled. "Anyway, B.B. Stylz said, word on the street is," Dario paused, looking around before leaning in and whispering, "O Jackson's missin'."

He sat back, eyes bulging, head nodding ever-so-slightly as a smile crept across his face. "Found that out from a friend-a his. Had to pay him fifty bucks for the info."

Eddie didn't flinch, but nodded in feigned surprise, as he continued digging into his food with his fork.

"Missin', huh? They sayin' anything else?"

Dario shrugged. "Just that. Nobody seen him in like—days. His dudes in the garage be straight-up trippin'."

"Why's that? He could be outta' town or somethin'."

Dario looked at Tau. "Tell him."

Eddie wiped his mouth. "Tell me what?"

Tau started talking fast. "I hear that Dax, O's partner at the garage, is real worried cuz there's a load of—" he made some air quotes, "'supplies' down in Arizona that's got to be picked up. And he's nervous about makin' decisions without O's approval. He's freakin' out. Doesn't know what to do."

Dario leaned in and whispered. "And I heard that somebody dropped off a load of meth at O's daddy's garage. They wanted their cash. When they found out O's been missin', they left. Said they'd be back. Took the meth with 'em."

Dario and Tau sat quietly, waiting for Eddie's reply.

Eddie took a bite of the halibut. "So, what kinda' supplies we talkin' about down in Arizona? Is that meth, too?"

Dario nodded. "Yep. Lil' Red, O's cousin, said they wanna' talk to you. Heard about you from people in the neighborhood. They heard you could handle big shit like this."

Eddie hid his excitement and answered calmly.

"That right?"

"Yup. Said they want you to take over. Handle them-Mexicans."

"How much meth we talkin' about? In Arizona, I mean?"

Tau shook his head. "I don't know. But he called it a 'load,' so I'm guessing maybe a carload or somethin'. Truck maybe?"

Eddie looked across at Micola, now loading cold cuts into the deli-case. He knew she couldn't hear them.

"Go on."

"I'm thinking," Tau said, "that me and Dario could make the run to Arizona. Bring the load back."

Eddie set down his fork and leaned back against his chair. After thinking about it for a minute, he shook his head. "Mules? No."

Dario and Tau's faces fell.

"What? Why not?" Dario asked. "Man, I thought you'd be interested. That's good money."

"I hear you can get twenty G's doin' that. For one load," Tau said.

"Too risky," Eddie said. "I don't want the heat. We're doin' good with what we got. We're makin' money." He shook his head as he chewed. "We work O's garage and those supplies. That's enough. Keep things in the neighborhood. If we start thinkin' too big, gettin' in too deep, we draw attention to ourselves." He shook his head and waved his fork at them. "Fa-get it."

Tau nodded. "You're probably right, Eddie. Driving across state lines with illegal drugs means big prison sentences if you get caught."

"But there's millions to be made, man," Dario said, frowning.

"I don't care about that. Listen, when you start gettin' greedy, things go south. Trust me. Here's what I want you'se two to do. I want you to go back to that garage—"

Dario raised his brows. "Say what now?"

Eddie frowned. "O's missin', remember? That guy, Dax? He's a chicken-shit."

"But he's a big and beefy chicken-shit," Dario said.

"There's nothin' to worry about," Eddie said. "You'se two are professionals now. Besides, it sounds like O's business is all fucked up without him. Dax? He doesn't know what to do. O was the leader. *He* ran the ship. Now, he's gone. Maybe he shows up, maybe he doesn't."

Eddie paused to let that sink in.

Dario's face lit up. "You know somethin', don't you?"

Eddie's expression darkened as he pointed his fork at Dario.

"Keep your big mouth shut Dario, understand me?"

Dario exchanged a glance with Tau.

"Sorry Mr. B." He made the "zip-your-lips" gesture.

"All I'm sayin' is, Dax is no leader. So, I want you'se two to go down to that garage and tell him that you'll start overseein' things. But tell Dax that he's the front man. We want Magic Man to see a familiar face. Tell him to take the product and pay Magic Man."

Eddie returned to his lunch.

Tau nodded at Dario. "We got this."

"Alright. Let's take this one step at a time. If O comes back, I'll go talk to him again."

Dario smiled. "You want me to get B.B. Stylz to—"

Eddie shook his head. "Too many people gettin' involved, Dario. Let's just take it slow. Keep it quiet. Got it?"

The boys nodded.

Eddie pushed his plate aside and straightened up, leaning back in his chair. Knowing full well that O was never coming back, he pointed a finger at Dario and Tau.

"I can tell you both right now, once I take this shit over, that's it. The business is mine. I don't care what O says when he comes back. So you tell Lil' Red — or whatever the fuck his name is — that you'll be down tomorrow morning to talk about it. When you go down there, tell-em you work fa-me and you're my representatives. All communications go through you from now on. Take Sal with you. He's good for scarin' the shit outta' people."

The boys looked eagerly at Eddie, drinking in all of his advice. It gave Eddie a strong sense of pride. "This is your chance," he told them. "You handle this, and you'll both have cash comin' outta' your asses."

Dario nodded. "Alright. Yeah. We got this, Eddie."

He stood and started circling the table, pacing. "So, Eddie? You got both my pieces, man. Can I get one back? I can't be walkin' into O's place actin' like I'm in charge without protection, man. I—"

Eddie pointed his finger and stood. "Hold that thought."

He left the table and disappeared. When he returned, he slipped Dario's .38 snub-nose into Dario's hand.

"Take it. I don't need it."

Dario's eyes popped, as he put the gun into the back of his waistband.

"You don't need it? Man, I've been doin' all this work, *all this time* without protection? Why'd you take *both* my pieces, and Tau got to keep his daddy's, huh?"

Eddie shrugged. "I forgot."

Dario fell sideways a bit and let out a gasp. "You forgot?" He shook his head, "Man I—"

Eddie put up his hand to hide his amusement. "You got the fuckin' gun, alright? Now shut up about it."

Dario nodded and sat back at the table. "Alright. Thank you."

Eddie turned to Tau. "Tau, see what else you can find out. See what else O's got goin' on."

Tau spoke up. "Lil' Red said O's been sellin' a lot of drugs and hot property on his own, too. Said he has a lot of his own customers—in addition to Magic Man's business."

Eddie tapped his fingers on the table. "That's what I'm lookin' for. Good. Go talk to Lil' Red and get the details. Word on the street passes along pretty fast. O's customers will find you."

Tau and Dario nodded.

"Get some new burners for this shit too," Eddie said.

"Got it," Dario said.

Eddie waved them off. "Get outta' here. I got work to do. You do too. Good luck with Dax." He slapped his hands on the table. "Keep up the good work. I'm proud-a you boys."

They stood to shake Eddie's hand, chuckling and smiling at the compliment.

"I wanna' hear from you'se two about this tomorrow."

Eddie grinned like a proud father, as he watched Tau and Dario walk out of the restaurant.

Fifty-one

Weeks flew by, and the cool fall weather made its timely, yet unwelcome, appearance. Dropping temperatures and early sunsets meant shorter days and swift night falls. The occasional snowflakes began to arrive as well, drifting and swirling about before landing on the cooling ground.

Kate shivered in the uncomfortable lawn chair as she tugged at her furry hood, bringing it down around her ears. Marco sat next to her, both bundled in winter coats, watching Renzo run around the soccer field, parents shouting and whistles blowing. The colder the weather, the longer the games seemed to last. She was thankful the season was nearing its end.

"You seem quiet," she said to Marco.

He gave her a frozen-faced smile. "I'm alright. It's just—ya' know … work. Micola's fine. That part of the job is a breeze. She's sweet and appreciative. But Eddie's really gettin' into some heavy shit. I think it might be time to pull the plug, Kate. Put our plan into action."

Kate held her breath for a second. She knew this was coming, but the whole thing scared her. It scared them both. They didn't want to get on Eddie's bad side, plus, the money was so good.

"What's going on? Did something happen?"

He shook his head, still watching Renzo and the game in front of him. "I'm not positive, but those boys—Dario and Tau—he's meeting with them a lot. Sometimes he drives himself, taking them with. Tells me he doesn't need me. That's when I know they're going somewhere off the books. And when I do drive him around, I keep hearing him talk about some guy named 'O'."

Kate frowned. "'O'?"

"O Jackson." Marco pressed on his forehead with his gloved hand. "I don't know. I'm not sure what that's all about except the guy is missing and Eddie seems to know what happened."

"Why do you say that?"

He shrugged. "Just a hunch. His mannerisms when they talk about it. I'm pickin' up on somethin'. And it's not good."

"Do you think he did something to this 'O' person?"

He turned to look at her. "I do, Kate. I do."

"Oh my God, Marco. Do you think he—"

A voice interrupted them from behind. "Hey. I thought I'd find you'se two here."

They turned to see Eddie strolling toward them wearing a long, black wool coat and a black brimmed hat.

They stood to greet him.

"Eddie, hi," Kate said, putting on her best fake smile.

"Hey Eddie," Marco said. "We were just talkin' about you."

Eddie smiled as he leaned in to kiss Kate on the cheek. "Nothin' bad, I hope." He chuckled at his own joke. "Kate, you're looking lovely, as usual."

She tugged her furry hood. "Thanks."

"No, nothin' bad at all," said Marco. "I was just tellin' Kate it's been slow. Haven't really driven you around much the past couple weeks."

"Yeah," Eddie said, "but don't think nothin' about that. It's just that, if Dario's sittin' out front and it's easier to pop into his car, I'll do it, right?"

"No, I get it. It's just, I hate to take your money, Eddie, ya' know, for nothin'."

Kate could see Marco trying to finesse a way out.

Eddie frowned. "No. I need you. I do. Micola needs you. Honestly, I don't know what I'd do if I had to tote her around all the places she needs to go in a day, am I right?" He laughed.

Kate and Marco laughed with him, as they stood and watched the game for a few minutes.

"Damn, it's cold," Eddie said. "I don't know how you'se two sit here like this—in this weather. Nothin' like the last time I watched the game. Beautiful fall day that was, 'eh? I really enjoyed that, by the way. Thanks for invitin' me. Makes me feel like I have a home. A family. Between you and Micola, it feels real good, ya' know?"

"That's so sweet," Kate said. There was an awkward pause, before she continued. "So, what brings you by?"

"Well, I saw the game and hoped it was Renzo's team. Then, I saw you'se two. I really wanted to talk to you, Kate."

"Oh? What about?"

"I gotta' a friend. Marco, you know him—Sal?"

Marco nodded.

"He's my cousin, actually. He lives with his mother—my Aunt Rita. She's no sweet pea if you know what I'm sayin'." He let out another quick laugh at himself, and Marco and Kate politely joined him.

"Anyways, he's makin' money now—" he pointed at Marco— "like you. And he ah' ... he wants to get his own place. Maybe a nice condo he could buy. Doesn't have to be right in the neighba-hood. Just somewhere ... a bit nearby. Maybe even downtown. Thought maybe you could help him find somethin'. Wha-d-ya say?"

"Sure. I can do that. No problem. I'll start looking tomorrow. Have him give me a call, so I can find out what he likes and what he's looking for. Thanks for the referral." She faked another winning smile.

"No, Kate," he pointed at her. "Thank *you*. I appreciate it. Sal too." Eddie gave them a quick wave. "I gotta' get goin'. Marco? See you'se tonight around seven? Gotta' few runs to make."

"Sure, Eddie. See ya' then."

He waved and they waved back. Marco and Kate watched him leave, his long, black coat swaying, as he walked through the bumpy grass of the soccer field in his expensive dress shoes. He got into Micola's car in the parking lot and drove away.

They sat back in their lawn chairs in silence for a couple of minutes.

"God," Kate said. "How does he do that? Did you see what he just did?"

"Yep," Marco said. "He's a smooth-talker."

"Smooth, fast, and charming. It's like you don't know what hit you."

"I know."

"We were just talkin' about how dangerous he is, and how we have to get out, and then he comes along and we're sucked right back in. Me included." She shook her head in awe of Eddie and in disgust with themselves.

"You know what also sucks?" Kate asked.

"What?"

"I have to deal with Sal, now."

She laughed quietly and looked over at Marco, who was shaking his head, his mouth twisted down.

"Just because we're both still in his grip, doesn't mean we can't keep planning our exit strategy, Kate."

"Yeah?"

He reached for her hand. "Yeah. And we're gonna' do it. Soon."

Kate nodded and gave him a weak smile.

A whistle blew and the soccer game ended.

Winter

Fifty-two

As the holidays approached, shoppers came out in full force bringing increased business to Fortunato's. Eddie loved walking the floor, and schmoozing with customers, sending over rounds of drinks or complimentary appetizers. Word had spread that the owner was a charming force. Eddie loved the attention and his ego gushed.

He especially enjoyed Saturday nights. This particular Saturday night was no exception. Fortunato's was bustling. He checked on customers, chatting with those he knew, and getting to know those he didn't. He felt like the king he'd always known he'd become. He loved to see people waiting for tables, and he especially loved the attention—people calling out his name, pushing past others to shake his hand and introduce their families. Eddie never disappointed. He was charming, funny, and affectionate. The staff loved him, Micola loved him, and he loved his new life.

There was just one person who would make it all perfect.

Kate.

He looked at her from across the restaurant. She and Marco were having dinner. He'd sat down with them for a few minutes, drinking in her perfume and beauty. More and more, he'd found himself wanting to be near her. He wanted to share his happiness with her. He dreamed of it. He imagined Marco gone. Out of the picture. Kate coming to him. Being with him forever.

Eddie tried to shake Kate from his mind and refocus on the evening. From the size of the crowd, it appeared to be the restaurant's best night yet. Things were running smoothly, and laughter and chatter filled the room, drowning out the piped-in Italian music.

After a couple of hours, Eddie took a break from his charismatic banter to get a drink at the bar—his usual scotch rocks. He took a sip as he scanned the dining room, smiling and laughing with staff and patrons, all while eying Kate and Marco.

With empty dessert plates in front of them, he watched, as they spoke intimately to one another. He imagined it was him at the table, Kate slipping her fingers across *his* hand, instead of Marco's, as she looked deeply into his eyes.

A dark figure appeared at the restaurant's main entrance and pulled Eddie from his thoughts. He waited and watched, holding his drink near his lips but not sipping. The tall, thin Black man wore an impeccable gray suit, his short black hair neatly and stylishly trimmed. He stood in the lobby for a moment, scanning the place, as Eddie watched from the bar at the back of the room. The man leaned in to ask the hostess something, causing her to look around and then point at Eddie.

Shit. Who was this, now?

The man nodded and smiled at her before making his way through the crowded restaurant, heading for Eddie in the back. He caught Eddie looking at him and nodded.

When he reached Eddie, he put out his hand, and Eddie shook it.

"Mr. Bracchio?" he said, through the noise of the crowd.

"Who wants-ta know?" Eddie shouted back.

"Detective Matthew Lance." He handed Eddie his card. "I'm here to discuss ..." He paused and looked around the busy restaurant, as he leaned in to whisper. "Other business."

Detective?

Eddie looked at his card. "What other business?"

"Can we go somewhere private to talk?"

Eddie hesitated. "Yeah, sure. My office." He put out his hand. "This way."

Once seated in the quiet office, Eddie asked, "So. What's this business you're talkin' about?"

Detective Lance's manner was sophisticated. He was very well-spoken. Professional. "I'm not sure if you've heard, but there's a man from the neighborhood who's missing. A Mr. O Jackson. Seems Mr. Jackson has disappeared, and his family is very concerned that something may have happened to him."

Eddie shrugged his shoulder and leaned back in his chair, trying to appear casual. "Never heard-a him. Too bad, though. What's that got-ta do with me?"

"Word on the street, is that you may have had some interaction with Mr. Jackson."

Eddie laughed out loud. "Word on the street, 'eh?" He shook his head. "Who's sayin' that?"

The detective paused for a second. "Mr. Jackson's girlfriend, Ms. Tanya Steele. She claims he had a physical encounter with a man fitting your description."

"My description? Meaning ... ?"

"Meaning: middle-aged, well-dressed Italian man, new to town."

Eddie smiled and nodded. "Are you ... profiling me detective?"

Detective Lance laughed. "You must admit, you fit the description."

Eddie blew on his pinkie ring and buffed it on his dress shirt before giving the detective a disinterested gaze. "Look, Detective. I don't know nothin' about this ah'—this Mr. Jackson—or his whereabouts." He gave the detective a nonchalant raise of his brow. "Don't know nothin' about this woman, neither. For all you know, somebody told her to point the finger at me. This is ridiculous. I'm a businessman. I got a legitimate and successful restaurant here. And I don't appreciate the implication, Detective Lance, that I had somethin' to do with this guy's disappearance. Maybe—" he pointed his finger at him—"you should ask some-a his associates. I'm gonna' guess this ah'—Mr. Jackson—has some friends or even relatives you could talk to. There might be a gold mine of suspects for you. I'm just sayin' ... Maybe one-a them knows somethin'."

"I have every intention of doing just that, Mr. Bracchio. I'm covering all my bases. You understand." He shrugged his shoulder. "There's a process."

"Yeah, sure." Eddie leaned his elbows on the desk. "So, what? You think this guy's dead or somethin'?" He tipped his head to the side. "Or maybe he skipped town? What are ya' thinkin'?"

The detective shook his head. "Too early to tell. Anything's possible."

Eddie stood, indicating the meeting was over.

"Well 'ah, thanks for stoppin' by. I'd better get back upstairs."

"Of course."

Detective Lance stood too, giving his shoulders a barely-noticeable shrug to adjust his suit. He smiled and nodded.

"We'll be in touch, Mr. Bracchio. I'll see my way out."

Eddie said nothing in response and they did not shake hands.

The detective turned and left the office, quietly shutting the door behind him.

Eddie returned to his drink at the bar, an air of foreboding lingering over his mood.

Fifty-three

Several days later, Eddie was busying himself with vendor orders, when a heavy rap on his office door interrupted his train of thought.

"Yeah. Get in here."

Tau and Dario strolled in, arguing about something Eddie had no time for.

"Will you'se two shut the fuck up for once in your lives? Jesus. You're like a couple-a old ladies."

"Sorry, Eddie," Tau said.

"Yeah, sorry, Mr. B.," said Dario. He opened his mouth to explain their argument, but Eddie put up his hand.

"What'd I say, 'eh? What part of 'shut-the-fuck-up' don't you understand?"

Dario closed his mouth, as the two boys sat in the chairs in front of Eddie's desk. He noticed their dress shirts and dress pants and smiled to himself at their transformations.

Sal announced his presence with a quick knock on the door before lumbering in.

"Hey."

"Sal, come on in, cuz. Dario–"

Eddie shot his thumb in the air.

"Up."

Dario frowned but gave his chair to Sal.

Eddie leaned back in his chair. "That's for all that arguin'. You need to learn to shut your hole."

Dario opened his mouth to argue but quickly closed it.

"So?" Eddie said. "What'd'ya got?"

Dario leaned against the wall beside the desk. "Man. Cops came back to the garage today. Two detectives."

Eddie raised his brows. "Oh yeah? What'd they want?"

"O's *still* missin," Dario said. "Nobody's seen him—goin' on weeks now. I think he's dead if I'm being honest."

Eddie gave Dario a harsh stare.

Dario's eyes popped. "What?"

Eddie shook his head. "The way you talk sometimes. Too much. You need-ta learn-ta keep your mouth shut. Stay outta' shit that's none-a your business because people will start to think it *is* your business. *Capisci?*"

Dario hung his head, nodding.

"Now, what happened with the cops?"

Dario shrugged. "Dax said there were two of 'em. One white guy, one Black guy, both in suits. They stopped by to talk to O's daddy for a while. Dax told me he talked to the cops, too."

"Did he mention our visit?"

Dario shook his head. "Naw. Dax said he and Jones-ie'd never say nothin' about that."

Eddie frowned. "Jones-ie?"

"The big dude. Remember? Wears his clothes like a sack-a shit?"

Eddie nodded. "That guy. Right." He flipped casually through some papers. "So nobody's talkin' about me bein' there? About the screwdriver thing?"

"Nope. They're too scared-a you."

"Good. Did Dax say what the cops were askin' about?"

"Just asked when the last time he saw O—stuff like that. I guess his girlfriend and parents are freakin' out because he's been gone so long. They're thinkin' the worst. And the girlfriend—her name is Tanya Steele—she's mad at O's daddy cuz' he's actin' like he don't care. She's stirrin' up some trouble."

Eddie nodded. "Okay, well forget about all that. What else? Tau?"

Tau handed him a package of cash.

"How much?" Eddie asked.

"Five K," Tau said. "Same as last time."

Eddie turned to Dario. "Where's yours?"

Dario hooked his lip and rubbed his head. "Had some issues with collection. I'm gettin' it tonight though. I'll run it over."

Eddie scowled and jammed his finger onto the desk. "I want that tonight, Dario."

"I'll bring it. I promise."

"And? Are Mike and Stevie still workin' the meth over on Phalen?"

Dario nodded rapidly. "For that kinda' money? They're workin' hard. Doin' a great job."

Eddie nodded. "Good. Now, for the good stuff." He leaned down and reached into the lowest drawer of his beat-up desk and pulled out three packages wrapped in brown paper. He tossed them out to Dario, Tau, and Sal.

"Your cuts."

Dario's eyes lit up as he put his fist to his mouth. "No way, man. Are you for real?"

Tau shook his head. "Is this what I think it is?"

Eddie grinned. "That's right gentlemen. Merry Christmas." He looked over at Sal who was trying not to smile.

"How much, Eddie?" Tau asked.

"Ten K each."

Tau jumped out of his seat and he and Dario did a celebratory dance around the room.

"Oh my God! Eddie, I can't believe this. Thank you!" Tau shouted.

"Holy shit!" Dario screamed. "I ain't never had this much money before in my life."

Sal hooked a smile as he glanced over at Eddie.

"Thanks, man."

"Hey, Tau," Eddie laughed. "I don't think I've ever seen this side-a you before. I kinda' like it."

The room roared with laughter.

"Couldn't-a done it without all your hard work. This is only the beginning," Eddie said. "There'll be more from that last load, so you guys are gonna' be swimmin' in fuckin' cash in a matter-a weeks."

"Man, I'm already swimmin' in it," Dario said, kissing his package of cash.

"Alright. Enough celebratin'. Go on, now. Get back to work."

Dario and Tau turned to leave.

"Hey," Eddie called out. "One more thing, Dario."

"Yeah?"

"What's the update on your mom's shop?"

"Oh, real good, Eddie. It's been quiet. My mom said ever since Mike and Stevie did their thing, she's had no trouble. Still pretty early though. They're keepin' an eye on the place. I'll let you know if anything happens."

"Good."

Dario nodded. "My mom said the guy who owns the laundromat next to her wants to talk to you about helpin' him, too. Said he'd pay a monthly fee if it's somethin' he could afford."

Eddie clapped his hands. "Alright. Good. Go talk to that guy. Make an arrangement. You can keep the money."

"Wait, what? All of it?"

Eddie shrugged. "I told you, if you did good work, you'd be rewarded. This is the start-a that. Keep hustlin' and usin' Mike and Stevie to clean things up, and you can keep all-a that cash." He pointed at him. "Pay those boys right though, ya' here? You need them to make this work."

Dario nodded as he hid his smile behind his fist. "Thank you, Eddie. Thank you for trustin' me." His eyes popped as he looked over at Tau.

"Congratulations, Dario," Tau said.

"Same goes for you, Tau." Eddie said. "You're doin' good work with the cigarettes. But—" He held up his finger. "I want sixty percent-a that. I still gotta' do a lot of overseein' of that shit. For now. That may change down the road, alright?"

Tau smiled. "Sounds great, Eddie. Thanks."

Dario frowned a little, but then hit Tau's arm with a smile.

"Congrats, man."

"And don't worry, Dario. I know it sounds like you're gettin' less than Tau for the neighborhood stuff, but you'll be surprised at the money we're all gonna' make with the meth. You'll both see."

"For real, Eddie?"

"For real." Eddie smiled at them. "I'm proud-a you boys. You're makin' real progress."

Tau and Dario did a handshake hug.

"Now," Eddie said. "Get outta' here. Don't go spendin' that like crazy. Don't be stupid and call attention to yourselves. Cuz' if you do, you'll have *me* to answer to, got it?"

"Got it," Tau said.

"I got it, too, Mr. B.," said Dario.

Eddie waved his hand at them as they left.

Sal stood to leave too, but Eddie stopped him.

"So, what's goin' on with your new place? Kate findin' anything good to look at?"

"Ah', yeah," Sal said. "We've looked at a few places." He tipped his head and frowned. "They weren't a good fit, but now she knows what I like, and we're meetin' up tomorrow to look at more."

"Good. Bring her in for lunch. I haven't seen her in a while. I'd like to catch up."

"Sure thing, Eddie. Hot lookin' broad. Too bad she's married, 'eh? I'd like ta'—"

Eddie scowled at Sal as he jammed a finger at him. "Don't you ever fuckin' talk about her like that. Don't ever disrespect her, you got that?"

Sal's eyes popped as he raised his hands and leaned back.

"Whoa, Eddie. No disrespect. I didn't mean nothin' by it."

"I mean it, Sal. Do not fuck with me on this."

"I got it, Eddie. I got it, alright?"

Eddie let the boiling blood release from his face.

"Alright. Good."

Sal tipped his head. "We good?"

"Yeah. We're good. See you'se tonight?"

"Sure, Eddie. See ya' tonight."

Eddie had already dismissed him and returned to the stack of bills on his desk, as Sal quietly shut the door behind him.

A few minutes after Sal left, Eddie threw his empty scotch glass against the door.

Fifty-four

A cold front had swooped in, its bitter air biting Eddie's cheeks and burning his lungs. Winter finally had its grip on the city. His body's involuntary shiver forced him to button up his coat and pull on his gloves, before swinging the strap of his briefcase over his shoulder. He walked over to Marco's awaiting Mustang a few cars down from the front door of Fortunato's. Exhaust plumed out the back as Eddie opened the passenger door and hurried into the warm car.

As Eddie settled in, Marco handed him a package of cash.

"Sal said to give you this."

Eddie took it and flipped the bills in a fan before placing it in his briefcase.

"Thanks."

They headed north on Payne toward the garage when Eddie's burner rang.

"Tau. What'd ya got?"

"Eddie. We got problems."

"What's wrong?"

"I just heard from Dario that Stevie got pinched on his way back from a pick-up."

"Shit! What about Mike?"

Eddie looked at Marco who gave him a questioning glance before returning to watch the busy traffic ahead.

"Mike's good. It was just Stevie," Tau said.

"How'd you find out?"

"Apparently, Stevie called his mom from jail. She called a lawyer, and then she called Mike's mom. Mike's mom called her sister … and I don't know. Somehow, somebody told Dario. Dario is freaking out."

"Dammit! This is bad, Tau."

"I know."

"So they arrested him and confiscated the load?"

"Yep. It's gone for good."

"Shit! How the hell did this happen?"

"I don't know. That's what we're trying to figure out."

"Dammit," Eddie said. "Is Stevie gonna' talk?"

"I don't think so," Tau said. "He's too afraid of you. But what are we gonna' do about the missing product?"

"I don't know. Let me think about this. I'll call you back." Eddie flipped the phone closed.

"Sounds pretty bad," Marco said.

"It is bad. Real fuckin' bad." Eddie pounded the dashboard. "Shit! Pull over. I gotta' think."

Marco pulled the car to the curb across the street from Yarusso's and Eddie told him what happened.

"Eddie," Marco said. "I wanna' help you, but I can't get involved in this shit. Kate would—"

Eddie's face twisted. "Tough shit, Marco. You're up to your ears in this. Just don't tell Kate, ya' hear?"

"But—"

"Marco. Please—shut the fuck up. I gotta' think."

Eddie eyed Marco's dark reaction—the way he bit the inside of his cheek and shook his head—before gazing out the front windshield. Marco was the least of his worries.

Eddie's phone lit up in the dark car. He flipped it open.

"Talk to me, Dario."

He could feel Dario's pacing through the phone, but surprisingly, he sounded cool.

"Eddie. Don't worry. I got this. I'll talk to Dax and let him know what happened. Dax'll call Mateo's guy and tell him we had a situation, but that we've got the cash for them. We'll have to take the hit for now and see how they react. Not sure how they're gonna' feel about this, but it's all we got right now."

"Good. We'll see if that holds 'em. I don't like it, but ...."

"Yeah, but Eddie. This is how it goes. Shit gets pinched. We all take the risk. We just gotta' deal with it. Part-a business, know what I'm sayin'?"

Eddie was surprised by Dario's take-charge attitude.

"You're right, Dario. Thanks for handlin' this like a professional."

"Thanks, man. That means a lot. I won't let you down. Don't worry. I got this."

"Good. Keep me posted. I want to know everything. Find out what's goin' on with Stevie, too. I'm worried about him spillin' to the cops."

"Alright, Eddie. Talk to ya'—"

Eddie slapped the phone shut.

"Come on. Let's get these errands done. I gotta' get back to the office."

Marco kept quiet.

At the restaurant, Eddie opened the passenger door but paused before getting out. "Listen, Marco. About earlier, I—"

Marco lifted his hand. "I won't say anything to Kate. It's fine. Sounds like you have everything under control."

"I do. It'll all work out. No need to worry Kate about any-a this, *capisci*?"

"I won't say a thing."

"Alright. Good. I'll see you'se tomorrow afternoon, 'eh? Oh, and here." Eddie dug into his pocket and gave Marco a wad of cash.

"That's a grand. Okay? Nothin' to Kate, right?"

"Thanks. And ah', yeah. Nothin' to Kate. I'll see ya' tomorrow."

Eddie pulled himself out of the car and slammed the door. He watched as Marco made a U-turn to go home.

Fifty-five

Kate came out of the bathroom towel-drying her hair, the steam from her recent shower glazing the cold bedroom windows with a light layer of fog. Marco sat up in bed and rubbed the sleep from his eyes.

"What a great day we have ahead of us," she said. "I have to tote that big lug, Sal, around town trying to find a condo, and you have to tote the other lug around town."

Marco rubbed his forehead. "I know, Kate. It sucks, but we just need a little more time. We like the two townhouses we've found for ourselves, and I'm feeling pretty good about my interview at that last place. We're almost ready to leave."

"Thank God," she said. "I'm so sick of Sal. I swear he is dragging this out on purpose. The way he leers at me—it's creepy! I don't know how much more I can take."

"Want me to tell Eddie he's leering at you? He'll make him stop."

Kate walked to the dresser and started digging around in the drawers. "No. I can handle this. That'll just make it worse next time I have to see Sal. It's fine. Don't say anything. We need this commission."

"True. I'll stop by later and grab some more boxes from the grocery store for packing. Renzo hasn't even started packing his room."

"I know." Kate's voice raised. "He's still raging about this whole move. It's that girlfriend of his. He doesn't want to leave her."

"Can you blame him? It's like us. I mean, what if you had to leave me? You'd hate that, right?"

She smiled and walked over to him.

"I *would* hate that. I don't even like thinking about that. I suppose we need to give him our understanding and make arrangements for them to still see each other. It'll be annoying, but hopefully it won't last."

Marco climbed out of bed and grabbed her around the waist. "Time will tell how that plays out. Right now, I gotta' get in the shower. Micola has a bunch of errands this morning. She doesn't like to be kept waiting."

"I know. Get going. I'll get breakfast started."

Marco kissed her. "Be down in a few."

She slapped his naked ass. "Hurry up."

After breakfast, Kate left in their new SUV to meet Sal, and Marco left to pick up Micola for the day's usual errands. He pulled up to her house promptly at ten-thirty.

"*Buongiorno*, Marco," she said, lumbering into the passenger seat. "Cold day today."

"Sure is, sweetheart. But I'll keep the car nice and warm for you."

"*Grazie*. You-a good boy." She patted his hand.

They drove in silence. Marco turned from Payne onto Tedesco next to Morelli's Market and parked.

"I'll wait here and then help you put the stuff in the trunk."

Micola paused, her hand lingering on the door handle.

"Marco," she said.

"Yeah?"

A dark look crossed her face. "I have to tell you something."

Marco frowned. "Okay. Anything wrong?"

Micola wrung her gloved hands and stared at them for a moment before looking at Marco. "I hear something." She paused. "Eddie and Sal. Arguing."

"Arguing? About what?"

She pointed. "You."

"Me?"

"*Sì*. About money. Sal say to Eddie that you take-a money."

"Me? I took money?" Marco whipped his head back and forth. "Micola, I never took money from anybody."

"*Sì*, I know this, Marco. I know you. You-a good man. But Eddie, he-very angry. Sal said you took two thousand dollars."

"What the f—" Marco held his tongue as he shook his head.

"I'm sorry. I must tell you. I—"

Marco took her hand and kissed it. "Thank you. I appreciate you tellin' me this. I'll talk to Eddie. Let him know I didn't steal nothin'. Alright? It'll be fine."

She bit her lip and nodded. "Okay Marco. *Molto bene*. This will be fine. Yes?"

"Yes," he said. "Go on in. I'll see you in a bit."

After Micola left the car and headed into the Italian market, Marco slammed his hand on the steering wheel.

"Shit!"

Fifty-six

*T*he following morning brought bitter below-zero temperatures. The January frost clung like frozen marshmallows to the stark tree branches lining the streets of Payne Avenue. Micola stood behind Eddie, shuffling to stay warm, puffs of her frozen breath billowing around his shoulders as he fiddled with the keys to the front door of Fortunato's.

Eddie struggled to hide his anger at having to come down to the restaurant so early on a Sunday morning. All this trouble, just so Micola could be sure she'd have enough heavy cream and mascarpone for the tiramisù.

Payne Avenue was quiet, the only sound coming from the occasional passing car.

"I don't know why this couldn't-a' waited 'til later, Micola," Eddie said, clearly irritated as he pushed open the door to the restaurant.

"*Scusa*, Eddie. *Un minuto.*"

She shuffled off to the kitchen as Eddie stood near the door, waiting, his head pounding from too much scotch the night before.

Ordinarily, he would have slept it off, no problem. But Micola had come barging into his room earlier, waking him from his amorous dream about Kate, and fussin' about mascarpone. He'd barely understood what she was sayin' to him. As his mind cleared, he was reminded of Marco's deception, which further fueled his dark mood.

Micola hurried out of the restaurant kitchen, smiling. "Okay, Eddie. I have what I need."

Eddie gave her a half-smile and moved toward the door. He let Micola out first, while he locked up.

The sound of an approaching vehicle off to his right caught Eddie's attention. A dark SUV had slowed down a half-block away. Micola babbled on in her broken English about her recipes and how none of the other women in the kitchen followed them like she did.

"Eddie. Isabel, she no-whip the eggs." She flapped her hands in the air. "They no-get fluffy and my tiramisù is no-good!"

Eddie shivered as he took her elbow, helping her maneuver patches of ice on the sidewalk, as they headed toward her parked car.

The black SUV slowed as it passed in front of the restaurant. Eddie looked up and saw a woman in the passenger seat pointing something. Sudden pops of light flashed in his direction as three shots rang in his ears.

"Micola!"

Eddie's brain and heart seemed to stop as he threw himself onto Micola, the two of them crashing violently onto the icy pavement. The brunt of his fall was taken by his knees. The rest of him landed directly on top of Micola. He ignored his piercing sharp pain and pushed himself off, rolling her onto her back.

He ignored the screech of rubber against asphalt as the SUV thundered down Payne Avenue. He briefly looked up to see it screech again as it barreled right and sped down Seventh Street.

He grabbed Micola's shoulders and shook her.

"Micola—sweetheart! You okay?"

She let out a low gurgle as her glazed eyes looked up at Eddie, almost as though looking through him.

"No! No! Micola!"

Her mouth opened to speak, but she had no breath for words. Eddie saw the dark blood oozing around her wool coat, now ripped to shreds by the bullet that hit her near her throat. He tilted his head toward the gurgling sound, and began to press firmly on the wound.

"Jesus Christ!" Eddie hooked one arm under her neck. "Micola! Micola! Stay with me, sweetheart! Stay with me! You're gonna' be okay, ya' hear me?"

Eddie's panic and heartbreak crippled him. His throat froze to a numbness as he fought the cold air for a breath. He lowered Micola's head and fumbled furiously in his coat pocket for either of his two phones. His hand grabbed the bigger phone and he pressed the emergency button at the bottom of the locked screen.

"911, what's your emergency?"

"I got a woman here—she's been shot. She's losing blood fast. Please—get somebody over here. Hurry!"

"Sir, what's your location?"

"Fortunato's Restaurant on Payne Avenue near Seventh. We're right outside the restaurant. Hurry! Please!"

"Sir, I have an ambulance on the way. Put pressure on the wound. Do you understand? Put the phone down and put pressure on the wound. Keep the line open though, okay?"

Eddie threw the phone onto the icy sidewalk, leaving the line open. Through his sobs, he climbed onto Micola's body. With one palm over the other, he pressed into the gaping hole near her throat. Her warm, thick blood slipped around his cold fingers, as he looked down at her, her eyes now closed, her body motionless.

Tears burned his eyes, his breath coming out in bursts of cold fog. He hadn't realized until that moment how much he loved Micola. She'd taken him in. Changed his life. He felt overcome with a haze, a dizziness of disbelief. He continued to press as he shook his head, his tears freezing on his cheeks.

"No," he whispered. "Please, God. No. Come on, Micola." His voice grew louder. "Come on! Can you hear me? Stay with me! Micola!"

He heard the 911 operator's voice on the phone near his leg but couldn't understand what she was saying. He continued pressing on Micola's wound as he looked up and down the empty street. Finally, the distant sound of a siren grew as he begged Micola to stay strong.

"They're comin', sweetheart. Here they come. Stay with me now, ya' hear? I need you. Come on. Stay with me!"

Even as he pressed and begged, he knew he'd lost her. He'd killed her as if he'd pulled the trigger himself. This was his fault. His gut felt sucker-punched and his lungs could find no air. Still, he never stopped pressing.

The ambulance screamed louder from the direction of Seventh Street. It rounded the corner onto Payne Avenue and came up fast. Eddie stayed in position, never looking up, frantically working to keep Micola alive. He screamed at her. Begged her to stay with him.

Someone pushed him aside, causing him to fall back onto the cold, hard sidewalk. He watched the backs of the paramedics as they crowded over Micola, shouting words he couldn't comprehend. His ears rang from all the noise. He ran his bloodstained hands through his hair and across his cheek, shaking his head, unaware he was crying.

Someone knelt down next to him. A woman. "Sir?"

He'd barely heard her. It was as if he were under water.

"Sir? Can you hear me? Are you alright?"

His brain cleared a bit as he looked at her face — a pretty young Black woman in a uniform. She looked concerned and was reaching out to him with a towel. She moved closer to help him clean Micola's blood off his hands.

Eddie took in a deep breath and nodded, letting her wipe up the blood. She grabbed his hand and pulled him up to his feet. His knees stung and throbbed, his legs felt weak, wobbling underneath him, as he walked over to Micola, who was now sprawled across a gurney, a blanket covering her head.

"No, no. Please," he said. "I need a minute."

The paramedics all nodded and stepped aside, as he pulled the blanket from Micola's face and looked down at her. She already looked pale and lifeless. Gone.

He leaned down and whispered in her ear. "I'm sorry." He brushed the back of his hand across her cheek, kissed her forehead, and then stepped away.

They quickly moved in, pushing him aside as they loaded her into the ambulance.

"Sir?"

Eddie turned to see a police officer standing next to him.

"Sir, we need to talk. I'm very sorry for your loss, but I need to ask you what happened."

Eddie nodded and looked around, taking a hand down his entire face to wipe away his hot tears and Micola's drying blood.

"Ah', yeah. We can go inside."

He fished out his keys and opened the restaurant. He described to the officer the details of the events, the black SUV, and the woman who shot Micola.

Even though Eddie had never seen the woman before, he knew who she was.

O's girlfriend. Tanya Steele.

Eddie tucked his rage deep in his gut, and kept that bit of information to himself.

Fifty-seven

*A*fter saying his final goodbyes to Micola at the hospital and filling out the necessary paperwork, Eddie returned to her house late that afternoon to notify her daughter of the news, and to call Primo, Micola's brother-in-law. Both calls added to his grief, a heavy weight piled on top of an already devastating day.

Micola's daughter could barely breathe after hearing the news, and all he could do was sit there quietly on the phone listening to her choke and cry.

Primo's reaction was more subdued, but his simmering fury and insinuating blame on Eddie proved more than he could take. He knew his head was now on Primo's chopping block. He'd need to watch his back because that could happen at any time.

Still, he couldn't stop thinking about Micola. She'd been his new world. He really loved her. She'd changed his life forever, and now she was gone. Because of *him*.

He sat at the kitchen table with a bottle of scotch and drank long into the night. He felt her presence, imagined her bent over the stove stirring a pot of boiling pasta, turning to smile at him, as she carried over a plate of one of her miracle dishes.

There'd be a funeral. He wasn't even sure if he was supposed to handle it. He couldn't bear to think about such a heavy task. The events of the day were seared into his memory, and the scotch hadn't numbed any of it.

The phone rang and rang. First Dario, then Tau, and then Sal. Word was spreading. He let the calls go to voicemail. His thoughts were occupied by the woman who killed Micola.

He thought about her a lot.

Fifty-eight

Eddie's phone buzzed at the bedside table, jarring him from his weakened slumber. The morning light peered around the edges of the window shade as he pulled the comforter closer to his chin, protecting him from the cool room. Dark memories from the previous day's horrors rushed back, as an ache grew in his chest.

He glanced at the phone and let it go to voicemail, though he knew he couldn't avoid the calls much longer. The restaurant would need to close for a few days, in Micola's honor. He'd get Regina to handle those details. Next, he'd meet with Dario, Tau, Sal … and Marco, to discuss the cops and how to answer all their questions.

Fuckin' Marco.

Marco stealin' from him was another matter that made his head spin. Of all the people Eddie thought he could trust, it was Marco. It didn't make sense, but Tau confirmed it. The cash packages Eddie'd received from Marco had been short, and Tau had no idea how long that had been going on.

He rubbed his face before sitting up. It hit him that Micola wouldn't be downstairs fixing his breakfast, no aroma of coffee swirling up the stairs. He showered, went downstairs, and fixed his own meager breakfast and coffee, before making his calls.

After getting Regina on board, and confirming with Micola's daughter that she'd be handling the funeral, he scheduled a meeting with Tau, Dario, and Sal. They were his top priority, and he'd asked them to arrive at the house within the hour.

Marco wasn't answering. If he didn't hear back from him, Eddie would try Kate.

Fifty-nine

Marco's phone buzzed incessantly, waking Kate from a deep slumber. She rolled over to look at the clock before nudging Marco.

"Babe. Your phone keeps ringing. You'd better see what's up."

Marco moaned as he reached for his phone, squinting to see the number before it stopped ringing.

"That was Eddie. Wonder what he wants?" He sat up. "Jesus. Tau and Dario called. Sal too. Something's going on."

"You'd better call," she said.

Marco climbed out of bed, pulled on some sweats and dialed Eddie's number.

"Eddie, Marco. What's up? I gotta' lot of missed calls."

Kate watched Marco's face fall, as he looked at her. He ran his hand through his hair and paced.

"Jesus, Eddie. What the hell happened?"

Kate watched him shake his head at her. She sat up and waited for the call to end.

"Marco, what's wrong? What happened?"

"Micola. She—she died. She was shot yesterday morning."

"Oh my God! No! What happened? How?"

Marco relayed to Kate the few details he'd received from Eddie.

"He wants me over there. Now. At Micola's house. I gotta' go."

"Of course. You go shower. I'll fix you some toast and coffee."

"Okay. Thanks."

Marco hurried through his shower and breakfast and kissed Kate on his way out the door.

"Keep me posted. I'm worried."

"I will," he said. He shut the back door and left.

Kate watched Marco from the kitchen window. He backed the Mustang out of the driveway, as a sickening sense of dread began to flutter in her stomach.

Sixty

*E*ddie let the boys in from the cold. They gave him a hug with their solemn condolences, before Eddie directed them into Micola's living room, where they removed their winter jackets and took their seats on the sofa and chairs. The doorbell rang again, and Sal lumbered in, his head lowered in mourning. He too embraced Eddie before kissing him on both cheeks.

Sal grabbed Eddie by his shoulders. "How you doin', cuz?"

Eddie shook his head as he closed his eyes. "Hangin' in there, I guess. I'm gonna' miss that old broad."

He guided Sal into the living room and took his coat. Tau and Dario stood and shook Sal's hand before they all sat down.

Marco arrived next. Eddie let him in and accepted Marco's condolences but with a callousness he hoped Marco sensed.

Marco took off his jacket and threw it over the arm of the sofa. He squeezed in next to Tau and Dario. Eddie and Sal sat in the two chairs across from them.

"I made some coffee," Eddie said. "Not as good as Micola's, but ah' … anybody want some?"

The four men shook their heads and the meeting began. Eddie relayed the details of yesterday's killing of Micola. He struggled to keep his voice strong, swallowing often to press back the lump in his throat. He appreciated their pretending not to notice his show of weakness.

They sat in the living room for hours, discussing their roles with Eddie, and their official roles with the restaurant. Eddie wanted to get their stories straight on what they did for him so they'd be ready when the cops came snooping around, asking questions.

Dario and Tau were to say they worked on marketing customers—hustling to get them into the restaurant, as well as handling various pickups and deliveries. Marco, as Eddie's driver, was already a truthful response. And Sal was to be considered the muscle. Security. Hopefully, it wouldn't come to the point where they'd ask for documentation of anybody's pay. Eddie would worry about that later.

They next discussed the shooter. The woman. Eddie wanted immediate surveillance done on O's girlfriend and of her family members and friends. He was fairly confident she was the shooter.

"A white girl. I want photos. She had on a puffy black jacket and a black winter hat—a knit one. I saw some blond hair hanging out of it. So I think it's short, but maybe not. A black SUV. High-end. Big. Newer model. Find out what kinda' car O drove. Find her house. I want it all."

"Dario," Eddie said, "you said you knew where O's house was over in Minneapolis?"

Dario nodded. "Yeah. Lake of the Isles or one-a them high-class lakes over there. I can find out for sure where it is."

"Good," Eddie said. "Be discreet, though. Be careful who you ask." He waved his hand across the room. "All of you'se. Be careful who you talk to, got it?"

They all nodded.

"I'm pretty sure I could pick her out from a photo," Eddie said. "I mean, it happened fast, but I saw her face. I'll know when I see her."

He reiterated that he would handle the retribution. He *wanted* to handle it. He was looking forward to it.

"I think that's it for now," Eddie said. "You'se all know what you gotta' do."

They nodded.

"That's it."

He pointed at Marco. "You stay. The rest-a you'se can go." Eddie stood, and Dario, Tau and Sal followed him to the door. Dario gave Marco a quick look before turning to leave.

Eddie shut the door behind them and returned to the same chair in the living room, across from Marco.

Marco raised his hands defensively. "I know what you're about to say to me, Eddie. Micola told me."

Eddie blinked as he tilted his head. "What? How would she know anything?"

"She said she'd heard you and Sal. You were arguin'. She wanted to warn me."

Eddie sat back and stared at him, thinking.

"I denied it to her then," Marco continued, "and I'm denying it to you now." He sliced his hand in the air. "I did *not* steal from you. Never would. I have a family. I'm not that stupid."

"Well," Eddie said, leaning forward, his elbows resting on his thighs, "how do you explain it then? Tau said he gave you packages of five grand. I get the packages from you, and two of them were forty-five hundred, one of them was four grand. How do you fuckin' explain that, Marco? Huh? And how many other times were there, that we don't even know about, 'eh?"

Eddie watched Marco's reaction. He appeared to be stalling, but then, his head popped up like he had an idea. He looked up at Eddie, wide-eyed.

"There were a couple-a times when Sal gave me the packages."

Eddie frowned. "Sal? What? No." He shook his head, taking in what Marco was telling him. "Sal's my cousin. He wouldn't do me like that. No fuckin' way. Uh-uh. Not Sal."

"I'm tellin' you, Eddie. It wasn't me. Sal's the only explanation. Ask Tau. He gave a few packages to Sal, and then Sal gave 'em to me."

Eddie leaned back in the chair and rubbed his forehead.

"Jesus Christ."

He sat there thinking, while Marco squirmed. Eddie finally spoke.

"Alright. Let me talk to Tau and then to Sal. "I gotta' get to the bottom of this, on top of all the other shit that's goin' on. Who knows how long I've been gettin' ripped off here? Go on. Get outta' here. I'll be in touch."

He picked up the phone.

"Who you callin?" Marco asked.

"Sal."

Marco stood, rubbing his hands on his thighs. "Ya' gotta' believe me, Eddie. I didn't do it. I swear. Never would."

Eddie flicked his hand at him in dismissal.

Marco paused. Eddie stared at him, still holding the phone.

"What?"

"Eddie, I've been meaning to talk to you about this." Marco looked at his feet and brushed his fingers through his hair.

"Spit it out. I got shit to do."

Marco bobbed his head. "Yeah, right. So, ah'. I ah'—Kate and I have been talkin' and we ah'—"

"Jesus H. Christ, Marco, what?"

"I'm out. I'm outta' all-a this." He shook his head at Eddie, crossing his hands, one over the other. "I can't get any deeper into this shit. Kate and I—"

Eddie jumped to his feet, his mouth twisted into a scowl, as he screamed at Marco.

"I don't give-a shit what you and Kate think about all-a this. You're *not* leavin'. You got that? You're *in*. *All* the way in." He glanced at the floor and tipped his head as he laughed. "You—of all people—know that. So, no, you're *not* out. You're in. Alright? *Capisci*? You and Kate are just gonna have-ta fuckin' deal with it."

Eddie waited, as Marco opened his mouth to say more, but he shut it. Then, after a few seconds, Marco said, "Nope. I'm out." He threw down his hands and walked out the front door.

Eddie watched Marco leave and then threw his phone against the wall, smashing it to bits.

Sixty-one

Kate paced the living room and kitchen waiting for word from Marco. She bit her nails, as she peered out the window for the hundredth time. When Marco finally stormed in through the back door, she ran to him. The cold from the opened door floated across her feet.

"What happened?" She wrung her hands, waiting.

Marco stood near the door staring at her, breathing heavily, his eyes wide.

"It's time, Kate."

"Time for what?"

"To get outta' this neighborhood." His pitch grew higher, louder. "Time to get away from Eddie. Things are bad. Out of control."

"Calm down, babe. Take off your coat and tell me what happened."

They moved to the living room. Marco took a deep breath, as he ran his fingers through his hair. He looked around.

"Where's Renzo?"

"He's at Everett's. He'll be there all day and then sleeping over."

"Okay. We gotta' go get him, and then we gotta' leave. Now. Things are really heatin' up."

"Marco," Kate said. "What happened?"

Marco spent the next hour telling Kate everything: what happened to Micola; the meeting; the woman—O's girlfriend—or so Eddie thinks; and Eddie's implication that this woman needed to be "handled." He told her about their marching orders with the cops; and the likely investigation into all of Eddie's operations. Finally, Marco confessed to Kate what Micola had told him—that Eddie had accused him of stealing.

"Tell me you didn't steal from him, Marco."

Marco shook his head. "No! I didn't steal from him."

"Thank God."

"But Kate, I told him."

She searched his eyes. "Told him what?"

"That I was out. I was done."

"And? What did he say?"

"He told me I couldn't leave. He wouldn't let me. But I left anyway. Which is why we gotta' go, now. He's burning mad, Kate. I think he might come after me."

Kate rushed her hands to her face. "Oh my God, Marco."

The wind howled outside the frosted living room windows as the two of them huddled together on the sofa, planning their escape.

"This is all my fault," she cried. "If I hadn't been so easily charmed by Eddie, we never would have had dinner with him, and we wouldn't be in all this trouble." She dabbed her eyes with a tissue.

"Don't say that," Marco said. "We made all of the decisions together. How were we to know it would all come to this?"

He moved in closer, and she put her head on his shoulder. A soft pelting on the window took hold and they turned toward it. The day's light was fading quickly.

"Damn," Marco said. "It's snowing."

Kate shook her head and whispered, "and we have to go."

Marco nodded. "We do. Let's pack up some stuff. We can send for the rest another time."

"Okay," Kate said. "I haven't listed the house yet, but once we're safe, I will."

They climbed the stairs and hurriedly packed as much as they'd need for the foreseeable future. Then, together, they packed for Renzo.

After running back and forth in the frigid January air packing the SUV, they stood in the kitchen, breathless, chilled to the bone. Darkness had descended, and it was time to go.

"Renzo will be waiting. I told Everett's mom it was an emergency. Renzo's been texting me, but I've been stalling, telling him we'd explain when we were all together."

"Okay," Marco said. He leaned down to kiss Kate. "I'll go get him. See if there's anything else we might need."

She nodded. "Be careful. Keep an eye out—for anything."

Marco held her hands. "I will. Don't worry. We'll be back to get you and be on the road before you know it." He walked to the kitchen door and turned to her.

"Love you," he said, with a sad smile.

"Love you."

Marco walked out the door to the car. Kate wrapped her oversized sweater tighter around her body, as she stood in the kitchen watching him through the frosted glass window. He backed the SUV, packed with their stuff, down the driveway, turned right and drove down the street. She continued to stare into the darkness after his tail lights had disappeared, her mind whirling.

A flash of light to her left caught her by surprise.

Headlights.

Cloaked in darkness, the car immediately pulled out onto the road. Briefly illuminated by the streetlights, the light colored car passed her driveway, accelerating as it sped down the street in Marco's direction.

Sixty-two

As she fussed around in the kitchen, Kate moved to the back window for yet another glance out at the cold, dark driveway. The yard was still. No sign of Marco and Renzo. Time seemed to have stopped.

Where are they?

Her phone rang. The display showed Marco's picture.

"Hi, baby. Where are you?"

"Kate." Marco's voice sounded strained.

"What's wrong?" she asked. Her heart skipped, as she pulled her hand up to her throat. "Where's Renzo?"

"He's with me. We just got a flat tire."

"Oh my God, Marco—"

"—I think somebody was following us, Kate. I don't see any cars now. I took Arcade over near that brake place. The one where I applied for a job. Remember?"

"I think so, yes."

"I wanted to get away from all the traffic. I have to change this damn tire—in ten-below weather—but we'll be there as soon as I get it done. We're gonna' have to leave right away. I gotta' bad feeling, Kate."

"Me too. Do you need me to call someone?"

"No. I'll be fine. I've done thousands of tire changes, this'll be quick. Give us twenty minutes. I'll go as fast as I can."

"Okay. No sign of that car?"

"No. Maybe I was just imagining it."

"Okay. Hurry up."

"Don't worry. We'll be there soon. Love you."

"Love you, too."

Kate ran upstairs to gather some last-minute items. After about a half-hour, she returned downstairs, gave the living room a once-over, then pushed through the swinging door into the kitchen.

They still weren't home. Butterflies did a tiny dance in her gut, as she opened the back door to listen for his car, the cold air startling her. She stood at the top of the steps, hugging herself while she waited, her head tilted, as she prayed for the sound of tires turning up the driveway. But it was eerily silent, except for the occasional cracking of branches from the tense, frigid air.

She waited a couple of minutes out in the cold, straining to see headlights before finally giving in to her body's shivers. She returned to the kitchen, but remained at the back window, waiting. Watching.

The butterflies turned to a slow flicker of panic. This was taking too long. They should have been back by now. She took her phone from her sweater's pocket and dialed Marco's number again.

Voicemail.

Where did he say they were? What was taking them so long?

Over a half-hour and no word. She couldn't wait another minute. Her heart pounded in her ears. She threw on her coat and boots, as she grabbed the keys to Marco's Mustang and her purse. She whipped open the back door, slamming it, as she ran out into the dark yard toward the car, snow cracking under her steps.

The coldest night of the season nipped its invisible claws at her ears, stinging her cheeks and burning her nostrils. The porch light did little to illuminate her path, and she tripped over something as she stumbled to the car. Her nervous legs wobbled as she struggled with the keys, climbed in, and slammed the door.

Clouds of her breath shrouded her face, the light from the house giving them a life of their own. She took in a deep breath and tried to slow her racing heart, as she started the engine. Her hands shook as she grasped the wheel. She told herself to pull it together. She carefully backed down the driveway and turned left onto Desoto heading toward Payne Avenue.

As she drove, she fumbled for her phone in her purse and hit redial.

"Come on, Marco. Pick up!" Her voice cracked.

When his voicemail message returned, she screamed into the phone.

"Marco! What is happening? Where are you guys? I'm freaking out. I'm on my way to find you. Call me as soon as you get this message."

She was about to end the call, but before she did, she said, "I love you, babe. Hurry up and call me."

She tossed her phone on the passenger seat and thought about Marco's call to her. His voice. The way he sounded. It was like nothing she'd heard from him before. Panic.

Someone was following them? Who? Was it that car she saw pull out after he left?

As she headed north on Payne, she tried to remain rational. Maybe Marco had trouble changing the tire in this cold, and they started to walk. No, he would have called her to pick them up. Maybe something was wrong with his phone. She scanned the shadows and doorways along the icy sidewalks for any sign of people walking, hoping to see her husband and son, but it was apparent this cold was keeping everyone indoors.

Maybe they'd crossed paths, and Marco and Renzo were already home. That didn't make sense, though. He would have called her. She drove the Mustang slowly, looking side-to-side and up and down each street, praying.

She headed east on Minnehaha and south on Arcade, until she came upon a couple of darkened streets to her right. She took each one before turning back and continuing down Arcade. No businesses, no houses. Nothing but masses of brittle, leafless trees and vegetation, now reduced to sticks from winter's grip.

Finally, the brake store appeared on her right, obviously closed for the night. She continued along the lightless road, unsure where it would take her. She gripped the steering wheel as she looked to the left and then to the right, scanning for any sign of their SUV. She inched down the road, seeing nothing.

A curve in the road appeared, her headlights illuminating its dark path. She followed it slowly. As she maneuvered the bend, she let out a breath. The SUV was just ahead, pulled over on the right side of the road, lights off. Relief coursed through her body, as she choked back a lump that had been in her throat for longer than she'd realized.

She pulled up behind the SUV, her headlights shining directly
into it. It was definitely her car, but there was no sign of Marco or
Renzo.

Sixty-three

*K*ate put Marco's Mustang in park, but left it running, the headlights on, to provide the only illumination available on the deserted road. She left the warmth of the car and felt the fierce slap of bitter wind as it whipped across her face. She zipped up her coat and tugged on her knit cap, as she headed to the SUV parked up ahead, struggling against the strong, biting gusts.

Where were they?

She shouted into the empty darkness on either side of the SUV.

"Marco? Renzo?"

Panic rose in her throat, as she struggled to see in the black cold night. She paused, and then hurried back to the Mustang to retrieve the flashlight from the glove compartment. She clicked it on and headed back. A quick pass of the flashlight over the car's windows told her it was empty. She waved the light across the wooded area to either side of her.

"Marco! Renzo! Are you out there?"

The only response was the freezing wind roaring in her ears.

"Marco! Renzo! Can you hear me?!"

A car approached and passed her, heading in the direction of civilization—Arcade Street. She reached into her pocket for her phone, wondering where that car had come from and whether that person had seen anything.

She dialed Marco's number, willing him with a prayer to answer. She heard the ring of Marco's phone in her ear, just as she heard the muffled sound of a phone ringing to her right, near the SUV.

Holding the cellphone to her ear, she ran through the darkness, following the narrow beam of the flashlight, and listening to the ringing of the phone, until she was standing at the driver's window. The window was down, and Marco's phone was ringing inside. She raised her flashlight into the car and let out a high-pitched, feral shriek, a sound she didn't recognize as her own.

Marco's body and head lay slumped across the steering wheel, the side of his temple tilted upward and covered in a dark, shiny mass, its odor smacking her nostrils.

Sixty-four

Cold darkness swirled inward, throwing off Kate's equilibrium and causing her knees to buckle. She lowered her phone from her ear, feeling it slip through her numb fingers and drop, her leaden body pulling her with it.

She caught herself and stepped back, her gloved hand instinctively covering her mouth and nose, as she furiously shook her head. She refused to believe this lifeless soul was her husband. It couldn't be. Her legs wobbled as her head spun, but she fought the dizzying fog that tried to slip in and take her.

"No! Marco, no," she sobbed, as she yanked open the car door. "Renzo! Renzo! Where are you?"

The wailing in her ears sounded strange and distant, outer-body-like.

"Renzo!"

She pushed her head into the car, over Marco's slumped body and near his gaping head wound in search of her child, tears now burning her frozen cheeks, her heart beating and fluttering and seeming to stop, all at the same time.

Kate leaned deeper into the car toward the passenger's side, her knee on the driver's seat in front of Marco's thigh, as she fell onto him, her hand swinging in the darkness like a blind madwoman. She touched a puffy jacket sleeve and wailed again.

"No, no, no!"

She pulled herself out of the car and raced around the front of it, stopping short at the passenger door. She yanked it open. Renzo's body slipped near the edge of the seat, almost falling into the street. She caught him and pushed him gently back in, his back and head resting against the back of the seat. With short, staccato breaths, she called out to her son in the darkness.

"Renzo! Renzo!"

She grabbed his shoulders and turned his face toward her. The silver moonlight lit a dark mass covering the front of his chest, his face and body spattered with blood. Her weak scream cried out his name.

"No, no! Renzo! Renzo, baby. It's mommy. Can you hear me?"

She felt for a pulse, her hand moving up, down, and around his throat.

Nothing.

She stopped short and took his hand, pulling back when she felt his fingers twitch.

"Oh my God! Renzo!"

Kate knew Marco was gone, but she called out to him just in case.

"Marco! Stay with me! Renzo! I'm here baby. Hang on! I'm getting help!"

She pulled herself out of the car and fumbled into her coat pocket for her phone. It wasn't there. She screamed, as she remembered she'd dropped it and ran back to the driver's side. She fell to the ground with her flashlight searching for it. When she found it, she raised her shaking and bloodied glove and tried to slide her finger across the phone but was unable to unlock it. She ripped off the glove and pushed the word "Emergency."

"911. What's your emergency?"

"My husband and son have been shot!"

Kate's voice cut through the darkness, tearing and shredding, echoing through the leafless trees.

"I think my husband might already be dead. I don't know, they're bleeding and unconscious! Please hurry! Please, please! Hurry!"

The male operator continued. "What is your location, ma'am?"

With the phone to her ear, she ran around the front of the car to Renzo's side, her knee on the open door's ledge, taking his hand. It felt icy.

"What?"

"Your location? Where are you?"

Kate looked around and down the road. No street sign could be seen in the darkness.

What was it? She took that third right.

"I—I'm not sure. Oh, no. Ah', let's see." She sobbed and cried, her words breaking, but still, she tried to concentrate. "I took

Minnehaha going east to Arcade. Yes, that's it. Then, I took, ah'—oh, God. What did I take? I ah', I took a right. Then, I drove right three different times, and then each time, I turned around, back onto Arcade. So, I'm at the third right off of Arcade ... south of Minnehaha. Yes, yes. That's it. I'm sorry, I don't know the name of the street."

"Okay, ma'am, emergency vehicles are on the way. Stay on the phone with me, please."

"Okay. Hurry, please! My son—"

"What's your name, ma'am?"

"My name?" Kate didn't know why she had to waste time with this. "It's Kate. Kate De Luca. My husband's name is Marco." Kate began to cry hysterically. "And my son's name is Renzo ... Lorenzo De Luca."

Still kneeling on the open door's ledge, Kate squeezed Renzo's hand and brushed his hair away from his face. She leaned in and kissed his cheek, shouting at him to hang on.

"Ma'am. Are you in danger? Do you know if the shooter is nearby?"

Kate hadn't thought of that. She looked around into the darkness and began to feel lightheaded. She thought she might faint. The dispatcher's voice faded in and out. She wiped her forehead with her bloody hand.

"I ... I don't know!" Heat rose up her face as more dizziness set her off balance. "I don't know. I don't see anyone. No cars. It's so cold. Please!" Her own loud cries pierced through her. "Please hurry! He's dying!"

"The ambulance is on its way. They'll be there soon—"

"I hear them!"

Kate dropped her phone, pulled herself up, and ran around the SUV to flag them down, screaming and jumping as she waved her arms. Flashing lights rounded the corner coming up fast.

She ran back to the driver's side door and leaned in, pushing and shaking Marco's shoulder as if trying to rouse him from a deep slumber. She clung to the hope that he might still be alive.

"Hang on, Marco! Help is on the way, baby. I love you. Please don't leave me, Marco. Please!"

She again ran around the front of the car to lean in next to Renzo. She used all of her might to rein in her hysteria, to appear calm, as she spoke softly.

"Renzo, baby, can you hear me?"

She heard her son's quiet voice.

"Momma." He pointed toward Marco, his eyes still shut. "Dad." He let out a weak whimper. "Help him. He's shot."

Kate let out all available oxygen. This nightmare could not be real.

"I know, baby. They're here now. Hang on. Help is here." She blinked away her endless tears. "Who … who did this to you? Do you know? Tell me, Renzo. Who did this to you and daddy?"

Renzo appeared to use all of his might to speak.

"Se 'eh …"

She shook her head. "Who baby? Who did this?"

Her vision blurred in the night's darkness as one of the emergency vehicles screeched to a stop next to the SUV. She heard voices screaming, yet they sounded so far away.

As more blaring sirens approached, Kate left Renzo and ran, waving her bloody arms and hands.

"Over here! Hurry! Please—hurry!"

She returned to Renzo so he wouldn't be afraid. She kept wiping her tears from her face, unaware of the blood on her hand, now all over her face.

"Stay with me baby. Momma loves you. Can you hear me?" She tipped his chin. "Renzo?"

Scooping her arm under his neck, she wiped the dark wetness away from his mouth and nose with the tips of her frozen fingers and wrapped her arms around him to keep him warm.

"Help is here, sweetie. Hang on. They're here now."

An ambulance and two police cars pulled up beside the SUV. Two paramedics, a man and a woman, jumped out of the ambulance. The woman jogged around and opened the back doors of the ambulance, while the man ran toward Kate and Marco's cars, just as another ambulance approached.

"Please, hurry!" Kate swung her head back and forth screaming at whomever would listen. "Please hurry!"

"Step aside, ma'am."

The paramedic then shouted orders to the woman near the ambulance, as Kate moved to the front of the car. Two more police cars pulled up behind the ambulance, sirens wailing and then shutting off, their echoes ringing in Kate's ears. The female paramedic ran toward the car, a bag in hand, and ordered Kate to stay back.

Plumes of white clouds surrounded the mouths of so many strangers now running around. Kate held her hand to her mouth trying to muffle the screams pressing in her throat, as her weakened legs buckled.

Two male police officers, one white and one Black, both tall and muscular, approached the SUV, hands on their holstered weapons. Glancing in through the opened SUV doors, they passed the paramedics, and took Kate by her elbow, pushing her further from her husband and son, while the paramedics, now leaning deep into the vehicle, barked orders at each other, as the crew from the second ambulance jumped to work.

Kate fought the cops and tried to run, escaping at first, until the beefier of the two grabbed her in a bear hug and talked quietly near her ear.

"Okay," he said, almost whispering. "Stay with me, now. I need you to stay with me, here, okay? They're working on them. Come on, help me understand what happened."

She nodded her head and relaxed a bit, so he released his grip. Looking down at her, he said, "Can you do that?"

She grabbed her head with both hands as tears rolled down her cheeks. She nodded again as she gasped for breath and let him guide her. She lost her balance under her shaky legs, and he hooked his strong arms under hers, catching her.

Then, with an arm around her shoulder, he guided her toward the squad car and sat her in the back seat. It felt warm inside despite the door remaining open.

They asked many questions and she impatiently answered them as she sobbed.

…*"Yes. That's my husband and my son. Marco and Renzo."*

…*"No, I don't know who shot them."*

She leaned out to look back at her SUV as the weight and reality of what was happening crept into her consciousness. Her heart felt destroyed.

The officers continued to pepper her with questions. Kate answered them with a quaking voice while straining to watch the paramedics as they dragged her husband and son out of the car and onto stretchers. She tried to get out, but the white cop put his hand on her shoulder, forcing her back into the squad car.

"Please," she whispered, "I need to be with them."

He looked at the other officer who nodded and helped her up and out of the car.

"I'm riding with them to the hospital," she told the officer.

He nodded. "I'll see you there. We're not done talking."

She ignored him and ran toward her husband and son. Her legs felt numb—as though she wasn't moving at all. She finally came upon the two stretchers carrying the bodies of her husband and child and climbed into the ambulance with Renzo. Once inside, she watched as Marco was lifted into the vehicle next to them, motionless, his face and winter jacket stained black with blood.

Sixty-five

*K*ate sat on a side bench inside the ambulance, the harsh lights illuminating her son's gaping chest wound. She held his cold hand, averting her eyes from the deep hole in his young body. The two paramedics yelled orders at each other while one of them pressed on the wound. From under the oxygen mask, Renzo lay motionless, his once pink and glowing youthful complexion now gray, his body still.

The medics urgently, yet calmly, worked on her son as Kate kept her head near his, holding his hand and leaning in close. She whispered in his ear, as she smoothed his brown curls from his forehead.

"Hang in there, baby. Mommy's here. I love you." She kissed his cheek and hand over and over. "Stay strong, baby. You and daddy are gonna' be okay." Her voice cracked. "You hear me?"

She didn't believe her own words. Renzo already looked different. Gone. She was certain Marco didn't survive, though no one had told her so.

They made a sharp turn, as the ambulance driver shouted orders into a two-way radio preparing the emergency personnel for their arrival. He took another fast right into the Regions Hospital emergency parking lot. He swerved around a sea of parked cars, finally making his way up to the entrance. Kate's breath grew shallow as things happened quickly.

Her hand was yanked from Renzo's as they whisked his gurney out of the ambulance to a crew of five waiting for him. One of the officers from earlier blocked her view as he leaned in. She rose and let him help her down. Icy snow lashed at an angle under the bright lights, but a large overhang above the emergency room entrance shielded them from the storm.

She shouted up at the cop. "Where are they taking him? I need to follow them!"

At that moment, the siren from the ambulance carrying Marco interrupted his response. Kate's head snapped back into focus as it pulled up. She put her hand to her mouth and choked back her screams as Marco too, was quickly whisked inside.

She moved to run after them, but the cop grabbed her arm.

Kate tried to pull away from him, digging in her heels. "Please! I need to be in there!"

She yanked her arm from his grip and took off. The doors where they took Marco and Renzo had locked shut, so she darted in through the lobby entrance. Passing a crowd in the waiting room, she ran up to an intake desk where a clerk was with a patient.

Pointing and crying, Kate sobbed and wailed. "I'm sorry, but they just brought my husband and son in. I need to get back there. Please!"

The heavyset woman apologized to the patient she'd been helping and stood up. She pointed Kate to the next desk over. "Ma'am, ma'am," she said to Kate. "Calm down. We'll need some information."

Kate furiously waved her head. "No, no, I—"

"Please, ma'am. Someone will take you back in a second. We at least need their names, dates of birth and address. If you give us that, I promise we'll take you back. Okay? You can give the information to this young lady. The smiling woman gestured for Kate to sit.

"I'm not sitting," Kate said. She railed off their names, birth dates and address and threw the insurance card at her. Looking back at the first woman, she pointed. "Take me back to my husband and son. Now."

The woman nodded and gestured another apology to the person she was helping. She rose and started walking. Kate followed her to a secure area. The woman swiped her badge and hit a silver button on the right wall. They paused for the huge doors to swing open. She jogged with Kate down a long hall, and then turned right, down another hall.

Shouting could be heard from inside an operating room. Kate ran ahead, leaving the woman behind. As Kate pushed back the curtain, her head spun at the sight.

A crowd of nurses and doctors were frantically working on her son's motionless body, the bright spotlight blazing down onto his bloody chest. She ran toward Renzo but was grabbed at the waist.

A tall dark-skinned man in baby blue scrubs was bent over, his fingers working inside Renzo's chest. Kate's legs buckled as tears poured down her cheeks.

"Oh my God, is he ok? What's happening?"

With a slight accent, a male nurse shook his head. "I'm sorry ma'am, but your son is very weak. We are doing our best to save him."

An unfamiliar crack in her voice escaped, as she shook her head. "No." She pressed the tears from her eyes and sniffed her runny nose. "Come on baby. Please, stay with me."

She looked around at the nurses and doctors working on the machines, checking Renzo's tubes and jotting down notes.

"Where's my husband? Marco? Is he okay?"

One of the nurses gave her a strange look as another one said, "He's down the hall. They're working on him now, ma'am."

"Can I see him? Can someone show me where he is? I want to tell him his son is okay."

"Not yet," said the doctor, who was leaving the room as she spoke.

"Please! Is he okay?"

He shook his head. "No ma'am. He is *not* okay. And I'm sorry. Neither is your son. She'll take you to your husband."

She stared at Renzo as she left the room and turned the corner following the nurse to her husband's room. She entered, took one look at Marco, and everything went black.

Sixty-six

Kate moaned as she slowly blinked open her eyes. The face of a dark-haired heavyset woman was inches from her nose. Her kind, brown eyes looked concerned. Voices and the sounds of machines faded before growing loud and then quiet. Her body felt heavy. Numb. She struggled to keep her eyes open, but they refused to cooperate. She liked it there—in the dark. It was peaceful, warm. A harsh, painfully bright light came across her face from above, seizing her from her serenity. She squeezed her eyes and prayed for the return of the blackness. The dark, noiseless hole.

Another faraway voice.

"Ma'am? Can you hear me?"

I'm dying. I want to die.

A searing sharp pain in her head and shoulder snapped her to attention.

Awake.

Wide awake.

Then gone again, the black hole sucking her away.

Sixty-seven

A gentle tap on her arm and something cool on her forehead pulled Kate from a depth she'd never felt before. As she stirred, intense pain zigzagged across her temple. Though it throbbed even to blink, she opened her eyes. That woman, the nurse who'd looked at her funny in Renzo's room, was now looking down at her, smiling.

Wait. Was that just a minute ago?

Kate reached for her head and moaned. "What happened?"

"You fell. Got a nice bump on your head, sweetie."

As Kate's head cleared, she remembered. Despite the crashing pain in her head, she pushed herself to her elbows.

"My husband! My son! I gotta' go."

The nurse pushed her down as the doctor she'd seen working on Renzo walked in.

Kate looked at his expression and froze.

"Mrs. De Luca," he said, his voice quiet and kind, as he pursed his lips and gently shook his head.

Kate's eyes and nose burned. She shook her head, worsening the pain. Her voice failed her as she whispered, "No." Her burning throat grew thick as she fought for air.

"I am so sorry. We did everything we could, but your husband and son lost a lot of blood. They did not survive the gunshot wounds. I'm very sorry."

Kate wanted to scream and yell at them, but her strength was sapped. She looked up at the doctor, holding her breath as she shook her head at him. Tears washed over her eyes, her nose both runny and congested.

"No," she whispered again. "That's not right. Check again. *Please*." She shook her head and pointed beyond the curtain to the hall. "I saw them. They were alive. I—I. Please! Check again!"

Heat surged in her face as she tried to sit up, but an agonizing pain slammed across her skull, causing the room to spin. She fell back onto the pillow and covered her face with her hands. A heaviness fell across her defeated body as she shook with sorrow and rage. She wanted to scream but lacked any energy. She wiped her hands down her face as she fought the searing pain crossing her head. She refused to accept this nightmare.

The doctor slipped out the door, but the nurse stayed and held Kate's hand as she spoke to her quietly, calmly.

"Try not to move, ma'am. Is there anyone we can call for you?"

Kate pressed the palms of her hands on her eyes as she turned to look at the nurse.

"Can you call my mom?"

She barely recognized her own voice. It sounded so small. Like a toddler's.

The nurse patted her hand. "Of course."

Kate gave her her mom's name and number. The nurse left the room leaving Kate alone with her living nightmare.

She whispered quietly.

Marco. Renzo. Please come back to me. Don't leave me. Why is this happening? Who did this? I hated seeing you guys looking like that. I hope it didn't hurt. I hope you weren't too afraid. Please. Please. Please. Walk through that door and take me home. I'll make you a nice spaghetti dinner with some gravy. I promise I'll call it gravy, Renzo. I promise you don't have to get your hair cut, and you can put your feet on the coffee table, and you don't have to make your bed anymore. Just please come back. I hit my head and it hurts so bad. Maybe that's why this is happening. It's just a dream, right? I got a concussion and this is all a dream. Marco, please walk through that door smiling and surprise me with Renzo holding flowers or something. I want you to help me out of this bed with your strong arms and take me home and take care of me. Please, please, please....

***

"No! Please! Please Marco! Please!"

Kate's mom, Louise, pushed back the curtain and ran to Kate's bedside.

"Kate!"

Feeling something shake her shoulder, Kate pulled herself up through the deep fog.

"You're dreaming, Kate. Wake up, sweetheart."

Kate stopped thrashing and opened her eyes. The hospital room was dimly lit, but she recognized the face in front of her.

"Mom?"

Seeing her mother's worried face hovering above her brought Kate to the devastating reality: her husband and son were dead. She began to wail, but then stifled it to a quiet whimper. She reached up to her mother's face with a weak hand.

"I'm here," said Louise. She wiped Kate's sweat-drenched hair from her forehead. "Dad's here, too. We've been sitting outside waiting for you to wake up."

On seeing her dad, John, standing behind her mom, both looking sorrowfully at her, Kate let out an agonized moan. She sat up and reached out to them. They huddled together as Kate buried her face in her mom's chest. She cried as her parents wept in silence. After several minutes, Kate pulled back and wiped her eyes and nose with the handkerchief her dad held out for her.

She blew her nose and sucked in jerky puffs of air, letting them out slowly. Her head pounded and her eyes, nearly swollen shut, ached as she looked up at her parents.

They looked old. Tired.

Her dad walked around to the other side of the bed and sat next to Kate, reaching across to take her hand. As they cried, Kate's mind whirled between the realization that Marco and Renzo were gone and her refusal to accept it. Suddenly, she straightened, eyes wide, her mind clear. She smeared her hair from her face, pushed back the sheet and blanket, and threw her legs over the side of the hospital bed.

"I want to see them."

Her mom's mouth hung open, as her dad stood and shouted at her. "What? Kate, no."

Kate nodded furiously. "I want to see them. Now."

She scrambled out of bed, pausing to let the dizziness pass, as the cold linoleum drifted up through her stocking feet. She saw her winter jacket and purse laying across the end of her hospital bed, her winter boots dripping on the floor below. She noted her attire: her sweatpants and sweater. No hospital gown—yet. Louise gently touched her arm.

"Kate. No." Her mother's voice cracked. "You're *not* ready."

"I'll *never* be ready for something like this, Mom. I *need* to see them."

Louise let her daughter go. Kate pushed back the curtain and walked gingerly out into the bright hallway, her head pounding. She looked up and down the hall but saw no one. She took a chance at the first left she encountered and turned, walking a short distance. Halfway down and to her right was a nurses' station. She stopped and shouted at the group of nurses busying themselves with various tasks behind the counter.

"I need to see my husband and son. Now."

The strength and determination of her voice surprised her, considering how weak her legs felt and how much she'd struggled to stand upright. A peripheral view of her parents walking toward her from her right didn't sway that determination.

One flustered nurse said, "Okay, let me see what rooms they're in."

"They're not in a *room*," Kate shouted. "They're *dead!*"

Her angry, loud voice surprised her. Surprised everyone.

The other nurses stopped what they were doing to look at Kate, as Louise wrapped an arm around Kate's waist.

"Please, sweetheart. Come back to your room."

Kate yanked her shoulder and pushed herself from her mom. She took a step back from everyone.

"No! Where are they? Why is everyone staring at me? Find out where they are! I need to see them. Please."

She felt the hysteria building in her stomach, crawling toward her throat.

Hold it together, Kate. Now's not the time to collapse. You may never get another chance to hold them.

The nurse who'd been sitting with her earlier ran up the hall to Kate and waved the other nurses off.

"Mrs. De Luca?"

Kate turned to the familiar face, her arms outstretched. "Please. I *need* to see them," she whimpered. "Please."

"Okay," said the nurse in a calm voice. She took hold of Kate's arms. "Let me—" she looked around and then back at Kate. "Let me see where they are ...." Kate felt the woman's sincerity and saw it in her concerned eyes.

"Wait right here. I'll get them ready for you, okay?"

Kate's quivering hand went to her lips as she nodded.

Get them ready ...

Her head felt as if it would split down the middle. She was grateful for her dad's strong arm around her waist as they waited. She rested her head on his shoulder where, at that moment, it seemed to fit perfectly.

"Try to breathe, honey." His deep voice was quiet, soothing. "Just try to breathe."

She nodded at him and tried to do as he suggested.

Kate's mother stood in front of her, as Kate took slow, unsteady breaths. She couldn't bear the look of her mother's pained face, so she squeezed her eyes and pressed back her own burning tears. She continued to mimic her dad's dramatized slow breathing.

In and out. In and out.

Kate heard the distant voice of the nurse and opened her eyes to see her walking toward her. "I have them ready for you, Mrs. De Luca. Come with me."

Kate looked at her mom and up at her dad, who kissed her forehead before letting her go. She left her parents standing under the bright lights of the cold hospital hallway, and walked alongside the nurse down an endless corridor. They took an elevator that brought them down two flights. They turned left off the elevator and continued down another long hall. This one seemed gloomier. Deserted. At the end of the hall stood a set of double-doors. The nurse used her badge to open it, and then put her arm around Kate's waist as they walked in together.

After a short walk, they turned left.

"They're in here," said the nurse, her words stopping Kate's heart and breath. The woman opened the door and stepped aside, giving Kate a sad, but compassionate, smile.

Kate looked past the metal-framed door and into the room. The nurse backed out and quietly shut the door.

Her steps felt heavy as Kate entered the chilly steel room. Medical equipment, now quiet, was pushed to the side, no longer needed for the lifeless patients lying before her. She felt a choking panic rise in her throat as her dizziness returned.

Her first glimpse was of their dark curls. She scanned their bodies, covered by clean, pale blue sheets. Their arms lay over the sheets, resting at their sides, their beds touching. The room was silent. Still. No life-saving machines or pumping noises. Just the distant sound of life outside the morbidly serene, dim room.

She struggled to believe the lifeless bodies were those of her family. Her life. Marco and Renzo's thick, dark hair, as beautiful as if they were still alive, fell back and away from their gray, wax-like faces. Their extreme stillness sickened her.

A fog swirled inside her head as she moved slowly toward them, the crisp sheets hiding the ugly reality.

Sixty-eight

Kate moved toward them, her hand first touching the footboard of Renzo's bed. She let it glide along the soft sheet, and then the mattress, as her husband and son's faces came into view. She put her trembling hand to her mouth to quiet the scream rushing to her throat. Air choked and sputtered in her lungs and her head jerked back and forth as she forced her wobbling legs to continue.

She separated their beds and walked between them, dragging her fingertips along the side of each bed until she was face-to-face with her motionless family. Their faces looked stiff, drained.

Dead. They're both dead.

She reached out a weak hand to touch Renzo's forehead. His skin felt cool. Like rubber. She shook her head as she reached over to touch Marco's forehead forcing her eyes away from the gaping wound in his left temple. She leaned down and kissed his cheek and moved across to Renzo and kissed his cheek.

Staying close to their faces, she whispered. "I'm scared, you guys. Why did this happen to us? I want you to come back. I need you."

Kate hated seeing them like this. Though they were together, they seemed—alone—empty. She reached out her hands and placed one on each of their clammy cheeks before grabbing a chair and pulling it between the two beds. Instant relief flowed through her legs as she sat down.

She cried heavy, loud and mournful tears. The pain in her heart filled the room, though she barely heard herself. She stood to kiss them, or fuss with their sheets, or make sure they were covered. She whispered to them.

Her heart sank when light from the swinging door crossed the floor as it brushed open, signaling the end of her final visit with them.

The nurse peeked in. "I'm sorry ma'am. It's time."

Kate moaned. "No!"

The nurse walked in and stood next to her. She leaned over and put her arm around Kate's shoulder. "I'm sorry. We have to go."

Kate sobbed as she gave them each one last kiss. "Goodbye my loves. See you soon."

She looked up at the nurse who gave her an odd look. As they left the room, Kate stole one last glimpse of her husband and son before the door closed behind her.

Sixty-nine

*E*ddie's face flushed red as he pounded his fist into the center of the desk. "What the hell are you telling me, Sal? Jesus H. Christ!"

His heart pounded as he pressed his fingers to his temples. He could barely stand to look at Sal, who stood before him with that stupid fucking remorseful look on his face. Eddie lowered his hands and mustered all of his restraint to stop himself from jumping over the desk and strangling Sal to his last breath.

The heat that was about to come down on them barely mattered. The only thought rattling in his brain was Kate. His hope that they could one day be together vanished in the split second it took for that fat fuck Sal to walk into his office and tell him that he'd killed the kid.

"I told you to kill that thief, Marco, Sal. What the fuck happened?"

Sal stood in front of Eddie's desk and looked at the floor and then back at Eddie. "I'm real sorry, Eddie. It all happened so fast."

"Yeah?" Eddie said. "Tell me." He pounded his fist again. "Tell me!"

"Well, ah' … first I ah' … I drove to Marco's house, like you told me to, so I could keep an eye on him and follow him if he left." Sal paused to check Eddie's reaction and then continued. "But his car wasn't in the driveway, like it usually is. Just Kate's white SUV. So, I left."

"And?"

"And—I came back here—to the restaurant and sat in the car for a while, across the street in the parking lot. And then, it was gettin' dark so I drove back to Marco's house. The Mustang was in the driveway. That's when I decided I'd just wait. I mean, you said you wanted it done right away. So, I parked about three houses down." Sal shrugged. "Waited maybe an hour, hour-and-fifteen, and that's when the SUV pulled out of the driveway. Thought it was Kate at first, but then another car came from the opposite direction and its lights shined in on the driver. It was Marco. I waited a few seconds and pulled out. I followed him down to Payne.

Eddie leaned back in his chair, bouncing slightly, arms crossed, jaw clenched. It was all he could do to keep himself from shooting Sal right in the face.

"Then what?"

Sal gave Eddie a quick side-glance before continuing. "I followed him down to Minnehaha. He took a few turns into a neighborhood. Turns out he was going to pick up the kid."

Eddie growled, ready to rip into him, but Sal raised his hands.

"I swear, Eddie. I didn't know who it was. I saw Marco walk up to this house. Didn't know whose house it was. And so, ah' ... while he was in there, I ran out and gave the tire a light pop with my knife. Ya' know, for a slow leak, hoping he'd pull over. Make it easier for the hit."

Sal again looked down at his feet before starting up again. "Then, Marco walks out with the kid, but, like I said, at the time, I didn't know that, right? The kid's pretty tall. Almost as tall as Marco. And, and ... I couldn't tell in the dark .... They both had on those puffy winter jackets and hats. I swear, Eddie. I didn't know who it was. And, like I said before, you wanted it done that night and I ah', I wanted to get it done fa' you."

"So," Eddie said, "I guess I didn't know Sal, that you are *so* fuckin' stupid," Eddie pointed at him, "that right then, you *knew* you'd be taking out *two* people, even though you didn't know who the second guy was. Is that what you're fuckin' tellin' me?"

Sal looked up at the ceiling and let out a puff of air before nodding at Eddie.

Eddie kept a brutal gaze on Sal. "And then what?"

Sal continued. "They got in. I followed, staying back a bit, waitin' for the tire to flatten. I could see Marco started havin' trouble around Arcade. He took a left and pulled into one of them three little roads down there, not even a road, really. Then, he pulled over cuz-a the tire, and I pulled up behind him."

Sal continued. "I ah' ... got out and walked over to Marco's car, pulled out my piece, had it at my side."

"Go on."

"I ah' … went to the driver's side. Marco saw it was me and rolled down his window. Was glad to see me, asked me to help him with the tire." Sal shrugged. "That's when I popped him. And when I did that, the kid opened his door and started runnin'. So I chased him around the back — met him by the trunk — and shot him. That's when I saw it was the kid."

Eddie slammed his fist on the desk three times. Sal blinked, but otherwise kept his composure.

"Then," Sal continued, "I dragged the kid around and put him back in the car — the passenger seat. He was still alive, so I thought he might be okay."

"Oh, is that right? You thought he'd be okay? Huh?"

Eddie reached into the side drawer of his desk and pulled out O's .45. He stood, walked around his desk and shoved it into Sal's temple.

"Whoa, whoa," Sal shouted as he stepped back, his hands raised in surrender. "Eddie, please! Jesus Christ! I'm sorry!"

"I oughta' waste you right here, you stupid fuckin' piece-a shit."

Eddie's face twisted and contorted as he continued to press the pistol into Sal's head. Sal stood motionless, hands still raised, eyes squeezed shut.

The office door flew open. "Eddie!" Tau shouted. "What are you doing? Stop!"

Dario came in behind Tau and both of them put their hands out cautiously, as they approached Eddie and Sal.

"Come on, Eddie," Dario said. "Put it down. You don't wanna' do this. Think-a the mess. We don't *need* this right now. Not here in your office, man. Not worth it. Come on now, Eddie. Put it down."

Eddie released the gun from Sal's head. "Fuck!"

He hit him in the head with the butt of it. Sal dropped to the floor against the wall, groggy, but still conscious. Eddie moved in, leaning down. He again smashed the butt of the gun into Sal's cheek and then kicked him in his gut with his pointed dress shoes three times, before Dario and Tau pulled him off. Sal lay still, in a heap, blood pouring from his forehead.

Eddie was breathless as he pushed them away. He pointed down at Sal. "Get him outta' here."

He turned back toward his desk as Tau and Dario struggled to pull Sal to his feet. They hauled him out of the office, his head hanging and his feet dragging behind him.

Eddie slammed the door and paced the office. He stopped in front of his desk and pounded both hands on top of it.

"Fuck!"

KATE

Seventy

Kate watched the light traffic from the front passenger seat of her parents' silver SUV, her dad next to her, driving. The ride home from the hospital was brief. She'd hoped for more time to prepare herself for the return to her empty house.

She turned to look at her mom sitting quietly in the back seat. She gave Kate a reassuring smile and nod, but it didn't help. The lump in Kate's throat grew as her dad turned the car up her driveway. She looked at her house, eerily silhouetted against the darkness, the lights still on from when she'd left in a frenzy a few hours earlier.

John pulled up the driveway and parked. Kate realized her SUV and Marco's Mustang were still on Arcade—at the *scene*. Her dad turned to her. "Kate, sweetheart. Are you *sure* you don't want to stay with us for a few days?"

"Thanks, but I'll be fine."

"I'm happy to stay with you, dear," said Louise.

Kate turned back to look at her. "I know, Mom. Thanks, but I *need* to be alone."

Her mom reached her hand out and Kate stretched back to take it before letting it slip away. She opened her door and got out slowly, her wobbly legs reminding her how weak she felt. Her parents got out too and came around to her side, hands out. Kate stopped them.

"I'm fine. I can walk," she said, sharper than she'd intended. She squeezed her eyes for a second and reached out to touch her mom's shoulder. "Sorry. I—"

Her mom gently kissed each side of her face and whispered, "I know, honey. We'll come in for a minute. Get you settled, check to make sure you have enough to eat, and be on our way."

Kate nodded as she fought back burning tears. Her dad took her arm and they climbed the back steps together. He took his extra set of keys to her house and unlocked the back door. Kate followed him. She sucked in a breath and held it, as she saw

Renzo's sweatshirt hanging on the chair and Marco's work shoes neatly on the mat next to the door. She touched her throat and looked around before setting her purse on the table.

Slowly, she blew out the air. "This is gonna' be harder than I thought."

Her parents stood there. Silent.

"Mom?"

"Yes, Kate?"

Would you mind calling Marco's mother, Mary, in Brooklyn? I don't think I'm up to it."

"Of course. Give me her number. I'll call her while you go upstairs and change."

Kate dug in her purse for her phone and found Mary's number.

Her dad kissed her cheek. "Maybe a nice bath would feel good. Do you want me to get it started for you?"

"That does sound good. But I can do that after you leave. I'll go up and change. Be down in a bit."

"Okay, sweetheart," he said.

Kate walked through the living room. She felt numb as she slowly headed up the stairs.

At the top, she stopped at Renzo's room. It took all her might not to flip on the light and walk in. She stayed near the doorway and gazed around. Her young son's life was evident in every corner of his room. His bed was made, messy job as usual. The never-ending pile of dirty clothes on the floor near the closet, and his schoolwork, unfinished, on the old wooden desk, his chair neatly pushed in. Kate pressed her hand to her mouth holding in the cry, but that didn't work. More tears burned her cheeks. She forced herself to continue down the hall to her bedroom.

She flipped on the light and stood near the door before moving to sit on the bed. She smoothed her hand across the bedspread, as she thought about her last conversation with Marco.

His shoes and gym clothes lay in a pile just inside their closet. She rustled through a mound of her own clothes and found a pair of sweatpants and a nightshirt. She dropped the shirt and picked up Marco's t-shirt. She held it to her face. The scent of his cologne brought him to life. She put it on and went back downstairs to find her mother going through her cupboards calling out things to her dad, who was making a list.

Her mom's voice sounded shaken, upset, as she turned to Kate. "How's your headache? Is it feeling any better?"

"A little," Kate lied. "Did you get a hold of Mary?"

Louise stopped going through the cupboards and nodded. "Yes. I—that was one of the most difficult things I've ever done. She insisted on talking to you, but I told her you weren't up to it."

Kate nodded. "Thanks for doing that. I'll call her tomorrow. You can go now. I'll be fine."

John stepped in. "Come on, Louise. Let's go."

"But—"

"*Now.*" He handed Louise her coat and purse.

Kate's knees felt ready to collapse beneath her, as she waited for her parents to gather their things. She couldn't wait to be alone. Her mother walked to her and kissed her cheek, and her dad gave her a strong hug. He pulled back, gently touching her chin. "We'll call you tomorrow, sweetheart. Take that bath and try to get some rest."

She nodded, but her quivering chin kept her from speaking.

Her parents left out the back door into the darkness, leaving Kate standing motionless near the table where she and her family had shared so many conversations and memories. She moaned as she realized they'd never sit there or anywhere for dinner again.

She left the kitchen and trudged back upstairs, her head pounding from the fall at the hospital. At the top of the stairs, she again paused at the door to Renzo's room, but this time, she didn't look in.

She walked into her bedroom and headed for the bathroom. Turning the bath water as hot as she could tolerate, she stripped down and stared at her reflection in the mirror. She barely recognized the tired woman looking back at her. As she tied up her hair, she noticed something on her face. She leaned in to the mirror and saw a smear of dark blood near her ear. She used her tears to loosen it. Her sobs grew as she continued to wipe the blood long after it was gone.

She stepped into the tub. Her shoulders trembled and her stomach muscles contracted, as she drifted into the hot water. The sound from the faucet drowned her sobs. She shivered and cried, waiting for it to fill around her cold body. With the warmth, came the grief she'd been holding back all night. She sat motionless in the tub, crying off-and-on, allowing her sorrow to win its battle with fatigue.

The horrifying image of Marco and Renzo bleeding in her car was pressed into her mind no matter how hard she tried to will it away. She realized then, as she mourned, that she'd live with that memory etched as a permanent scar until the day she died.

After a while, her tears subsided and the water cooled, sending a shiver through her bones. She climbed out and dried off. She took something for her pounding head and climbed into their bed for the first time as a widow. She lay back and closed her eyes, unable to fight the exhaustion any longer. Her slumber was restless, the nightmare of the day's events vivid in her dreams. It was the first of many more to come.

Seventy-one

Kate spent the following week with her parents in a fog-like trance as they made the copious arrangements needed to bury Marco and Renzo.

The first stop was O'Halloran & Murphy Funeral Home. Her dad maneuvered south through the always-busy Snelling traffic, and brought the car to a stop in the funeral home's huge parking lot, piles of snow plowed high around its perimeter. Kate sat motionless in the back seat until her mother opened the door and leaned in, reaching for her hand.

"Come on, dear. I know you don't want to do this. I'll do my best to get you through it as quickly as possible."

Grateful for her words, Kate took her mother's gloved hand and slid out of the car. A bitter wind slapped her face before sneaking into the crevices of her tan wool coat, sending a shiver through to her bones. Wool in January was never adequate, but her mother insisted on "dressing up" for such a solemn occasion.

The grim sky pressed downward, its cold, gray clouds seemingly close enough to touch. Kate's dad opened the trunk and removed the garment bag holding the clothing her husband and son would be buried in.

The three of them walked gingerly across the icy parking lot, side-by-side. They stepped onto a short sidewalk toward a stout, white-pillared entrance, canopied with a peaked roof bearing the name of the facility in tall, gilded letters. Kate had been to many wakes in this red-brick building, but had never noticed that sign or the white shuttered windows.

Her dad held open the door for Kate and her mother, and followed them into a sizeable foyer with chandeliered lighting and soft, beige carpeting. Kate welcomed the room's immediate warmth. Silence filled the space, prompting them to whisper. To their left was an office with glass windows. A tall, middle-aged man with thinning brown hair looked up and came out to greet them, speaking softly.

"Good afternoon. You must be Mrs. De Luca." He reached for Kate's hand. His touch felt warm, a bit sticky. "My name is Lewis Patterson. I'm so sorry for your losses."

Losses. Plural.

"I'll be helping you with the arrangements today."

"Thank you, Mr. Patterson," said Louise. "Yes, this is our daughter, Kate De Luca. I'm Louise O'Brien and this is my husband, John."

Kate forced a weak smile but felt distracted. Marco and Renzo were somewhere in the building. Their presence was the only reason she could put one foot in front of the other. She suddenly became acutely aware of her burning face and eyes, raw from wiping the never-ending flood of tears.

Lewis led them into a moderately sized office with a window facing Snelling Avenue. After the paperwork was completed, he then showed them where the wake would be held.

Kate let her mother handle the details. She followed behind, saying nothing. Her dad's firm grip on her elbow kept her steady, as the now-familiar numbness returned and grew heavy. She preferred the feeling of nothingness. She didn't care about any of the details, nor did she have the energy to argue with her mother about them. She felt barely conscious, let alone sane enough to make decisions.

A familiar wall of darkness began pressing Kate's mind inward as though she were wrapped in a straitjacket. She felt lightheaded and breathless as her parents' voices grew distant. She continued to nod in agreement no matter the decision.

Thankfully, her mother knew Kate better than she'd thought and most decisions were adequate. Louise waited though, for a nod from Kate before finalizing anything. There was one decision they'd disagreed on. Kate insisted on open caskets for the wake. She didn't articulate the reason, but the truth was, she *needed* to see them one last time. Once this decision was made, they followed Lewis along a carpeted hallway and down some stairs to what Kate could only describe as a casket store.

The room held a faint odor of newness that burned her nostrils and made her body go rigid. She put her hand to her mouth to stop her lips from quivering. In front of her were rows and rows of caskets, one more elaborate than the next. Death boxes of all sizes, colors and finishes. Each on its own cloth-covered pedestal for better eye-level viewing of their satin bedding and pillows.

Kate's vision darkened. Everything seemed to compress and shrink. Nausea curled in her belly, as her head began to spin. She squeezed her eyes before finding herself looking upward. Her breath grew shallow. Voices muffled. The walls closed in and quickly faded and disappeared. A translucent light grew, bright at first, but then quickly dwindled to a murky gloom before darkness enveloped her.

> *Kate opened her eyes to find she was sitting alone in a field of long, green grass, a forest of trees surrounding her in the distance. Before her, were two deep openings in the ground. A mountain of black dirt, six feet high, surrounded her and the holes. Two open caskets holding Marco and Renzo were perched above the openings, suspended mid-air, as they gently swayed back-and-forth. Dressed in black suits with white dress shirts and black ties, Marco and Renzo's arms were folded across their stomachs, eyes closed. They looked alive, but asleep.*

> *The earth began to rumble. Kate tried to stand and flee but slipped, and her feet fell out from under her. She scrambled back up as the mountains of dirt shook and tumbled down like an avalanche. It quickly formed mounds around her legs and waist, trapping her movement. The cool, moist soil then crashed on top of her, across her head and into her eyes and mouth. She coughed and choked, as she reached across both boxes with her arms, the dirt's weight nearly breaking her bones as she screamed soundlessly. Her efforts to shield Renzo and Marco from the landslide were futile. They pleaded with their eyes but her dirt-filled mouth prevented her from crying out. All she could do was choke and watch them disappear under the heap of black soil.*

Kate awoke to her father's face close to hers. Her eyes darted around the room, as he spoke to her.

"Sweetheart. Are you alright? Can you hear me?"

She coughed and choked but it wasn't necessary. There was no dirt in her mouth. No dirt anywhere. She blinked.

"Kate?"

"I can hear you, Dad."

She squeezed her eyes shut, trying to press back the burning tears, but she was unable to stop the warm drips from traveling down both cheeks toward her ears.

Her voice cracked. "I'm sorry. I don't know what happened. I—" She shook her head back and forth.

"Shush," he whispered with a sad smile. "You fainted. Can you get up? Or do you need to stay put a bit longer?"

Cloth-covered pedestals and the bottom sections of caskets encircled her. Her mother's nyloned legs and burgundy pencil-skirt were to her left. Kate twisted her head to look up at her. Louise was bent over, wringing her hands, her hair falling forward around her face.

Kate pressed herself up onto her elbows. "I'll be okay. Help me up, Dad. Let's get this over with. I need to get out of here."

John helped her up, keeping a firm hand under her elbow. With the spinning of her head subsiding, Kate nodded her willingness to proceed.

Louise opened the door and allowed Lewis back in. He gave Kate a sincere and concerned smile.

"You need to pick them, dear," her mom said softly.

Kate inhaled deeply, took a quick look around, and walked to a shiny, black coffin with white satin interior. "These will do. Doesn't really matter, does it?"

"Okay, Kate," said John. "Let's get you some fresh air while your mother finishes things up."

Kate gave Lewis a slight nod and allowed her dad to help her out of the hellhole and back outside. The icy air knocked her senses straight. It was exactly what she'd needed.

"Do you want to sit in the car and wait?"

"No. I need the air. You get in. It's freezing. I just need to be alone for a minute."

"Sure, kiddo." He kissed her cheek and got into the car, starting the engine.

Kate looked up at the steely sky and tried to rid herself of the terrifying dream. She knew, though, that she'd never forget the look of terror in her husband and son's eyes as the dirt filled up around them.

She cried quietly, wiping the tears before they froze onto her cheeks. She wished she were anywhere else in the world.

Seventy-two

The sounds of church bells and traffic were muted behind the heavy, dark wooden doors of the Church of the Assumption. Momentarily blinded by darkness, Kate paused and waited for her eyes to adjust to the soft light. The faint scent of holy incense tickled her nose and provided an instant sense of comfort. Her parents stood next to her, quietly waiting for Kate to take the first steps into the lovely old-world church.

As they paused inside the narthex, the quiet echo of footsteps and coughs bounced across the stone floor and up to the church's towering arched ceiling. She looked out across the nave at the growing congregation of mourners, most dressed in black, and amply represented on both sides of the aisle. Their bowed heads were gracefully illuminated by extravagant chandeliers and natural light filtered in through brightly colored stained glass windows perched high above the altar.

Some of the bereaved stood, speaking softly to acquaintances, hugging, crying. But most sat quietly, the harmony of creaks created by their movement on the old wooden pews, adding to the solemn mood.

Kate held her gaze straight ahead, grateful for the brimmed black hat and veil her mother insisted she wear. It made it easier to evade the sad eyes watching her from both sides of the aisle. Her simple black dress and string of pearls were also her mother's idea, but the dress felt loose and disheveled. Her high heels pinched her toes—numb from the bitter January temperature—and felt unsteady under her feet. She longed for her gray and white flannel pajamas, her soft snuggly socks, and her bed with its thick, puffy comforter.

Piped notes from the church's organ reverberated throughout the holy room with a familiar hymn, as Kate and her parents made the long walk to the front pew. Ahead, the closed caskets of her husband and son loomed at the front of the altar, draped in the traditional linen pall.

As they approached, Kate stood in front of the caskets, setting one hand on each.

Her husband and son. Sealed inside.

Her dad guided her to her place in the front pew to the left of the caskets. Kate's parents sat on either side of her—to keep her from escaping—she guessed. She glanced over at Marco's grieving mom, who blew her a sad kiss as they exchanged a moment of grief together.

Kate began to lose herself in the past but was shaken to her senses by her dad. He'd tightened his grip on her arm and gave her a strange look she'd never seen before. So sad. So worried.

What had she just done? Did she say something out loud? Why was he was looking at her like that?

"Are you sure you're alright?"

"No dad," she whispered. "I'm *not* alright. But what am I supposed to do? Run?" She glanced around the church. "'Cuz, I *want* to run."

He wrapped his arm tight around her shoulder and leaned in his head to touch hers.

"Come on, baby. Stay with me."

The strength of his hold on her, and the encouragement in his voice, helped her carry on. She stared past him at the caskets. They seemed to be moving further away. Shrinking backward.

From behind her, in the loft high above, choir singers began a beautifully mournful rendition of *Ave Maria*. The melody startled Kate, taking her breath for a moment. She listened intently to the soprano's clear tone, and the accompanied harmonies, so beautiful it made Kate's heart ache.

She wanted to cry out loud. Instead, safely hidden behind the black veil, she swallowed the choking lump in the back of her throat, but let her quiet tears fall.

She heard a low whimper and looked up at her dad, as he fought back tears. He'd always tried to be strong for her, and seeing him like this broke Kate all over again.

Her mother's arm came across her shoulders from her right, and the three of them bowed heads and released their pain together. She felt her mom's body shudder lightly next to her, and she fought to hold herself together as the funeral pressed on.

With each passing reading, intermittent song, and prayer, Kate felt more and more shattered. Father Byrne's words of death, immortality, faith, afterlife—it was all too much. She felt guilty for wanting the service to end. For rushing the final moments with her husband and son, but her weariness was winning this fight. It had sapped her strength and her will.

After communion, the congregation sat quietly, as Father Byrne finished his holy duties and began his final remarks. Kate barely listened, eager to flee, but, when she heard him mention Marco and Renzo, and something about the *Tango*, her head popped up. At that moment, the sweet high melody from violins accompanied by an accordion graced her ears. *Their* song—the *Tango*—filled every crevice of the church.

She looked at her dad, the lights from above reflected in his flowing tears. Never had she loved him more. He knew the depth of the meaning that song held for her. *He* brought this song to the service. *He* made this happen. She collapsed into his arms. She'd never known he was capable of such thoughtfulness.

She lifted her head from his chest and scanned the congregation. They had joined in her pain, many wiping their eyes, all of them watching her with sadness and melancholy smiles.

She finally realized that they understood her pain.

Seventy-three

*A*fter the service, Kate stood at the back of the church, her parents and Marco's mother standing with her, as they greeted well-wishers.

As she hugged a co-worker, she heard a familiar and inappropriately loud voice. She glanced to her right and saw him. Down the aisle, mingling near the pews, stood Eddie. He wore a stunning black suit with a white dress shirt, and a splashy pink and yellow paisley tie. A line of people stood waiting to speak to him. His thick, black hair was set in its usual polished manner, his laughter and hand-shaking—like a celebrity—contrasting almost comically against Kate's grieving.

Look at him. Acting as if this was about him.

Kate watched him survey his crowd of fans, obviously wallowing in his popularity. He looked up to see her watching him. His face quickly fell into an appropriately somber expression. The insincerity of this subtle move struck a nerve. It was telling. She watched as he gave her a slight wave and a smile. He fought his way through the crowd toward her, his squad following behind him like poorly dressed robots.

Eddie reached out his hand. Kate paused before taking it. His side-glance at her hesitation pleased her. His hand felt cool and strong. Smooth. Manicured, of course. But still, in her mind, his grip felt like acid. She wanted to yank her hand away. To wipe the filth onto her skirt. But instead, she let it slide slowly down to her side, so as not to cause a scene.

For the first time in a while, Kate felt alert, her mind clear, as she looked into Eddie's eyes. Then, tilting her head, she looked past him and into the eyes of his goons.

"Oh. S'cuse my manners," Eddie said, stepping aside so the three men could also pay their respects.

"You remember my cousin, Sal."

Sal.

Sal, with a swollen black and blue cheek and a bandage near his brow, stuck out his meaty paw and gently took Kate's hand.

"Condolences." He wouldn't look her in the eye and stepped back quickly.

"And I think you've met these two: Dario and Tau."

Dario bowed as though greeting a queen. Eddie gave him a quick smack on the arm.

"Sorry for your loss, ma'am," he said, stepping back behind Sal.

Tau shook her hand. "Sorry," was all he said. He nodded and stepped back.

Kate took a good look at all of them. Burning their faces into her memory.

Dario. Young. Tall. Skinny. Black. Out of control—if she recalled Marco's description of him.

Tau. Young. Tall. Asian. Reserved.

Sal. Old. Beefy. Italian. Dangerous.

Eddie put his hand to his chest. "Kate, I'm gonna' find out who did this. This ain't right. And if you need anything, you come see me, ya' hear?" He shook his head and flipped his fingers. "I mean it. Anything."

"Thank you, Eddie. I'll try to remember that."

She felt something sour build in the pit of her stomach. She wanted to run. Thankfully, her mother interjected. "Kate. Time to go."

Eddie dropped his hand and nodded. "Take care, Kate."

She stared at him for a second before turning to walk away with her parents.

She stopped. "I'll be right back."

"You alright, sweetheart?"

"I'll be fine, Dad. Go wait in the car. I won't be long."

Kate walked as quickly as her high-heels would allow to the wooden door at the end of the narthex. She shut the door behind her and turned herself around inside the tiny bathroom. She fell to her knees, vomiting into the toilet. She tried to quiet the sound of her heaving so as not to disturb the churchgoers, or God. Lifting herself from the floor, she took a step to the sink, turning on the water, as she looked at her reflection in the tarnished, cracked mirror. She lifted her chin to see beyond her veil.

God. I look like hell.

Kate bent down and splashed her face with cool water, and used her hand to rinse the sour taste from her mouth. She then dampened a paper towel and held it to her face as she stared into the mirror. She no longer recognized the person staring back at her. Her gaze looked empty. Lifeless.

Still, there was something stirring inside of her. Though her body felt numb, her mind had begun to race. There was something cold tugging at the depths of her belly. Eddie had triggered it. She'd felt it with his handshake. She'd seen it in his eyes and in the eyes of the other three standing with him.

He'd always been the perfect gentleman to her, to Mrs. Fortunato. Yet, Marco's words had suddenly come to the forefront of her mind. Some of the things Eddie had done were far from legitimate. Dangerous.

A quiet knock on the door brought her back to her reflection in the mirror.

"Kate? Everyone's waiting to go to the cemetery."

"Coming, Dad."

She dried her hands, ran them through her hair, and pinched her cheeks before adjusting her hat.

"Sorry," she said to her dad, who met her with a worried look.

"You okay?"

"I'll be fine. Let's just … get this day over with."

He held open one of the tall, heavy doors, and they walked out to where her mother stood waiting for them. Though the gray clouds still lingered, the day's brightness burned Kate's eyes, causing tears to form. She sucked in a deep breath and let the frigid air clear her foggy mind, as they made their way to the car to begin the procession to Sunshine Memorial Park Cemetery.

The service at the cemetery was a blur for Kate. She sat on a cold folding-chair, just far enough from the two silver caskets, that she couldn't reach out to touch them. Her frozen, numb toes throbbed from the vicious cold. A biting wind raged against her face and sent shivers to her bones.

A small group had braved the arctic weather and settled into chairs all around her. Others stood. All were ready to hear the priest's final words about her husband and son, yet anxious to leave the frozen grounds and get somewhere warm.

Through the wind, Kate heard Eddie's voice.

"No. Get the car ready."

Kate stiffened when, out of nowhere, she remembered Marco mentioning the stolen money. Her grief had been so consuming, and she'd been so numb to everything, she hadn't had space in her mind to recall the details of their hurried departure, until now.

"We gotta' leave. Things are really heatin' up ..." and ... *"He's burning mad right now, Kate. I think he might come after me."*

She sucked in a deep breath of frosty air and held it tight in her lungs, as she tried to clear the image of her dead family, with Eddie standing over them.

The priest's muffled voice barely registered. Kate heard none of his words, nor did she comprehend the words of her mother, who sat next to her and whispered endlessly into her ear.

Instead, her thoughts drifted to Marco and Renzo. If only she'd held Marco's hand tighter, kissed him longer; if only she'd looked at Renzo's face closer and listened to his words more carefully. Maybe then, her memories would be sharper, clearer.

A loud cough startled Kate back to her new bitter reality. The dark green tarp, serving as a temporary cover, flapped noisily above the caskets. She was certain the cough had come from Eddie and that made her want to scream. Instead, she sat quietly, unable to feel her numb limbs, as Father Byrne recited more holy words.

When he'd finally finished, those in attendance walked single-file to the caskets to deliver flowers, or place their hands on them for a moment of prayer before hurriedly leaving for their warm cars.

Kate found herself once again staring at the shiny silver boxes. Draped in floral sprays of pink and red, they loomed before her. For the first time, she noticed the caskets were sitting on long rods, hovering over deep holes dug into the dirt. Their permanent resting place.

She thought of her nightmare from the funeral home. Her heart burned at the thought of them lying inside, sealed tight, forever. She blinked away her thoughts and stared ahead. She knew she was looking for the last time, at the vessels that would take away her precious Marco and Renzo's bodies from her forever.

She let her body and mind drift. It was a relief, a numbness, that she embraced. She felt nothing and the reprieve was comforting. It was her newfound inner hiding place.

Voices nudged her to the present, but she didn't stay there long. She drifted again, falling back into her head, her thoughts.

Back at home eating dinner together.

For now, pretending was all she needed.

Seventy-four

*A*fter a small gathering of family and friends at Kate's parents' house in Hudson, Wisconsin, Kate, John and Louise dropped Marco's mom, Maria, off at the airport. The three of them then drove in silence until they turned up the driveway to Kate's house. The sun had set, and Kate both dreaded and yearned to go inside.

She heard seatbelts unclicking.

"We'll come in and get you settled."

"No, Mom. Please. I'm fine. I just want to be alone. And you must be exhausted."

Louise opened the back door. "But—"

"Of course, Kate," said John. "Come on, Louise."

Louise huffed, but moved to the front passenger seat. Before shutting the car door, Kate leaned in. "Thanks again for everything. I really appreciate it. I couldn't have gotten through this day without you both."

"We wanted to help, sweetheart," said her mom.

"And we still want to help," said her dad. "Remember, we're here for you. Lock up when you get inside."

"Okay. I'll call you tomorrow."

Kate shut the car door and climbed the stairs. After unlocking the kitchen door and stepping inside, she switched on a light and turned to wave to her parents. She watched as their car's lights faded down the street. She continued to stare out into the shadows of her backyard long after they'd gone, as if in a trance. The house was eerily silent. This reality was more frightening than she'd imagined.

Home. By herself. Forever.

Leaving the light on over the stove, she walked into the living room and headed upstairs. She stopped at Renzo's door and flipped on the light switch. Her hand rushed to her throat as she choked on her own breath. She pressed her fingers to her lips to hold her scream, as her heart revved and pounded.

She stepped inside his room. Her hand touched his desk and the books and pencils scattered across it. Her fingers grazed the wooden shelves holding his soccer trophies and ribbons. Her feet brushed his favorite sweatshirt with his school's name and logo. It sat in its usual pile, near, but not in, the laundry basket. She picked it up and inhaled his scent, squeezing it tightly as she pressed the fabric into her eyes to absorb her burning tears.

Her little boy, her baby. Gone.

Her lips quivered and her nose burned, as she looked around his room. She took in every little thing, including his knee pads and soccer ball laying in the corner next to his bed. None of them could have known that the past season of soccer would be his last.

Kate sat on Renzo's bed and grabbed his pillow. She sat there for several minutes, before bringing it to her face and soaking in the scent of his shampooed curls.

More tears welled in her eyes, and she let them stream quietly down her cheeks. Images of Marco and Renzo's bloodied bodies blazed in her memory, flashing as bright as the police sirens at the scene. Those images popped in and out, and over and over in her mind. The pain of those visions was too much.

After days of holding it together for everyone else, she couldn't hold it in any longer. Her body began to seize and shudder. She fell off the bed to her knees and howled and rocked for nearly an hour, as she tried, unsuccessfully, to shake those horrible bloody images from her memory.

Sapped of all strength, she struggled to her feet. She grabbed Renzo's pillow, walked across the hall to her bedroom, and climbed into bed. She placed Marco's pillow near her face, taking in the subtle scent of his cologne, and held Renzo's pillow close to her heart.

She cried off and on, grateful for the solitude to finally let go. Loud, uncontrollable sobs purged her body, numbness and weariness the only breaks in her agony.

Her eyes grew heavy with fatigue and she finally relaxed, grateful to be alone, away from the looks of pity, the words of sorrow. It was all too heavy a burden for her to bear.

Her tears had dried for the moment, but her throat ached and her heart felt scorched, blackened. She flopped around for an hour before finally succumbing to complete exhaustion.

Seventy-five

*T*he morning light burned red through Kate's eyelids as it stirred her awake. The painful reminder of her sorrow quickly reappeared. Her night had been restless. Happy dreams of Marco and Renzo laughing at the dinner table, the three of them sitting in front of the TV, had transformed into nightmares of Renzo calling out to her, his bloodied hand stretched out, reaching for her. Darkness surrounded him. She couldn't see his face. Only his bloodied hand, which she couldn't reach.

Mom. I can't find you. I'm scared. Are you there, Mom?

The memory of that nightmare made her moan.

Her phone buzzed on the nightstand and startled her back to reality. Her body ached as she reached for it. She looked at the screen.

Mom.

She wasn't ready for her yet. She put the phone back on the nightstand and let it go to voicemail.

Ding.

The voicemail message had arrived. She'd never listen to it but would call her later.

Kate lay in bed, looking up at the ceiling. The house was so quiet. She inhaled deeply and held it, before letting it out and upward so it hit her face. She squeezed her eyes shut and forced herself to sit up. The heat was running, but still, the room felt cold making her shiver. She hated to leave the warmth of her bed. After a wave of lightheadedness passed, and the brief throbbing in her temples subsided, she forced herself to her feet as she glanced at the clock on her nightstand.

Ten-fifteen.

Later than she'd thought. She needed a shower but didn't have the energy. Coffee first. She put on some warm wool socks and grabbed Marco's fluffy sweater, her favorite—because it was extra-large and cozy—before heading down to the kitchen.

She left the living room blinds closed and walked into the kitchen to make a pot of coffee. Soon, its aroma filled the kitchen.

On normal days, she'd inhale it slowly, savoring it. On normal days, she'd turn on some music and sway around the kitchen as she waited for the brewing to finish.

But nothing was normal anymore. Today, silence was all she was given, and it was all she could handle.

After pouring herself a cup of coffee, she sat at the kitchen table and stared blankly at the swinging door, willing Marco and Renzo to walk through it in their usual loud and chaotic fashion. Instead, the silence continued. She sat there sipping, but not tasting, the coffee as the throbbing in her head slowly crept back near the base of her skull.

Her buzzing phone startled her.

Mom, again.

She wasn't sure why, but these calls were making her angry. To make them stop, Kate answered.

"Hi Mom. Yes, I'm fine. Mm-hmm. I showered. Yep. Eggs and toast. Just tired. Really tired. Mm-hmm. Love you too. I will. Okay. Bye."

The call was quick and her mother seemed to believe her. Kate hoped this would keep her away, at least for a few hours.

She walked to the fridge and opened it but found herself mindlessly staring into it. She went back to her seat at the kitchen table, wrapped her hand around her cup and closed her eyes. A cold chill startled her back to reality. With her hand still wrapped around the now cold cup, Kate glanced over at the clock on the stove.

Eleven-ten.

She looked around the kitchen and put her hands to her face as the tears again burned up and out. The pain in her heart and chest grew—fast this time around—and she found she couldn't contain the tears.

Why? Why was this happening? Please. Let this be a dream.

She stopped crying as suddenly as she'd started, and again stared at the swinging door. She wanted to be up in bed, in the dark, but had no energy to climb the stairs. She lowered her head into her arms and rested them on the kitchen table. She stayed in that position until the phone buzzed.

Mom, again.

She let it go to voicemail. The clock read one-forty.

Kate willed herself up to bed and slipped away into darkness. She was beginning to like it there.

Seventy-six

A faint buzzing pulled Kate up from a deep slumber. She forced her heavy head to turn and look toward the nightstand. She stared at her buzzing phone until her mind came into focus. She glanced at the clock before answering.

Ten a.m.

She grabbed the phone. The caller I.D. showed it was Detective Steber.

When did I add this name to my phone?

Kate's failed memory concerned her as she hit the button on the screen.

"Hello?" Her hoarse voice surprised her. She cleared her throat.

"This is Detective Steber. Is this Mrs. De Luca?"

"Yes."

Kate sat up and wiped her face with her other hand as she tried to snap herself awake.

"Good morning, Mrs. De Luca. I wanted to give you a quick call with an update on your husband and son's case."

"Okay." She wasn't sure she wanted to hear what he was about to tell her.

"The most important information we have so far, is that the bullets removed from your husband and son came from the same weapon. So it's likely we're looking at a lone shooter."

Kate's mind raced. "Okay, but do you have any idea who that could be?"

"We're working on it, ma'am. But unfortunately, there are no real leads. We had one homeowner tell our officers he saw a guy walking about a block away from the scene around the time of the murd—," he paused and changed his language. "Around the time you drove up to your husband's vehicle. And, while it's unusual to see people walking outside in the dark when it's this cold, obviously, that's not against the law, and we have no way of knowing who it was."

Kate noted his slip-up but her heart quickened at the thought of a potential suspect. "Did he give any kind of description?"

"The witness said he thought the guy was short, stocky. He couldn't tell anything else—race or whatnot. It's not much, unfortunately."

"I understand. Anything else?"

"Uh, yeah."

Kate heard his hesitation and braced herself.

"We believe your son exited the vehicle immediately after his dad was shot. He made it around to the back of the SUV and that's where he was shot. He was then dragged back to the car. Blood on the snowy street with signs of him being dragged in the snow, along with no gun residue around the passenger seat, lead us to believe that that's what happened."

"Oh my God," Kate whispered. "He ran? For his life?"

"I'm real sorry ma'am. Yes."

"What kind of monster does something like this?"

"That's what we're trying to find out."

Kate's head swam. She was thankful she was still in bed. Her poor baby. He must have been so terrified.

"If I could ask one more question, it would be helpful," said the detective. "I know this is difficult for you."

Kate barely heard him. "Yes."

"You said your husband mentioned a flat tire on your call with him?"

"Yes. He said he was pulling over to change the tire."

The detective cleared his throat before speaking. "The tire had been punctured, Mrs. De Luca. With a knife or some other sharp object. We believe this shows premeditation."

"Premeditation? I—I don't ...." She paused. "Did they find anything else? Fingerprints or ... anything?"

"No prints, but that's not surprising. We're making another sweep of the scene and the vehicle to make sure we didn't miss anything."

"I can't believe it. I don't understand why—" Kate stopped speaking as it hit her.

Eddie.

It was so strange how her grief continued to play games with her memory. She needed to get out of this fog, but it was so difficult, like a weighted blanket pressing down on her brain. Of course this was all Eddie's doing. It suddenly became so clear.

"Ma'am?"

"I'm sorry, Detective," Kate said. "I'm having a hard time absorbing all of this."

"I understand this is difficult for you, Mrs. De Luca. Are you sure you don't know anyone who might want to harm your husband and son? No enemies? Someone with a grudge? Anything would be helpful."

"No," she lied. "No one."

She wasn't sure why she was lying to the detective, but maybe it was because she wanted more time to sort things out, and for her head to clear.

"Well, if anything comes to mind," said Detective Steber, "please let me know."

"I will. Thank you, Detective. And you'll call me if you hear anything?"

"Absolutely. I'll be in touch. Have a good day."

"Thanks. You too."

Kate hung up the phone and laid back on the pillow, staring at the ceiling.

Have a good day. Sure.

She put the back of her hand over her eyes. A guy walking? That could be anybody. But the punctured tire? Like the detective said, that shows premeditation. And there's only one person she could think of who'd want to harm Marco.

Eddie Bracchio.

But why would he kill Renzo? It didn't make sense. Even Eddie wouldn't do something like that. Would he? She rolled over and went back to sleep as visions of her dead husband's bloodied head resting on the steering wheel, flashed over and over in her dreams.

Seventy-seven

*K*ate spent the next week under a hideous spell of depression. Fatigue turned to restlessness and then to insomnia and back to fatigue. She answered her mother's daily calls to keep her at bay.

Her nights were spent staring at the ceiling, pretending Marco and Renzo were downstairs watching baseball, or in the kitchen, eating. Sometimes, she thought she'd heard their voices, their laughter. Other times, she'd walk around the house, up and down the stairs, or she'd find herself gazing out the window. She had urges to pull out her hair or throw dishes at the wall, but had no energy for such things.

She paced as she sobbed. She blamed Marco, but mostly herself, for their deaths. If only she'd come looking for them sooner, or ... or, what? What should she have done?

Something. She should have done something.

After a couple of weeks of deep depression, and as the familiar heavy blanket of fatigue had once again begun to fall across her shoulders, Kate's mother called to tell her they were coming over. Despite Kate's insistence that she was fine, her mother refused to change her mind.

Panic took hold as Kate observed her surroundings. She rushed around picking things up, and then ran to the bathroom to wash her face and brush her teeth. She looked at herself in the mirror. With her toothbrush still in her mouth, paste swimming around her lips, she let out a quiet gasp. Her hair fell limply around her face in greasy knots, but it was the dark cavities under her eyes and her hollowed cheeks that startled her most.

When was my last meal?

She couldn't recall. If her mother saw her like this, they'd have her committed. She ran down to the kitchen and forced herself to eat some toast and drink a glass of milk. She had an hour to pull herself together. She did *not* want a fuss from her parents, so this had to be good.

Stepping into the shower, Kate felt a wave of comfort as the hot water poured down her head and shoulders. After a few minutes, she washed her hair and reluctantly stepped out to dry off. She brushed and dried her hair and applied a light coating of lipstick to brighten her gray pallor. She then rummaged through a pile of her clothes laying in a heap on the closet floor, and found a clean pair of gray sweatpants and a long-sleeved black t-shirt. She stopped at her dresser mirror to check herself out.

Better.

Her hair drooped lifelessly around her shoulders, but at least it was clean and brushed. Her clothes seemed to hang a bit more than usual, but hopefully, her parents wouldn't notice. She pulled her shoulders back and stood straight. She'd have to remember to do that in their presence.

Still feeling out-of-sorts, she made her way downstairs and into the kitchen. She found some crackers to munch on, as the toast seemed to have triggered her appetite. She ate a bunch of them and drank a glass of water while she waited for her parents. She yearned for their visit to be over, so she could climb back into bed and again fall into darkness.

Seventy-eight

*T*he doorbell rang and Kate greeted her parents with a fake smile.

She knew her disguise hadn't worked when her mother's jaw fell at the sight of her.

"Kate! You look awful."

"Thanks, Mom."

Her dad kissed her cheek. "You alright, Kate?"

"I'm fine," she lied.

Kate sat on the sofa, prompting her parents to join her. She sat quietly for an hour while they chastised her about her health, eating, drinking fluids, getting rest, and getting out into the world. Her mother even suggested drinking wine.

Kate smiled and agreed with everything they'd said. She cried occasionally as she talked about missing Renzo and Marco, but had to admit the comfort and companionship of her parents felt nice.

Her mother made Kate eggs and pancakes which she didn't want, but ate them anyway. They offered her words of comfort, all while her mom sent her not-so-subtle hints.

"You know you can't stay pent up in this house all alone forever, Kate."

"Yes," Kate snapped. "I am aware of that."

"Well, I'm sorry, dear. I'm not trying to upset you. I'm just trying to give you a little motivation. Maybe you need a project. Keep yourself busy."

"I'm sorry. What do you want me to do? Take up knitting? Huh? My family was *murdered* two weeks ago, Mom. Your *son-in-law*. Your *grandson*."

"Don't use that tone—"

"Alright, alright," Kate's dad interrupted.

"Come on, Louise. Time to go."

Louise opened her mouth to protest but shut it fast. "Fine."

Kate walked them to the door where they exchanged hugs. "I'm sorry, Mom. I didn't mean to—"

Her mom shook her head. "No, *I'm* sorry. I'm rushing you. I don't mean to push, honestly. I don't."

"I know."

"Let us know if you need anything," said her dad.

"Thanks, Dad. I'll talk to you guys later."

Kate noted the setting sun, as her parents drove off. The renewed silence of the house hit her. She sat on the sofa with her head back, staring up at the ceiling, as she began to cry for the millionth time. When she'd settled down again, her mom's mention of wine prompted her to go to the kitchen and open a bottle.

She returned to the sofa with a glass of chardonnay in one hand, the bottle in the other. The living room was dark, but she left the light off, welcoming that mood, as she put up her feet and slowly sipped from the glass.

When half the bottle was gone, she took it upstairs. In her bedroom, she slid to the floor and leaned against the side of her bed. As she stared at the white slatted closet doors in front of her, she drank straight from the bottle. After a couple minutes, she leaned over and pulled open the closet doors.

She stared at the messy shelves of shoes and bags, before crawling in and rustling through Marco's clothes, chuckling at his bad habit of throwing everything into a pile in the corner. It had always infuriated her, but now, she'd do anything to have him next to her doing just that.

She flipped through Marco's stuff, inhaled his t-shirts and sweatshirts, and imagined him sitting there with her. She closed her eyes and pictured his face, his thick black hair.

After a couple of minutes, she blinked to clear her tipsy head, as she stared at the closet wall. A tan canvas bag was wedged inside a cardboard box of old car magazines she'd begged Marco to toss. She didn't recall ever seeing that bag before. It clearly looked as though Marco had been trying to hide it from her.

Kate crawled toward it. It felt oddly heavy. She dragged it out from under the magazines and into the bedroom. She dug her hand deep into the bag and pulled out a large silver pistol.

Seventy-nine

Kate's pulse raced, as she tried to push down her rising nausea.

Woozy from the wine, she stayed on the floor and held the cold gun in her hand. Where did Marco get a gun? Why did he need one? She shook her head and pressed her hand to her mouth. She'd believed him when he'd said he hadn't stolen the money, but maybe he'd been more involved in Eddie's street business than he'd let on.

Kate thought about how terrified Marco seemed that last day after his argument with Eddie. Pointing the finger at Sal for stealing; and then telling Eddie he was out; standing up to him; defying him; and how filled with rage Eddie had been. Marco *knew* Eddie would come after him—*after them*.

She recalled how Marco had been running around the house in a frenzy that evening, frantic for them to leave town. But, even before that terrible day, he had seemed troubled. And each day, he seemed more anxious. Fearful. They both knew that the only way out was to run. Why hadn't he grabbed the gun when packing for their move? Maybe he'd planned to run up and grab it once she and Renzo were belted in the car, ready to go. Maybe he didn't want her to know about it. Or maybe he didn't want to frighten her more than she already was. Kate scanned her memory fighting to remember the details of that day. Still, no matter how often she'd analyzed other theories on who killed Marco and Renzo, it always came back to Eddie.

Kate stuffed the gun into the canvas bag and pushed it back into the bottom of the box. Her head pounded as she crawled into bed. Her thoughts were out of control. She fell asleep with the lights on, tossing and turning, as recurring visions of the gun consumed her dreams.

The sound of a car revving past the house startled Kate from her slumber. She looked at the clock.

Four thirty-three a.m.

Her bedroom light was still on. The furnace hummed, but her cool face told Kate the room was chilly. The warm bed and her foggy head and heavy body kept her still. The wine had seemed like a good idea at the time, but now, she was paying for it.

She forced herself out of bed and put on her heavy robe and fluffy slippers. In the kitchen, she made toast and coffee and brought them into the living room. She sat on the sofa and thought about her last conversation with Marco, right there in that very spot.

She pushed herself back and swung her legs up into a fully reclined position. As her head cleared, she began to feel more alert at that moment than she had since the night of the murders.

As she looked up at the popcorn ceiling, that sleek, silver gun and Eddie's missing money crept back into her mind. She thought about some of her conversations with Marco and about his experiences with Eddie.

A vision of Eddie's face flashed in her mind. His cocky smile. She recalled his vain performance at the funeral. The way he shook hands and laughed like a celebrity. His phony sympathy.

What did he say?

> *"Kate, I'm gonna' find out who did this. This ain't right. And if you need anything, you come see me. Ya' hear?"*

Kate bolted up from her prone position and paced the tiny living room.

Eddie thought Marco had stolen from him. Marco had told her as much. He'd heard it from Micola and denied it to Eddie. But Eddie didn't believe him. *He* didn't know Marco like *she* did. Marco would *never* steal from Eddie. He'd never take such a risk with his family.

Kate next thought about Marco's role in Eddie's circle. She assumed she'd known everything about his job, but maybe he'd kept certain things from her. Maybe he needed the gun for protection.

The other problem was that Marco *knew* too much. He knew things that Eddie wanted kept secret. When Marco told Eddie he was quitting, it probably enraged Eddie and worried him at the same time.

All of this led Kate to conclude that, if Eddie truly believed Marco *had* stolen that money from him, coupled with Marco leaving the organization and taking valuable intel with him, Eddie would want Marco dead.

Kate put her hands to her head and squeezed her eyes shut. This *was* all her fault. She'd introduced Marco to Eddie. She'd encouraged Marco to take the job.

Her husband and son were dead and it was all her fault.

An uneasy tingling swept through her body and landed with a sick punch in the pit of her stomach. Black spots crossed her vision as she headed for the kitchen. Once there, she bent forward, her hands on her knees as she breathed heavily, fighting for air. She tried to calm herself so she wouldn't pass out, but as her head cleared, the nausea rose. She ran to the sink and vomited, moaning and crying as she gagged. When the lurching finally settled, she straightened up and wiped her mouth with a dish towel. She stood there, breathing heavily before releasing a howling cry into the towel.

She leaned against the kitchen counter and slid to the floor, pushing her knees up, her head buried in her arms. After a while, she dragged herself back into the living room. Spent from the vomiting, she fell onto the sofa. This nightmare was her new existence and it had blackened her heart forever.

Eighty

*K*ate opened her eyes, unsure of the time. She stretched her legs and looked around. The memory of how she'd returned to the sofa was a blur. It was still light outside, but the sun was setting. Her body felt like she'd awakened from a coma.

The realization that Eddie was behind it all washed across her body like cold water. Clarity had shattered the fog she'd been swimming through for the past two weeks. She'd known at the funeral it had been Eddie who'd killed her family, but since then, her mourning process had clouded that reality. The truth about Eddie was evident, despite any proof or witnesses, she knew he was behind it.

A spark stirred deep in her belly. She rose from the floor and paced the entire lower level of her house, as her mind spiraled to a place she'd never been. Her thoughts went back to her first meeting with Eddie. He'd been so charming. She'd been lured by a genuine manipulator. She felt so stupid. So gullible.

And those three guys with him at the funeral? Eddie's cousin, Sal. She knew him from helping with his condo search. He'd given her the creeps from the first time she'd met him. But the other two ... Marco had talked about them often. She'd met them a couple of times. Even Renzo had met the three of them a time or two. Until the funeral, she'd never given them a second glance.

Could they be the killers? Operating at Eddie's bidding?

Sal.

Dario.

Tau.

All three had hovered behind Eddie. Their king. Yes, these were the guys. Eddie's flunkies. Kate bet that they'd do anything he'd ask of them.

Detective Steber had said that the tire had been punctured and that the bullets removed from Marco and Renzo's bodies came from one gun. One shooter.

Who else would do such a thing?

No one.

Kate knew they were all in on it. All four of them. This new energy turned her in an unexpected direction: from hopelessness to a rage she couldn't explain.

She grabbed her cell and began scrolling through her recent calls to find Detective Steber's number. She was about to make the call when she paused. He'd never believe this was even close to a lead and certainly not enough for an arrest.

Kate threw her phone down on the sofa and plopped alongside it, arms folded, thinking. She pinched the bridge of her nose to stop the ache shooting across her eyes.

She spent the next half-hour going back in time, trying to force her memories to the forefront. All of those visits to the restaurant, Eddie's dinners, his visits to their house. Marco had always seemed in good spirits. Now, she wondered, besides the gun, what else he had kept from her.

She needed to check things out at the restaurant. She needed to see Eddie.

Eighty-one

*I*t was a quiet afternoon at Fortunato's. The frigid February weather had kept business slow for a couple of weeks. Eddie stood at the bar watching the Timberwolves when he heard the front door open. A tall, middle-aged man in a gray suit stepped in and looked around the empty restaurant.

Cop.

Eddie strutted toward him. "Afternoon. Can I help you?"

"Good afternoon. Lookin' for Eddie Bracchio."

"You found him."

The man held out his business card and Eddie took it.

"Detective Steber, St. Paul PD. Wanna' ask you a few questions about the murders of Micola Fortunato, Marco De Luca and his son, Lorenzo."

Eddie's face turned sorrowful as he shook his head. "Terrible thing. I still can't believe it, ya' know?"

The detective nodded.

"And," Eddie said, "I don't know if you know this, but I already talked to another one of your guys—a detective too, I think."

"Yes, I do know that. Detective Lance is helping me out with this case since the murders happened just a day apart from each other. We're trying to connect all the dots."

"Sure. We can go to my office. It's more private." Eddie led the detective to his office and shut the door. "Have a seat."

Detective Steber took a seat in front of the desk as Eddie sat in his place behind it.

The detective flipped open a notepad. "Just a few questions, Mr. Bracchio."

"I thought you guys were all finished with me. I mean the other guy asked a *lot-a* questions."

"We have a lot of people to talk to, Mr. Bracchio, and there's always follow-up. And, as you know, we have three murders and one missing person, and the only common denominator in all this," he raised his brows as he pointed at Eddie, "is you." The detective tilted his gray-haired head as he waited for Eddie's response.

"Listen, Detective Steber," Eddie said, "I'm a victim here."

The detective frowned. "How so?"

Eddie stuck out his head and whipped his arms out to either side. "Seriously? I was standin' right next to Micola when she got shot. I could-a' been shot, too. I didn't have nothin' to do with that. How could I? That's fuckin' ridiculous."

"And the De Lucas?"

Eddie let out a breath and hung his head for a second. "Marco was my friend, okay? Renzo? Great kid. I'd *never* hurt them, or hurt Kate. You're barkin' up the wrong tree here, alright?"

"I'll move on—for now," said Detective Steber. "Let's get back to Mrs. Fortunato, if I may?"

Eddie frowned, but nodded. "Terrible thing. I loved that woman. And to see it happen right in front-a me like that?" He rubbed his forehead and sucked in a deep breath. "I got nightmares about it, ya' know?"

Detective Steber nodded. "I imagine it was a horrifying experience. I understand you two were very close."

"Yeah, we were. *Very* close."

"I've learned some of the details from your manager about your relationship with her—that you two lived together. And in fact, you were the one who helped her open this restaurant, is that right?"

"That's right," Eddie replied.

"I understand from Mrs. De Luca, Marco's widow, that Marco worked for you, is that correct?"

Eddie's elbows were on the desk, his hands clasped in front of him. "That's right."

"I understand he used to work as a mechanic, but quit that job to work fulltime for you, is that right?"

"Yeah, that's right."

The detective continued. "And did Mr. De Luca work here? At the restaurant?"

"No. He was my driver."

Detective Steber looked at Eddie and paused for a second before nodding. "That's right. I do recall Detective Lance mentioning he was your driver. Did he have any other duties?"

"Yeah, you could say that."

"Such as?"

Eddie tipped his head side-to-side. "Well, I suppose you could say he was my bodyguard, and ran personal errands for me and whatnot."

"Bodyguard? You need a bodyguard Mr. Bracchio?"

Eddie nodded. "Yeah."

"Why's that?"

Eddie shrugged. "No big deal. It's just—the neighborhood, ya' know? It's rough. I like to have somebody watchin' my back, know what I mean?"

Detective Steber wrote something in his notepad. "I suppose I do, yeah."

"Yeah, I bet you do," Eddie said chuckling.

Detective Steber looked back up at Eddie, his pale blue eyes darkening. "Can you tell me what types of errands he ran for you?"

Eddie scratched his head to stall. "Mostly, he drove Micola around for her supplies and errands. She liked her ingredients to be top-notch, so he took her around for that kinda' stuff. And ah', ya' know, other usual stuff. Bank runs, stops at the store, or for supplies. Sometimes, personal deliveries for me—shit like that."

"Do you mind if I ask what types of personal deliveries he made?"

Eddie felt heat rising up his cheeks. "Yeah, actually. I do mind."

The detective nodded and paused. He set down his pen and notepad and looked directly into Eddie's eyes. "I understand from various interviews of people in the neighborhood, that you've made quite a name for yourself. People speak very highly of you."

Eddie smiled and tipped his head. "That right? Ain't that nice?"

"It is. They say you've cleaned up the Payne Avenue neighborhood—seemingly single-handedly."

Eddie shrugged. "It ain't a hard thing-ta do."

Detective Steber smiled. "Most would disagree, Mr. Bracchio, the police force included."

Eddie stared into the detective's eyes. "I ain't most people."

"I see. Care to elaborate?"

"Not really, no."

"Alright. I'll move on," said the detective. "Where were you on Monday, the eighteenth, around seven-thirty p.m., the night Marco and Renzo were murdered?"

Eddie reached into his desk drawer. "Let me get my notes. I knew you guys was gonna' keep askin' me that, so I wrote it down. Didn't wanna' forget." Eddie flipped through a notepad. "Got it here, somewhere. Let's see …. Oh, here it is. On the eighteenth, Marco drove me home. Said he had to take his kid to a friend's or some shit like that. I don't pay attention to that sorta' thing. I was home all night."

"Can someone verify that?"

"Yeah. Sal Gagliardi."

"And he's your cousin, correct? Salvatore Gagliardi?"

"That's right."

"He was with you at the time of the murders?"

Eddie nodded. "Yeah, he was."

"Okay. I believe Detective Lance will be meeting with him to verify your alibi—and his. Now, I know you gave the officers at the scene a full statement about the morning of Mrs. Fortunato's murder, so I just have a few follow-up questions, if you don't mind."

Eddie shrugged. "Suit yourself."

"Great. Thank you. So, ah', Mrs. Fortunato? How did you know her?"

"She's got relatives where I'm from," Eddie said. "They sent me to check on her. Make sure she was okay on a-count-a' there's been some problems in the neighborhood. Shootin's and whatnot."

"I see." The detective checked his notes. "I see here that you're from Brooklyn, New York. Is that right?"

"That's right."

"And on the night of Marco and Renzo's murders, you say you were with Sal?"

"That's right."

"Where were you? You and Sal? "

Eddie didn't hesitate. "Micola's house. He was helpin' me with funeral arrangements and sittin' with me while I was grievin'."

"I see." Detective Steber made some lengthy notes before looking up at Eddie. "And did you see Dario Tucker, and ah'," he flipped through his notes, "Tau Vang? Did you see them the day after Micola's murder? At her house, as well?"

"Yeah. They were there for a while, too."

"And Marco? Was he at the house at that time, too?"

Eddie paused, pretending to think. "Ah', yeah. Yeah, I think he was there for a bit, too. Mostly, they came over to give me their condolences. Nothin' else."

"Well, I think that's it for now, Mr. Bracchio," said the detective, standing. "I'll find my way out. I'll be in touch if I have any more questions. Have a nice day."

Eddie remained seated. "Thanks."

He stayed in his office for another half-hour going over everything that was just asked of him. The more he'd thought about it, the more concerned he'd become. He needed to talk to Sal.

Eighty-two

*K*ate left the house for the first time in weeks. It was four p.m. and the day's overcast light was fading fast. She'd dressed hurriedly in sweats, her winter jacket, and ankle-high snow boots. She grabbed her bag containing Marco's binoculars and stumbled across the snow-packed driveway to Marco's Mustang. It wasn't her preferred vehicle, but the police still had not yet released her SUV.

As she backed out of the driveway, a sense of uncertainty clawed at her nerves. Her heart pounded and her adrenaline raced as she found herself driving at a pace too fast for the neighborhood. She was unsure why she'd felt a sudden urge to check out Fortunato's, but she guessed it was because Eddie and his flunkies had begun to consume her thoughts.

She slowed her pace and drove down the quiet side streets, though she barely paused for stop signs, until she got to Payne Avenue. She turned right, watching the activity at the restaurant up ahead.

As she approached, Kate saw a man leaving the restaurant. She sat up, straining through the low light to see if it was Sal. The man got into a car before she could really tell. She hit the steering wheel with her gloved hand.

"Damnit!"

She turned left into the overflow parking lot across from the restaurant and maneuvered the Mustang around until it faced the restaurant's front doors. She parked and scanned the area before pulling the binoculars out of her bag and slumping low in her seat.

Surveillance: Day One.

Kate sat there for two hours and saw Eddie just once, through the window. No one else of interest had come or gone. Her frustration only led to a stronger determination to prove that Eddie and his crew killed her family. Despite the car's heat pumping through the vents, she grew cold and uncomfortable. She decided that had been enough for her first night.

She returned each day, adjusting the time, and watching the restaurant through the binoculars from the safety of her car across the street.

On her third day, it was early after lunch when she saw Detective Steber pull up a few spots away from the front door. Seeing him made Kate's heart skip. He must have been there to talk to Eddie about Marco and Renzo's murders. This gave her a slight sense of satisfaction knowing the police were indeed working on her family's case.

She ducked as the detective emerged from his beige sedan. He looked around, his gaze passing her direction, but he seemed unaware of her vehicle. It made her realize the black Mustang was too conspicuous. She'd have to rent a car. As the detective walked to the door of the restaurant, she sat up and homed in on him through the binoculars. She wished she were a fly on the wall. She would have loved listening to him interrogate Eddie.

After about thirty minutes, Detective Steber left the restaurant. He casually walked back to his car and drove off. Satisfied with her surveillance for the day, she put the car in drive and returned home.

Once inside, she put on the kettle for tea. When it began to hiss, she poured the boiling water over her tea bag and walked to the living room. She sat there quietly sipping it as she imagined Detective Steber's visit with Eddie.

Her phone rang. She looked at the screen.

Eddie.

She let it go to voicemail.

She then turned her thoughts to her budding plan.

Eighty-three

The following morning, Kate returned to the parking lot across from the restaurant. She'd hoped the change in time would lead to more information. It had been nearly a month since the murders with no sign of the men from the funeral. Eddie must have told them to lay low.

She arrived in her rented navy blue Nissan and spent another couple of hours in her usual location, though nothing remarkable presented itself. She returned home feeling a sense of doubt weakening her resolve. Maybe she was wrong. Maybe they weren't involved. Maybe they'd just been friends of Eddie's who'd accompanied him to the funeral as a show of support. She didn't believe this, but without a sighting from any of them, she had nothing to go on. No one to follow.

Two more weeks went by without anyone of importance showing up at the restaurant. Still, Kate continued her surveillance, each day renewing her conviction that she was on the right track. Yet each day her confidence waned. Was she wasting her time? She didn't want to believe that. This was the only thing giving her purpose. Without this, she had nothing.

After another disappointing afternoon watching Fortunato's, Kate again returned home feeling defeated. She sat in the quiet living room sipping tea. With temperatures finally on the rise, the annual tease of spring was within the city's grasp, as March came in like a lamb. Though still cold, the snow began to soften and the rain made its first appearance in months. As she listened to it gently bouncing off the windows, she began to doze.

The sound of a car pulling up Kate's driveway caused her to bolt upright. Evening had fallen and darkness had moved in around the house. Her hands began to shake, her nerves heightened. She inhaled deeply and tried to pull herself together. It was probably just her parents coming to check on her.

Kate slipped into the kitchen and peered out the backdoor window just as someone emerged wearing a brimmed hat.

Eddie.

Oh God. What was he doing here?

Kate turned and walked in circles in the middle of her kitchen.

She considered not answering the door, but instead reminded herself that this was an opportunity to observe him. It's what she'd been hoping for all along.

Still, having him in her home repulsed her.

She opened the door just as he lifted his hand to ring the doorbell.

"Eddie—what are you doing here?"

"Kate. I'm sorry. But I've been worried about ya'. You haven't answered my calls. I wanted to check in—see how you was doin'." He lowered his chin. "Hope it's okay."

"I'm fine."

Eddie shrugged. "Can I come in?"

Kate moved aside and let him in. He removed his hat and wiped his wet feet on the rug. She thought about stabbing him with the butcher knife sitting in the block just feet from her reach.

Eddie turned to her. "Mind if we sit down? I wanna' hear how you're doin', Kate."

"Okay."

She invited him into the living room and gestured for him to sit. He took a seat on the sofa, still in his winter coat, holding his hat. Kate took the chair across from him. He looked drawn, fatigued. She'd almost forgotten that he was in mourning, too.

"So, Kate," Eddie asked. "How you doin'? You holdin' up okay?"

She shrugged. "How do you think I'm doing, Eddie? My husband and son were murdered."

He looked down at his hat. Kate thought she saw remorse quickly cross his face.

"Kate. I can't fuckin' imagine. Marco—he was my friend. I mean, yeah, he worked for me, but we was just gettin' ta' know each other, ya' know? I liked the guy—a lot. And Renzo..." He made a *psst* sound as he shook his head and looked at her, wiping his eye. "Can't even imagine that shit, Kate. What you're goin' through, I mean."

Kate said nothing. She stared at him and let him talk. She *wanted* him to talk.

He shifted in his seat. "Kate. I came by to tell ya' that I've been thinkin' about you a lot. And, like I said, I've been worried about ya'. And if you need—"

Kate shook her head, fighting the tears welling in her eyes, the crack in her voice. She refused to cry in front of him. She waved her hand back-and-forth. "You don't need to—"

Eddie put his hand to his chest. "Kate. If you need anything—*anything*—you can come to me. I wanna' take care-a you, ya' know?"

Kate thought his performance seemed sincere. Thoughtful, even.

"Thank you, Eddie, but I—"

He flapped his hand. "I know—you don't want nothin' from me. But seriously, Kate. Anything at all, you come see me, okay?"

"Thanks. I appreciate you coming by to check on me."

Eddie stood. "Alright. And Kate—me and you? We got similar situations. I lost Micola, ya' know."

"Yes, I know. I'm sorry. She was a wonderful, sweet woman."

"Yeah. She sure was."

"And I'm sorry I—I missed her funeral. I just—"

Eddie raised his hand and shook his head. "You couldn't, Kate. I understand. It's all too much."

Kate nodded. "Any idea who did it? Micola's killer, I mean. Do they know anything?"

"Naw. Not yet. But I'm gettin' close to findin' out."

Kate nodded, wondering what he meant by '*I'm* gettin' close.'

"Are you getting any help from the police?"

He shrugged. "Fuckin' cops, am I right? Are they helpin' you on your case? Did they find any prints? I mean, I ah', I thought maybe they'd find some, or maybe have some ideas about the flat tire or somethin'."

Kate's heart skipped. *How does he know about the flat tire?*

She hid her surprise. "No. Not really. Haven't heard from them in quite a while."

Kate thought she saw a look of relief on his face, but maybe she was just being hopeful she had the right guy. She could be wrong about him, though she doubted it.

Eddie put on his wet hat. "Alright, Kate. I'd better get back." He looked out the window. "I hate this shitty weather."

They returned to the kitchen where Eddie paused. He turned to her and pointed. "Remember, now. You need anything, you call me. Better yet, come see me. Okay?"

She nodded. "Okay."

"Alright. Good. Take care now, Kate."

"I will."

Through the splattered rain on the kitchen window, she watched him back the car down the driveway until the car turned the corner and disappeared.

Eighty-four

Eddie backed Micola's car out of Kate's driveway, a feeling of satisfaction washing over him. Despite her grief and fatigue, she was still beautiful. He'd felt a rush just being near her, but it was painfully obvious she didn't feel the same. She wanted nothin' to do with him. Somehow, he had to change that.

Every time he thought about Sal fuckin' everything up, it pissed him off. Marco was one thing. He'd been stealing, and none of them had any idea how much. Big mistake for not watchin' things more carefully; for trustin' his crew too much. That would never happen again. So, Marco? He had to go. No question.

But the kid...

He shook his head and hit the steering wheel as he turned onto Payne.

His thoughts drifted back to Kate. Even in her sweatpants and robe, without makeup, she was sexy. Beautiful.

It'll be a long damn time before his dream became a reality.

His plan was to keep checking in on her. Get her back on his good side. He was confident that would work. His plans always worked, and he always got what he wanted. Just not always *when* he wanted.

For Kate, he'd wait forever.

Eighty-five

*K*ate ran to the kitchen sink and lurched up the small amount of water and tea she'd had earlier. She reached for a glass, her hand trembling as she took it from the cupboard. She rinsed her mouth several times before taking a big swallow. It felt cold going down and instantly relieved her nausea.

She wiped her mouth with a dishtowel and paced the kitchen. Eddie knew about Marco's flat tire. How would he know that? She made a note to call Detective Steber to ask if he'd mentioned it to Eddie. Despite how awful it was to have had him in her house, that little nugget of information made it worth it.

Exhausted from the day, and shaken by Eddie's visit, Kate forced her heavy body up the stairs and into bed. She closed her eyes, hoping for sleep, but the bloody images of the love of her life and their sweet boy had returned. Like a strobe, it flashed endlessly in her head as it had done so often since that terrible day. She tried to think of other things—things she should be doing, or happy memories. But whenever she had a moment where she thought she felt better, that horrifying vision returned. She could not make it go away and she knew she never would.

Kate rolled onto her side, her head falling deep into the pillow. She welcomed the evening's darkness and let it envelope her. She wished she could stay there forever. Her life's path had twisted in an unwanted, hellish direction. How could she pretend to carry on? For what? Her purpose had vanished with the flashes of two pulled triggers.

As she had many times before, Kate wondered what Marco and Renzo's last thoughts were, what their terror must have felt like. She began to cry as the feeling of guilt returned. She should have saved them. She should have protected them. She wished she'd never met Eddie Bracchio, and she punished herself for pushing Marco to take that job. It was all her fault. They were dead because of her.

When the tears ran dry, she lay there, bedridden with grief, her body stiff and aching. She reached over to touch Marco's pillow. The emptiness of the bed and the hollowness of the house stung her heart. She knew there was no one who could possibly understand the depths of her devastation. Numbness swirled and waved up her body from her toes to her eyes before she fell into a restless sleep.

> *The frigid air burned her lungs as panic caused her to gasp. She removed her gloves and reached for her son. Renzo's neck and face were covered in dark wetness, blood pulsing out of his neck in thick waves.*
>
> *"Renzo!"*
>
> *The world went black. Then, light returned.*
>
> *"Who did this to you, Renzo? Do you know? Who did this to you and daddy?"*
>
> *"Se 'eh,"*
>
> *"What? Who?"*
>
> *"Se eh-l, Se-hel."*

Kate's eyes flew open, the dark room silent but for her loud gasp. She scrambled upright, holding her chest, reliving the dream.

> *Se' eh-l. Se-hel. Se-hel.*
> *Sal.*
> *Sal.*
> *Sal.*

Kate screamed out into the empty bedroom.
"He said 'Sal!' Renzo said 'Sal!'"

Eighty-six

The following morning, Kate awakened to the sound of a garbage truck driving past the house.

What day was it? Tuesday? Garbage day?

She'd missed it again, two weeks in a row.

Her mind and body felt groggy with fatigue. Her sleepy eyes refused to take in the sunny morning. Kate was still shaken up about her dream—Renzo trying to tell her it was Sal who shot them. She couldn't get it out of her head.

As she pulled herself up from her restless slumber, she was startled by an inexplicable sensation. She paused, frozen. For the briefest of moments, she thought she'd felt Marco—his presence—almost as if his bare arm had brushed across hers.

Was he trying to talk to her? Was he haunting her?

She both loved and hated it. Heavenly, yet agonizing. She'd felt similar sensations from Marco before, but so far, nothing from Renzo. She longed for a sign from him, as well. She knew these visits weren't real, but they helped her get through the toughest days.

She let out a long sigh.

Renzo.

She walked to his room, flipped on the light, and sat on his bed. She missed him so much she sometimes thought it might kill her. His furrowed brow; his warm smile; his shy giggles; the way he was always hugging everyone. So loving. She missed all of his playful noises. His humming, his talking with his friends in his room, or out on the porch. His constant drumming on the countertops and any table he could find. It was as if the music had died with him.

She didn't stay in his room for long. It was too painful. She switched off the light and returned to her bedroom. Her thoughts moved to Sal. She hated that his awful face came into view whenever she thought of Marco and Renzo. The simmering rage returned, burning in her belly. He was the shooter. She was convinced of it.

She walked to the closet and stared at its doors.

The gun.

She moved slowly to the folding doors and pushed them apart. The tan canvas bag was back in the corner where she'd put it, under the big box. She could see it sticking out.

She went to her knees, sitting back on her haunches. Pausing, she blew a breath of air upward before moving in. She reached back and dragged the heavy box toward her. She then dug deep into the bag for the pistol.

She'd never held a gun before. Its weight felt daunting. Powerful. She wiggled into a seated position and stared down at the weapon. Feeling its heft. Its might. In her home. And now, in her hand. The steel barrel felt cool to the touch. She was terrified she might do something wrong to make it go off, yet ... fascinated. This could be useful.

Then, unexpectedly, she envisioned herself pulling the trigger, the bullet exploding into a face that looked like both Eddie and Sal.

The vision startled her. She held her chest and collected her breath as the realization of the change happening inside her took hold. She put the gun back, tucking it away, deep into the bag. She put the heavy box of magazines on top of it and shoved it all into the corner. She stood and stepped back, staring at the inside of her closet before closing the doors and leaving the room.

She spent the rest of the day in a fog. As evening fell, she ate a light meal and settled in on the sofa, the TV on, the sound down low. She stared at the screen, but her thoughts were on the gun.

A movie on TV caught her attention. A cop was holding a gun and moving slowly, cautiously up a set of stairs. She watched his use of the weapon with keen interest.

When the movie ended, she climbed upstairs and into bed. Sleep eluded her. She stared at the ceiling, thinking about Eddie. About his restaurant. The restaurant that she helped him get. About his recent creepy visit. His crew. Her mind was a mixed mess of intrigue, fear, depression and fatigue.

No wonder she couldn't sleep.

It was time to get back out there. Time to continue her surveillance. Now, it wouldn't be only Eddie she was following and watching, but Sal, too.

Eighty-seven

Kate woke early the next morning. Too early. There'd be no activity outside the restaurant for a couple of hours. She paced the living room and kitchen, anxious to get started. When it was finally time, she threw on her winter coat, grabbed her bag, and hurried out into the cold. She stumbled through the soft, matted-down snow to her latest rental, a navy Prius.

The crisp March morning creeped through Kate's coat making her shiver, the temperature hovering at a chilly thirty-five degrees. The sun deceived, shining high and bright against the white snow in the backyard, illuminating the brilliant blue sky, yet it held no warmth. Spring was not ready to show her hand; no buds yet on the trees; no robins flitting overhead.

Kate drove the Prius down the few blocks to Payne, turned right, passing Fortunato's on her right and then took a left at the following light, making a U-turn back around. The streets and sidewalks were dry and clear of snow, but mounds of it remained on the boulevards lining the blocks of old buildings.

She turned right into the empty lot and backed into her usual spot under the huge oak tree, ready to start her surveillance. She'd hoped for some activity, but was prepared to be patient. She'd continue this plan until something played out. She felt confident that something would.

After three hours sitting in the car without any action, Kate's back and knees started to ache. She needed a break. She paused, though, when she saw Eddie come out of the restaurant, heading toward Micola's car.

Kate's heart jumped as she held her breath.

She scooted down and watched him climb into the car and shut the door. The faint sound of its engine prompted her to start her car. She pulled to the parking lot's exit, pausing to wait for Eddie to drive away. He headed down Payne Avenue toward Seventh Street. She followed him, staying behind other cars to avoid detection.

Eddie turned right at the light on Seventh and Kate did the same. She followed him for several blocks, passing the Lafayette Bridge and continuing into downtown St. Paul. He passed The Assumption Church where Marco and Renzo's funerals were held. He then passed the Xcel Energy Center, crossed Kellogg Boulevard, and passed the bar and restaurant district.

Eddie's turn signal indicated he was turning right onto North Chestnut Street. Cossetta's Italian Restaurant and Market loomed on the corner. Kate continued straight but looked to her right in time to see Micola's car turn into the small, back parking lot. She made a U-turn and headed back, passing the parking lot, opting for street parking a block ahead.

The walk to the entrance was quick. Kate looked around before pulling open the heavy wooden doors. She'd never been inside the legendary Italian restaurant and market, and the aroma of garlic and fresh pizza dough was a scent more pleasant than she'd experienced in a while. The sounds of clanging, clattering and voices came from all four corners, and from above. A massive staircase near the back entrance welcomed customers, some climbing it with trays of food, others descending.

Amongst the sounds of those working and dining, Kate heard Eddie laughing. She followed the sound to her right and saw him at the far corner of the deli counter under a sign that read "PIZZA." She ducked behind the staircase and walked through an entrance that led to a sizeable Italian market and grocery store, pausing near the door. When she realized she no longer heard Eddie's voice, she started to panic, but stopped short when three familiar looking men entered through the Seventh Street doors.

As they made their way into the deli, Kate got a better glimpse and confirmed they were Dario, Tau and Sal. She nearly backed into a table of Italian breads as she tried to hide. She studied them from her location, their faces, their builds, and even tried listening to their voices, as they climbed the stairs.

Kate needed to see the four of them together, as a group. They'd all played a role in the massacre of her family. As Eddie's voice dissipated, she gathered a tiny shred of nerve and walked slowly out of her safe little corner to the staircase and started climbing.

She kept her head down and stared at her feet as she ascended the wide, dark and worn wooden stairs. Holding the railing, she kept her ears tuned for any sign of Eddie coming in her direction.

At the top, was a spacious casual dining area encircling the opening of the grand staircase. Kate was grateful for the bustling crowd. She mustered enough courage to glance in various directions, but Eddie's voice was the clue she needed. It came from behind her, so she turned left keeping her back to them. She found a table near one of the waitress stations about twenty feet from Eddie's table. She crooked her chair until her view was clear.

She stared at the four of them.

Killers.

She pretended to look at her phone while straining to hear their conversation, though she couldn't make out much. Their mumbling conversation continued for another ten minutes, when one of them let out a loud belly laugh at something Eddie had said. The others erupted in laughter. Their casual and carefree afternoon made Kate seethe as bile burned in her empty stomach and fueled her rage.

Despite the strong urge to do so, she refrained from going over there. She needed a plan, but had no idea what that plan might entail. For now, this unexpected stakeout was enough. She took advantage of her perfect view, soaking up the details of their faces, their voices, their clothes, and their mannerisms. She looked at each of them and made mental notes. After today, she'd never forget their names or faces.

Sal. The shooter. The *killer* of Marco and Renzo. There he was—right there. She reined in her frenzied anger and looked closely at him. Stocky, middle-aged, Italian. Eddie's cousin. He had a threatening, angry demeanor about him. He *looked* like a killer. Muscular, with a gruff frown. Similar features as Eddie, though nowhere near as good-looking: black hair, but thinner, more gray; sinister eyes; big, hooked nose that was darker than the rest of his face. *Heavy drinker.*

Tau seemed quiet. His olive complexion, smooth; his thick, black hair swooped back, shiny from the quaint chandelier above the table. He smiled, but never seemed to laugh. Reserved. Or disinterested. She wasn't sure.

Dario seemed to be the most outspoken of the bunch. Boisterous; high voice; always interrupting the others for a laugh. Based on his attitude and body language, he seemed eager to please Eddie.

And then of course, there was Eddie. He appeared to be running the meeting. Their moment of fun had subsided, and now, the other three were leaning in, quietly listening to their leader.

After thinking about it, and working up the nerve, Kate made a decision she felt was imperative.

She stood and walked confidently to the table where the four men were seated.

"Hello, Eddie."

Eighty-eight

Eddie's eyes popped at the site of Kate standing before him. The other three sat silently, staring at her. She wondered what they were thinking.

"Kate," Eddie said, standing. "What a surprise. What brings you down here?"

She smiled, feigning innocence and a genuine interest in him and his crew. "Oh, I love this place. I came for lunch and thought I'd treat myself to a little tiramisù for later." She smiled and teased them with a hair tousle.

Eddie giggled, which surprised Kate. "Yeah. I know what-cha' mean. The tiramisù here?" He kissed his fingers. "One-a-the-best in town. Not as good as Micola's recipe, a-course."

Kate smiled. "Of course."

Eddie brought his hand to his chest. "'Scuse my manners. You remember my cousin, Sal."

Sal lifted his head, without really looking at Kate.

"Yes, hello, Sal. I saw you at the church. Thank you for coming." She took a good look at him.

You fucking killer.

"My honor," he mumbled. He seemed flustered, unable to look her in the eye.

Eddie moved on. "You remember Dario."

Kate did a quick flip of her hand in greeting. He was seated next to Sal nearest the window, too far for a handshake, and she wasn't interested in faking any more niceties than was necessary.

"Hello, Dario."

You're in on it, I know you are.

"How you doin, Kate? Good to see you. Again, so sorry for your losses—ya' know, you're husband—and ah'—your kid."

"Shut the fuck up, Dario," Eddie said, shaking his head. "Sorry about that, Kate. He's a fuckin' moron."

Kate opened her mouth to speak, unsure how to respond, but Eddie had already moved on.

"And this here's Tau."

You're in on this, too, Tau.

"Hello," Tau said, also too nervous to look at her.

"Well," Kate said with a smile, "I'm sorry to have interrupted. I just wanted to stop and say hello."

"Kate, please," Eddie said. "Join us. We can pull up a chair."

Sal pressed his back against the booth and looked at Eddie like he was nuts.

Kate shook her head, waving her hand. "No, thank you. I have to go. My parents are—she struggled, her excuse unprepared. "They're coming over later, and I—ah', my place is a mess. You know how mothers are, right?"

Dario laughed. "Boy, do I! My mom—if I leave a big mess in the kitchen—"

Eddie stuck his neck out in Dario's direction. "Dario. Shut. The. Fuck. Up."

Dario rubbed his hands nervously up and down his thighs. "Sorry, Mr. B."

Eddie turned to Kate. "Great to see you, Kate."

Kate lit them up with her best fake smile, flipping back her hair and giving them all a slight wave. "You too."

"Don't be a stranger, now. You bring your parents in fa' dinner to Fortunato's real soon, 'eh? My treat."

"Thank you, Eddie. Maybe we'll take you up on that."

"You do that. Take care now, Kate."

She gave the group a nod. "Bye."

Kate walked to the staircase and made her way down and out of Cossetta's. Once in her car, her whole body started to tremble. She placed her cold hands on her face to calm the tears that seared her eyes and streamed down her cheeks. She sat there on that side street for several minutes trying to collect herself, before putting the car into drive and heading back home. By the time she pulled into the driveway, her heart rate had settled and her tears had slowed.

She hurried into the house and upstairs to her bedroom, falling to her knees in front of the closet. She sat there for a few minutes, before opening the closet doors, reaching in for the bag, and pulling out the pistol. She held it in her hand, examining it, her finger on the trigger.

At least two of those men had a hand in killing Marco and Renzo.

Eddie and Sal.

She'd figure out how Dario and Tau fit in soon enough. She slowly lifted the gun, pointing it, imagining Eddie standing in front of her, hands up, begging.

Eighty-nine

Still standing at the table after Kate left, Eddie looked down at Sal, Dario and Tau. "Let's go," he said, grabbing his sunglasses and turning to leave.

He heard their bustle and then footsteps clamoring down the stairs behind him.

"That Kate sure is fine though," he heard Dario say.

Eddie stopped and turned, jamming his miniature screwdriver into Dario's side. "Don't start with that, Dario. I'll fuck you up right here on these stairs."

Dario's eyes widened. "Eddie—I'm sorry, man. No disrespect. Alright?"

Eddie stopped. "You need-ta learn some self-control you miserable piece-a shit."

"Come on, Eddie. I said I was sorry."

Eddie paused before turning to him. Dario had barely blinked and Eddie's hand was squeezing his throat, whispering in his ear. "I should-a killed you back on the first day we met."

Dario's hands went up in surrender, but he said nothing. After a second or two, Eddie felt Sal's hand on his arm.

"Don't make a scene, Eddie. Not here."

Eddie quickly let go of Dario's neck, sending him falling onto a step, coughing and holding his throat. Eddie ignored him and continued down the stairs without looking back.

Outside, Eddie walked to the driver's side of Micola's car. He looked over the hood at the three of them hurrying toward him.

Before getting in, he called out. "I don't wanna' see any of you'se for a while. It's still too soon. I can't believe we ran into Kate. Of all fuckin' people seein' us like that."

He shook his head. "Stupid. Go do your jobs. Keep your heads down and stay outta' trouble. And—I repeat—" He pointed his finger, dragging it left-to-right in front of them. "Don't come around the restaurant 'til I tell you'se. *Capisci*?"

They nodded and walked away. Eddie slipped into the car and drove off.

Ninety

Kate spent the evening sipping Chardonnay and reliving the events from her afternoon at Cossetta's. She sat in the recliner, Renzo's favorite chair, and flipped endlessly through TV channels, never staying on one for long.

After finishing her second glass of wine, she felt drawn to her bedroom. She climbed the stairs and flipped on the light, astonished to see her room in such disarray. The bedding unmade; clothes strewn about the floor and chaise; a wet towel from her morning shower still in a heap on the floor where she'd left it; and shoes scattered about.

Chaos. The clear picture of her life.

Kate ignored the mess and again faced her closet, staring at the white slatted doors. She couldn't help herself. She was drawn to the canvas bag. She again dropped to her knees, leaned into the closet and shoved the box of magazines to the side. She tugged the heavy bag, dragging it toward her, pausing before digging around inside.

She pulled out the silver pistol and held it in her hand. She shifted its weight back and forth, as she examined it. She wondered if there were bullets inside. She didn't even know how to check. There was that rolling thing that she always saw on TV.

What did they do? They popped it somehow, and it opened. The bullets were in the tiny holes inside that thing. The chamber? Is that what it's called?

She caught her reflection in the full-length mirror to her left — holding a gun.

What did she think she was doing?

She had no idea how to use a gun—how to load it—and she certainly had no idea how to shoot it. This was ridiculous. She put it back in the bag, slid it into its secure place and covered it with the box of magazines.

She went back downstairs, poured herself a third glass of wine and returned to the recliner. She found a channel and watched it mindlessly, unable to concentrate, the gun reappearing in her thoughts. She changed the channel. Then the next channel, next channel, next, next.

Then ... she came upon an old Clint Eastwood movie. He portrayed a cop and was shooting at people. She watched him closely, paying attention to how he held the gun, how he aimed it.

Clint Eastwood's gun was much bigger, more menacing than the one sitting up in her closet. There were other characters with guns. She'd never paid attention before. Never noticed how often guns appeared in different scenes. Some of the guns snapped open, to the side, to insert the bullets.

Bullets.

She put down her glass of wine and ran back upstairs.

Bullets. Bullets.

She moved the box of magazines and pulled open the canvas bag. She reached in and again pulled out the gun, setting it on the floor next to her. She shoved her hand back inside the bag, feeling the bottom of it with her hand, looking for side zippers or bumps or a box. Looking for bullets.

No bullets.

She sat there, staring at the gun sitting beside her.

What were you thinking, Marco? Why did you have this gun? Where did you get it? Why are there no bullets? What was your plan?

She squeezed her lips, thinking. Her eyes began to dart around the closest in front of her. She got onto all fours and started knocking things around. Clothes hanging from above swayed across her head making her hair flip in all directions.

Pushing her hair away from her face, she sat back, breathless.

No bullets.

She leaned over and picked up the gun, twisting it around in her hand, examining it. Were there bullets inside?

Forget the gun. Move on.

She returned to her movie and glass of wine. Her phone buzzed on the sofa. Her mother. She let it ring.

Intrigued by the violent movie, she focused on the guns. She finally saw one of the criminals stop to reload. He did something to make it open to the side.

"Oh!"

She ran upstairs to try to duplicate what she'd seen in the movie. She smoothed her hand all around Marco's gun, turning it, until she felt a raised knob. She pushed it and the chamber opened. Kate's heart began to pound. Six holes with a bullet in each.

The gun was loaded.

"Oh my God."

She slapped it shut and put it back, tucking the canvas bag back into its hiding place. She hurried back downstairs and tried to forget about it.

What would she even do with it?

She had no idea how to shoot it. She'd need lessons, which she'd never do. She couldn't even reload it if she had to.

Still … she could not stop thinking about that gun.

Ninety-one

The following morning, Kate brewed a pot of coffee and went to sit on the sofa in the living room. She tucked her feet underneath her and thought about what she knew:

Eddie believed Marco had stolen money from him.

On the night of Marco and Renzo's murders, Marco had told Eddie he was out of the organization. He'd returned home terrified, ready to take his family and run.

Then, there was that mysterious car parked outside their house when Marco left to pick up Renzo. It quickly followed him.

Marco called to tell her about the flat tire.

Renzo tried to say "Sal." He struggled to say it as he lay dying in her car.

Eddie knew about the flat tire. *How*? She'd never mentioned it to him. Did the cops talk to him about it? She wouldn't bother checking with Detective Steber. Finding hard evidence wasn't her concern.

Sal killed Marco and Renzo. Kate was convinced Eddie knew every detail about it, and most likely ordered it.

That was good enough for her.

She was unsure of Dario or Tau's roles in all of this, but in her mind, they were guilty by association.

They all had to go.

Ninety-two

Kate's mother called often, nagging Kate about her plans to return to work, and asking how she was paying her bills. Kate appeased her by saying the insurance money had kept her afloat, which was true. But she didn't tell her mother that she'd been tossing all of Marco and Renzo's medical bills in the trash. They died. In Kate's opinion, they didn't deserve to get paid, nor did she care about any repercussions.

She didn't care about anything. Her job, her bills, nothing. She only cared about one thing. And that plan was in motion.

***

Three weeks later, during one of her evening watches, Kate finally got some action. Sal rounded the corner and walked into Fortunato's. She grabbed her binoculars and was able to get a good look at him just before the door shut behind him. Her heart raced. She looked at her phone. Ten o'clock. She was surprised she'd stayed that late but was glad she had.

Kate watched and waited, her fingers gripping the binoculars every so often to make sure she hadn't missed him leaving. She ducked low, constantly wary of customers coming to retrieve their cars and encountering a strange woman spying on the restaurant.

After a half hour, she shut off her car and stepped outside. The cold March air slapped her awake. She had no plan as she crossed the dark street and headed for the door to Fortunato's. A couple was leaving as she arrived and the gentleman held the door for her.

"Thank you," she said.

He nodded as Kate went inside. The scent of garlic and everything Italian, coupled with the warmth of the room, calmed her nerves, but her guard remained intact.

A young woman approached her. "Good evening, ma'am."

"Yes, good evening."

"Kate!"

Seeing Eddie approach, the woman smiled and retreated.

He took her hand and kissed it. Kate cringed at the gesture, but fought the urge to yank her hand from him. Instead, she graced him with her best fake smile.

"Hello, Eddie."

"What brings you down here this late?"

She was surprised by how excited he seemed to see her.

"I—ah'—was visiting my parents and thought I'd stop in for a glass of wine. You know, after a visit with the parents, one needs wine." She laughed at her little joke and Eddie joined her.

"Yeah, so true."

He put his hand on the small of her back as Kate scanned the restaurant. Sal was sitting at the bar, his back to the rest of the room.

"Come on," Eddie said, "I'll get you a table."

"Oh, no. That's not necessary. I can just sit at the bar—if that's alright."

"Sure."

She followed him to the bar and deliberately took a seat next to Sal, who appeared lost in thought, hunched over a caramel-colored lowball beverage of some type—on the rocks.

"You remember, Sal?"

"Yes. Hello, Sal."

He sat upright and looked at her, shooting Eddie a strange look.

"Ah', yeah. How you doing Mrs. ah'—"

"Kate. Call me Kate."

"Kate."

"I'm fine. Thanks for asking."

Eddie turned to the bartender. "Bobby—get this lady a—" He turned to Kate. "Chardonnay, right?"

She nodded. "Very good, yes."

"Chardonnay. And make it quick, alright?"

Bobby nodded, quickly returning with her glass of wine.

Sal fumbled in his pockets. "I gotta' go, Eddie."

Kate touched his arm, hiding her distaste for the gesture. "Don't go on my account, Sal. Stay. Have a drink with me."

Sal looked at her sideways, as if she were a ghost. He frowned and shook his head, but Eddie slapped his back.

"Where you goin'? 'Eh? Where you gotta' go?"

"I told Mitzie I'd meet her at The Corner Bar, ya' know. For a drink."

Eddie laughed. "Forget Mitzie. Stay. Have one more drink."

Sal looked at Kate like she was poison. "I-dunno. I tole-her I'd be there by now."

"Bobby!" Eddie shouted to the bartender. "Get Sal one more. Put it on my tab."

"Awe, geez, Eddie. Come on."

Eddie slid the drink from Bobby over to Sal. "Sit down. One more, 'eh?"

"I won't bite, Sal," Kate said, with a gentle laugh. She looked at him, gazing at all of his features, hiding her scrutiny with a fake, warm smile.

"Did you say you were going to The Corner Bar?"

Sal grunted. "Yeah."

"I've heard of that but can't place it. Where is it?"

Sal sighed before answering. Kate observed his right leg bouncing up and down as he clutched his drink.

"It's ah'—you go down Payne. Several blocks up, I don't know. To ah'—Beaumont. Take a right. It's on the corner."

"Oh, yes," Kate said. "I know the place. I guess I've never paid much attention to it before. "'Corner Bar.' That's rather cliché, isn't it?" She laughed.

Sal nodded. "Cliché. Yeah. I guess so."

"The Corner Bar's a shithole," Eddie said laughing. "But that's Sal's hangout. Been hangin' out there all his life. Ain't that right, Sal?" He again slapped Sal's back. Sal looked irritated.

"That's right."

"So, Kate," Eddie moved into the bar stool on the other side of her. "Tell me. How you doin'?"

Kate took a sip of wine. She hated the question. It seemed that was all anyone asked her these days.

"I'm okay."

"Thinkin' about gettin' back to work soon?"

She took a deep breath and let it out loudly. "Oh, I don't know. I need to, financially, but honestly, it's the last thing I want to do. I have no energy, ya' know?"

"Listen, Kate. You need money?"

She waved her hand. "Oh. No. No. I couldn't. I wouldn't."

"You sure?"

"Yes. I'm sure."

"Well, if ya' change your mind, promise me—" he pointed a finger at her "—you let me know." He waved his hand across the bar to emphasize his point. "You need anything. You call. *Capisci?*"

She nodded and smiled. "Okay, Eddie. I appreciate that." She finished her wine and dug for her wallet.

Eddie reached for his chest. "Kate. Please. Don't insult me. Your money's no good here."

She opened her mouth to object, but he put his finger to her lips to silence her. Thankfully, he released it quickly. "Don't even try it."

She wrestled herself out from the bar stool. Eddie was quick to take her hand to help her.

God. She wished he'd stop touching her.

"It was nice visiting with you, Sal."

Sal looked at her without smiling back. "Yeah. You too."

Eddie put his arm around her, *again*. "Come on. I'll walk you to your car."

Kate hated being treated like his possession, but she knew arguing would be a waste of time.

Outside, the frigid air was sobering. A chill crept up her legs.

She pointed. "I'm right across the street. If you could just watch from here, that would be great."

"Not on your life. I'm walkin' ya'."

Great.

When they arrived at her car, Eddie said, "Jesus, Kate. You park way back here? That's no good. It's dangerous."

She shook her head and hand at the same time. "It's fine. It was crowded when I first got here."

"Well, next time, you call me. I'll find you a close spot, alright?"

"Okay, Thanks."

He gave her car the once-over. "What? You get a new car? What's this?"

"Ah', yeah. The cops—they still have my SUV and I don't—I can't drive Marco's Mustang. And I—I don't think I'll ever be able to get into the SUV again either, so I—it's—"

Eddie put up his hand. "I get it. You don't have to explain."

"Well," she said, "thanks again for the drink."

He kissed her hand. "My pleasure, Kate."

God.

"Goodnight, Eddie."

"Goodnight, Kate. You take care-a yourself."

She nodded and shut her car door, letting out a sigh as he headed back to the restaurant.

She sat there for a moment, letting the car warm up, putting her quivering hands to her face.

Ninety-three

Over the following weeks, the weather had taken a pleasant turn toward spring, yet the melting snow and bright sun had done little to improve Kate's state of mind.

She'd busied herself with her latest obsession: following Sal. It hadn't been difficult to learn his routine. Since her drink with him at Fortunato's, he'd been easy to track. And after her dream about Renzo, she'd known for weeks what she needed to do.

She was ready for Sal.

Ninety-four

Kate sat in her usual place near the back of the parking lot of Fortunato's, this time in a rented champagne colored Chevy Impala.

Despite the cool March evening, droplets of perspiration formed around her forehead, as she tried to calm her trembling hands. She stared across the street at the customers coming and leaving in a steady stream. She watched couples laughing, holding hands, some hugging each other. Envy burned in her throat. They had no idea how lucky they were.

As the parking lot thinned, Kate rubbed her face. It was eleven p.m., hours since she'd seen Sal enter the restaurant, and hours since she'd lost her nerve.

She turned on the headlights and buckled her belt, preparing to leave. The restaurant door opened as it had done several times throughout the night, but this time, it was him. Sal was leaving. Eddie stood in the doorway speaking to him for a moment before they parted ways.

Kate's heart jumped. Sal seemed unsteady on his feet as he rounded the corner. She put the car in drive, pulling out of the lot and entering onto Payne.

She turned right, driving a block up before making a quick U-turn. She passed Fortunato's and saw Sal up the street. He'd stopped for a second before walking to the driver's side of his car. He seemed to be having trouble with the keys, at one point dropping them and stumbling around to pick them up.

Kate passed him slowly, not wanting to lose him. He didn't seem to notice her as he flopped into his car. She turned into a driveway a block ahead and waited, her lights off.

At first, nothing happened, but after a couple of minutes, the headlights illuminated, and Sal drove off. Kate followed, staying far enough behind to avoid detection, though she wasn't too concerned given his obvious state of intoxication.

Sal took a quick U-turn and Kate followed him, as he made his usual route to The Corner Bar, parking on the same side-street where she'd watched him many times before. She passed him and drove up a block, before turning around so her car faced Payne.

The street lighting was minimal, and Kate was grateful to be shrouded in the shadows. She watched from inside her car, as he stumbled out and headed the half-block down the dark street toward the front door of the pub, pulling it open and walking inside.

She sat in the quiet darkness of her vehicle. Her pounding heart could not be controlled and sent waves of anxious electricity throughout her body. This was the moment. Could she do it? Could she walk into that bar?

Kate grabbed her bag, feeling around for the gun. It was there, at the bottom, under her long, red wallet. Satisfied, she opened the car door and stepped out, pulling Marco's black knit cap over her ears, her long hair bound and tucked beneath the collar of her black leather jacket.

She sucked in a cold gulp of oxygen hoping it would fuel her sanity and calm her. It helped a little, but her nerves still felt like rattling bones. She was ready, though. The emptiness that had replaced her heart told her so. She'd waited long enough.

She closed the car door and walked across the street toward the bar's entrance. Muffled music grew louder as she approached. Someone opened the door, and it grew even louder, causing her to pause. Her heart raced, but she swallowed the lump of fear in her throat and pressed forward.

She pulled open the rundown wooden door and stepped into the dirty little bar filled with dirty-looking men.

Ninety-five

The stench of stale popcorn and sour liquor seared Kate's nose as she entered The Corner Bar. The Rolling Stones played loudly overhead as she scrutinized the room with a glance. Neon signs above the restroom doors, a pool table, and an actual juke box, made it feel like she'd stepped back in time.

As she entered, the bar patrons stopped their conversations to stare at her. The sudden attention rattled what little confidence she had and made her question her motives. She considered leaving, but instead, played it cool. She walked toward Sal, one of the few who hadn't turned, too engrossed in his liquid orgasm sitting on the bar in front of him.

Pig.

Kate did her best to ignore the eyes bearing down on her and slid into the red, torn patent leather stool next to Sal.

"Hello, Sal."

On hearing his name, Sal slowly turned his inebriated head in her direction, his brown eyes glazed over like a sheet. His long, bulbous nose with a sharp bump at the top looked like a bird's beak, its purple, broken blood vessels displaying Sal's long love affair with the drink.

He seemed confused and stared at her, her face not registering. After a few seconds, he sat upright a bit, turning to look around the bar, as if to confirm his location. If she'd thought *she* was afraid of *him*, it appeared at that moment *he* was more afraid of *her*.

"Remember me? Kate?"

He lifted his head, almost as a nod, but not really. With slurred words he said, "What—" He looked around again and hiccupped. "What-er you doin' here?"

"Oh, I was out running errands and thought I'd stop in for a quick beer, and here you are!" Her voice sounded cheery. Innocent. Inside, she wanted to run, wondering how she could be doing something so stupid.

She called out to the bartender over the loud rock music. "Can I get a lite beer?"

The bartender frowned. "Sure. What kind?"

Kate shrugged. "I don't care."

He nodded and brought her a bottle, setting it in front of her.

"Thanks," she said. "And bring another for my friend Sal, here."

The bartender looked suspiciously at the two of them, but returned with a whiskey-looking drink on the rocks for Sal.

"Thanks," he said, killing off the last of his first drink and sipping the one she'd just bought him.

"You're welcome. Cheers." She clinked her glass on his. He looked at her strangely.

"Remind me," he grumbled. "What the f' —I mean ah', what are you doin' here? I mean—nice lady like you, in a place like this? Ya' shouldn't be here."

"Why not?"

He chuckled and gave her a creepy smile. "Look around. This ain't a place fa' you. This is a rough place and Eddie—" He stopped short.

Kate sat back in her seat. "Eddie? What about Eddie? What's he got to do with it?"

"Never mind. Fergit-it."

"No. What? What about Eddie?" She tried to sound light, still cheerful. Innocent.

"Eddie don't want you in a place like this. He'd kill me if he knew you was in here."

"Why in the world would Eddie care where I spend my time? What's he got to do with anything?"

For the first time, Sal sat upright. "Ya' kiddin', right?"

Kate stared at him.

Sal continued. "Eddie wants to protect you. He likes you. Wants us to keep you safe."

"I'm confused. Why? What do you mean he *likes* me?" Kate's stomach started to swim.

"Ya' know. He *likes* you. Wants-ta take care-a you, all that. He'd fuckin' kill me if he knew I tole-you all-a this. So, keep this between us, okay?" Sal started to sway back and forth before putting his elbows safely back onto the bar.

"I-ah'. Wow," Kate said. "I'll keep it between us, yes. Of course. You can trust me, Sal. I promise I won't say a thing. She tightened the grip on her beer bottle, unable to drink it.

She shouldn't be here. What was she doing?

She thought back about Eddie's care toward her, the kind words, the offers of help, money. The way he looked at her. His arm around her, and his constant touch-ie-feel-ie behavior.

Oh God.

She considered leaving. This was all too much to take in. Marco and Renzo were dead. Why? Because of her? Because of Eddie *liking* her?

She killed her family. Not with a weapon, but it might as well have been. So many thoughts crowded her mind. It was all pouring into her head too fast. This couldn't be true. Was all of this so Eddie could possess her? Her stomach swirled and lurched as her head spun.

"Excuse me, Sal. I need to use the restroom."

Sal shrugged and returned to his drink.

Kate stood and walked toward the back of the room, immediately remembering where she was. Greasy-haired men in leather jackets and equally scary women hanging on their arms, turned to watch her. She heard whispers and chuckles, but they left her alone.

Thankfully, the sole unisex restroom was empty. She locked herself in, the scent of clean soap surprising her. She leaned against the wall and put her hands to her face, as she tried to pull herself together.

Panic rose in her chest as her breathing became labored. She rocked forward and back, unsure of what to do with this new information.

She moved to the sink and looked at her reflection in the dingy mirror. She was surprised how together she appeared given the state of her nerves. She nodded to her reflection and splashed her face with cool water before drying herself with a couple of sheets of cheap brown paper towels.

Pull it together, Kate. You can do this. More now than ever. You have to do this.

She took a deep breath and left the restroom. Her heart sank as she saw that Sal's seat was empty. She rushed to the bar and asked the bartender if Sal had left, which was a stupid question since there was only one bathroom and she'd been in it.

The bartender nodded. "Just left."

Kate moved to leave, her bag held tightly in her hand.

"Hey," said the bartender.

Kate turned to him.

"You owe me twelve bucks."

"Oh, right. Sorry." Kate returned to the bar and dug in her wallet, paranoid someone would see the gun. She pulled out a twenty. "Keep the change."

She exited the bar, her heart pounding as she put on her driving gloves. She looked around before turning right and walking around the corner. Up ahead, Sal was standing at his car. Even from her distance, she could see him staggering, trying to hold himself up.

She called to him as she picked up her pace. "Sal!"

Sal turned and stared back as though he couldn't understand why she was talking to him.

"Sal," Kate said breathlessly, as she approached.

"What-da-ya want from me, lady? Go away. I shouldn't even be talkin' t-ya." He continued fiddling with his keys.

"You shouldn't be driving. You're drunk."

"Do it all the time. Now go. You're gonna' get me killed."

"I don't understand why you keep saying things like that. Eddie wouldn't—"

Sal started to laugh. "Oh, no?"

He returned to the difficult task of unlocking the driver's side door.

Kate approached him. "Here. Let me." She yanked his keys.

"Hey!" Sal shouted. "Gimme' those."

"Let me drive you home."

Sal's face frowned into a wrinkle as he shook his head. "What? No fuckin' way."

"Please. I insist. What would Eddie say if I let you drive and something happened? To you? Or you hurt someone else? You wouldn't want that …. would you? Come on, Sal, let me drive you."

Sal moaned. "Jesus H. Christ! Fine. You can fuckin' drive. Just shut up, will ya'?"

Kate sucked in a breath and released it. "Okay. Good." She moved to open the passenger side door. "Come on—over here."

Sal rolled his eyes but complied. He walked around to the passenger side of his car and handed her the keys. He lumbered in, immediately laying his head back onto the headrest, eyes closed.

Kate hurried around to the driver's side, her eyes darting around for any witnesses, as she slid inside. She inserted the key and started the engine. Taking in a deep breath and holding it for a second, she looked over at Sal, his head back, eyes still closed.

She put the car in drive and maneuvered her way out of the street parking spot. She drove up Beaumont, unsure where she was about to take this drunken killer. But she had him, sitting right next to her—and she could barely believe it.

Ninety-six

*P*ulling her bag close to her thigh, Kate drove Sal's car and its intoxicated owner up Beaumont Street in the opposite direction of Payne Avenue. After a short drive on the dark and isolated little road, a curve to her left brought them onto an even shorter road named Drewry, which led to the parking lot of a community academy. She slowed near a deserted area just before the parking lot. To her right was a wall of trees, their leaves only beginning to bloom this early into spring. Nestled beyond the barren forest sat Swede Hollow Park.

The only possible activity would be from the academy, but that was shuttered and dark this late at night. Kate tried to calm herself with steady breathing, but her trembling hands gripping the wheel told her that wasn't working.

She pulled over to the side, close to the wall of foliage, forcing the car deep under the overhanging tree branches. She shut off the car's engine and lights. The moon's glow illuminated down through the branches onto Sal's face, a flicker of concern falling across his stoned eyes, as he realized they'd stopped.

Inside the car, it was dark and quiet until Kate heard Sal's stomach moan like an old building. He turned his head slowly to look at her. Her body began to tremble at the sight of this man staring at her, helpless, really. Vulnerable.

She squeezed her eyes shut.

Marco and Renzo's faces came into view. Marco was rolling down the window of the SUV that frigid January night. Renzo leaned forward to look past his dad at the person standing at the driver's-side window. Both smiling with relief that help had arrived.

Sal's face came into view. A gun appeared. Marco's smile slid down, disappearing. Renzo's did, too. Terror crossed their faces before the gun popped. Marco's head slammed

*onto the steering wheel, blood spilling down the side of his
face.*

*In that split second, Renzo knew he was next. He opened
the car door and ran. Another shot from the gun caused
Renzo's excruciating pain, as he fell to the icy ground. Sal
then dragged him back to his place in the car.*

*Together, Marco and Renzo's bloodied bodies lie slumped
in the front seats, as Sal turned and walked back toward
the very car, she was now sitting in.*

The image of her dead family enraged her anew. She shook
her head, letting hot tears spill down her cheeks.

No turning back.

She'd come too far.

It was time.

Sal struggled to sit up, as he looked around into the blackness.
"Hey," he said. "Where the hell are we?"

"Doesn't matter," Kate said. She locked the doors.

"What-da'-ya' mean? I thought you was takin' me home."

Kate reached into her bag and pulled out the heavy silver
pistol. Using both hands, she pointed it at Sal's head, working
furiously to keep her grip steady, her breath controlled.

"You're not going home."

"Whu-?" Sal turned to see the gun pointed at him. He pushed
himself away from the gun, pressing his head against the
passenger window, fiddling for the door handle.

"Hey, where'd ya' get that gun? Put that away. You don't
know what you're doin' with that. It's dangerous. Jesus. Put that
away."

Kate shook her head, ignoring the stray tear rolling down her
cheek. "I'm not putting this away, Sal. You're gonna' tell me why
you killed Marco." Her voice cracked. "And my boy. I know you
did it."

Sal seemed to instantly sober up, as he lifted his hand toward
her. Kate pulled the gun back close to her chest, the barrel still
pointing at him.

"Listen, lady. You get the fuck outta' my car. Now."

"You killed them, didn't you?"

She was angry at her tears, her shaky voice. She'd imagined she'd be stronger. More confident.

Sal lowered his hand and shook his head at Kate. "This is a *bad* idea, lady. You—sittin' there with a gun on me?" He chuckled. "I mean, look at-ya'. It's obvious you don't know what the fuck you're doin'. You're gonna' hurt somebody."

Kate blinked back the burning tears. She did *not* want to start crying.

Stay strong.

"I know what I'm doing, Sal. I've been thinking about this for months." She suppressed the hysteria building in her throat. "Do you hear me? *For months.*" She reined in her terror and fed on her building rage. "And now, I need *you* to tell me. Okay? Did you … kill … Marco and Renzo?"

Kate's jaw stiffened as she steadied her hands. Despite the weight of the gun, she sensed a reawakening of her confidence. Sal pressed his back against the passenger door, his hands up, but Kate didn't like the look in his eye. He looked angry, ready to pounce.

"You gotta' know," Sal said, his words thick and slow, "it was all Eddie's idea, okay? You happy? Is that what you wanted to hear? Now, put down the fuckin' gun. You ain't gonna shoot nobody. Look at ya'—shakin' like a leaf." He let out a quick snort.

"Why?" Kate shouted. "Why did Eddie want them killed? I don't—"

Sal started shaking his head. "You got this all wrong." He frowned. "Well—a little wrong. He didn't want your kid hit. Alright?"

This made Kate pause and lower the gun a bit, but Sal was eyeing it, so she tightened her grip. "What do you mean? He wanted Marco dead, but not Renzo?"

Sal nodded, hands still up, back still pressed against the door.

Kate shook her head. "I don't understand. Why then? Why was Renzo killed?"

"Look," Sal said, "Eddie's got this wild thing about you. I mean, I think he's in love with you, if ya' ask me. He won't admit it." He gave her a slimy grin. "But that husband-a yours?" Sal shook his head. "Eddie was pretty pissed about him stealin' from him. It's mainly what got him killed."

Kate could not comprehend or stomach this talk of Eddie in love with her. It made her skin crawl, but she needed to keep Sal talking. She needed the information that only he had.

"What exactly did Marco steal?" She asked, though she already knew the answer. He stole *nothing*. Still, she needed to know what *Eddie* had been thinking.

Sal stared at Kate, pausing for a beat before laughing. "Eddie was raging when Marco walked out on him that night. Do you know that?" He paused, as though recalling the moment. "Yeah. Raging. So he ah', he ordered the hit. Told me to go take care-a him." Sal pointed at Kate. "Your husband. Not the kid." He shrugged. "As it turned out, when Marco stopped to picked up a *guy*, I didn't know it was your kid, right? He was tall. Looked like a man. I had no clue. I only knew Eddie wanted it done that night. So I handled it." He wiped his forehead causing Kate to stiffen. "But you know the funniest part?" Sal chuckled.

Kate refused to respond. There was nothing funny about any of this.

Sal's eyes closed for a second and then opened wide. "I knew all along that Marco didn't take nothin'," he said. "But *Eddie* didn't know that. He *still* don't know." Sal shrugged. "But I, ah' — well ... I follow orders."

"Who took the money?" Kate yelled. "Who?"

Sal let out another drunken' chuckle. "It was me." He waved his hand in the air. "They're all fuckin' stupid. Every last one of 'em. Yep. I took the money." He laughed so loud it rang in Kate's ears.

Sal continued. "For a while, nobody even noticed ... until they did. Not really sure how it all went down, but Tau figured it out. He knew the numbers. He knew money went missin'. I pointed the finger at Marco, and they believed me. They all did. It was that simple."

Sal lowered his hands a bit. "Now, put the gun down, lady. You ain't gonna' shoot me."

Kate couldn't control her tears. This drunken pig *framed Marco* and then killed him and Renzo. She used all of her might to stay focused as a flushing heat began to throb in her cheeks. Her tears turned to anger. Her pulse roared in her ears. She shook her head and straightened her arms. The gun felt heavy. Powerful.

Sal lurched for the weapon. Kate saw his quick move and tightened her grip, along with every muscle in her body. In that instant, she squeezed the trigger and felt the gun's powerful jar as it jerked back toward her face. The vibration and power from the blast sent a buzzing seizure racing up her arm.

The bullet exploded into Sal's jaw. His head whipped back and smashed into the passenger's window. Kate's eardrums seemed to rupture, as the thunderous blast ripped through the inside of the car. In the instant it took the gun to detonate, she let out a scream she couldn't comprehend as her own, until she felt it shredding painfully in her throat.

A brief but forceful spray of blood and other human debris slapped across Kate's face. Her mouth instinctively opened in surprise, causing her to suck in a deep breath and possibly some of Sal's vapors.

Her body stiffened, immobilized by shock and revulsion. Endless fragments of Sal's insides decorated the windshield, the interior roof and everything else in the front seat of the car.

The combined sounds of the exploding gun and her scream ripped through the car. Then … silence, except for a piercing ring in her ears so loud, she barely heard the last moans of Sal's body.

She lowered the gun and placed it in her lap. Sal's bloodied face had twisted away from her, yet it was still within arm's reach of her own. Everything had happened so quickly. So closely. And it was over as suddenly as it began.

She looked out past the mosaic of blood and skull fragments spattered across the windshield, at the darkened road, frantically checking for anyone who may have heard the blast. The street was still.

At that moment, Kate knew her life was over. She could not undo this. The sound of that bullet smashing into Sal's jaw was unlike any she'd ever heard, and she feared she'd never lose it from her thoughts.

It was what happened to Marco. To Renzo.

The ringing in her ears continued. A steady, sharp and endless timbre.

The stench that overtook the car—of gunpowder, of blood and Sal's loosening bodily fluids and gases—was overwhelming. And unlike the fog she'd hoped would engulf her during this murder, she was clearheaded. Still, she had no idea what to do next. She hadn't thought that far through.

She looked over at Sal, his twisted head was smashed against the side window. He looked dead—really dead. She had trouble believing she'd actually just killed a man, but on a deeper level, she felt satisfied. Sal got what he'd deserved.

Hysteria rose from her gut as panic set in and nausea bubbled in her stomach.

Oh God. I can't throw up. I cannot spray my DNA all over the car or the road.

She pressed the sour waves down and tried not to stare at the gaping wound in Sal's jaw. It had only been a minute, but it seemed as though she'd been sitting there in Sal's bloody car for an eternity.

Time to move.

She used her gloved hands to wipe the blood from her face, which moved it from her mouth but smeared it all over her cheeks. She put the gun back into her purse and got out of the car. She stepped onto the dark street, the cool air a blessing to her lungs and wits.

She listened through the ringing. Silence, except for cars passing in the distance on Payne Avenue and the whistle of branches from nearby trees. No sirens, no curious neighbors running toward her.

She looked at the car and groaned. Sal's dead head was on display for anyone who happened down the deserted road. She leaned back into the car, grimacing as she grabbed his arm and pulled him down toward her so his head was resting on the middle console. There was nothing she could do about the bloodied windows, so she shut the door and stepped back to assess the view of the car from a distance.

Satisfied that Sal could no longer be seen by a passerby, she hurried back down Drewry to Beaumont. She took off her gloves and threw them into her purse as she jogged the three blocks down toward her rental car sitting outside The Corner Bar.

Inside the car, Kate's hands shook as she turned on the engine. She tried to calm her nerves and resist the urge to speed. She didn't want to attract any attention from the bar patrons leaving as the bar's closing loomed.

Was she really breathing this loudly?

Her heart pounded, blood pumped in her ears, but the breathing—it was so unbelievably deafening—she was nearly hyperventilating.

As she sat at the red light pressing down her nausea, her left turn signal clicked loudly, each click rhythmically counting down the seconds to her escape.

How long is this light?

Cars turned toward her from the opposite direction, people staggered out of the bar, and everyone seemed to be staring at her, knowing.

Finally, the light turned green and she made the appearance of taking a casual left onto Payne Avenue, forcing herself to remain calm, despite her jittery hands and weak legs.

She let out a loud sigh as she pulled into her driveway. She left the rental car running, while she backed Marco's Mustang out of the garage and drove in the rental. She couldn't take any chances of it being seen from the street. Once that was complete, she hurriedly staggered into the kitchen, ran up the stairs into the bathroom and vomited.

Ninety-seven

Kate knelt on her bathroom floor and hugged the toilet as her whole body tried lurching out the fact that she'd just murdered a man in cold blood.

Her life was over.

She spent an hour on the floor until her body began to shiver. As she pulled herself up, she inadvertently looked into the mirror and gasped at the horror that was her face. Blood smeared dry across her cheeks, her hair a rat's nest of fury.

The fresh memory of her wiping Sal's bloodied remnants from her mouth returned. The first of many such visions, she imagined. With this recollection, came more lightheadedness, more nausea.

She couldn't get into the shower fast enough. She stripped off her clothes and left them in a heap. The hot water blanketed her body in warmth and soothed her frayed nerves. She scrubbed harder than necessary, watching as Sal's dried blood rinsed down her body and spun around the drain.

After her shower, Kate put on her robe and slippers, and wrapped her wet hair in a towel. Next, she brought a bedsheet to the floor and kicked all of her bloody clothes and the rug beneath them onto the sheet. She wrapped it all up, hurried to the washer and tossed it all in. She'd wash it all again when that cycle was complete.

Once that was done, fatigue set in. Kate climbed into her bed, snuggled deep under the covers, and turned off the bedside lamp. Her pulse thumped heavily in her neck down to her fingers and toes, as she tried to relax and calm her nerves. With the weight of her predicament falling heavily across her body, sleep was elusive. When she finally succumbed to her fatigue, nightmares of bloodied faces consumed her dreams.

First, Marco's bloodied head, lifeless on the steering wheel. Then Sal's jaw exploding over and over, each time, the gun's blast getting louder and louder. And then, Renzo's weak voice as he tried to tell her what happened despite the gaping hole in his chest. She fought through the muddied dreams, wishing they'd stop, but it was as if they were on a loop. Those three visions, repeating, over and over.

The only change in her morbid dreams came just as morning's light began peeking through the blinds.

Eddie's face.

It was so close to hers. He was shaking his head and talking to her, but she couldn't understand his words.

Kate bolted upright, out of breath. The clock read ten a.m. She forced herself out of bed. She had work to do. Her first task was to clean the blood from the rental car and then get it detailed and returned. She'd rent a new one at a different location.

When Kate returned home with a different car, she flipped on the TV, anxious for any news of the discovery of Sal's body. She flipped channel after channel and checked her phone incessantly, but nothing showed up.

She was tempted to drive over near the area, but knew that was stupid. She stayed in the house, sitting in the recliner, numbly watching TV, sometimes walking the floor, sometimes peeking out the window. Paranoia had moved in and followed her everywhere.

She flipped on the six p.m. news. Still nothing about Sal, but there was a story that piqued her interest and rattled her nerves.

> *A woman believed to be the girlfriend of the missing O Jackson had been gunned down outside her Minneapolis home. No suspects.*

Eddie had succeeded with his vendetta. Micola's death had been avenged. Kate shook her head. She knew how he'd felt. That urge to settle the score. She'd felt it too. Still felt it. Things weren't finished. It was an urge that couldn't be quelled whether she liked it or agreed with it.

Ninety-eight

*A*fter a brief meeting with Eddie in his office, Dario and Tau
stood to leave. Eddie called out to them.

"Lemme' know if you hear from Sal, 'eh? Been callin' him all
day. Keeps goin' ta' voicemail."

Tau nodded. "We'll have him call you."

Dario closed the door behind them. Eddie leaned back, raising
his hands and resting them behind his head as he thought about
all the recent events.

Tau had really come through handling O's girlfriend like he
did. She got what she deserved. All the talk on the news about
the orphaned child and what a tragedy it was, made Eddie
chuckle. The kid'll be better off without parents like them.

He picked up his cell and dialed Sal again.

Voicemail.

Where the fuck is he?

Must be on a bender. He grabbed his keys. Time to go look for
him.

Ninety-nine

K ate woke from an afternoon nightmare. This time, Sal was beating her over the head with Marco's gun, Sal's gaping gunshot wound to the jaw spilling blood down onto her face. He pressed her back against the driver's side window, a force she could not overcome.

Her own scream was what jarred her to her senses. She bolted upright, breathless. Her heart pounding. She sat there for a moment, gathering her wits before running to the window to peek out. This new constant sense that someone was watching her had intensified.

Seeing no one in the yard, she returned to bed and turned on the TV. She flipped through the local channels and stopped short at the newswoman speaking to the viewers. The words "Man Found Dead" hovered under her image. Raising the volume, Kate watched the news of Sal's murder unfold before her as panic rose in her throat.

She jumped from the bed and began to pace in front of the TV. The news story mentioned an "unknown woman" who'd been at the bar with him Saturday night. Police were interested in speaking with her.

Oh God.

Her cell phone rang, startling her. She looked at the phone's screen. Her mother. She let it go to voicemail, again, making a note to call her back. The last thing she needed was her parents coming over to see her in this state.

Kate continued pacing the entirety of the house, her nerves thinning, as she tried to remain calm, reminding herself that this had been the plan all along. Things were going as expected. Still, being the subject of a manhunt was not something she'd ever imagined.

Kate found herself sitting on the floor at the end of Renzo's bed, his pillow in her arms, a framed picture of her, Renzo and Marco in her hand. She sat there for a while before climbing on top of his bed. She wrapped his blue and red basketball comforter around her, and curled into a ball as she stared at the photo. Tears flowed as a fire reignited in her belly.

After hours of grief surrounded by bouts of panic, Kate had regained some of her composure. Marco and Renzo returned to the forefront of her thoughts. They were her everything and, going forward, her primary motivation. She needed to stop caring about the outcome of her actions. An almost impossible thing to ask of herself, but she needed to numb her emotions in order to continue.

She called her mom, reassuring her enough to keep her parents at bay—at least for a while. She then called Detective Steber inquiring about any updates to Marco and Renzo's case, hoping to keep her out of his realm of suspects for Sal's murder. She thought her voice sounded rattled and nervous, but the detective hadn't seemed to notice.

Her next thoughts were of Dario, Tau, and then, Eddie.

By evening, Kate's resolve had returned—somewhat. She climbed back into her latest rental, a black Hyundai sedan, and resumed her surveillance at the parking lot across from Fortunato's.

Her primary target: Dario. Over the next several days, she'd followed him all over the Payne Avenue area, quickly learning his hangouts and the timing of his routines. But he was with Tau a lot, which made it tough for her to plan anything. She could not handle both of them at once.

After a few frustrating days struggling to keep up with Dario, she decided to switch directions. She'd save him for later.

One hundred

Eddie learned of Sal's death from Tau, who'd heard it on the news. The cops said he was found in his own car. Passenger seat. They think he knew who killed him. Eddie disconnected the call and walked down to his office. The lunch rush was picking up, but he needed to be alone.

Who would have killed Sal? And why? He supposed there were many who didn't care for the guy. He was a monster, after all. Even in the last year, he'd roughed up many people on Eddie's list. Killed a few, too, including O Jackson.

He thought about Marco. That one stung. He regretted ordering that hit.

The kid.

Eddie shook his head and ran his hand through his hair.

Kate.

The last time he'd seen her, she'd seemed okay. Sitting there at the restaurant. Talking to him and Sal. But Eddie knew it was a front. She was still hurting bad, even three months later. He made a note to call her to see how she was doing.

He'd have to call Sal's ma', too.

Shit.

He'd have to go over there. Console her. Another damned funeral. His head spun. Things were out of control. With Marco gone and now Sal, he was down to just two guys he could really trust, and business had been expanding. He'd need Dario and Tau to promote Mike, and add some new runners.

The whole thing made him uneasy. Cops would be crawling around again, asking questions. He needed to get Dario and Tau on the same page, and try to figure out who did this to Sal.

He felt his blood pressure rise and let out a long, slow breath. He'd really have to start watching his back.

Maybe he was next.

One hundred one

Kate sat on the cold, cement steps outside of Micola's backdoor, her knees clenched together as she shivered in the April evening air. Her jeans and light jacket were no match for the chilly spring wind bearing down on her.

It had been a few days since the news of Sal's murder, and she was growing accustomed to the idea that she now was a killer. What she hadn't considered was the growing paranoia and how much it would fray her nerves.

She stared out into the blackness of the backyard, ignoring the revving engine of a car down the street, and the beginnings of a heated argument coming from a few doors down.

When the lights from Eddie's car bounced up the driveway on her left, she scrambled to her feet. She smoothed her jacket and jeans and secured her bag over her shoulder, patting the bottom of it to confirm the gun was in its place. She waited at the bottom of the stairs for Eddie to park Micola's car and exit the garage. As he pushed the buttons that commanded the garage door to close, she called out to him.

"Hello, Eddie."

Eddie turned. "Who's there?"

"It's me. Kate."

He walked toward her, straining to see her in the darkness. "Kate? That you?"

"Yes."

Eddie waved his hand toward the driveway. "I didn't see your car."

"I walked," she lied. Her car was parked around the corner and down an alley.

"What're ya' doin' here, Kate?"

She swallowed. "I—I … this is embarrassing."

"What? What is it?" he asked, patting his hair as he walked in her direction. "You need somethin'?"

"I guess I was just looking for someone to talk to." She watched his expression soften.

"Yeah. Sure. Come on in. I'm glad you came."

He fumbled with his keys as he tried to open the back door. Once opened, he flipped on the kitchen light and stepped back, watching Kate as she crossed the threshold.

"I could use somebody to talk to, too," Eddie said. "I suppose you heard about Sal on the news."

Kate stopped, her mouth open.

Sal.

"Kate? You okay?"

"I, ah'. Yeah, yes, I heard. I'm so sorry, Eddie. This must be ... I'm just ..."

She looked at her hands and then bit her lip, as she looked up at him. She watched his eyes quickly scan her body. He looked thinner, his skin pale.

"Please. Where's my manners? Come into the livin' room, Kate. Sit down. Let's talk, okay?"

She smiled. "Okay."

Eddie nodded and walked quickly down the dark hall, flipping on lights as he passed. Kate followed him into the antique-looking living room, admiring the mahogany grandfather clock ticking in the corner.

"Go ahead. Sit down. I'll get us—" He paused and turned to her, arms out. "What can I get fa-you, 'eh? Coffee? Water?"

"I'd love a glass of wine—I mean—if you have any."

She watched his eyes pop a little. "Ah', wine? Sure. Yeah. I think I got some. White? Red?" He snapped and pointed his finger at her. "White. You like White."

She smiled and nodded, looking directly into his eyes. "That's right. Thanks."

"Great. I'll go—"

"Do you have any music?"

"Ah'. Yeah. Micola had quite the selection. Anything in particular?"

Kate looked at her hands and back up at him. "Something quiet. So we can talk, I mean."

He nodded. "Right." He walked over to Micola's console stereo and started flipping through her old albums.

"Wow," Kate said, walking toward him. "This stereo is amazing." She stroked the dark glossed wood. "So vintage."

He moved his hand through his hair and nodded. "Right? I just about fell over the first time I saw this thing. It's in pretty good shape, too. Sounds fantastic."

Eddie flipped the lever and they watched the vinyl album fall to the turntable, and the needle move to the exact spot where the first song began. The sound of Tony Bennett's smooth voice filled the room. Eddie adjusted the volume so they could talk.

"Tony Bennett," Kate said. "Perfect."

Eddie smiled. "Yeah. Perfect."

He removed his suit jacket and tie, laying them across one of the two chairs facing the sofa. "I'll go get that wine. Have a seat. Make yourself comfortable."

He called to her from the kitchen. "Can I get you somethin' to eat? A sandwich or maybe a snack or somethin'?"

Kate called out over the music. "No, thanks. Just the wine."

He came back in, strutting, she noticed.

Cocky bastard.

He leaned down and handed her the wine.

She looked up and gave him the look Marco always told her made him melt. "Thanks." She took a pretend-sip and watched Eddie gulp his.

They sat in uncomfortable silence, listening to the crooner sing about San Francisco. She sensed Eddie's nervousness and savored it. He took another long drink of his wine and she pretended to take another sip.

"So," he said. "What'd'ya wanna' talk about? What can I do fa-ya'?"

She gave him the *look* again and shrugged. "It's pretty embarrassing, actually. It's just … I've been so … lonely. I miss Marco and Renzo so much, I don't know what to do with myself. I can't talk to my mom. She's grown so impatient with me. She wants me back at work. She acts like it was just a little blip in the road. But I can't …"

She shook her head, real tears burning her eyes, as she looked down at her hands.

"And my dad—I can't talk to him about it either."

Her shoulders fell and she started crying. She hadn't envisioned herself looking and feeling this genuine.

Eddie stood. "I ah' ..." He rubbed the side of his cheek with his knuckles. "Shit. I ..."

Kate looked up, wiping her eyes. He walked over and handed her his drink napkin. She took it and he moved to sit next to her.

She let him.

"What can I do, Kate? I'm sorry you're so sad. Shit. I hate seein' ya' like this, ya' know?"

He reached out his hand and gently brushed a strand of hair from her eye.

She let him.

He sat uncomfortably close, but she didn't move. The Tony Bennett album moved to the next song. Finally, she mustered up the nerve to sit back against the sofa. Eddie sat back too, and Kate tipped her head and rested it on his shoulder. She heard his breathing over the music. He was trying to slow it down, but Kate sensed his struggle. She worried he could hear her heart pounding in her chest because, to her, it seemed to be drowning out the music. They sat motionless in the dimly-lit room for several moments.

In her head, Kate contemplated her next move. She didn't like being exposed through the huge picture window behind their heads. She shimmied a little, and he looked at her.

"Kate, I'm sorry—if you don't—"

She shook her head. "No. This is nice, really. It's just—" She turned. "I feel like the whole world is watching us through that window."

Eddie pulled away. "Oh, yeah. I can fix that, I think. Lemme' see."

He stood, walked around the sofa, and peeked behind the drapes, looking for a way to close them.

"Shit. I don't see how you close these." He turned to look at her, letting out a loud breath. "Sorry, I ..."

Kate stood. "I think ... maybe I should go."

She reached for her bag, feeling through the fabric for the gun. She really felt she should go. This was a mistake and he'd soon see right through her.

"No, no." Eddie was next to her in an instant. "Don't go. Really, Kate. I want you to stay." He held her arms, sliding his hands down them, as he looked into her eyes. "Please, Kate. Stay." He chuckled. "Maybe you could help me figure out these drapes, 'eh?"

She looked into his eyes. She'd never been this close to him. His eyes were so dark, black almost. Long lashes. He wasn't unattractive to the ordinary woman, but he made Kate's skin crawl. She hated everything he stood for, all the damage he'd done since he'd arrived a year ago. She swallowed and held her nerves.

"Sure. Let me see …" She walked around the sofa and pulled the drapes away from the wall. "Oh, here." She found an attached string on a pulley and moved it. Slowly, the drapes pulled together until they were closed.

"Good," Eddie said.

He put out his hand inviting Kate to return to the sofa. She paused, before nodding and sitting back in the same place. Eddie joined her, a little closer this time.

"Now," he said. "Where were we?"

"It's just …" Kate lowered her gaze. "I needed someone to talk to. I have no one. I hope it's okay I came. I …"

"Kate. I'm glad you came. Stop worryin' about it. Let's just sit here, drink our wine, and listen to the music. Sit back, now. Like you was doin' before. Put your head back here." He patted his shoulder. "It felt nice. I've been lonely, too. First Micola, now Sal. It's like a damned nightmare, ya' know?"

Kate nodded, holding the stem of her wine glass, as she twisted her head to look into his eyes. "I do know. It's so terribly lonely. I feel like I've stopped living."

He nodded.

She moved to sit forward, rubbing her hands on her thighs.

"Maybe… I don't know…"

"Maybe what?"

Losing her nerve, Kate stood again, taking her bag in her hand. "I don't know, Eddie. Maybe this is a bad idea. I should probably go. I think it's this room. This house. Micola. Everything. I feel like she's here, watching us. I shouldn't have come."

Eddie leapt to his feet. "Kate, no. Please. Don't go."

Kate hesitated, thinking. "Is there somewhere else? Upstairs …? Your room? Maybe the reminder of Micola won't be there." She wasn't sure if he'd heard her over the music. She barely heard herself.

He nodded, a slight look of desperation in his eyes. "Sure. Yeah. We could do that. Come on."

Kate bent over to pick up her glass of wine.

Eddie grabbed his glass too and moved to turn off the upbeat song.

Hating the silence, Kate said, "Do you have anything else you could play?"

"Sure."

He set his wine glass on the coffee table and walked to the console. Moving quickly, she grabbed an opened packet of crushed sleeping pills from her jacket pocket and tipped it into his glass, spilling half of it onto the table. She frantically swept it onto the floor, while watching Eddie's back. Her hand quickly returned to her pocket as he continued flipping through Micola's album collection, humming. Kate watched his wine, praying the room was dim enough to hide the remaining white particles as they fell to the bottom of his glass.

"Here's a good one," Eddie said. He turned to her smiling. "Bing Crosby. Sound okay?"

"Perfect."

After the music started, Eddie left for the kitchen to grab the bottle of wine. When he returned, he was smiling.

"Follow me."

One hundred two

Kate threw her bag over her shoulder and followed Eddie up the dark staircase, each step creaking under their weight. Photos lined the walls, but the lighting was poor, and Kate didn't care to look at them anyway. The smell of must grew as they climbed. She took the opportunity to reach quickly and quietly into her bag and slide the revolver into her deep jacket pocket.

This was it. No going back now, and if he felt the gun in her pocket, it was all over.

A landing with a window high above their heads broke the long climb. Eddie turned and moved up four more steps. Kate followed his silhouette, the stairwell cloaked in darkness. At the top of the stairs, Eddie flipped a switch, illuminating a landing surrounded by four doors. They stopped at one of them.

Eddie entered a bedroom and flipped another light switch to turn on a lamp placed on one of two dark wooden nightstands on either side of a queen-sized bed.

Kate followed Eddie into the room. The bed to her left was covered in a white bedspread and navy throw pillows. She grazed her hand over an old trunk at the foot of the bed. Eddie did a quick sweep of some clothes on a chair near the window, tossing them into the closet. The glow of the evening's moon streamed through the single window, and Eddie moved to lower the navy shade.

Kate slipped out of her jacket, placing it and her bag on the trunk, making sure to hide the pocket carrying the gun. She sat on the edge of the bed and kicked off her black flats, shivering as nervous goosebumps crawled across her body.

The music from the living room drifted up the stairs and into the bedroom. Eddie walked toward her, sitting next to her on the bed. He scooted closer, leaning in, as she stared into his eyes. She too leaned in, moving slowly, testing his reaction.

He brushed her hair away from her face, as his lips met hers. She let out a slight moan, one he mistook for passion. He pressed harder, pushing her back onto the bed, their feet still hanging over the side. Kate wrapped her arms around his neck, encouraging his passion, moving her body with his, forcing him out of control.

His moans made her want to gag, but she kept going, letting his heavy hands travel around her body. He moved to the buttons on her blouse, and she let him. He moved to the button on her jeans, and she let him, helping him pull them down and off of her ankles, revealing her lean, bare legs.

She watched as he scanned her body. The chill she felt wasn't because she wore only her unbuttoned blouse, lacy white bra and panties. It was Eddie's eyes. They held a certain power she couldn't place. He shook his head with a hungry smile.

"You're more beautiful than in my dreams."

She smiled, but it must not have been convincing, because Eddie paused, frowning. "What's wrong, Kate?"

"Nothing. Keep going."

"You sure?"

She glanced toward the foot of the bed at her jacket on the trunk. "Yes, I'm sure. I just … I thought I heard something. I'm sorry. I'm a little nervous … about this."

"Me too."

Kate reached up and wrapped her arms around his neck, gently kissing him. She knew from his moans that he now believed her.

The gun was out of her reach, so Kate let his fondling continue. He stopped for a second, looking at her, questioning her with his eyes. She returned his look before gently pushing him down onto his back. Climbing on top of him, she straddled his waist with her long legs.

He lay back, staring up at her, and then blinked. "Whoo. Hmm."

She stopped. "What's wrong?" Her heart skipped as she glanced at her jacket.

Eddie put his hand across his forehead and rubbed it down his face. "Nothin'. Must be the wine. Just got a little dizzy there for a second."

"You sure? Are you okay?" She looked closely at his eyes. He was blinking fast, a mist of perspiration beading near his hairline.

"Yeah, yeah." His words were slowing. Slurring. "I'm fine. Is-tha-wine. I'm go-o-o-d." He pawed at her breasts. "Kate. Kate. I've … I've always loved you. Since that first day. You were so beautiful. I couldn't stop thinkin' 'bout ya'."

He wiped his face again and opened his eyes wide, trying to stay awake, but it was an obvious struggle. His eyes closed again.

Kate waited. Straddled on top of him, she stayed motionless, her hands on his bare chest, cringing at the touch of his wiry gray and black curls. Eddie's breathing slowed, deep and steady.

She moved a little and he opened his eyes, smiling up at her through the waves of her long, chestnut hair. "You're so-o-o beautiful."

She smiled at him and waited, afraid to move, as she eyed her jacket pocket.

After a few more minutes, his breathing steadied. Eddie was still. Relaxed. Kate gingerly climbed off of him, hurrying to her jeans, as her unbuttoned blouse whipped around her. She pulled them on, zipping and buttoning them and then fumbled around for her jacket pocket, feeling for the gun.

As she pulled it out, she heard rustling from the bed. She turned just as Eddie's fist came flush across her face. Pain exploded across her cheek and jaw. She fell to the floor, darkness closing in around her.

One hundred three

Eddie's voice screamed in Kate's ear. "You fuckin' bitch. You tryna' kill me?"

He laughed as he climbed on top of her, ripping at her bra with one hand, the other hand pushing into her throat and squeezing.

"You won't need that gun just yet, Kate."

Kate's face throbbed and ached, heat and panic filled her body, as she fought for air. She threw up her fists, striking anything she could to get him off her neck. She connected with what she thought was his nose, which set Eddie back on his haunches, screaming.

She turned onto her stomach, scrambling, as she reached for the top of the mattress, trying to get up and out the door. He grabbed her ankle, and she kicked him in the face before getting back to her feet.

Eddie wailed from the hit. "So ya' wanna' fight, huh?"

She turned to see a purple wound swelling quickly near his eye, his black and gray hair falling wildly around his face. She coughed and gasped, as he rose to his feet, lunging. He landed a vicious slap across her face, wrenching her head sideways and sending her into the end table nearest the door. Her hip scraped the corner as she fell into the lamp, taking it and the table with her crashing to the floor.

Kate landed violently onto her side, the blow knocking the wind from her lungs. She choked and fought for air and tried reaching for her throat, but her arms felt numb. Heavy. Darkness faded in and out as did the sound of Eddie's yelling.

A forceful tugging around her waist kept her conscious. Something hot dripped from her mouth, the bitter taste of iron searing her tongue. The carpet burned her stomach as she was dragged, then lifted and flipped onto her back. She opened her eyes to a gray fog. She blinked to clear her vision but the effort was futile. She stared at the wall just under the bedroom window, the bottom of the curtain moving gently above her.

Eddie's weight pressed down on her. She looked up at him. His face an angry blur. Despite her efforts, her body refused to put up a fight. In her semi-conscious state, Kate stared under the bed, refusing to look at Eddie, as he worked on the button to her jeans. She kept her gaze on the carpet under the bed. At the far side, something shiny caught her attention. She squinted, which helped clear her vision.

Across the carpeted floor on the other side of the bed, and next to the toppled nightstand and lamp, was a set of keys, a bunch of coins, a wallet, and something else she couldn't make out.

The tugging at her waist continued. Eddie's violent words and rough hands faded in and out. Kate's body felt numb except for the yanking of her jeans.

After finally releasing the button and zipper, Eddie slid backwards off of Kate and worked to pull her jeans down from her waist. She kicked at him, but her legs were weak and useless. She turned her head away from his face, which caused the room to sway. With her head tilted to the side, and her body numb from the attack, Kate focused on that shiny item under the bed. It looked like a small silver tool. Her head cleared enough to see the top of Eddie's head bent downward, his hair strewn about his forehead as he tugged on her jeans.

He let out a growl. "Goddamn jeans!"

He dragged Kate's body away from the window and wall and near the center of the room at the foot of the bed.

Kate raised her arms above her head hoping to grab onto her gun which had fallen under the bed near the wooden chest. She felt around until her fingers grazed a shoe. She grabbed it and smacked Eddie across his head with it. Eddie fell to the side and Kate rolled away from him, crawling weakly, searching for the gun. She touched it just as Eddie grabbed hold of her legs, tearing off her jeans. He pulled himself toward her as she wrestled to grasp the trigger. As he came at her with a fist, she smacked him with the side of it, the gun landing square on his jaw. Eddie let out a wail as he fell back.

"Jesus fucking Christ!"

He knelt back, breathless, pressing his hand to his jaw. Kate fumbled to get a better grip on the gun and pointed it at him. Holding it with both hands, she scrambled backward near the foot of the bed toward the door, her hands quivering with fatigue.

On his knees, Eddie looked at her and laughed.

"Is that what this is about? 'Eh? You comin' over here to seduce me, and then kill me? Huh, Kate?"

Blood now flowed from his cheek, a crazy grin spreading across his face. His usually-perfect hair fell about his face, as he laughed breathlessly.

With weak and shaky hands, Kate continued to point the gun at him. She stared back, motionless, breathing heavily and coughing, the pain in her face explosive.

Eddie stood and unbuttoned his pants. "You asked for this, Kate."

"Don't come any closer, Eddie."

Eddie ignored her command and moved in quickly. Leaning down toward Kate, he slapped the gun sideways from her hand, sending it bouncing across the carpet. Kate screamed as she leaned out for it, but he stood above her, legs spread. He slammed the door shut and put his back to it. She had nowhere to go. She cowered near the toppled nightstand, with no room to back away.

Eddie made no motion for the gun, his hands now on his hips. He shook his head, as he looked down at her.

"I've always cared for you, Kate. You were the girl of my dreams, right?" He shook his head. "But now?" He frowned and shrugged. "I can't trust ya'. You gotta' go. Just like your husband. Couldn't trust him neither." He laughed as he wiped his wound, looking at the bloody results.

"First though—you're gonna love what I got fa-ya'. You'll wonder why you were ever married to that loser, Marco, with his tiny prick."

He stripped off his pants and pulled down his underwear. Kate squeezed her eyes shut to block the vision of the bleeding man in front of her, his violent state of rage on full display.

Eddie moved in closer, leaning down. He slapped Kate across her swollen cheek and then shoved his hand onto her chest, sending her back to the floor, her head taking a bouncing blow near the closed door. Kate fought him and slapped his hands away, as she tried to throw him off with her hips, but he was too strong, and she was too worn out.

Tears burned her eyes as she knew what was about to happen and hated that she wasn't strong enough to stop it. Eddie ripped at her underwear, as Kate turned her head to the side praying it would be over soon. Eddie smeared his hands all over her chest, knocking her legs apart with his knees, growling like a rabid dog.

She felt herself leave her body for a moment and then opened her eyes. Within her grasp were the keys, the coins, and the wallet she'd seen under the bed from across the room. But it was that shiny silver tool that caught her eye. She blinked.

A little steel screwdriver.

She reached for it just as Eddie lowered his head to look between her legs, his hand reaching.

One hundred four

Kate dug her fingers into the carpet, fighting to get closer to the screwdriver, but she was still too far to grab it. She wriggled and fought with Eddie for a couple of seconds, which cost her another burning slap across her face, but it was enough to get the screwdriver's handle into her grip, blade down.

Eddie's body, now lowered onto hers, crushed her, cutting her oxygen. She felt his breath, hot on her cheek, a faint scent of wine grazing her nose.

Kate's strength waned, yet she mustered what little she had left. Releasing a high-pitched howl, she raised her arm and jammed the screwdriver into the side of Eddie's neck. It slid in easier than she'd thought, but stopped short after hitting something solid. His Adam's apple, she presumed. Blood sprayed out of the wound as Eddie's head jerked up, his eyes bulging. His mouth opened to scream, but no sound emerged. His hand instinctively reached for his neck, as he pulled himself up from Kate's chest.

Kate coughed from the release of his weight. Crimson streams of blood were sprayed across her bare chest, bra and unbuttoned white blouse. She scrambled to push Eddie from her lap. Her heart pounded in her chest and her cheek ached and throbbed. She watched Eddie, while eyeing the gun a few feet away. He didn't fight her. He seemed uncertain as to what had just happened, a confused and twisted look wrestling across his face.

He croaked and gagged as he fought with the screwdriver. He finally yanked it out with a howling shriek. Kate gasped, backing away, watching. Blood oozed between his fingers as he held the wound tight with both hands, plugging the flow, as gurgling and whizzing sounds eked from the new opening in his neck.

Eddie tried to stand, but ended up spinning in a half-circle before falling to his knees in the center of the bedroom. Kate fell on the gun, fumbling to get a steady grip. When she did, she turned and pointed it at Eddie.

"Kate. What are you doing?" Dark blood dripped from Eddie's mouth and spattered across his face as he spoke.

Kate watched him try to crawl toward her. Holding the gun as steady as she could, she backed herself up to the closed door as he continued toward her. He grabbed at her leg and she kicked his hand.

"Please. Kate ... I..." Each word gurgled, as he drowned in his own fluids. He blinked and raised his bloody hand in a pleading gesture. The gun began to quiver in Kate's hands. Eddie reached again. She kicked his hand again.

"You ..." Her voice cracked. "You killed Marco and Renzo—my baby boy!"

"Kate. I ... I thought we could ...."

She laughed at his nonsense and screamed at him. "I wish I'd never met you! You killed my entire purpose for being alive! My family!"

As she sobbed, the tears spilled down her bruised and swollen face, her hair knotted and twisted about.

Eddie, now curled into a ball on the floor holding his neck, struggled to speak. "Kate, I swear. You gotta' believe me. Renzo was not part of the plan."

Kate's eyes darkened and she raised the gun higher, pointing it stronger in Eddie's direction.

"Don't!" She cried, shaking her head. "Don't talk to me about my son like he was some project!" She heard the rising and cracking hysteria in her voice. "I don't want to hear about your 'plan.' Stop. Just stop ... talking ... about my family. You killed them. And when you killed them ...," she sniffled, "...you killed me. Don't you understand?"

"Kate .... Please."

"You killed me, too," she whispered.

Kate tightened her grip on the gun and squeezed the trigger.

One hundred five

"9 11, what's your emergency?" The male dispatcher's voice was deep.

"I … I just killed somebody."

"Ma'am. Did you say you 'just killed somebody'?"

Kate's voice broke. "Yes."

"What's your name, ma'am?"

"Kate. My name …" she sniffled and coughed. "… My name is Kate De Luca."

"Okay, Kate. Where are you? What's the address?"

"Um—I don't—I don't know. It's a big house, brick. On Burr Street. It's off of Minnehaha. It's owned by Mrs.—ah'—Mrs. …"

Kate squeezed her eyes shut and shook her head. "Oh God. I can't remember that old woman's name." She thought of the restaurant. "Mrs. Fortunato. That's it. I don't know the house number, I'm sorry. But Mrs. Fortunato. I'm in her house."

"Okay. Are you on a cell phone, Kate?"

"Yes."

"Is it yours?"

"I—yes."

"Okay. Stay on the line with me, Kate. I've found the address and I'm sending a unit over there now. Do not leave your location. I repeat, do *not* leave your location. Do you understand me, Kate? I have officers on the way."

Kate sniffled.

"Ma'am? Can you hear me? I need you to respond to me."

"Yes, sorry. I can hear you."

"Alright. Now, who did you just kill?"

"I ah' … oh God," Kate cried. "I just killed him. I killed Eddie. Eddie Bracchio." Her jagged voice choked as she gasped and sucked in air. "He lives here. Mrs.—ah'. Mrs. …"

"Fortunato?"

"Yes, Fortunato."

"Eddie lives here—lived here. In her house."

Kate ran her hand through her knotted hair, feeling something wet and warm on her forehead near her hairline. She pulled back her hand to see a bright smear of red covering her fingers.

"She died. She's dead, too."

"She's dead? Did you kill her, too? Mrs. Fortunato?"

"No," Kate shouted, shaking her pounding head. "I didn't kill her. Somebody else killed her. A drive-by... I ah'... " She coughed and began crying into the phone. "I killed Eddie. Just Eddie."

She considered confessing to Sal's murder as well, but didn't have the strength. That would be for a later time.

"Okay. Where is the body? Mr. Bracchio's body?"

The sound of the word "body," shook her. "Upstairs. He's upstairs in his bedroom. I—I'm downstairs. In the kitchen."

"And you're sure he's dead? Did you check for a pulse?"

"I checked. I—I didn't find one. I'm sure he's dead."

"What happened, ma'am. How did you kill him?"

Kate sniffled. "I ah'—there was a fight. He punched me. And choked me. He tried to rape ... me." Kate tightened her cracking voice. "I stabbed him. In the neck." Kate whined as she relived it. "He had a gun. And I ah'—..." She sniffled and pushed her sweaty hair from her face. "He was gonna'—" Kate sobbed uncontrollably. "He was gonna'—"

A faint sound of sirens growing louder steered Kate's focus from the 911 dispatcher.

"They're here. I hear the siren. I gotta' go."

"Kate!"

Kate pushed the button on her cell and scrambled to her feet. She hurried from the kitchen, down the creaky old hallway, slipping as she turned at the foyer. She pulled open the heavy mahogany door, just as two St. Paul police officers climbed the front steps, one talking into a two-way radio on his shoulder. The man on the radio was a bulky white man, the other, a tall, thin white female.

On seeing Kate open the door, the officers drew their weapons. "Put your hands up," the female officer yelled. "Now!"

Kate felt the blood drop to her feet as her vision spun. "Okay, okay," she shouted, raising her arms. "I don't have any weapons on me." She braced her body for another assault.

"Are you the one who made the call about killing someone?" asked the female officer.

Kate no sooner nodded when they both approached her. The male officer slammed her against the closet door, her cheek taking the brunt of it. Pain split across her already pummeled face and head. The voices of the cops faded and, for a second, everything went black.

She heard one voice shouting near her left ear. "Stay with me. Shit."

"Come on man! Take it easy!"

Kate felt a yank of her arms as they were pulled behind her back, causing a guttural moan to rush up from her stomach. Though she'd never in her life been cuffed, she knew that was what was happening. She felt the cuffs cutting into her wrists before a quick click locked them tight.

"You have the right to remain silent ... Anything ..." She barely heard the rest of it.

"Oh my God, that hurts. Please. Can you—"

The male officer began screaming at her. "Anybody else here? In the house? Upstairs?"

She shook her head.

"You sure?"

She nodded. "I'm sure. Just—"

"Just what?" asked the female officer.

"Eddie," Kate said. "He's upstairs. He's the one I killed."

"Okay," said the male officer. He walked the hall and peeked into the living room. "We're gonna' put you in here for now." He disappeared. Kate heard a click and the living room lit up. He walked back out and tipped his head in the direction of the living room.

The woman pulled on Kate's arm. "In here. Come on."

Kate felt the weight of her battle with Eddie press onto her shoulders. Her legs buckled under her as she was guided into the living room.

Eddie was upstairs. Dead.

She had trouble grasping the reality of it all. His dead body, the fight, his strength and speed. She felt herself falling.

"Whoa, whoa. Stay with me."

She led Kate into the living room and sat her in one of the two chairs facing the picture window, the curtains still drawn from her earlier encounter there with Eddie.

"Where's the body, ma'am? Which room upstairs?" asked the male officer.

"First room to the right at the top of the stairs," she whispered.

"Who is it?"

"Eddie Bracchio." Speaking was becoming too much for her.

He raised his brows and looked at the other officer.

"You killed Eddie Bracchio?"

She nodded, squeezing her eyes shut. Her shoulders began to shake uncontrollably.

Another siren arrived.

"Ambulance. Send 'em up," said the male officer. He left the living room. The last thing Kate heard was his heavy footsteps climbing the stairs. Her head began to spin. The female officer spoke to her, but her words seemed garbled. Darkness swirled, first in her peripheral vision, but soon it was everywhere.

The silence that followed was a gift.

One hundred six

"Mrs. De Luca. Can you hear me?"

The voice was faint. Distant.

Kate felt something. A pushing on her shoulder. She winced and opened her eyes to a light so bright it burned. She felt her eyes roll back into her head. Her lips felt cracked. Her mouth dry, like cotton. But the voices grew louder.

"She's waking up."

"Mrs. De Luca…"

Kate took a deep breath and opened her eyes, squinting and blinking. A sharp pain crossed her back. Her head felt split in two. She shut her eyes again. The pain seemed to worsen as she moved. Two tall figures in dark clothing, one in front of her, the other beside her, came into view.

"Where am I?"

"You're in the hospital. We need to talk to you, Mrs. De Luca. About Eddie Bracchio."

"How long have I been here?"

"Twelve hours." Another voice. Another man.

Kate vaguely recognized his voice. She blinked to clear her vision and looked over at the man standing next to her.

"Detective Steber?"

He nodded and then read her her rights. Once she agreed to talk without counsel, Detective Steber continued. "Do you remember what happened, Mrs. De Luca? Why did you kill him?"

A rush of memories flooded through her like a cold ocean wave. Tears burned and overflowed, rolling down her cheek and over her nose.

"He murdered my family. My husband. My son." The sound of her cracked and broken voice seemed strange.

The two detectives looked at each other. "Mrs. De Luca, do you mind if I record this conversation?"

Kate flipped her hand and shook her head. "Go ahead. I don't care."

After the recording device was running, Detective Steber continued with his questions.

"Mrs. De Luca, I need you to be more specific. You say you *know* Eddie Bracchio killed your husband and son. What led you to believe this?"

Kate squeezed her eyes shut and then blinked. Her blurred vision began to clear.

"We talked about it," Kate said. "I accused Eddie of orchestrating it and he admitted it. Didn't matter, though. I already knew. I've known since the funeral."

"What made you so sure?"

Kate's mind drifted to the funeral.

"Mrs. De Luca?"

Kate blinked.

"Mrs. De Luca, how did you know Eddie Bracchio killed your husband and son? You said you've known it since their funeral."

Kate nodded.

"How?"

"Marco," Kate said. "I got him the job. With Eddie. And ah'–" She sniffled and wiped her eyes with the back of her hand. Her arm felt weak from the gesture. "Marco told me he was getting into things with Eddie that he didn't like."

"What kind of things?"

Kate shook her head at the memory. "Heists. Minor ones at first. Shaking people down for money they owed Eddie. Then, it started getting more serious."

"Like what? How serious?"

"Drug runs. Drug deals. That's when Marco started getting scared. He didn't want to do it anymore. We'd made plans to leave. But by then, it was too late."

"What do you mean?"

"Marco went to see Eddie the day after Micola died. Eddie accused him of stealing. Marco denied it and told Eddie he wanted out, but Eddie said no. And when Marco got home, he told me how furious Eddie had been about him leaving. Marco was terrified. He said we had to leave *that night*—after he picked up Renzo. But he left to pick up Renzo and they never came home." Kate turned her head toward the window. "You know the rest."

Detective Steber pulled up a chair. "Okay, Mrs. De Luca. Tell me about Eddie. Tell me what happened. How did you end up killing him? I need specifics."

"We should start with Sal."

Detective Steber looked at his partner and then back at Kate. "Sal? Got a last name?"

Kate shook her head.

"I killed Sal, first," she said. "He's that guy you found dead in the car near The Corner Bar."

Steber looked at the other guy who quickly left the hospital room.

Detective Steber folded his arms and leaned back, waiting.

Kate continued. "He was the one who actually shot and killed Marco and Renzo. He was the shooter."

"So this guy, Sal, murdered your husband and son, correct? Eddie didn't shoot them?"

Kate nodded. "That's right."

"And how do you know that?"

"I know." Kate closed her eyes to rest for a moment. "Sal is Eddie's cousin, and Eddie ordered him to kill Marco and Renzo. Wait. No. Not Renzo. That was an accident. Eddie didn't order him to kill Renzo."

"And how do you know that?"

"Sal told me."

"And when did he tell you that?"

"In the car, just before I shot him in the face."

The room went silent for a moment. Detective Steber wiped his forehead. "Go on."

"Sal told me that Eddie ordered him to do it because Marco stole money, and because Marco dared to stand up to Eddie and tell him he was leaving the organization. But Sal told me that *he* was the one who stole the money, not Marco. I knew all along Marco would never do something that stupid. I *knew* he didn't steal from Eddie. But Sal blamed it on Marco, and Eddie believed Sal because he was Eddie's cousin."

Kate took a breath. All the talking was exhausting. "So I killed Sal and I killed Eddie. I never got around to killing the other two."

She put her hands over her face. "That will haunt me for the rest of my life."

"What other two?"

"Eddie's other flunkies. Dario and Tau. I don't know their last names, but I swear, they never left Eddie's side." She waved her hand across the room. "They were all in on it."

Her chin quivered, as the tears flowed once again. "Sal killed my boy for no reason." She shook her head. "Said he didn't mean it. Said Renzo looked like a man. And, he wouldn't have done it if he'd known it was Renzo."

Kate began to sob, so Detective Steber waited until she settled back down.

"Mrs. De Luca. Can we talk about Eddie? What happened. Let's start at the beginning."

Kate took a deep breath, and through intense physical and emotional pain, she told Detective Steber the whole story, beginning with that fateful call from Eddie Bracchio a year ago, asking Kate to find him a place to open a restaurant.

One hundred seven

*T*he bright spring day brought unseasonably warm temperatures, and Kate was grateful she'd chosen her sleeveless navy dress. It felt a little roomier than usual, an expected casualty of not eating. She pushed her oversized, dark sunglasses up and fluffed her long, dark hair forward to hide some of her face before opening the passenger door.

As she and her attorney exited his car, she panned the crowd that had gathered around the looming courthouse doors, each waiting to catch a glimpse of the female cold-blooded killer.

The pink and white floral scarf Kate had selected to hide her identity, really only hid her emotions. She wrapped it tighter around her neck and dipped her head, stealing the photographers' chances at a prize-winning front page photo. The bright lights from cameras flashed endlessly as she walked toward them, her attorney gripping her elbow and guiding her through the throng of gawkers toward the courthouse entrance.

As she and her attorney neared the glass doors of the towering Ramsey County Courthouse, Kate focused her gaze on her tan pumps and the swirls embedded in the concrete steps. She was relieved her parents weren't there to see this spectacle.

Soon, she'd be standing before Judge Margaret Haley, the woman now in charge of Kate's fate. Life in prison would be the likely sentence, though a future behind bars meant nothing to her. She felt nothing. Numbness was her newest companion. It helped her move through these necessary processes.

Kate's focus was interrupted by a screech from a speeding car approaching from her right. She turned and blinked. A silver Ford Fusion was careening toward the courthouse plaza. It flew past so quickly, it was almost a blur.

Almost.

Kate locked eyes with Tau, sitting in the front passenger seat, the barrel of some sort of weapon under his chin, pointing it directly at her. Above the natural hum of the crowd and shouting from journalists, came several muffled popping noises that echoed across the plaza and into Kate's ears. The wall of the courthouse and glass door before her were pummeled by quick zipping hits, causing glass and concrete to explode into fragments, shards, slivers, and rocks.

Screams from the crowd and the rush of feet racing for cover began just as Kate felt something rip open her face and smash into her neck. A stinging and burning sensation spread through her as her arms instinctively rose to stop the onslaught.

A warm liquid dripped into her eyes and she smeared it away, tearing at her scarf as she felt herself falling.

A set of strong arms wrapped around Kate and pushed her head downward. Then, another pop was heard as more hot pain hit her, this time in her side. Her neck and head lurched back, and she fell violently to the cold, hard stone. She squeezed her eyes closed, an instinct that did not improve her pain. When she opened them again, she saw feet. Feet—running. Scattering feet. Desperate to escape the gunfire.

Someone rolled her flat onto her back. She opened her eyes and looked up, as she choked and gasped for a breath. Heads hovered over her. She couldn't make out faces. A voice near her left ear shouted things she couldn't understand. More yelling. More jostling of her body. She tried lifting her head, but it wouldn't comply.

The pain in her side was an excruciating fire that stole her air. She wondered how anyone could endure such agony.

Marco and Renzo endured this.

Burning tears formed under her closed eyelids, as she let out a howl, not only for her own pain, but for her husband and son's. *They'd* felt this pain, too. *They'd* suffered this way.

She deserved this pain. It was all her fault. Everything.

She didn't want to go on. She felt herself drifting into darkness. Then, returning.

Darkness. Silence.

Then, chaos again.

She preferred the silence.

Someone—a man—started pressing on her side, causing her to cry out. The pressure continued, but after a while, the pain began to diminish. She felt sleepy and hated all the faces so close to hers. All of the shouting.

The rigid cement pressed into the bones in her back, but slowly, numbness began to replace the pain in her side and her legs. Some of the faces moved away, allowing the vast blue sky to come into view. A bright cobalt glow and long rainbow-like sunrays, more vibrant than she'd ever remembered, captured her attention. A gentle breeze brushed against her cheek, as she focused her gaze on two puffy white clouds moving ever-so-slightly in a swirling motion. Her body relaxed as she watched them. Faces and voices faded.

A radiant peace wrapped around her like a warm bath. She smiled up at the clouds, lifting her bloodied hand toward the sky. Reaching.

Faces reappeared. Someone held her other hand, but she'd barely felt it. She devoted her gaze to those two clouds. She felt her body rise, as the image of her beloved husband, Marco, appeared in the white tufts above her. He smiled down at her with his big brown eyes and thick, black hair, one curl falling across his forehead. Next to him, her son, her beautiful Renzo. His tufts of brown curls bounced, as he smiled and waved her toward him.

She whispered weakly, quietly.

"Marco. Renzo."

One hundred eight

Brooklyn's unusually cool temperatures kept the streets empty. A heavy wall of gray clouds quickly moved in, bringing rain that tapped lightly on the window outside the aging brick house. The phone rang and the old man reached for it from his usual place on the sofa.

He coughed before speaking. "Is it done?"

He listened for a moment and then said, "You know what to do next. I'll be in touch with the final payment."

Primo Simonelli flipped the phone shut and returned to gaze out the window at the tiny sparrows flitting around a puddle in his yard.

One hundred nine

*T*au hung up the phone and nodded to Dario, who returned the nod. He whipped the revolver into the black Mississippi River far below, its heaving waves dimly lit by the moon's light. Tau followed suit, tossing the burner phone into the river.

"He says the rest of the money is on its way."

Dario smiled and fist-bumped Tau. "Looks like it's just you and me now, man."

Tau smiled and nodded. "Yep. You and me."

ACKNOWLEDGMENTS

I would first like to thank my readers for the opportunity to share my passion for writing and storytelling. I appreciate your willingness to join me on this adventure. Writing this book and delivering it to you has been a true blessing.

I would also like to extend my heartfelt gratitude to my husband, Geno Bartone, for his unwavering support and patience as I hid in my office banging at the keyboard night after night. Without his ideas, constant support and encouragement, this book never would have come to fruition.

Special recognition must go to my daughter, Brittani Bartone, for her countless hours spent reading and editing the manuscript, as well as her heartfelt encouragement, especially when my own self-doubt reared its ugly head (which was often). Her contributions to this novel have been invaluable.

Thank you also to my first readers: my sister, Kathleen O'Connor, and my dear friends, Allison Brady, Allison Stohlmann, Jelena Nik, and Jerry Spiegelberg. Your insights into the depths of the characters have truly opened my eyes and helped guide me through some challenging issues, ultimately leading the story toward its best outcome. Your comments, recommendations and encouragement mean the world to me. I appreciate your generous time and support.

I would like to express my appreciation to the City of Saint Paul, Minnesota, for serving as the backdrop of my story, and for providing me with the inspiration to write this novel.

Finally, I would like to thank my parents, David and Patricia O'Connor, for instilling in me the fire and passion for writing. I miss you Dad.

From the Author:

Thank you for reading *PAYNE Avenue*. I hope you enjoyed it. While it's fresh on your mind, I hope you'll write a review and let me know what you think. I appreciate your feedback.

Would you like to know when M.T. Bartone's next book becomes available? You can sign up for her new release e-mail list at: www.maureenbartone.com

Follow Maureen on social media!

Twitter (X): www.twitter.com/@BartoneMaureen

Facebook: www.facebook.com/maureenbartoneauthor

Instagram: www.instagram.com/mbartone40

TikTok: www.tiktok.com/@bookwriter225

Threads: mbartone40@threads.net

Goodreads: www.goodreads.com/mbartone

Linkedin: www.linkedin.com/in/maureen-bartone-25804953/

Middle Grade Books by Maureen Bartone:

- *Life in the Gumball Machine*
- *Life in the Gumball Machine – Vinnie and Gordy's Return*
- *Tilly's Top-Secret Trapdoor* -- National Indie Excellence® Awards FINALIST